MW01611046

The White Gold Caper

Janet McDermott

Copyright © Janet McDermott
All rights reserved.

ISBN: 978-0-9969746-1-5

DEDICATION

I am dedicating this book to my brother, Roger who passed away early spring. Good climbing, Roger. May the winds blow your way always. 1943-2016.

CHAPTERS

The White Gold of
Snow !

Janeth M Dentt

2018

ACKNOWLEDGMENTS

I fully declare that my writing is a fictitious collection of thoughts and feelings that I have absorbed and accumulated over my lifetime. As a writer scribbling thoughts on the computer to the aspiring author finding a pathway to publishing, there is a multitude of friends and places to recognize. To my hiking buddies who respect and understand the majesty of the Rocky Mountains and to all the people who freely shared a facet of insights on the internet or in person, thank you. My places, ev ents, people and incidents sift through my imagination then appear as fiction. I also need to thank Craig Ebel for designing the clever book cover after listening to my comments. Plus, of course, a loving scratch goes out to my stouthearted Schnoodle who slept through the entire book! Thanks all!

CHAPTER 1

AVALANCHE

McPherson Gulch was historically christened McPherson's Funnel by the Summit County locals. This ordained moniker described the gulch's formation to a tee. Cut a funnel lengthwise and there you had it, a perfect image. Drive west on I-70 from Frisco, Colorado toward Copper Mountain, take Highway 24 south toward Leadville and shortly, thereafter, on the left was a post holding a small hand written sign announcing McPherson Gulch. Skiers speculated that there should be numerous avalanches back in there because of the contour but for years it had held firm. One cabin plus one man was occupying 200 acres.

Johnny McPherson, who now owned the entire gulch property, lived an obscure life as one of the few known mountain men left in the county. He was, according to gossip, a recluse in his early 60's. Johnny had retired from the technology computer field in Denver almost ten years ago. His grandfather, Arnold McPherson, had willed the entire gulch to Johnny in a trust fund some 30 years ago.

Johnny had spent the last 20 years building his off-the-grid home. Grandfather Arnold McPherson had first built a one room log cabin in the 1930's. Johnny had simply added onto his grandfather's construction. He had successfully expanded the cabin adding spacious rooms, electricity, water and the internet all operated by solar power with generators. Even his steady girlfriend of ten years, would now visit his comfortable modern home holidays and during the magnificent summer season. His present living conditions were a far cry from Grandfather McPherson's.

The iconic old cabin was an existing symbol of the prospector's history. Growing up Johnny had been fortunate enough to spend several summers with 'Pops' learning to mine and respect the lifestyle. From his grandfather Johnny learned to understand the mountain history and economic growth.

Pops would never pass up an opportunity to tell his story. During the early days prospecting had been lucrative for him. Arnold McPherson went off to the gulch every summer to mine. In the winter he lived with his wife, Mary, in Frisco. When Mary McPherson died in the early 60's, Arnold made a decision to move permanently back to the gulch. Life had become just too citified in town for him.

Arnold sold their home in Frisco, paid off the loan on McPherson's Gulch and buried his wife, Mary, in the Frisco Cemetery. Their home in Frisco

sold for a pretty penny what with the tourist trade
beginning to invade the mountains.

History was a-changing the area completely,
Arnold observed. Even the production of Rounds
and Porter Lumber was slowing down; their
company's tree cutting contracts were dwindling.
Now tourists and water had become the name of the
game for Summit County. Suddenly, Dillon
Reservoir became more than just speculation. In the
early 1960's Denver's lawyers had learned that one
could buy water as a commodity and promptly
forced the town of Dillon to move one more time.
The bulldozers were digging a great big hole to hold
Denver's water reserve.

Even Frank Rounds, the lumber mogul, decided
to invest in the growing land value. He bought 5000
acres near Breckenridge. After his son Bill returned
from WWII, all Frank's investments began paying
off. Bill along with his Army buddy Paul Duke, had
become skiers in the 10th Mountain Division. The
two young men could now answer the question,
'What would tourists do in the winter?' Bill Rounds
got the ski area permit and then hired Paul Duke as
the first ski resort manager. Breckenridge Ski Area
opened for business!

Hell that was really the last straw for Arnold
McPherson. His decision to live in McPherson
Gulch had definitely been the right move for him.
He remained there until his death in the early
1980's. The old days of lumber and mining were
over!

Now, two generations later, Johnny McPherson
also sought a simpler life. Johnny did have some

concerns about the gulch contour. A financial investment for him meant that the gulch had to sustain his developmental construction needs. Naturally, the data about the avalanche potential had been read meticulously. A simpler life was one thing but science was another. The terrain where 'Pops' had built the first cabin seemed to be stable; no evidence of avalanches so far. Even his sister and husband ,who hated the backcountry, felt safe in Pop's cabin. This year they all had even celebrated Thanksgiving in the gulch. Yep, Johnny's girlfriend, Sadie and his remaining family, were coming around.

The summers now were the busy seasons when Johnny hauled in provisions. Flour and dried supplies were stored in Pop's old mining shaft that had become a perfect food cellar. Winter, meant trips out once a month to socialize and purchase items that could be carried in his backpack. Solitude was priority; Johnny liked it that way.

He had even made sure that his narrow trail to the home was not fit for motorized vehicle travel. Johnny didn't want the noise, exhaust fumes or unwelcome visitors to interrupt his lifestyle. The 'private property no motorized vehicles' signs along the path and the narrow metal footbridge over Ten Mile River had done the job. Also, skiers were leery of potential avalanches so his gulch was perfect for a McPherson.

He intentionally travelled by skis or snowshoes during the winter. Three miles of skiing was an easy price to pay for privacy. He did not own a snowmobile. If he really had health issues then

Johnny would contact the outside world. He had installed a 30' communication tower near his log home. A helicopter landing pad had been constructed for invited business guests and emergencies. He did various computer projects for companies all over the world. Johnny McPherson was a famous computer consultant who led a very private comfortable life off-the-grid.

***

It was a pristine morning as sunrise provided the atmospheric optics of sun pillars shooting far into the deep blue sky. The already fallen flakes appeared as cocoons of shard ice clustered together in the bitter cold. December 21 temperatures registered excessively cold this year barely reaching -20 in the morning. It had been a warm October followed by numerous freeze-and-thaws in November. The cold mask finally decided to stay for a while. Tomorrow was the Winter Solstice when the world would go slightly off balance; true, winter was about to begin.

A solitary figure, cloaked in a hooded white parka, broke the morning tranquility. The deliberate snowshoe steps produced a crackling sound as the intruder approached Johnny McPherson's domicile. Sticking out from the intruder's backpack was a rather heavy cylinder shaped object. The weight slowed down the progress as the figure began to ascend toward the gulch's rim. Traversing the climb while huffing and puffing like a train, the stranger groaned from the strain. An hour later with much effort extended, the assailant unloaded the small howitzer and placed a rather large shell in the chamber. Inspecting the wind swept lip of the rim, the assassin determined the direction of fire.

The explosion was then followed by two more blasts; a wait- and- see began. Slowly the snow awoke with a deep rumble and a ground shaking shudder ensued. The solitary figure ran backward in defense as the rim split off in a large fracture some 50' long. The hanging ledge tremored for a few fatal seconds. Finally, the gravity and massive weight brought the tremor to an end and the fracture fell. What man had instigated had become Mother Nature's unstoppable force. Not a mere light switch turning off and on but a monstrous power that would only conclude when the energy was spent.

Down it all came. An active formation of bonding snow drawing strength from gravity and speed. A rolling white tidal wave dumping boulders and trees into the mix. It was a recipe for chaotic disaster; the snow track spilled into the gulch funnel destroying the face of McPherson's Gulch. 100 years of environmental terrain had been given permission to finally move.

There was no hesitation as the tidal wave raced toward Johnny's home. It howled then heaved the communication tower out of its' way like a match stick. The twisted tower flipped high in the air then rolled 20'on the mobile surface. As if the hissing snow had become a deep sea monster, the tower was then sucked into the depths and disappeared completely. The wood home was no match for the avalanche force. There was not even a pause to consider human life as all traces of habitation vanished. Erased. Gone.

After the avalanche had filled the silhouette of the funnel, it slowed down to stuff the spout. The snow rapids compacted into one singular massive formation then belched out near the footbridge. Slowly the runoff lumbered to a stop. Done.

And then McPherson's Gulch became totally quiet as the white formation took only three seconds to settle. The snow had seeped into the gulch contours and was christened as the new stable surface. The sun began to sparkle on the snow. It had been a long three minutes. The wildlife would soon learn to trust the contour again and forget the past.

Winter Solstice would come and go. The calendar pages would turn as winter's grasp held the high country firmly for months. And then , the sun would change position and slowly begin the snow melt. The ground would begin to breathe and become alpine green once more. The Crocus would bloom. Mother Nature, who had held her secrets tightly, would finally have to reveal the truth. How would history record McPherson's demise?

CHAPTER 2

A CASE?

Detective Jennifer Holly, hands on hips, inspected her new office. In the last two years Jen had been promoted to detective by the Buena Vista, Colorado Police Department. She had settled into Ernie Burger's position when he had retired. In early spring Summit, Lake, and Chaffee Counties had decided that a new combined task force needed to be created. The High Altitude Pursuit Team had suddenly come into existence. Even though the normal Frisco Police Chief job had become vacant, HAPT provided the promotion that Detective Holly really wanted.

Jen Holly, on a whim and a push from her mother, Arlene, had submitted her name when the memo came out. She had spent every available hour writing a job description and potential goals for the new task force. Low and behold her efforts had paid off; the three Police Chiefs met and decided that she was a perfect fit. Not only was she the first lady boss but the first Captain of HAPT. Precarious situation to say the least she thought. Hard to tell if the other officers thought the position was too short-lived or they just didn't want it.

When a new department was created with grant money from the Federal Government, one had to wonder how long it would last. It still was an incredible opportunity for her, she calculated. The question was that if HAPT ran out of money next year, would it disappear and be called a demotion for her future? It was a chance that Jen was willing to take. No one to her knowledge had volunteered to work on the force yet. Jen Holly, needless to say, was nervous as she prepared for the first HAPT meeting.

"Lord help me," she mumbled inspecting her newly decorated office. Jen had brought in some gently used comfortable furniture. It stood to reason that if a family was in pursuit of a missing loved one, they needed a little comfort. Her office in the Community Center between Breckenridge and Frisco had plenty of corner windows. The sun's warmth positively heated the space. As her job description described, the office didn't reflect a police station atmosphere. It was inviting and secure; divided into office and conversation center.

The liaisons from each county were scheduled to meet in her office right now. It would be enlightening to see who would show up. There could be either Chiefs or their employees. Jen was curious about a lot of things these days. Breathe she told herself as the door opened.

Chief Josh Anderson of Breckenridge was the first to arrive. He eyed the black ponytail and big brown eyes curiously. She sure was the best looking of the leadership team; you could melt in those eyes he thought. It was the first time that they had met since the interviews. He nodded and held out his hand. "Welcome, Captain Holly. I approve of HAPT whole heartedly. That was a great proposal."

Jen motioned for him to sit. Josh Anderson picked one of the stuffed chairs and settle in. His intense blue eyes scan the area with approval. He was young for a Chief; his slight build was wiry yet physically fit.

"Thank you. I really appreciate your support, Chief Anderson," she said.

"Call me Josh please. These meetings are usually very informal and hopefully on task. Titles get in the way," he added checking out her office. "I like what you've done here. Nice space."

Jen grabbed her tray with coffee in a carafe and muffins for the occasion and placed it on the coffee table. "Well I hope that the other Chiefs are as enthusiastic as you are," she commented.

"Oh Carl will grouch about it being too comfy but deep down he's a teddy bear and will appreciate what is provided. Leadville has their own environment you know."

"I know. My mother lives and runs The Single Canvas Art Gallery in Leadville. She always tells me that the people may seem stand-offish but the houses were built narrow and close to neighbors so everyone shared their warmth . It's a community thing," she added with a smile.

Never heard that before but I like it," Josh said as he poured himself some coffee and extracted a muffin.

"Hey, I know you, young lady," Chief James Marten said as he came in stamping his feet on the doormat. "I like what you've done with the place. Can I move in?" James was stocky and tall; he towered over them.

"Absolutely," Jen said. She didn't hesitate before giving him a hug. Captain Holly had spent many hours with this officer from Buena Vista and felt like he was her adopted father. He smelled like home, she thought as they hugged. He pulled her ponytail playfully before he sat down.

Carl Hagen, the elder Chief from Leadville, filled the doorway watching the interaction. His face rather tense as he surveyed the office. Portly, fit Carl's description. "Doesn't look like a police department to me," he judged.

"That's the point, Carl," said Josh sipping his coffee. "Putting people in a situation to remove some stress is the point so sit down and have a muffin. You look like you could use it."

"You can say that again." He hung up his coat and flopped onto the couch. Chief Carl Hagen wore a very frustrated expression. It was obvious that he was going to share immediately. "Hell yes. Another day with the McPherson clan rattling my cage. No, I can't sign a death certificate without a body. The man died in an avalanche for God's sake. It's a known fact that winter isn't totally over. Anyone knows that we can't recover the body until the melt is over. Hell there's mud all over that gulch right now," he grumbled. "It will be June before I can talk the ME into going up there. The man didn't have a highway to his house for heaven's sakes."

"Well, he did have a helicopter pad," Jen added quietly.

"Don't make no difference. It ain't stable now," Carl shot back gruffly.

"Well moving on," said James Marten. "We need to discuss your staff here. "From my staff, Bill Smith wants to join Captain Holly. He lives in Frisco and also has worked with Jen before. Jerry Neal and Tyler, the wonder dog, wanted to come too. " I can't let you have both of my officers, Jen, but Bill is coming and Jerry will help when we can spare him. Is that okay?"

"Wonderful," Jen said with relief. Suddenly she was feeling far more confident. Those two men had worked with her before and she really respected them.

Josh nodded his head and added, "Well from Breckenridge I have an employee willing to work here, Officer Libby James. She has worked with me for three years and is very capable. The hiking and camping is right up her alley. A good officer. I think her computer ability will definitely be another bonus. She'll be here tomorrow morning."

The focus of the group then landed on Carl who finally disclosed his offering. "Frank." They all knew Frank; he was infamous. The man hated uniforms and bureaucracy. He didn't fit in any police department. For Carl to make such a ludicrous offering did not escape any of them.

"Come on Carl, you can do better than that,"

Josh scolded.

"It's like you really don't want this department to succeed," Chief James Marten from Buena Vista said then added, "that is ridiculous."

"Well I don't think so and neither does Frank. He asked for the damn move." Carl leaned back on the couch and folded his enormous arms as he divulged his secret. The top of his balding head had turned slightly red.

The room went quiet as everyone processed this piece of information.

"He did?" James Marten questioned not believing his ears.

"He did," Carl repeated. "I asked him twice and he told me that I was fucking hard of hearing." Carl dumped three teaspoons of sugar into his coffee and waited. "Besides, nobody else wanted to move. They all have family in Leadville and don't like Summit. No offense, Josh."

"None taken," Chief Anderson said shaking his head in disbelief. "Frank huh?" Josh murmured.

The focus then turned to Captain Holly who had turned slightly pale while she listened. "How's he feel about having a woman as a boss?" she asked.

"I asked him and he said that it couldn't be any worse then having me as his boss. You tell me, guys, what in the hell was I supposed to do? Frank has been in the police department since Moses wrote the Commandments. I don't even know where he came from; besides who cares?" Carl finished.

The silence was deafening as they waited for Jen's input. "He would handle the radio once and awhile," she stated. "What do you think?"

"I have no idea," said Carl. "Look we can't deny him any opportunity at this point. The man has seniority over everyone in my department including myself. He knows the history of our counties because he's lived here. He read your proposal. What could I do?" For the first time Carl Hagen's frustration became obvious.

Jen realized that Carl wasn't trying to destroy the program but had truly been trapped in this situation. She couldn't ever remember Frank saying anything to anyone in any of the counties. He just looked in disgust at folks. His training in backcountry had to have been excellent. The man lived in a tent as far as she knew. He was the quintessential local. "Oh my," Jen murmured then took a breath and continued, "I am fine with Carl's decision. I have to say that this is the first I have ever experienced a decision made by Frank. I believe we have to honor it. If he doesn't work out, I will let you know. What is his last name by the way?"

"Bless your heart, little lady," Carl said. "I will back you anyway that I can. If he starts drinking again then we, as a group, will have to fire him. That's all I can say. Mason." Carl added.

"What?" James asked.

"Mason. That's his last name."

"Hmmmmm," mumbled Josh Anderson.

"Then it's settle for now," Jen said. "I assume there is no pursuit cases right now since we are between summer and knee-deep in mud season?"

Everyone nodded and the room became quiet. She could practically hear their minds spinning.

Jen ventured forward carefully. "Carl, would you mind if I looked into the McPherson Case? It fits the down time definition of action for my department. Can we consider it a cold case?" She looked around at the faces.

Chief James Marten was the first to respond, "I think that's a great idea for a couple of reasons. One, being that McPherson Gulch is truly between two counties, Lake and Summit, according to the GPS maps. That's a fight for another day and, theoretically, Johnny McPherson died in December and it's now May; we could easily call it a cold case. What do you think, gentlemen?"

"It sure would be a load off my calendar," said Carl Hagen from Leadville. "I sort of feel like you got dumped on today, Captain Holly. However, having said that if we ain't got the money next year for your department, I would still have to vote to close it. Just saying so you know where I'm coming from. The Feds have a way of giving and taking away as you well know. Leadville is a mighty poor county next to Summit. Are we clear, gentlemen?"

"Bout as clear as you can get," replied Chief Marten.

"Well that's our dose of reality for today," said Josh Anderson from Breckenridge pulling himself out of the chair. Let's meet in a month?"

"Sounds good," Jen said. "Carl, can I come over today to get the files on the McPherson Case?"

"How about I send them tomorrow with Frank?" he asked shaking her hand.

"That will be fine," Jen said. And with that the Chiefs exited her sunny office.

She then went to the window and looked out at the mountains trying to think about where to start HAPT tomorrow. Bill would be here bright and early. Libby sounded great and it was good to have another woman in the mix. Frank would be Frank whatever that meant. One thing she did know was that the best approach would be to truly try and start clean with him. Straight on like his reputation didn't exist. Just maybe…she thought. Jen checked her watch. Time to meet Bix she thought and locked up the office.

***

The restaurant was just dimming the lights as Jen Holly entered. Bix Bixler was seated at a table near the front by the windows and waving. She got out of her chair and gave Jen a warm hug.

"Good to see you and, once again, congratulations. Quite a coup I'd say! Not without risks but that's life, right?" Bix stated ending her hug with an intense inspection of Jen's face. "How was your first day?"

"Better than I imagined after a sleepless night as you know. Thanks for putting me up last night. I was able to get a jump on the morning and that really helped," Jen said as she picked up the menu.

The ladies paused to make dinner decisions. "A couple pizzas since we're here for happy hour?" Bix suggested glancing at Jen. "Maybe Truffle Fries and salads?"

"Sounds fabulous. I am really tired of making decisions today. A beer would be my contribution.

Want one?" They surveyed the beverage menu as the waitress took the order. Finally, it was time to lean back and relax.

"I have officers that want to be moved into HAPT. Can you believe that?" Jen said happily.

"As a matter of fact, I can. You aren't a slouch, you know. Who?"

"Well Bill is coming over and Jerry on occasion from Buena Vista then Libby James from Breckenridge and Frank." Jen waited to see Bix's reaction.

"Frank? Never thought he'd move from Leadville. Well…well quite a surprise. You know he lives in Frisco?"

"What? I figured he lived in a tent," Jen sputtered!

"Actually far from it," Bix said then sipped her beer and waited for her dramatic pause to register. There should have been a drum roll, she thought.

"Where?" Jen couldn't stand it any longer.

"He lives in a million dollar home here in Frisco. Frank is a trust fund baby from the 1980s."

"Shit! You're kidding me," Jen sputtered again. "Does anyone but you know that?" She eyed Bix's weathered complexion and gray hair closely. Bix, as a friend, was one of Jen's greatest assess.

"Not a lot but a few locals keep tabs. The ones who have been around for at least 20 years like me know him. Frank Mason lives here for a reason," Bix smirked. "Masontown is named after his relatives; the family was originally from Masontown in Pennsylvania."

"Unbelievable." Jen Holly took a long sip of her

beer and stared at Carol Bixler nicknamed Bix for a long time. This turn of events had changed her total perspective. It was one of those earth shattering events that just sort of landed in your lap, she reconnoitered. So the whole 'tent thing' had been a ploy that Frank had used to his advantage. He obviously liked it, she calculated. Very nice to know, Jen thought to herself. It sort of made her disgusted but she'd get over it.

"Before our conversation takes another turn, did want to thank you for helping me pick out the office furniture. I think the Chiefs actually were impressed even good old Carl. And, by the way, it was the Chiefs who showed up today instead of liaisons. I guess my task force is solvent for a year at least."

"My guess would be for longer than that, Jen," Bix added as the fries with sauce arrived closely followed by the pizza and salads. The ladies found themselves in appreciation of great tastes. They split one more beer and proceeded to devour the meal. Bix was relieved that Jen's day had gone well. Her take on Frank was that he understood the opportunity that HAPT provided and jumped on it for reasons only he knew. Bix couldn't wait to watch the developments. It would be truly interesting. Jen Holly would make an incredibly good leader and Bix would help in anyway that she could.

"By the way, thanks for the room last night. You were right, it did make things easier today. I did feel grounded. Sure my cats are getting lonely, however. Guess I will have to find somewhere over in Summit to live. Buena Vista is quite a drive. Maybe this weekend I can look around.

"How about a one bedroom condo on Boreas Pass?" Bix asked. "Got a friend who is ready to rent her condo up there."

"When could I look at it?" Jen asked leaning up in her chair.

"I'll call her tomorrow early and let you know. Could you look tomorrow after work? Places don't last long in Summit as you well know."

"Perfect," Jen said. "Tell her maybe around 5:30?" Jen tossed her napkin on an empty pizza pan and finished her beer.

"Done," Bix said then popped her last bite of pizza into her mouth.

"Planning to do some snowshoeing Friday. Want to come?" Jen asked eyeing Bix's reaction.

"Sure. Where?" Bix asked.

"Near Copper. We could meet at the Officer's Gulch Trail Head. So Bix, guess what my first case is?" Jen revealed her cold case as she gestured to the waitress to bring coffee. She began to feel more comfortable with her decisions that seemed full of change. It just might all work out with the help of good friends, Jen mused.

CHAPTER 3

MEETINGS AND SUCH

Thirty minutes early Captain Holly unlocked her new office. She had muffins for the morning and was about to make coffee when the front door opened.

A short young lady entered and nervously smiled. "Captain Holly? I am Officer James from Breckenridge. Nice to meet you. Can I help you with the coffee. This is a great office by the way. Not what I was expecting but it does fit the job description."

Jen waited until Libby James had calmed down. She handed her the pound of coffee and then got a word in, "Nice to meet you and I am glad that you came over from Breckenridge. I hear you love camping and hiking?"

"It's my passion, yes," she said while depositing three scoops of coffee in the machine. Her red curls bouncing with each scoop of ground coffee.

"Glad to hear. I am hoping that this task force

will be able to challenge you." Jen proceeded to open the box of muffins and added some fruit to the plate. She eyed Libby and watched. The lady was maybe 5'4" and looked physically fit. The red hair and blue eyes kind of sparkled. Jen liked that. "So where are you originally from, Libby?"

"Kansas City, Missouri until three years ago. Got my degree and promptly moved to the mountains. I love it up here and Chief Anderson has been great. My folks are still in Missouri. Where are you from, Captain?"

"Colorado native if you can believe that. My mother resides in Leadville and owns an art gallery."

The front door opened and Bill Smith plus Frank Mason entered. "Congratulations, Captain Holly. It will be a pleasure to work with you," Bill said. Ever since Bill Smith had been shot during the Holden Murder Case, he had walked with a slight limp. Bill now hiked more than he ran. Determined to be physically active was obviously his goal. He couldn't help himself so he gave Jen a hug enthusiastically. His short brown hair had slightly begun to grey, Jen noticed

"Thank you, Bill. I am so glad that you have decided to join us. I hear Jerry will be with us from time to time?"

"Yep. Chief Marten just couldn't let both of us go. I'm sure it will work out just fine."

"I understand," Jen said. Her eyes moved to Frank Mason who had come in and dropped a box of files on the floor then sat down on the couch. He had grabbed a muffin and was pouring himself coffee. Obviously, he was used to being ignored, Jen observed. She went over and stood by the couch. It got quiet in the room as she stood waiting for Frank to recognize her. The silence spoke volumes.

Shocked and slightly uncomfortable, Frank put down his coffee and got up. He stared at Jen Holly for a few seconds and then realized that it was up to him to say something. "Frank from Leadville. You needed an officer from our department. I'm it."

"Glad you are with us, Officer Mason," Jen said and held out her hand for him to shake.

He looked at the hand like it was a dead fish for a few seconds then moved to shake it. "Nice to meet you," he mumbled then slouched back on the couch to think about the situation.

The rest of the officers filled in the chairs and sat down at this point. Libby had introduced herself to Bill and they were on a first name basis already discussing hikes and bikes. Everyone spent the next thirty minutes chatting and eating.

The atmosphere was relaxed and workable, Jen thought. She finally got up and brought the McPherson box over and sat it on the coffee table. "So shall we get started," Jen said. "Frank brought the files over from Leadville for our first case. It is to be considered a cold case at this time." Johnny McPherson's death on December 21 of last year has never been verified as an accident or homicide." Jen picked up a picture of Johnny and hesitated for a second. Frank and Johnny could have been brothers, she noticed. At least they were about the same age and build. She then continued, "The

avalanche in McPherson's Gulch might have caused
his death. We need a body, ladies and gentlemen.
We need evidence."

"Is there any doubt what happened?" asked Bill.
"The locals assume that he was taken out by the
avalanche." He popped an orange slice in his mouth
and munched.

"At this time we will assume that since there has
been no body found, Johnny McPherson is
missing," Jen concluded. "We can't assume
anything," Captain Holly added.

"You won't find much else in those damn files.
Everyone assumed everything in that case. The case
was closed by Leadville and left to spring," Frank
contributed.

"Did you know Johnny, Frank?" Jen asked.

"What do you mean by that?" he snapped.

"Since you have lived in Frisco for more than
thirty years, I would assume that the possibility of
you knowing the McPherson family is good," Jen
returned casually as she sipped her coffee. "Maybe
all three generations," she added.

Frank's mouth opened and closed as he realized
that this lady knew his background and, indeed,
more than he had suspected. Who in the hell had
she been talking with, he wondered. "Well as a
matter of fact, I did know Johnny. He was a good
man and so was his grandfather, Arnold. Quite
frankly I never knew of any avalanches in that
gulch before this one. It don't make sense to me."

The group looked at Frank. They were shocked
to hear that many sentences come out of his mouth .
No one in the group had realized that he lived in

Frisco and that he was a local with community ties.

Jen's brown eyes scanned the Leadville box. She pulled the box over and dug all the information out and proceeded to sort. There were now three piles on the table; she lowered the box to the floor and leaned back. "The way I see it is that we need to investigate the McPherson family, Johnny's business interests, McPherson Gulch plus past history and the crime scene. I would like to start the day by dividing up the research. Who wants to do what?" Captain Jen looked at the eager faces. "Frank, what is your preference?"

Frank flinched and then calmed down to think. It was pretty obvious to him that this Captain wasn't going to let him slide. It was a whole new ball game, he reconnoitered. "Where would you like me to start? I figure you've got an idea." He watched her cautiously while determining her agenda.

"How about the past history and local friends. Talk with his close friends who kept tabs on him. He was a recluse but my guess is that he spent time with various people in the county."

"Then I can work by myself and travel around the county to get the information?" Frank Mason asked trying to establish his perimeters.

"Exactly. People, at this stage of the investigation I want everyone to work individually. Tomorrow morning we will meet and share every bit of information uncovered. No one will be allowed to sit on their findings. We're not competing but working as a team. These morning meetings will launch the day's activities. So, Libby, what gets your fancy?"

"Well, if it's okay with everyone, I'd like to take McPherson's business ties. Sounds interesting to investigate an international computer consultant." Libby selected the pile of research that seemed to jive with business.

Bill eyed the piles of papers and pointed to family information. "Well I didn't know Johnny McPherson at all even though we both had ties in Frisco. I'd like to find out about the family if you don't mind including any girlfriends." Bill looked at Jen to verify his choice.

She nodded and said, "Then I am taking the crime scene. I have made plans to snowshoe in this Friday. Think I need to understand the terrain back there before we venture on." Captain Holly got up out of her chair and leaned on the back as she felt the need to address the team. Her 5'8" presence produced the picture of a strong countenance as she began.

"I, personally, feel that your choices and our direction will be excellent. I want everyone to work on this project 100 percent. If there should be a rescue or search happen in the near future, we would then have to jump on that situation. HAPT's major goal is to be quick response. As we finish our cold case meetings in the morning, we will then try to work in a couple of hours of classroom and techniques for high country rescue teaming. My goal is that within a month's time we feel like a well working team who can handle emergencies and detective type research. We need to be conscious of each member's expertise so that when we deploy on a mission, everyone knows where and how they fit.

Clear?"

The team listened intently and began to realize exactly what Captain Holly demanded of them. It obviously wasn't going to be cookies and milk at 10 for sure, Libby thought. Bill Smith's assumptions about Jen as a leader were right on target. Frank was beginning to realize that his slate had been wiped clean from Leadville and he would be required to truly contribute. Good.

"Now, because we don't have someone to take over the communication center yet, we need to share the duty. Each day one of us will be the designated office contact. I have put the weekly schedule on the wall. Libby, today is your lucky day. Exchange cell numbers and Libby, organize the contact roster. Our phone PR has to be both official and friendly sounding. No one will be exempt from this duty and I really want the public to feel that instant help is on the way. We will need to move quickly when in response mode."

So it was settled. They adjourned from the morning meeting and took their pile of information plus an office key. Each chose a desk and began to settle in. Frank threw his few papers on the desk and began to make a list of locals to contact. Libby James brought out a few of her desk belongings and organized. Bill Smith sat down and began to read the information while taking notes. Jen got up and walked over to the Summit GIS office to gather topography maps and other information. She intentionally left the office so her officers would feel the freedom of their own activities.

By lunch time Libby was the only person left in

the office. Her search had now turned into phone inquiries. She had picked out three companies who had used Johnny's services during the last year. She decided to begin the calls after lunch.

Jen walked back in after lunch and began to organize for the snowshoeing project tomorrow. She and Bix would go in the afternoon after the weather had warmed up. She began with her list of equipment to take. Naturally water and snacks plus her smart phone for pictures was priority. Jen added her avalanche beacon to the pack just in case the snow decided to move. Her personal inflation vest for sliding on the surface was also tossed into the pack. She knew that avalanches weren't really started by noise but they couldn't afford to take any chances. Movement and weather made any slide possible. She also added a large light weight bag in case they found anything as evidence. They could slide the bag down to the car if need be.

Jen then spent the rest of the afternoon scheduling their trainings sessions. Tomorrow the forest service representative would come and talk about winter and summer over night stays. Avalanche authorities were high on her list plus getting the ski patrol leaders in for personal contacts had to be important. Maybe a morning social with the leaders of the various ski patrols was a good idea sometime before winter. Snowmobile training and a mechanic for maintenance on the trail was important. They needed to be able to repair their own machines just in case. Captain Holly admitted to herself that her lengthy list could be accomplished over the next year. The team's cold case had become priority at this time.

She began to listen to Officer Libby James digging into McPherson's business. The young lady was friendly and seemed to ask the right questions on the phone. Libby would be ready for tomorrow morning's meeting.

Jen had decided to wait before she contacted any guest speakers. If all the team was working like Libby, their time would focus on the case first. After the morning meeting she would have more of an idea of the schedule. Jen decided to wait and see before scheduling anything. She leaned back in her chair and sighed. For the first time in an hour, Captain Holly addressed Libby. "Call it a day, Libby. Thanks for your work on the phone organization and the sheet with our information on it. I think people will feel comfortable dealing with us."

"Thanks. I hope so," Libby said and began to stack and organize her notes.

"I need to go see a lady about a condo on Boreas Pass. Ever lived up that way?" Jen Holly asked.

"No but I do have a couple guy friends who rent up there. They like it," Libby answered.

"Good. I need to make the move from Buena Vista as soon as possible so I have my checkbook handy." Waving her book, Holly got up and put on her coat. "Will you lock up, Libby, and don't stay too much longer. You're off the clock at 5:00, young lady."

"Will do, Captain Jen. See you tomorrow."

"So you shall." And with a wave Jen left the office.

Libby watched Captain Holly disappear out the door and let out a contented sigh of relief. This job was going to really be a positive move for her. Libby could just feel it. Less routine and more intensity seemed to echo through her mind. "Nice," she mumbled out loud and quietly hummed as she locked up the office. Her expectations high and enthusiasm soaring.

Frank Mason was still working at 5:00. He had found himself at Marcy Hamilton's door. He hadn't seen her for months and the 85 year old lady had always kept track of all the older locals including their children. Frank would be one of those people on her children's list even though his black hair and beard were abundantly sprinkled with gray. More coffee to drink, he thought as Marcy opened the door with a smile.

CHAPTER 4

THE CRIME SCENE

"I don't care what you say, Frankie, Johnny McPherson wasn't caught in no avalanche! I'd bet my life on it," Marcy said in defiance. "The boy knew what to do and his grandfather lived his whole life there after Mary died. It was a safe place. Hell, we walked up to his cabin years ago and there was nothing apparent that said avalanche. You want another shot of bourbon, boy?"

"Please," Frank Mason said leaning back in the rocking chair and scratched his beard casually. He had forgotten how nice it was to be in Marcy Hamilton's living room. The woman could spin quite a yarn and even at 85 knew how to entertain. She sure as hell didn't waste words that was for sure.

About two hours later after night had settled in Frank, a little tight from the bourbon, found himself walking home. It was nice to walk. The evening was quiet and the stars were abundant. You could almost fall into those stars, he imagined. There certainly was a lot to think about tonight. Nice way to fill a day of work, he thought; he had spent the time talking with the people he respected and knew. It was police work and yet not police work in his mind. The detective role for cold case was certainly a different animal.

When he had seen HAPT forming, he had gotten up his hopes that maybe someone would look into the McPherson Case. Chief Carl Hagen sure as hell didn't want it. He smelled politics and Summit County ties. That stopped him cold in his tracks.

No, Captain Holly was a different type of leader and just what Frank needed. The McPherson Case had just plopped into his lap today. Bingo, Holly had requested the case straight on. It had been Frank's lucky day! He wanted to find the son-of-a-bitch who had killed his friend and Captain Jen was just the one to do it. Her reputation from Buena Vista had followed her; this lady had guts and persistence. Captain Holly had been one of the major cops to solve the Holden crime spree. Hell, she and Detective Jerry Neal had tracked through the forest and killed the one stalker. Her cruiser had chased the pricks on backcountry gravel roads even. The news media had a video of her arresting the woman who poisoned the old guy. She was a one woman terror. Hell this old boy liked that kind of shit, he thought as he opened his front door.

***

As Captain Jen Holly opened the door of the

office on Friday morning, she was surprised to see all her officers hard at work on their reports. There was energy going and she hadn't even been there. Most excellent, she thought happily.

"Are we ready to meet? I brought food for the second day. Appreciate it now because next week I'll come empty handed. Next week the officer on communication desk duty needs to brew the coffee. Sound good?" There were nods all around but the officers were intent to finish their reports. Jen found no reason to interrupt immediately. "Half an hour and we'll start."

Captain Holly spread out her topography maps to study before she and Bix would snowshoe this afternoon. Most definitely the gulch was shaped like a funnel, she assessed. The only maps were, of course, created before the recent avalanche. The GIS Office would begin to map the newly formed area in late June. Right now, it looked like one mile in and then they could travel either to where the cabin had been or up onto the rim if there still was a rim. She even wondered if the cabin remains had surfaced yet in the melt. Johnny's cabin had been located on a plateau that looked fairly stable, Jen thought. She flipped to another map which described the rock formations and types of stone, granite being the most prevalent. It looked sturdy enough, she assessed. Granite didn't crumble that was for sure.

No, the granite wouldn't move so either the weather or man had to be a huge factor in this catastrophe. She decided to start with nature's involvement first. Freeze-and-thaw fluctuations could trigger the movement of any snow slide. She made a note to contact the Forest Service for the snowfall weather reports starting in October. It could shed some light on the activity of that specific gulch. What was happening over at Copper Mountain Ski Area would probably be close to the gulch weather. Jen decided to call the ski area and request their records also. Comparisons would be more than valid for the court hearing.

Her eyes then began to scan the elevations in the gulch. It looked like from 9,800 to 11,400. Copper was higher but close to these elevations for an average. Good comparison she reconnoitered.

"Well shall we get started, folks?" Captain Holly asked. Ready for some coffee she closed her folder, picked up her iPad and moved toward a chair.

"Can I start this morning?" Frank volunteered. The air in the room was suddenly sucked up by the other team members. It was a very unexpected and shocking development for everyone in the room except Frank Mason. He wanted to start!

***

Bix pulled up to Officer's Gulch Trailhead a little early. She had wondered about this whole avalanche event since it had happened. The locals couldn't believe that a avalanche had really occurred. The Forest Service wondered why it hadn't happened sooner. All in all, it was fairly curious. Bix had spent yesterday calling a few friends who wandered around backcountry more than she did. Her major question to these backcountry explorers was what did she need to look for as they covered the area? Of course, everyone said 'be careful.' The locals speculated about how settled the gulch was at this time. Bix figured that it had healed quite nicely over the months. Lord knew the amount of melting must have made the area more compact.

She turned her face into the sun as she rolled down her car window. It was one of those incredibly beautiful days where you could simply feel the power of warmth through the sun's rays. Bix let out an audible sigh and was lost in the splendor of the moment when Jen drove up.

"Afternoon. Did you bring some snacks?" Jen asked.

"Yep. Wouldn't leave home without them. Bix jumped out and locked her door. She then went to the back of her Wrangler and got out her pack, poles and snowshoes. "By the way, did I tell you that I am happy you volunteered your team for this case? Johnny McPherson needed someone to take on his case," Bix added. She tossed her equipment into Jen's Ford SUV Interceptor.

Jen shut the back hatch and stared down at Bix for moment. "At least you and Frank Mason think so. Had quite a surprise this morning at our meeting. He's all over this case. I take it that Johnny McPherson was one of his best buddies. Now I understand why he decided to transfer from Leadville." She moved around and got in the driver's side. They backed out and got on the highway toward McPherson Gulch. As they exited onto 24 Highway, Jen glanced at Bix. "So what are you thinking?"

"Well, I'm sure that Frank is glad for the case but I would bet he also needed a job change. Don't count the power of a task force team for less than it is. It sounds pretty exciting to me," Bix said.

They neared the McPherson sign and Jen put on her blinker. "Frank thinks the avalanche was deliberately started," Jen added. "I could sense his enthusiasm for the investigation. Hey look, there's a car up here just emerging from under the snow." Captain Jen stated. The blue color was just beginning to peek through the accumulated mass of white. It was obvious that the car hadn't been moved for quite a while. "Wonder if that's Johnny's car?" Jen pondered. She got out holding a ski pole and pack shovel then burrowed down toward the license plate. Jen came back to her car and entered the plate number information into her computer. They waited a few minutes until the answer came up. "Yep, it is McPherson's car. It's like the time just stopped six months ago," Jen added.

"Well, it did for him. Sounds like a kind of motive to me," Bix mumbled as she got out of the car. "There's a lot of locals that feel Frank is right. McPherson was more of a controversial character than I figured. I thought he just sat up here quietly computing whatever that means. Now, I am beginning to understand that your research isn't always good for your health. Johnny was an international authority who could create quite a stir." Bix got out, leaned over and slid her boot into the snowshoe binding then buckled.

They approached the footbridge. There were no human footprints going up into the gulch. No one had climbed since the last snow anyway. They began to cover the mile up the spout of the funnel. The elevation climb was more gradual than steep. Bix could feel her lungs getting a good workout, however. The snow had a wet crust that held their shoes up from the depth. She watched each step sink about three inches. Not bad, Bix thought. The time was noon so they had a good four hours to explore.

"So you're thinking that maybe we might be looking at an intentional avalanche also?" Jen asked stopping to catch air and drink water.

Bix thought for a moment then said, "Yep."

Bix's silent composure spoke volumes to Jen. She knew Bix. This silence meant that Bix didn't want to influence her but those were her thoughts. Local intuition was nothing to laugh at especially when it came from good sources, Jen reconnoitered. 15 years Jen's senior, Bix had become one hell of a good source.

They had met during the Holden Case and traveled to Denver for assault therapy meetings each month thereafter. She had promised Bernie Holden back then that she would look out for Bix; Captain Holly intended to keep that promise. What a wonderful couple Bix and Bernie had become. One lady, a North Dakota rancher and the other, a Summit County author and retired teacher. They connected two or three times a year. Seemed like that was enough for now. Anyway, there was a whole heap of respect present.

The climb continued until they reached an area where the decision to go rim or cabin had to be made. Both ladies looked around assessing the contour. "I'm thinking we ought to go up since there still is some of the rim left," Jen said. She pointed her pole at the ledge remains.

"I second that notion. If indeed there had been someone tampering with the snow slope, it would seem that they would fire into the area from there. Bix pointed at a small plateau about 50 feet above their present position.

"Ready?" Jen asked.

"Let's do it," Bix answered.

The ladies began the ascent slowly traversing the surface. Both, checking the terrain carefully for crevases. Their ascent was deliberate but extremely cautious; 30 minutes later they found themselves on the plateau looking down at where the cabin must have been located. Down there were some snow mobile tracks that circled the cabin area. Leadville's preliminary case inspection, Jen surmised.

Bix began inspecting the rim surface carefully. Being on the south side, the sun had melted off a couple of feet of snow, she observed. The rocks were peeking out. Bix moved closer to the granite ledge and began feeling around in the rock crevices. Jen inspected the snow surface. "Jen?" Bix said as her eyes caught a slight sparkle from an object some 10 feet up wedged into an obscure shelf. She pointed with her pole and Jen's eyes followed the direction.

"Bingo. What do you suppose?" Jen said in a

whisper. Her mind began calculating if her height plus ski pole would allow them to retrieve the object.

Bix stretched higher to get a better look at the object. She brought out from her pack a small pair of binoculars. After a closer inspection she said, "Best get pictures." It clearly looked liked a large shell casing to her. Mother Nature could very easily have had some help here, Bix thought. She aimed her imaginary finger gun in the direction of the possible shot. Perfect line for instigating a slide Bix then calculated.

Both ladies had seen the small howitzers that the ski areas used to start avalanches. Either Johnny McPherson was playing around or someone had intentionally fired the shell. The empty casing had discharged onto the existing snow surface or had been pushed into the crevice by the sheer force of the explosion. Now 10 feet up and exposed, the evidence had surfaced. Could be that the shooter had not seen where the shell had landed and left it. Maybe after more melting the police would be able to find more evidence. Who knew, Jen speculated.

"Well, that's an incredible surprise," Jen said a little louder as she took several pictures of the casing's position. She took off her pack and got the plastic trash bag out to put the casing shell in carefully. "I'll bet there's no finger prints but it will need to be tested. The chances that the person who fired the howitzer didn't wear gloves is slim."

Jen was able to get her footing on a small ledge two feet higher and used her pole to flick the casing free. It plopped and rolled toward them. They inspected the casing as if it were a carcass that landed on the snow next to them. The shell casing was definitely from a howitzer verified by caliber, 150 mm. The ladies stared. Jen used her glove to carefully pick it up after several more pictures.

She released a breath of air that her lungs had unconsciously been holding. Captain Holly then let the tension of the discovery register and said, "Okay, so now I am a believer." She carefully tied the bag shut and placed it in her pack. "A very interesting turn of events. Glad that we didn't wait a couple more weeks before venturing up here. It might have not been seen."

"Look at the direct shot that someone would have had from here. Wow," Bix said. She glanced at Jen for emphasis. To speculate homicide was one thing but to come upon the evidence was another. Granted, there were different scenarios here but Johnny McPherson destroying his cabin wasn't at the top of the list, Bix concluded.

Jen aimed her camera phone across the gulch divide then clicked panoramic pictures in the various directions. Her thought was that an avalanche expert could figure out where the explosion landed for best results. Lots of investigating to do, she thought.

Ten minutes later the two began the descent down toward where they suspected the cabin had been located. Bix had been up here years ago and she was fairly certain of the location. The descent was much quicker than the climb. The only problem was that there was zero evidence of a cabin. The avalanche had swallowed the evidence completely.

One could hope that after a complete melt some remains would surface and help solve this case. Of course they needed a body, Jen thought. Where would they find Johnny she wondered?

"I find it truly amazing that there is nothing here," Bix said. "I know that the force of one of these slides is incredible but to just completely take it all is crazy. Kind of like a tidal wave isn't it," she added poking around in the snow slowly.

"Chief Hagen was right. After 24 hours, recovery of an avalanche body becomes almost impossible; the warmth is gone which means no thermal imagery. I bet Tyler, Jerry's dog, might be able to find Johnny. That dog has a great nose," Jen said checking the area as thoroughly as she could. "Of course the body would still be frozen now. Haven't got an Infrared Beam Detector yet. Not sure if that would even work at this point. Should be lots of debris underneath to confuse any detection machine," Jen assessed.

"It looks so clean up here," Bix said. "It is as if nothing happened. Mother Nature simply erased the chalkboard, didn't she?" Bix then began to look around more thoroughly. "Where's the mine shaft opening? That can't be totally gone forever," Bix said.

Both ladies began inspecting the area poking with their poles. Bix moved back from the site and concentrated on her bearings. "The cabin was there she pointed and the mining shaft was over there somewhere."

They headed where Bix had pointed. From the top melt one could begin to see a small cliff ledge.

Jen took out her pack shovel and began tapping along the ledge. Finally, a clump of snow dropped and revealed the door leading into the McPherson Mine.

Together, they pushed it open and immediately felt a surge of stale air surrounding them. They went into the darkness to explore. Both ladies, simultaneously, flipped on their flashlights. The storage unit shelves had been searched; Jen and Bix could see dustless outlines where objects had been lifted then set back down carelessly. They looked at each other understanding the implications. The flashlight beams quickly inspected the frozen floor for prints. Nothing.

They stared at each other for a few seconds. Jen broke the silence, "Hello? Anyone here? Police." Her inquiry was met with stone cold silence. As they left, they closed the door securely so that future inspections could take place.

Bix spotted some bear tracks about 20 feet from the mine entrance as they got ready to hike back down. "I'd say it won't be long before the wildlife get in that door," she warned.

"So noted," Jen said.

CHAPTER 5

WELL IT'S OUT NOW!

"Well it's out now!" Captain Jen Holly grumbled throwing the *Summit News* on the coffee table. The officers glanced at each other then their eyes landed on the newspaper. "Is there anyone in this room that discussed our case to the news?"

"Capt, remember that I did talk with numerous locals yesterday. I did tell them to keep it under raps but you know how that goes. If one of my sources mentioned it to the wrong person, I can't help it. Shit happens," Frank said raising his hands in the air in surrender. Libby and Bill both nodded in unison.

"Well shit," Jen murmured. "I hadn't figured that we would become front page news so soon. I guess that would be my mistake." She thought back to Bix's comments about chatting with her friends before their trip to the gulch. Yes, shit did happen, she realized. "Guess that's part of my job. I was hoping that I could talk with the other Chiefs first, but I guess it really doesn't matter. I think I'll call the newspaper editor quickly and invite him over for a chat. Meet it head on. So let's talk about what we do want to release so far. Let's start this morning with what your reply to the content of this article would be. Do you feel it's accurate or are there incorrect comments?" She handed the article copy to each officer.

After a pause for comprehension, Bill began first. "I think the immediate family would find this article offensive and inaccurate. It implies that Martha, Johnny's sister, disliked her brother. She admitted to not being close but there was no hint about a fight of any sort. Her husband, Howard Carlson, is an executive with Slope Incorporated but to imply that the company wanted to develop a ski area in the gulch is unfounded at this time." Bill Smith checked his notes quickly then nodded. "Yep. 'Unfounded' is the word that he used."

"Well, Slope Incorporated is one of the three companies that Johnny had a contract with this last year," Libby James added. "Johnny McPherson was hired to research various gulches in Lake County to see if a viable area could be found. He did an extensive search and really found nothing that fit their expectations. He worked for them during the last summer in June so Lake County was his focus. McPherson Gulch is in Summit, right?"

"Yes it is mapped by the GIS Department in Summit, however, Lake County might be able to contest those findings. Actually, it's never been that important until now. Do you have a CEO name to contact other than Howard Carlson?" Jen asked.

"Yes." Libby said searching her notes now. Officer James's fingers were scanning material on her iPad at a lightning pace. "Walter Connally. Shall I contact him this morning and set up a meeting? It would mean a trip to Arizona to do it personally."

"See if he will consent to a web conference and record the meeting. Make sure that you get his permission to use the interview. That way we'll see his visual reaction and he will become familiar with your face in particular. We'll send you to sunny Arizona if it is a good lead but let's investigate a little more." Captain Jen then added, "Folks, make sure that you do view Libby's conference call sometime tomorrow. Forward it to everyone, Libby. That will make life easier for us."

Jen then turned her attention to Detective Bill Smith. "Did you personally talk with both Martha and Howard Carlson on the phone together yesterday?"

"I did. Want me to take a trip to Denver and meet them personally?" he asked sensing where Jen was going on this one.

"Definitely, but how about meeting with them separately? Howard at his office and Martha at home. Sort of a spur-of-the-moment thing. Starting with Howard Carlson first then head over to Martha at home, unannounced," Captain Holly said.

"Will do this afternoon if that's okay?" he asked.

"Make it so." She answered. "Libby, how about getting a warrant, if needed, for the McPherson Contract from Slope Incorporated. Call this Walter Connally and get on a first name basis and see if he will offer the paper work or not. Then set up the sync meeting." Libby nodded and shut her iPad.

"Frank, will you get with Jerry Neal from Buena Vista and see if the two of you can head up to the gulch. Take Tyler the dog along in case we might get lucky on finding the body. Jerry has done a lot of tracking and I think you two will hit it off. Another shell casing would be great. If you don't have a smart phone for pictures, borrow a camera from Breckenridge or Frisco Police."

Frank's eyes glowed. "Got a smart phone, Captain Jen. I'll dusk off the damn thing and use it. Looks like I've walked into the 21st century over here. Libby, tell me what iPad I need to buy after the meeting?" Libby hesitated then nodded with a smile. Frank couldn't have been happier with his assignment. "We'll scan the area and take lots of pictures. Hopefully, we won't find any hungry bears. How far into the mine did you and Bix go yesterday?" he asked.

"Maybe around 20 feet. It was quiet but I guess a sleeping bear would be quiet. I did ask if anyone was home. Make sure that Jerry has Tyler on leash just in case. Hate to have anything happen to Tyler."

"I'll tell Officer Neal, Captain."

"Good. Now I want to show you all where we're going to store our daily paper reports for each other and various county authorities for now." Jen removed the food boxes from the coffee table and lifted the table top that had hidden hinges. "Here," she pointed and then finished with, "always place this ugly green bowl back on the top. Since we're all going to be out of the office now and then, I just want to take some extra precautions. The filing cabinet is too obvious. I would like us to eventually use iPads only and keep the paper down to a minimum. Then I wouldn't need to see you all bent over writing each morning. The reports could be done from home and forwarded to all of us. Seems like wasted time in the office to me. We'll get a wireless printer fairly soon for our needs. Until then, remember to replace the ugly bowl on the table. The table is accessible yet might be overlooked if we had an interested intruder. Are we good on this?" They nodded.

"Today, I will be talking with the media and delivering our shell casing to the Buena Vista Ballistics Department. Chief James Marten has an excellent crime research group over there who will do a thorough job. Buena Vista would be the most impartial department in our area. Then I need to locate an avalanche expert from one of the universities. Someone not from the county so that if we should come to a trial, the information couldn't be discredited by local influence or some such nonsense.

Now about the media, anyone ask you about the investigation, refer them to me at all times. That way, I will become the spokesperson who has to deal with the questions. When they approach you smile warmly then refer them. Anyone have a problem establishing this type of communication with the world?"

"Absolutely not," said Bill, "and more power to you, Captain Jen." The officers nodded in communal relief. Staying away from publicity and having a clear order to do so, was a dream coming true for them at this time.

"I'm half day on communication duty so you will know where to find me," Captain Jen said. "Great excuse to invite the media here. I think a meeting on my turf for the first news conference is best. Keep in verbal contact with location conversation only today unless you text me. Frank, have Libby give you text lessons today if you need them. Then Libby, when the newspaper reporters and radio folk arrive, find some place to go and that's an order," Jen said with a smile.

Libby nodded then added, "Can I contribute a wireless printer to the office so we can forward our reports to a website then print them? It would be so much easier. I can create an internet address for us and only this department would know the password."

"Make it so and work on it today please," Captain Jen Holly said. "We'll verbally talk about the actual password tomorrow. I don't ever want to see it in any text or email. Do not write it down; do not tell any other police officer or family member. It must be owned by this group and if one of you did, at sometime move back to another office, the password will be immediately changed for the rest of us. Okay any other business?" The room remained silent.

The meeting was adjourned.

***

Libby dialed Slope Incorporated's home office and waited patiently on hold. Captain Holly had left for Buena Vista. The media would flood the office early this afternoon. Since Libby's window for private business was now until one, she had given all the necessary information to the secretary. Hopefully, Mr. Walter Connally would deem this call important. So much for the government power, she thought. Some ten minutes later, Connally came on the line.

"Hello? Officer James? Sorry to have kept you waiting but it is a busy morning. How can I help you?"

"Sir, our police office has just recently opened the Johnny McPherson Cold Case and I am researching his contracts from last year. Slope Incorporated hired him last summer. Is that correct?"

"Actually yes. He was a great resource for your area. We try to hire local anytime that we can. Is there a problem?"

"Oh no sir, it is a routine investigation for us. I was wondering if you and I could have a web conference today when you have time and if it would be possible to have you forward the Johnny McPherson files to the office here in Summit?"

"Well let me have my secretary check my schedule. I believe we could meet later this morning. As for the reports, I think you need to issue a warrant so that there is a paper trail for all concerned."

"I will arrange for the warrant to be sent out today or tomorrow. That's quite all right," Libby purred. "Just a point of interest, sir. I was wondering if you ever came to Summit or had Johnny come there during your business contact. It would help me to phrase my questions for our interview if you wouldn't mind." Her friendly tone paid off.

"Actually, I did come to Summit County at the beginning of his contract time. Need to check but I think it was July."

"Thank you, sir. That is helpful."

"Well, I have a meeting in two minutes. I will transfer you back to Clara to arrange our conference."

"Thank you. Looking forward to talking."

"I do want you to know that I will probably arrange to have one of our lawyers here to join us. It is just good business," he said with a slight edge to his tone.

"No problem," Libby said then was met with a click as he disconnected. Clara came on the line and promptly arranged the meeting for eleven. "Perfect," Libby murmured. She spent the rest of the morning organizing her questions for Connally. Libby figured that she had a good hour to talk with him since their interview could go into the lunch hour.

Around ten Libby slipped out of the office and went home to get the printer. Lordy, she had missed being able to use that link at work. It was beginning to look like one of the jobs she fit into was HAPT's computer geek. How cool was that, she thought. Even good old Frank was delighted with the free tutoring. So far Captain Holly was eliminating much of the tedious office work by introducing technology. Things were going just great right now she thought. Her perspective on being transferred looked like a bright spot. "Yeah," she murmured.

***

Bill entered the city of Cherry Creek near downtown Denver. He hadn't had much trouble finding the location. This area of the city sprouted rows of office buildings for the rich and busy companies. The Slope Incorporated Offices were located in a luxury complex towering above the street with underground parking and large street numbers for easy recognition. Bill grabbed the newspaper from his car seat and tucked it under his arm before he locked. The elevator directory said that Slope occupied the entire 6th floor. As he opened the glass doors to the main office, a bevy of secretaries looked up from their computers in unison skipping at most two seconds. "Howard Carlson?" Detective Bill Smith asked as he showed his badge to the group. Heads went down and back to work. One of the front secretaries motioned him over to her desk. Bill almost felt that there should have been a service entrance for him. The badge hadn't impressed anyone. "Mr. Carlson is in a staff meeting this morning. Can I schedule a meeting for after lunch today?" the lady asked.

"No. I will need ten minutes at the most of Mr. Carlson's time. A possible murder investigation trumps a staff meeting every time. Kindly tell him that Detective Bill Smith is here from Summit

County in regards to Johnny McPherson's murder."

"Please come with me," she said moving swiftly out of the main reception area. He followed her through a tunnel of offices and finally landed in one luxurious corner suite. Plush furniture and windows all around offered a stellar view of Denver. The young lady then closed the door quietly and disappeared in the pursuit of Carlson. Bill wandered around evaluating the various views from downtown to the West where a person could detect the outline of the mountains through a small amount of pollution. The air must have been evaluated as moderate today, Bill thought.

Approximately three minutes later, Howard Carlson arrived looking fairly bothered. "What is this about Johnny being murdered? Is that what I heard. Unbelievable."

"Unfortunately, it is true," said Bill who noted that Howard had eliminated any need for introductions. They had hit the road running. "Now that HAPT has reopened the cold case, a preliminary search of the avalanche area has revealed a shell casing that would indicate premediated mitigation. Someone started the avalanche."

"Couldn't that shell be from another time when Johnny did mitigation? Never knew him to bother with all the rules and permits. That's the McPherson way. Even old Grandfather Arnold McPherson was his own man. He'd let the county know later when he would blast in that worthless old mine. Johnny takes after his granddad and you can bet on that. Rules were second and need was first for that clan. The man was perfectly capable of keeping a tidy gulch," Howard said after throwing himself into a large comfy chair.

"The Forest Service has no such record of that kind of activity anytime in the last five years. Johnny would have to file a report either when it happened or later," Bill interjected. "Besides, in today's world an explosion of that size would have at least been detected."

"Hell, so your office is looking for someone to pin his death or homicide on and I'm a suspect? Is that what you're saying? That is out-and-out ridiculous! Holy shit!" Howard Carlson bellowed. "The company bought his fucking services and then ditched the son of a bitch. Johnny was really too arrogant to work with Slope. I found his contract an embarrassment. There were no results at all. He simply couldn't find any area with skiing potential in all of Lake County. Just goes to show you that hiring family is a load of crap. Not even for Martha!" he grumbled. "We had Thanksgiving dinner with him up there anyway. All's fair in love and war. Right? Relatives." Howard mumbled. "How he handled Slope's request just wasn't good business in my opinion. And here you are threatening Slope Incorporated and or me with murder speaking of another load of crap! That's not the way we do business!"

CHAPTER 6

BUSY DAY

"Sir, I am sorry that you feel threatened by me coming here. I assure you that it is simply routine on my part," Detective Smith said in a calm voice. "Our office must pursue all avenues in this case. I need you to take a look at this article that just appeared in the *Summit News,*" Bill said then handed the paper to Howard Carlson who inhaled quickly as he began reading the accusations made about his family. His pupils grew large and his face grew red!

"You have got to be kidding me? I'll sue these fuckers! Our family may not have always agreed on everything but Martha and Johnny were not out there to murder each other. They were sister and brother for heaven's sake. We visited Johnny and he came to our house occasionally. No, Johnny and I didn't agree that often but we did have a truce on business, if you're going to ask. And yes, it did center around the gulch. They don't call mountain property white gold for no reason. Johnny was sitting on a gold mine that wasn't mineral anymore but precipitation. I would have developed the area and he was of the persuasion to keep it as is. You know it was his family legacy?" Howard waited until Bill nodded before he continued, "You can't fault me for trying but I guarantee you, I didn't kill him and neither did Martha." Howard sighed thoughtfully then leaned back in his chair loosened his tie and added, "In case you haven't looked around, we're not destitute. We have a very comfortable life, and God willing, I can retire soon. Plus, Slope Incorporated will survive nicely without Johnny's property. You say you have a warrant for his research project?" Howard, again, waited for a nod. "I'll have Millie get it for you." Howard dismissed Detective Bill Smith quickly with a wave of his hand and a sigh.

At least Bill was going to leave with the McPherson project notes in hand. Howard was quite a character, Bill decided as he descended in the elevator. And, who knew what was really going on at Slope, he speculated.

***

Libby checked her digital watch and dialed Arizona. This interview would be her first solo. She glanced at her list of questions as the phone rang. Her dialogue needed to be perfect.

"Hello, are we on?" Mr. Connally asked checking the computer screen.

"We are," Libby replied. "Thank you for meeting with me on May16, 2016 at 11:00 a.m. Mr. Walter Connally. Is your lawyer present," she asked?

"Ah yes. This is Arthur Jones who represents Slope Incorporated ."

"Hello, Officer James. Are you all getting snow today?" Jones asked in a friendly tone.

"Not today. The sun is out and it's beautiful," Libby answered. People always thought that it continually snowed or hoped it would, Libby mused. Tourists. "Shall we begin? I know that you are busy and I would hate to take up too much of your time."

"Sounds like a plan," said Lawyer Arthur Jones opening a legal pad then nodding to a woman who was their personal recorder at the far end of the table. "We are recording this meeting by the way, Officer James."

"I am also recording this meeting so all is well. Now, Mr. Connally, will you describe your involvement with Johnny McPherson for the record?" Libby asked opening her iPad to jot down personal observations if needed.

"It was purely business. I had never met the man until I visited in July. You know he is Howard Carlson's brother-in-law?" Connally slipped in. "Due to his computer expertise reputation and his personal tie to Howard, McPherson seemed like a perfect fit for Slope."

"Can you elaborate on your comment, 'he seemed like a perfect fit.'" Libby asked?

Connally glanced at Lawyer Jones then got the okay to continue. "Johnny was a little out there for

57

my tastes. I don't think that I fully understood what drives a mountain man. I mean the guy was oblivious to making money. Preservation was all that he would talk about. I finally struck a deal with him to search Lake County for any sort of property grab that might work for a potential ski area."

"Then he was not interested in selling his property to you? Is that what you are saying," Libby questioned? Could be a motive, she thought. She glanced up to see the reaction to her question; she noticed that there was no reaction.

"That is correct. He was against any discussion about personal gain and or selling."

"How long did you stay in Summit in July?" Libby continued.

"Three days then back to the office. The research contract was signed and there didn't seem to be any other reason to stay at that point," Connally stated. "Our meeting in the fall was when McPherson said that he wouldn't sell his personal gulch to us and there was no other property in Lake County so Slope's communication with the man was over. Didn't like him anyway so that was okay by me. Arrogance doesn't play well. Anything else?" he asked in a dismissal mode.

***

Officer Frank Mason was in his snowshoes when the Buena Vista patrol cruiser pulled in. A tall young man with glasses got out. From the back seat he let out his co-pilot, Tyler, a German Shepherd who wagged his tail. Tyler barked once with excitement when he realized there was going to be a hike. Detective Jerry Neal had also brought his snowshoes plus a pack. The two men shook hands first then began their conversation.

"So Captain Holly wants us to see if we can find anymore shells or a body. Hope Tyler is ready for that kind of activity," Frank asked. His voice was slightly skeptical, Jerry noticed. Frank Mason had never worked with a trained dog before was Jerry's take.

"He'll be fine," Jerry said. "He had three months of cadaver training last year." Jerry then began getting out other equipment from the trunk of his car. He had brought a metal detector plus an image detector. He grabbed Tyler's pack and placed a gadget in each side. Tyler's pack was bright orange and announced that he was a K-9 Service Dog in bold letters. Frank went back to his car and produced an old army pack that he had used all his adult life.

"Can I carry some of the equipment?" Frank asked holding out his hand.

"How about the water supply for us? I didn't have a chance to check the maps so I don't know the area well at all for streams and melt conditions."

"Well then I will definitely come in damn handy today." Frank then added another jacket and flashlight to his pack. "I've been up here both winter and summer," he offered. "I know McPherson's Funnel like the back of my hand; we'll need water this time of year after we cross the hiking bridge up ahead." He piled the supplies into his pack then glanced at Jerry before elaborating on what he wanted to reveal to this stranger. "Got to tell you that Johnny McPherson was one hell of a friend of mine for the last 20 years. Guess you could say that I have a personal stake in our investigation. The man was smarter than shit and knew computers like nobody's business. Johnny's cabin was self-sufficient and the man took all the precautions. Actually, I think he had an avalanche detector in the house."

Jerry handed Frank the water and snacks. He listened with intense interest; Frank was a wealth of knowledge. Jerry hadn't realized how close his hiking companion was to McPherson. The case was getting more interesting by the moment, he speculated.

Frank continued, "The detector would signal an alarm if the earth began to tremble before a slide; it monitored the various snow crusts along the rim. Johnny had the situation covered in his mind so he wouldn't be caught off guard."

Jerry stared up at the gulch surveying the contour. "Sounds like he was well set for survival. I guess you agree that it wasn't an accident?" Both men tightened their packs and buttoned their coats then dawned sunglasses for their trek. Tyler was off leash but still very aware of his surroundings and ready for any orders as they began to set the pace.

Frank finally answered the question, "It wasn't no damn act of Mother Nature. I couldn't get Chief Hagen to buy into my theory so when Captain Holly got the opportunity for this task force, I jumped on it. Well, that was one of the reasons and also that she seems to be one hell of a cop." They moved up the funnel of the gulch.

As they arrived at the abandoned car, Jerry asked, "Is this Johnny's car?"

"Yep," replied Frank. "He's had it for years. Wonder if it would start? Well, it makes no matter now I guess." His expression saddened for a few seconds as he remembered that Johnny was dead.

Jerry opened the car door and took out a few small articles from the front seat then placed them in a plastic bag. "You know I worked with Capt. Holly in some pretty strenuous conditions. She knows what to do and when to take action. Her instincts, when we followed that suspect into the woods last case, were top notch. She can't bird call worth shit but she sure can pursue." Jerry searched the glove compartment and seats thoroughly. "Looks clean to me," he said before closing the car door.

"Glad to hear your opinion about Captain Holly," said Frank with a chuckle then continued, "and I'll remember about the bird call thing. By the way, it was her idea to investigate McPherson; I didn't have to say a thing," Frank added as the men crossed the footbridge.

Their footsteps crunched the snow surface. It was cold no doubt but equally still and beautiful; the two officers had become lost in their own thoughts and pace. Highway traffic noise was replaced by nature's winter quiet. As a hawk flew over, the men stopped to appreciate the sound of wing motion. It was a magnificently soft sound whispering through the still of the morning. Backcountry hikers did admire subtle nuances. It was always magic; it was gold. When the hawk circled the rim then disappeared, they continued their ascent.

Frank spoke first, "You know there's never been any slide movement up here before. Arnold McPherson, Johnny's grandfather, lived up here and did mining for some 15 years after his wife died. He never told me nothing about any movement and the old guy would, once and awhile, set off dynamite in the mining shaft. Pretty damn sturdy up here until now." Frank pointed at the far rim where the avalanche had started. "See how that rim has now crusted over again like cement. You'd have to blow the hell out of it to get the snow sliding." He eyed Jerry to see how the last comment set. There was a slight nod.

"Time to see what we can find then," Jerry said. "Let's go to the cabin site first then up onto the rim. Sort of backward from the way Bix and Jen did their trip."

"That's what I'd do," Frank murmured. He watched Jerry take a glove out of the evidence bag and let Tyler sniff it.

"Find what you can, Tyler." The dog took off like a shot. According to Frank's later calculations, Tyler headed directly toward where the cabin had been located. The dog outlined the missing cabin's foundation. Tyler had circled it precisely then sat down looking at Jerry. Frank's dog appreciation took a giant leap of faith.

"Doesn't look like there's a body in this area. I'll send him over it again just in case," Jerry said. "Find, Tyler, find." The dog, once again, smelled the snow area. Nothing. Tyler sat. "So where else should we look?" asked Jerry.

Frank thought for a moment then said, "Let's try the mine shaft and see what's there." As they walked in the direction of the mine, a murder of crows lifted off the ground leaving a trail of empty food containers in their wake. The men followed the trail of cardboard some 50 feet toward a darkened hole in the side of the cliff wall.

Frank noticed first that the door had been completely ripped off the hinges and discarded some six feet away. It had been thrown like a toy. "That ain't what Captain Holly's pictures showed. Something has been in there since." He got out his phone and started taking pictures.

They approached the opening cautiously. Jerry had leashed Tyler. The dog, however, wasn't showing any alarm. Whatever had entered had by now left. Frank turned the discarded door over and discovered large claw marks traveling the entire length of the door. "Well I'd say if there wasn't a bear earlier, there has been one now and a big one." He took more pictures.

Both men headed toward the opening and peeked in. With flashlights on, they investigated the chaos. Their entrance was met with a sudden mob of small critters scurrying in shock. The place was littered with half eaten boxes of food. Didn't take a genius to figure out that after the last visit, the awakening animals had followed the smells. Bingo. Dining had officially begun. The men went at least a 100 feet back into the mine and found nothing at that point. Tyler had indicated that he did smell human scent but that could simply have been normal. Hell, Tyler could be smelling Bix and Jen's scent. The critters had pretty well taken care of any other evidence present. Jerry and Frank walked back and stood outside surveying the entire scene.

"So let's get the gadgets out and check this whole damn area," Jerry suggested. "Any evidence of a body or something interesting might just appear in the images. You want to do the honors with the metal detector and I'll do the image detector?"

They searched for everything and anything that might seem important. Both men took notes of what was identified. They discovered that the cabin remains were still some six feet under the snow and pushed about 20 feet distance by the avalanche force. Frank found remnants of the tower twisted like licorice sticks under the snow. Jerry found images of furniture and beams. Neither man found a body image. Tyler had been correct. Frank decided to move over toward the mining shaft area again just for good measure.

He watched the scavenger crows who had come back. The food smell had bolstered their confidence of course. Frank focused on one big old stubborn male crow pecking away at something that sparkled in the sunlight. It was obviously stuck tight in the ice. Frank wandered over to inspect. He shoed the old guy away and got out his pocket knife. Squatting down Frank began to dig. The metal detector squawked so Frank turned it off for the time being.

He extracted a silver key from the ice and held it up to the sun. There were some numbers on it.

Frank took a picture of the area then put the key into his pant pocket.

"Frank, come here. Check this image out. You said a avalanche detector? What do you think?"

Frank rushed back over to where they had found the cabin remains and checked out the screen of the image detector. There it was, he knew. "I'll be damned. Must be what four feet below? Let's mark it."

Suddenly a shot ripped through the frigid air sending Frank onto the snow. The bullet spun him like a top; the spin left him face up.

Jerry had also dropped to the ground and used a silent hand motion to keep Tyler with him. He grabbed his rifle and aimed in the direction of the shot and let off several rounds; there was no return fire. Another hand command then sent Tyler racing up the slope toward the rim.

Jerry crawled over to Frank and checked out the wound. He ripped back the pant leg and investigated the damage. The bullet must have gone right through his left leg leaving an entrance and exit wound. That was the good news. However, the bullet must have nicked the femoral artery. The body's warm blood let off steam as it gushed out. Frank was out like a light. The warm blood dug a small ditch through the white snow. Jerry began shaking Frank to get him awake. "Come on Frank wake up!" Jerry was watching Frank's now pale face regain some consciousness. He eyed the slope to check on Tyler's progress then focused on Frank's situation. It was quickly becoming an emergency. Jerry got out the blood coagulant crystals from his pack then added a tourniquet for good measure. The stream of escaping blood slowed slightly. "Thank God," Jerry murmured.

Frank began to mumble. Jerry checked out the rim again with his binoculars then whistled for Tyler to return. The sharpshooter had disappeared. Jerry then pulled out his radio and called Captain Holly's Office. "This is Detective Neal 10-20 location, McPherson Gulch. Come in, Captain. We have a 217 in progress and need assistance. 10-53 man down;" Jerry then added, "11-41, ambulance needed. It is a Code 40," he said making sure that the ambulance team knew the severity of Frank's condition.

After a few crackles in communication mode, Office Libby James came on the line. "10-4 Detective Neal. Contacting with Code 3, Captain Jen and the Summit Ambulance . Can you meet them at the bottom of the gulch for directions in 20 minutes, 10-4," she asked?

"I will be sending my K-9 down to escort them back up. Right now it is important to start a fire and keep Officer Mason from going into shock. Make sure the ambulance team has worked with me before. They'll know what to do. Be advised 10-45B is his condition. 10-4."

"Affirmative 10-4," she answered. Libby sprang into action. She had just finished her call to Connally so the timing was good. She alerted the ambulance dispatcher first then called Captain Holly. "Captain Jen, there have been shots fired in McPherson Gulch . Detective Neal just posted a 10-45B by radio. Frank is down. Neal is staying to assist Frank. Ambulance enroute. K-9 will escort them to the scene. Code 3!"

"I'm on my way. 10-4." Said Captain Jen entering Leadville from Buena Vista. She hit the sirens and lights then informed Chief Hagen's Office that she was coming through in haste with a Code 3. Damn, so soon, she thought. "Please, God, keep Frank safe. "We just got started," she murmured.

Jen could feel the sweat on her hands as she maneuvered through Leadville's main street. Her eyes actively scanning for any tourists trying to jay walk or a resident pulling out from the side streets. The stoplights turned green on cue as she moved through. Jen checked her watch and figured that she was probably 20 minutes away. She floored the Ford Interceptor as the city limits sign of Leadville disappeared in her rear view mirror.

CHAPTER 7

RESCUE!

Tyler sat patiently at the Ten Mile River bridge near McPherson's abandoned car. The Ambulance came to an abrupt halt some 100 feet away and four attendants leaped from the back. The driver remained to turn the ambulance around for the hospital run. The team loaded their equipment in packs and then began the trek up the gulch. One attendant carried the light weight red sled stretcher. They had worked with Neal before so the hand signal was given to Tyler. He gave one bark and took the lead.

Within 20 minutes they had covered the area and saw a campfire some 50 feet in the distance. Tyler let a bark and ran full speed to Jerry. Space blankets were immediately taken out and packed around Frank Mason. The emergency team inspected the wound then proceeded to take vital sign readings. The stretcher attendant clicked on the radio and began the conversation with the emergency room staff.

Jerry and Tyler now stood back out of the way. Through his binoculars he scanned the rim once again. Nothing seemed to move up there. Rifle in hand, Jerry would wait until Jen arrived to investigate.

His focus went back to the scene around the campfire. The radio had brought at least four more voices into the frenzy. The instructions came fast and furious. The leg was being securely packed and Frank was now on the sled stretcher. The team had added IVs and now had Frank snuggled in s silver cocoon for warmth and safe transportation. "He'll make it," the young lady said patting Jerry on the arm. "Good work, Detective Neal." He nodded and watched them load up all the equipment that was scattered around Frank.

Then as suddenly as they had arrived, they now were moving down the gulch leaving red stained gauze and tracks in their wake. Frank in his chrysalis was sliding safely on the sled; he resembled a self-contained mobile hospital room.

It became, once again, silent for Jerry and Tyler. Jerry felt relief now that Frank was in good hands. It was almost surreal, Jerry thought, as he tossed snow on the fire to bring it down. He then picked up Frank's incredibly old pack and gave Tyler food and water. He folded the old keepsake and stuffed it in his own pack. Frank deserved to keep it, he reconciled.

As Jerry glanced once more in the direction of the team's departure, he saw a lone figure jogging with snowshoes on toward him. He waved at

Captain Holly while marveling at her speed. Once a
runner always a runner, he thought.

***

Detective Bill Smith had just arrived at the
Carlson residence. A Lexus was parked on the
garage ramp. Did look like Martha Carlson was
home. Very convenient he thought for the family to
live and work in Cherry Creek. Very tidy, he
mused. Bill was pretty sure that Martha hadn't
sneaked up into the gulch and fired a howitzer.
Howard had an alibi and Bill would bet that Martha
did too. Of course they could afford to hire
someone, he observed, as he sized up the mansion
with a four car garage.

As he closed his Ford Interceptor door, Bill had
to wonder what he would learn from the lady of the
house. His knock at the door brought the maid.
"Det. Bill Smith here. I need to speak with Martha
Carlson about her brother's death." The maid
simply nodded and waved him into a living room
decorated in pastel colors. Bill sat down and waited
politely. He had to assume that Martha was
probably calling Howard at this very moment.
Whatever, he mused. About ten minutes passed.
Maybe these two hadn't done the crime but they
were sure being careful. Maybe money made you
careful, Bill calculated. One had to be sure that the
lawyers said it was a-okay to speak. What a way to
live he thought.

"Detective, what may I do for you?" said a very
regal lady while offering her hand to Bill.

He got up out of his chair and likewise offered his hand. "Thank you for seeing me, Mrs. Carlson. Sorry that I came unannounced but driving to Denver really creates a short schedule."

"I would imagine. Would you care for some coffee? Water?" she asked motioning him to sit back down which he did.

"No thank you. I have to tell you that we have opened Johnny's case again but this time as a cold case. We have discovered that there is substantial proof that the avalanche was started by the intentional firing of a howitzer. Therefore, the police must change the potential death certificate from accidental to homicide. I hope you understand?"

"Indeed I do," Mrs. Carlson said nodding her head with a troubled expression. "Do you have any idea who might have done such a thing? My brother was a kind man and really didn't have a lot of enemies that I know of. Granted, we didn't see each other often but we were in touch through emails. So hard to believe…."

"So Johnny didn't mention anything happening out of the ordinary? When was the last time that you two communicated?" Bill asked.

"Off hand I don't have the exact date but we did email around the first of December. You know, discussing what the Christmas plans looked like. Howard and I have two adult children who live out of town. Holidays have really become difficult especially now that there are grandchildren," she said leaning back in the chair letting out a rather frustrated sigh.

"I understand. Would it be possible to have your email communications with your brother for say the last year?" Bill ventured.

"Oh I deleted all of them after Johnny died. It was just too painful. Sorry."

Bill had two thoughts about that development. One, they were evidence and or the lawyers advised her to trash them. Or, she didn't want any keepsakes from him. Interesting Bill speculated. Not exactly sisterly. "Mrs. Carlson, do you know of anyone who might hold a grudge against your brother?" he asked changing the subject.

"Heavens no. I can't imagine unless…"

"Unless what?" Bill asked quickly.

"Well Sadie might know of something. She was closer to him of course." Her eyes explored Bill's face like an x-ray.

"Sadie? Please tell me who she might be?"

"Johnny's girlfriend of ten years. They were sort of an off-and-on number. One never knew. Her relationship might help you find out more details. Johnny and I talked about the kids and our plans. How we were feeling and how Howard was doing. Fairly harmless conversations."

Bill had known that Sadie Russel had been Johnny's girlfriend and in fact the case files had a recorded interview from her. He had listened to the interview. Right now it was interesting to get Martha's take on Sadie. Didn't look like there was any love lost between these two, he thought.

***

Officer Libby James kept in contact with the hospital in Summit. Frank's ETA was ten minutes out.

Captain Jen had just called in on the radio that she had met Detective Neal in McPherson Gulch. Libby had been advised to call the media people and tell them that Captain Holly would be delayed for two hours. Libby was to relate the fact about an officer was down and Captain Holly was on scene. The situation would certainly delay the meeting. That was it; no more information given at this time. Libby knew it was enough to peak the media's interest.

She then put in a call to Bill Smith's phone. He needed to know what was happening. Libby was directed to voice mail which probably meant that Bill was in an interview. She told him to call immediately. He would get with her soon.

Libby leaned back in her chair and sighed two volumes of air. Well, she had wanted a little more action other than traffic tickets and it was certainly working out for her. Boy, was it!

***

"Are you all right?" Captain Holly said first thing before any police business. Jerry Neal was a damn good friend. She finished her jog slightly out of breath and gave Tyler one good pet while inspecting Jerry for any harm. It was all good, she realized. Now, to police business she assessed.

"Where did the shots come from," she asked eyeing the gulch one more time.

Jerry pointed up near where Jen and Bix had found the shell. "One shot," he clarified. The position did hold a full view of Johnny's cabin. Without another word the three began the ascent.

From the rim, Tyler began to pick up a smell. His nose was pushed into the snow and his legs were moving. The two humans followed silently knowing exactly what was happening. On a small plateau, Tyler made a circle illustrating that the tracks had lingered in that area.

"Stay," Jerry said. Tyler sat and watched them for another command. "Let's turn on the image detector just for kicks," Jerry suggested.

Jen began circling much like Tyler had done. Her eyes focused on the foot prints in the snow. From her pack she pulled out some plaster to fill one of the prints for the lab. Size 11 she assumed as the plaster hardened. Snow boot of some sort according to the tread. "Hey Jerry, have you seen this type of tread before?" Captain Jen asked.

Jerry kneeled down and inspected the tread closely. "Doesn't look like an American name brand to me. I could easily be wrong of course what with all the cheaper boots coming on the market."

"Hmmmmm," was Jen's comment as she placed the plaster print in her pack. "Wonder if the guy leaned his rifle on the ledge for the shot," Jen offered. "Come, Tyler, let's take a look while your boss is busy. They moved slowly over to the cliff ledge and inspected. Tyler moved five feet in front of Jen. He then sat down next to a little shrub bush some three feet tall. "Bingo. Thanks, boy."

Captain Jen checked the scratch marks on the

largest branch. She took pictures and used a swab to check for DNA. The guy might have placed his hand on the branch and small ledge to steady his rifle, she thought. "It came from here, Jerry. He had a clear shot. Which now brings me to the question of why Frank and not you?" she asked and waited.

"Good question and I can't answer it. There was only one shot and it hit Frank directly. The shooter could have then aimed at me quickly and taken both of us out. Instead, he hightailed it out of the gulch. Tyler came up here and found no one right after Frank fell. Does look intentional doesn't it? Unless it was merely a warning shot of some sort," Jerry offered.

"Makes no sense for a shooter to come in three miles and then climb up here to fire a warning shot. Percentages, unfortunately, targeted Frank," she assessed. Actually, I think the sharpshooter thought Frank was Johnny McPherson. Have you seen the picture of the guy? Frank Mason could be his brother."

"Well that's different," Detective Neal said and turned off the detector. "The assassin then must think that Johnny is alive. Wonder what made him think that? Interesting turn of events."

"That, or he had followed you two and saw Frank from a distance and simply couldn't take a chance that it might be Johnny McPherson," Jen reconnoitered.

***

"I am extremely sorry to report that Officer

Frank Mason was shot by a sniper in McPherson Gulch at 2 p.m. today. Officer Mason has been taken to the Summit Hospital and is in critical condition. I do not have anymore details at this time." Jen then took a deep breath and continued, " I also need to relate to you that recent evidence uncovered by our team has made it necessary to reclassify the McPherson Case. It will now be classified as a homicide."

Questions exploded throughout the room! Hands flew up begging for attention; the reporters' voices grew louder in a frenzy.

"Please," said Captain Holly in a firm quiet voice. She watched the group get a grip finally. Jen waited patiently. The dramatic pause worked; the media began listening again.

"At this time we have very little information about the shooter and or Frank's condition," Jen added. "My officers are on the way to the hospital to donate blood in hopes that they can help Officer Mason. I will join them as soon as this news conference is over. I was hoping to serve cookies and lemonade to you," she smiled slightly. "My hospitality has been cut short. I apologize. I can do better the next time we meet. Because time is of an essence, I had Officer Libby James print out my HAPT informational facts sheet for you. Libby?"

Libby nervously smiled and proceeded to distribute the informational sheet. Thank God for my printer, she thought. Jen began shaking hands and personally introducing herself.

"Captain Holly? Captain Holly? Interrupted an eager female reporter from Denver who had rushed up from one of the TV stations. "What does HAPT stand for?" she shouted.

Jen smiled and said, "High Altitude Pursuit Team. We are a newly formed task force created by the three counties of Summit, Chaffee and Lake. You may thank your local police leaders for having the foresight in establishing our task force to handle just this kind of event. We are equipped and ready for the task. Thank you for asking," she smiled at the young reporter. "And thank you all for your concern and interest. We'll do our very best. Now I have to ask that we call it a day and dismiss."

Capt. Jen Holly breathed a sigh of relief as she and Libby headed for the hospital. Jerry and Bill had already gone there some thirty minutes earlier. Hopefully, Frank's condition was improving.

"I think that went well, Captain. At least they weren't growling at us," Libby said relaxing a little in the car.

"Well get ready to meet the reporters again at the hospital. I hope we can get the group to give blood if they want any details. Guess they call that blackmail by blood."

"Too cool," murmured Libby as they locked the car and rushed toward the hospital entrance. As they dived into the media crowd, Captain Holly motioned them to join her as she said, "Come on let's give blood!"

The reporters glanced at each other, then shrugged and followed Holly through the hospital entrance.

CHAPTER 8

BLOOD SISTERS

Some thirty minutes later everyone was either giving blood or relaxing after donating. Libby and Jen were the last two officers to volunteer blood. When they finished, Jen told the team to meet in one of the hospital's conference rooms. The news media received a little more information in return for their blood donation then left. The blood clinic had finally become quiet until the next emergency.

During the wait at the hospital, Bill had gone up to the ICU unit and checked on Frank. The doctors had stopped his bleeding and repaired the artery wall. Frank was resting peacefully but still sedated. It was now time to watch him. The medical staff had reported that if their repair job worked then Frank could stay in Summit. However, if he began bleeding again, the helicopter would need to transport him to Denver. Their fingers were crossed.

Bill and Jerry arrived first in the conference room. They sat down and finally relax. "What a day. Been busy for everyone I'd say. Hey Jerry, check out your phone. There should be individual reports from the team about what has occurred today on all fronts."

Jerry checked his messages and then murmured, "Wow. Nice." The two guys buried themselves in the investigation emails. Libby and Jen arrived five minutes later.

"Everyone up to date on the information?" Jen asked glancing around the table. Heads nodded. "We have one shooter, according to the footprints. He fired one shot and then left. We can assume that Frank was probably the target. Jerry and I found the exact position that the shooter had occupied. It was dead aim, premediated. I'll record the event later after I have time to think. Will you do the same, Jerry?"

"Yep," he answered.

"Tomorrow Libby may have time to set the website up with a new password...." The team began thinking what to use.

There was a knock on the door and a nurse entered. "And the winners were found in the police blood donation. Our two female officers with B positive blood are a match for Frank Mason. Congratulations, ladies; you just saved a life," with that comment and a smile, the nurse left.

"Bill suddenly came up with the first password for the team to use. "Blood sisters. You're now Frank's blood sisters whether he likes it or not," Bill proclaimed . It was a winner; he knew it! 'Blood Sisters' was a great team password.

It was suggested by Libby that each case should actually have a new password so that the confidentiality could be maintained and so that technique became their first tradition. Later, the team would devise a universal password to record their entire HAPT history. Funny how easy some momentous decisions simply happen, Jen mused. Easily done, team, she thought with satisfaction.

***

Bix's iPhone had just rung saving her from working on the house cleaning. Simon, her toy schnoodle, looked up from his bed just in case she was disappearing.

"Hello?" Bix listened intently then sat down on the couch. Her eyes registered surprise as Jen related Frank's story to her. "So you really think that the shot was postmarked for him?" Bix asked as Simon watched. "That is so hard to believe. That means your team's every movement is being watched. I suppose the option that someone hates Frank enough to kill him is out?" Bix questioned.

She nodded when Jen threw logic into the conversation . "We have to assume that the shot was intended for Johnny McPherson's look alike, Bix. It is the safest conclusion that we can take. If we get lost in Frank's history, the McPherson Case suffers."

"True. I hadn't thought of it that way. You are right. I guess one has to go on the assumption that coincidences just don't happen. So how can I help?" Bix asked.

"Well, I had a thought. You, being a local friend of Frank's, could visit the hospital and talk with him about what we're thinking. Between the two of you, maybe Frank can figure out what this sniper really wants? Personally, I have no idea. I've got the team investigating McPherson's business, family and the gulch, but as far as the local connection, we don't know anything. Possibly you and Frank could put your heads together and work on that concept."

Bix knew how important that piece could be. Possibly, Frank talked with the wrong local who was connected in some way to McPherson's death. It was interesting and intriguing she assessed. "I could do that. Certainly visiting Frank in the hospital would be viewed as friendly concern, don't you think?"

"Indeed I do," Jen answered.

"Bernie's coming to visit in a couple of days so I would have some help investigating. You okay with that?"

"Most definitely. Tell Bernie that we'll have to celebrate her return to the mountains very soon," Jen added.

"Will do. Think Simon and I might head to the hospital as soon as Frank wakes up today. I'll call my hospital sources and get the scoop on that."

"I figured you would. You go, girl. I'll call you tonight if that's okay?"

"Perfect." After Bix disconnected from Jen's call, she dialed the hospital and talked with Betty, her favorite nurse. The word went out on the ICU unit floor that when Frank awakened, Betty would need to know. Bix figured that he was probably several hours from consciousness.

Knowing Frank and his habits, Bix could figure

that it wasn't a love triangle. She had to smile with that assumption. That left his being old friends with McPherson. Johnny had both, a girl friend and property. Still, it really could be as simple as the two guys looking alike. Bix picked up the duster and continued the cleaning as her thoughts wandered. All the options were on the table.

The property angle meant the entire gulch and its' potential was important. Money and property went hand-in-hand in Colorado especially when one was talking about a large amount of mountain terrain. It wasn't the old half acre stuff and a million dollar home but 200 acres. Her hand stopped the duster for a second as the potential value of Johnny's property soaked in. 'White Gold. Bingo!' Bix then continued to dust. International money was also in the mix. It certainly didn't have to be Colorado originated.

Still, how did Frank enter into the case? He wasn't in the will as far as she knew. How the hell did he end up in the sites of a sniper? Bix plopped into her favorite chair for a moment as she considered Frank's involvement. It also might be something that Johnny told Frank? Simon jumped up on her lap seeing the occasion as quality naptime. She leaned back and thought. Her hand now idly scratching Simon's black fur. The little guy was in seventh heaven.

Maybe it was what Frank knew or what he possessed, she ventured. It was obvious that Frank probably didn't know how he was involved. If the secret was on paper or an object then Frank might know where or how to find it. If the secret was hidden in a conversation that the two guys had, Frank needed to remember. However, Frank had become a sitting target either because of his appearance or knowledge or both. Bix grabbed her phone from the table and quickly dialed Jen. "Jen, have you got someone watching Frank? A guard?"

"Got an officer sitting in the waiting room. I take it you think we need to be more vigilant?" Jen answered with an edge in her tone.

"Most definitely and now!" Bix emphasized. "Call me back after you sound that alarm. I truly believe Frank is in danger because of what he knows or what he doesn't realize that he knows or in fact, looks like. The sharpshooter might just think that Frank is Johnny in hiding. Call me back when you have talked with your officer."

The phone went silent. Bix felt relief that Jen had taken her warning seriously. If she was right, Frank was truly in danger until this whole case got solved or someone got arrested!

***

Officer Libby James was startled as her text message alert beeped. Captain Holly was texting her. She sat up and read quickly. Her fingers flew over the keys then she moved toward the ICU unit. Libby took a chair with her and now was posted outside the unit. A couple nurses observed her movement then went back to their own routines. The older nurse at the main desk, who seemed to be in charge, then came over to talk.

"I'm Betty Sanders, the head nurse on duty

today. I wondered if there is something our staff needs to know about Frank's situation. Can you relate anything to us that would be helpful?" Betty asked with a warm smile.

Libby thought for a second on how to handle the situation. It did seem like a good idea to inform the floor nurses that the order had come through to guard Frank closely. Why not? She ventured into the conversation quietly after standing up. "Your nurses need to know that I have been ordered to keep surveillance on Frank 24-7. If any of you become aware of strangers entering this floor, please let the officer on duty know."

"Can you give me anymore information," Betty asked? Her eyes intently gazing into Libby's. The difference in height was apparent to anyone observing these two ladies. Betty was of formidable size and Libby was short.

"I am sorry but my orders do not allow me to say anything more about the situation. Sorry," Libby said. "It is the HAPT team's hope that your nurses can keep this information quiet."

"Most certainly. Discreet will be the rule on the floor," Betty answered. "Well, thanks for what you could say. Can I inquire what your name is and will you make sure that the next officer does introduce themselves to us?"

"Will do, Betty. I am Officer Libby James." The two ladies shook hands and the HAPT Officers became known to the hospital nursing staff from that point on.

***

Detective Bill Smith had left the hospital after their conference. It just seemed to him that the job had to move forward immediately. The only problem was that the investigation was producing so many possibilities. With Frank injured the amount of work could have doubled, however, Captain Jen had now brought in Jerry. Chief James Marten from Buena Vista had given Detective Jerry Neal a transfer to their team. It was a relief.

Nevertheless, Bill figured that he needed to get going on his list of suspects. He had just set up a meeting with Johnny McPherson's girlfriend, Sadie Russel. So back down to the Front Range for lunch. Sadie Russel worked at Benter Technological Communications out of the city limits along Highway 36. BTC had taken Bill an hour and a half to reach from Frisco. Pulling into the parking lot, he observed a row of computer oriented businesses lining the highway. The area was perfect for low property values and computers. It was a cow field with a few trees.

Sadie Russel met him at the front door. She was an attractive blond lady of average height. They walked toward the cafeteria. "Thank you for meeting me here," she said. "Now that Johnny is gone, I really don't get to the mountains all that often and I don't want to. Too many memories," she murmured.

Bill noticed genuine sadness in her eyes. That, or she was a good actress. "You're welcome, Miss Russel. The ride down was fairly easy. Thank you for seeing me on short notice. I assume that you have heard about Johnny's case becoming a homicide?"

"I did. Yesterday. I am totally shocked. Johnny was a kind man who left people alone. I can't imagine…." Her eyes searched Bill's face for answers .

He, of course, had none. "I know this will sound pretty lame but we're doing everything we can, " he said. "The investigation just got started this week. Let's get some lunch and talk?" They moved through the cafeteria line and then found a table at the back away from the lunch crowd.

"Did I hear that an officer was injured?" she asked while placing her tray on the table.

Bill waited until they were settled and then said, "Yes. One of our officers was shot today in McPherson Gulch. He is making a recovery in the hospital. However, the shooting has definitely illustrated that we are on the right track. Needless to say, our questions have gone in a different direction at this point. We are now wondering about Johnny's business connections and his personal life. He had obviously upset someone to the point of either starting an avalanche or paying someone to instigate an avalanche." Bill took a drink of his ice tea and watched Sadie's expression.

She hesitated weighing what she would say carefully. "Johnny had at least two contracts that had definitely become dangerous in my mind." She glanced around the cafeteria to make sure that no one was listening. "Slope Incorporated and International Mineral Recovery Foundation. Both companies did not get the answers that they wanted from Johnny. It was obvious to him that his property was far more valuable to them than his consultant services. Ask Howard Carlson about Slope Incorporated. I don't think that Howard knew what his company really wanted when he offered Johnny services. I could be wrong on that one. Howard and Martha Carlson are very money savvy if you know what I mean." Sadie's fork paused for a second as she made sure that her full meaning was apparent.

Bill understood her precise meaning. The property value was definitely a huge motive. Obviously, he would have to dig deeper into both of the corporations or Libby would through her computer expertise. "Before we finish our conversation Miss Russel, I have to ask you about being Johnny McPherson's executor of his estate?"

CHAPTER 9

FIRE!

Officer Libby James was busy on her computer during her hospital guard duty. Libby glanced around for good measure first then proceeded to build the HAPT website on line. Frank Mason's monitors recorded his vital signs with a reassuring rhythm; the repetitive sound spoke of Frank's well being at the moment. Her ears monitored while she began to create their site. Captain Holly's news release information was a great introduction piece. Libby transferred it to the site in a simple cut and paste. Naturally, the wallpaper was a terrific mountain panorama; it looked good, she thought. Libby's bright blue eyes sparkled as she assessed her work. Her chair was positioned in the sunlight. It was warm and toasty. Hospitals sure had a calming effect, she mused.

Libby got up to walk the hallway leaving her computer on the chair. She glanced at the nurses' station and back at Frank who slept soundly. The constant beeps of the gadgets connected to him were definitely reassuring to her. She could by now tell which beeps were Frank's and not the lady in the next ICU bed. Libby watched the nurses doing their rounds as usual. Hospitals were predictable; it was just the patience who added drama now and then, she determined.

Libby was almost ready to take a break and check her email when she began to feel uneasy. Something had been added to the scenario; something had begun to smell. It was an odd odor that didn't exactly jive with the hospital routine. It began to pique her interest. She looked at the nurses' station. Her glance caught Betty's eyes. They both sniffed in unison.

Libby moved down the hall while Betty called maintenance. Out of the corner of her eye, Libby suddenly saw a small trace of smoke protruding from under the east stairwell exit door. She exploded into a full run and threw the door open! In the stairwell was a large pile of rags getting ready to ignite into a full fire!

"Fire!" she yelled at the top of her lungs! Libby's mind flashed on the fire extinguisher box next to the restroom signs. She flew back down the hall, crashed the window on the box and seized the extinguisher. The fire alarms dominated the atmosphere like an explosion. Nurses ran to the stairwell to help. Libby got the extinguisher working and began spreading the white foam over the pile. Abruptly, another thought filled her consciousness, Frank!

She tossed the fire extinguisher to Betty and charged back toward Frank. Her eyes riveted on a stranger approaching from the west side of the ICU floor. He was dressed in white like an intern. The problem was that she had never seen him before. "Stop," she yelled and pulled her gun. Libby was well aware that she couldn't shoot because of the oxygen machines.

The assassin, sensing her dilemma, charged then threw a right hook launching her body into the wall. She hit with a deadly thud. Libby, ricocheted like a ping-pong ball, recovered quickly, then kicked him in the groin with a full leg thrust. What she had lost in size she was able to match in strength and speed. The two hundred pound man let out a surprised yelp; a syringe flew from his left hand. With his weapon gone, the assailant fled toward the west exit. Libby followed in hot pursuit.

Down the stairwell they went until Libby deliberately stopped. The guy was two floors down and still moving. She assessed the situation and then headed back to the ICU. Libby quickly turned on her shoulder radio and yelled, "Officer in 10-31, east stairwell in hospital. Suspect should be leaving by front hospital entrance soon. White uniform, male, blond hair, over six feet tall. 10-39, assist. 10-17 apprehend suspect. 10-4."

Captain Holly pulled over on I-70, did a cross the median maneuver, switched on her lights and siren and said, "Code 3," into her radio. She had been heading to McPherson Gulch for the crime scene follow up. Now the game plan had changed. Captain Holly yelled into the radio, " ETA 5 minutes. 10-19 pursuit officer, return immediately to ICU. 10-4."

"En route, 10-4," Libby verified.

As Holly entered the parking lot, she observed that Jerry's patrol car was near the south exit. The lights were blinking but he was no where to be seen. "Detective Neal, come in," Jen said. Her eyes scanned the cars in the lot closely.

"Searching the south perimeter exit. Think his car was parked near this exit onto highway 9. 10-4."

Captain Holly immediately issued a APB out to the Highway Patrol and Summit Police Forces. "Any car description, Detective Neal? 10-4."

"None. Should be heading toward Breckenridge at a pretty good clip," Jerry added. "I do have some tire tracks over here that are new, however. 10-4."

At least Libby would be an excellent witness, Jen thought. She left Jerry to make a plaster cast of the tire tracks and headed into the hospital to talk with her officer. As Captain Holly entered the hospital, she noticed that the incident had attracted a fire truck. Chief Josh Anderson was waiting for her at the front entrance. "Your officer and Frank Mason are okay, Captain Holly. Quite an event I'd say. Talk with you later, Jen. Will you need our assistance?" he asked.

"I think we have it under control. I'll call you later with details," she said and then added, "Detective Neal might need some assistance out at the exit. He is processing that scene. Tire tracks and anything else that might help. Would you mind stopping by and seeing if he needs anything?"

"Not a problem," Chief Josh Anderson said then left in search of Detective Jerry Neal.

Jen was shocked to see the nurses working on Libby as she approached the ICU. It suddenly occurred to Jen that she hadn't inquired if Libby was okay. It was a huge mistake on her part. The first words out of Jen's mouth, whether she was a cop or just a friend, should have been immediate concern. Captain Holly made a note to herself that she would never make that mistake again. One had to always take a few seconds to ask that important question.

"Are you okay?" Jen asked touching Libby's shoulder and staring into Libby's eyes a few minutes later. Officer Libby James let out a breath of relief. The Captain wasn't mad at her but concerned. That show of support gave her permission to relax and report. Later when she could process the whole incident, Libby would understand and appreciate good leadership. "He got me with a pretty good hook," she stated.

Nurse Betty, enthusiastically, added, "Then, Officer James almost knocked his private parts right off with a great kick. Lordy for a little lady, you pack quite a wallop!"

Later after the team had taken the statements from the nurses and processed the scene, Jen called Chief Anderson to see if the police had located the fleeing car. As far as the Breckenridge Police could figure there were 'no cars of interest' passing through the area. The sniper had simply blended in with the tourist traffic.

***

Frank felt the fuzz slowly lifting from his mind. The anesthesia nightmare had stolen his energy; he was waking up feeling exhausted. There was a constant throb pulsating in his head; it felt like an immense hangover from tequila shots. A plastic tube under his nose hissed and smelled like sweet rubber. He tried to pull himself up with his elbow and discovered that his body just wouldn't cooperate. "What the hell?" Frank mumbled in a slurred drunken voice that he couldn't recognize. He tried swinging his legs over the side of the bed. Abruptly, his left leg sent a shock of massive pain throughout his body. He saw stars as his brain absorbed the trauma. A huge moan escaped from his mouth.

"Frank, it's okay. Do you need the nurse? You're in the hospital, Frank. You got shot, remember?" came a calming voice. Frank opened his eyes and there was Bix Bixler looking down at him.

"What happened?" he mumbled.

"You and Jerry Neal went up to Johnny's gulch to find clues. Sound familiar?"

"I remember that but what the hell happened and 'no' I don't need a nurse."

"Plain and simple, you got shot by a sniper up on the rim and the bullet was meant for you not Jerry," Bix answered.

"Hell, I feel like shit. My leg?"

"Bullet went right through but nicked an artery on the way out. They fixed you up here in Frisco," she added.

"You sure the bullet was meant for me?"

"Yes, Frank for sure. They tried to get you again here in the hospital. Next time you see Officer Libby James make sure that you thank her. She took down a two hundred pound thug was the way I heard it."

"Holly shit…." Frank whispered. "She had my back, huh?"

"She did. Ask Nurse Betty after you feel better. She saw all of it in the ICU."

"Betty Sanders?" he asked.

"Naturally. I don't think that she ever leaves the hospital. She moved you into your very own room a few hours ago after you began waking up. Remember?"

"No, but I am awake now. My leg just let me know and 'no' I don't want more pain killers. If I am in danger, I want to be awake," Frank added. He smiled just a little and then asked, "Where's Simon, my boy?" Frank, using only his head to inspect the room, looked around.

Bix lifted Simon up onto the bed. He, of course, had on his service dog jacket. Simon immediately recognized Frank and offered licks and wags. After a few moments Frank got him to lay down and snuggle.

"Now Bix, why are you here?"

"Jen, Captain Holly, I mean, has asked me to talk with you about what you know or have that would send an assassin to your door. We figure it has to do with Johnny or at least the gulch. Can you think of anything?"

"Haven't the faintest idea. Well hell, what do I know?"

"Did you find anything in the gulch?" Bix asked as she pulled up a chair.

"Wait a minute. Check my pant's pocket. Where's my pants?" Frank said looking around the room.

"Probably in the closet. Let me look." Bix did find his pants and a plastic bag with all the small articles from his pocket. "Here." She handed the bag to Frank.

He searched the contents. "Got it. Found this key right before the lights went out." He handed it to Bix. They both stared at it for a few seconds as Bix turned it over in her hand. There were no markings on it except Diebold Inc. Canton, Ohio. Bix began to think that the key looked familiar. "Hmmmmm…" she murmured. "Lock box or security key of some sort?" she suggested.

Frank took the key back and inspected it closely. "Could be…," he said while still scratching Simon with his other hand. Simon lifted his head up and checked out the object of attention. His little black nose wiggled slightly as he sniffed from a distance.

"Well, it will be interesting to see what the team can find out about this key," Bix said. "Captain Holly is coming by pretty soon so give it to her. Now, I was wondering what you and Johnny talked about the last time you saw him?"

"Don't think it was earth shattering. We met for a drink sometime before Thanksgiving. Johnny felt hassled by the amount of work he was doing. I remember that. I was grousing about my job in Leadville too. You know, two friends sharing frustrations. He told me that Sadie was coming up for a stay at Christmas. Think he was pretty happy about that. Oh, and he did mention that he was going to ask her to be the executor of his estate. I was sort of surprised that he wasn't going to ask her to marry him. Seemed a little odd to me but you know whatever floats your boat. The McPhersons usually did go about things backwards. Hell, Johnny was a lot like his granddad," Frank added with a nod. "Although in Johnny's life, computers took the place of mining."

"Have you shared this information with the team?" Bix asked.

"Well no… I figured it would be interesting to see if Sadie knew about the executor thing. If she said that she didn't know, it would be suspect. At least that's my way of thinking." Frank moved his right leg and tried to become more comfortable. The activity made him wince with pain. Simon snuggled closer.

"What did you think of Sadie?" Bix asked.

"She seemed like a nice lady that I've met maybe twice in the last couple of years. Don't think she was crazy about mountain living though. Johnny was happy and that's all that really counted in my book. Loving someone and not living with them seemed to suit his style of life perfectly. I do know that they communicated daily on the computer for what that's worth," Frank said.

"It is a new way of life, isn't it?" Bix said coming from her own perceptive. She and Bernie touched base once a day. If they missed a computer connection, things seemed out of kilter for the rest of the night."

"So what did Johnny know about Grandfather Arnold's mining operation? Anything there that might shed some light on this case?"

"I don't think so. Lots of snow but not a lot of gold as far as I know. What else might be back in that mine, I don't know and I don't think Johnny knew either. He didn't like exploring back in there; he was kind of claustrophobic. It was a storage place up front and that was about it. Dank and dark didn't really interest him. I can remember, once years ago, asking him if he had anyone survey it. He didn't really answer. I figured it meant that the mine was worthless."

Bix could tell that Frank was starting to feel tired. His eyelids were trying to close without his permission. "Well Frank, I am going to take off and let you get some sleep. Can I come back tomorrow to check on you?" she asked.

"Of course. Please do visit...." Frank's eyes closed as needed sleep settled in; his hand stopped scratching Simon.

***

"This is Detective Bill Smith coming down from Eisenhower Tunnel. ETA 15 minutes. 10-4," he announced into the radio.

"This is Officer James. I have instructions that all available officers are to meet at the office. Please come on in. 10-4."

"10-4." Bill had followed the hospital assault on the radio as best he could during his return travel from Denver. There were areas where his reception had been disrupted but he had gotten the majority of the transmissions. Man, Frank was definitely a target, he thought. What was all that about, he wondered. Bill pulled in and parked. He quickly entered the building to find Libby and Jen waiting.

"Frank okay?'

They nodded in unison.

"Poor guy's had quite a day and so have you, Officer James. Congratulations for knocking the crap out of that jerk. He deserved plenty of pain. What a weasel. Frank was sedated, right?" Bill asked.

"He didn't know that anything was going on which was probably best," said Jen. "Detective Neal is doing his hospital duty right now. I will take the night shift. Bill, will you then relieve me ?"

"Sounds like a plan." Bill sat down on the couch after stretching his legs.

"Have you seen our website?" Libby asked not being able to contain herself.

"No," How do I get there?" Bill asked activating his cell phone Wi-Fi.

"Put an app on your phone for HAPT," she instructed both of them. "Go to top right and double click staff. Put in the password." Libby waited in anticipation.

Captain Holly expression said it all. A big smile popped out. "Wonderful! We are now in business."

Bill smiled and then said, "Did you do this in between punches? Really nice, Libby."

"Thank you. I wish we had been able to apprehend the assailant. I just felt that I needed to get back with Frank and-"

"You did exactly what was expected of you. You were headed back before I had time to issue the order. If we could have spared another officer to watch Frank with you that would be another story. Hence being a small fish in a little pond like Summit," Jen added then stopped that thought. She erased that option and moved on. "Now, lets look at the evidence we have to decide what happens next. Oh by the way, Bix chatted with Frank an hour ago so I have some more information," she said. "Frank said that Sadie Russel was to be the executor of the estate." Jen looked at Bill for conformation.

"Correct. I talked with Johnny's lawyer before I left and he verified that information. I asked Sadie about it and she said that she knew. Johnny had asked her in November right before Thanksgiving. At first she had been hesitant about accepting but after listening to Johnny, she decided to do it."

"Hesitant, why?" Jen asked.

"Johnny, basically, said and I quote, 'he wanted to get his estate organized. Johnny also said to Sadie 'one never knew what might happen in life.' Those were his exact words according to Miss Russel. She felt that lately Johnny had acquired a couple difficult clients; she sensed that he was nervous about his safety."

"Who were the clients?" Jen asked.

"Slope Incorporated and International Mineral Recovery Foundation. So I was wondering if Libby could investigate those two sources some more?" he asked. Detective Smith had begun to understand the individual talents of their team. He stared at Libby then said, "You have proven your computer expertise. If I had a choice, it would be to talk with the suspects. I know that I am better with people and asking them questions is sort of my talent," Bill confirmed. "Computers, not so much." He looked at Jen for conformation; she nodded. Bill had been exactly right about how they could work together. Libby was eager to become the team geek; it was definitely an opportunity for her.

"Well, I've done a little research on Slope Incorporated," Libby began sensing the appropriate time to enter the discussion. "Slope Incorporated was trying to buy the gulch to start a new ski area. I had a distinct feeling after reading the project offer that Slope's goal would be to construct a private and rustic ski area for the rich. Maybe even a little bit exclusive in nature. Spend big bucks to come shoulder-to-shoulder with other wealthy entrepreneurs. It would not be your family venture but a very exclusive club."

"Well, isn't that interesting. Huge motive. I take it that McPherson wasn't interested?" Captain Jen inquired..

"Of course not, " Libby continued, "Howard and Martha Carlson were supposed to put as much pressure on Johnny as they could. What's family for, right? I found an email lost in the corporate communications from Walter Connally, Slope's owner, to Howard Carlson. Walter Connally, made no reference to the pressure or specifics, mind you, but it was obvious; he was pushing Howard to convince Johnny to sell. I was about ready to call good old Walter back and ask him just how the Carlsons were suppose to convince Johnny," Libby said.

"Should shock the shit out of him," said Bill. "I could call Howard back and shock him with that same information. Maybe one of the two might shed some light on the situation. By the way, Slope has not bought any property in Lake County yet."

"Interesting," Jen said. It definitely did sound like a lead to follow. "Jerry and I will share Frank's guard duty and see if we can uncover the assassin. I think he's still in the county hiding with the tourists. As long as Frank is alive, the job isn't finished. So how about the International Mineral Recovery Foundation?"

Bill and Libby looked at each other. No answers.

"Okay then," Jen said, "I take your silence to mean that we need to investigate them. Bill, ask Howard and friends about that foundation. Libby, search on computer and find out just what this foundation does. Do we have it covered?"

Nods said that they did. However, all of them knew just how thin they were spread. Even with Jerry's help, there were too many options to research not to mention the question of who would handle the office duties? How long could they keep guard duty at the hospital while investigating the assassin's hiding place?

Jen would have to solve those questions in the next couple of days. The case had become so complicated and potentially dangerous at this juncture. Captain Holly certainly wasn't ready to place any of her officers in jeopardy and that was a fact. They would have to go slow and meticulously. There was no room for errors. Her first case had to be done correctly, she knew. Their entire existence as a team relied on her leadership.

CHAPTER 10

SLOW AND METICULOUS

Captain Jen Holly locked the door of her newly rented condo on Boreas Pass and turned around in time to see the sun spill predawn into the valley's depth. She was spellbound by the sheer motion of the sunrise. Dawn chased the shadows away then plunged forcefully into the valley contours.

Bix had described Summit County's geographic topography as a large bathtub. Gravity, with nature's certainty, pushed the water flow from the elevated end, Hoosier Pass, to the tub plug, Dillon Lake. Jen's calculations determined that her condo was located on the left side of the tub. It was a great image; the whole concept was spot-on. Bix's point about water being Summit County's most valuable commodity wasn't lost on her either. Much of Colorado water supplies were born deep in the high gulches where snow quantities tripled the accumulations of the valley floor. Twenty feet of snow depth was possible at twelve thousand feet; it was a fact.

The large metropolitan cities had taken legal action to control the water flow. Lawyers, representing Colorado Springs and Denver, marched the water into their reservoirs. Eventually when Colorado's thirst was quenched, the water had permission to flow into the Colorado River heading toward California. Pretty amazing, Jen thought.

Last night Jen had gotten home at 3 a.m. and fallen into bed exhausted. The cats, needing some warmth, joined her. She had been around long enough to observe, Myrtle and Milt, finding their kitty paradise in the sunny windows. Fortunately, a small teaspoon of human attention was also needed as they snuggled together last night.

My family has adjusted, she thought while turning the ignition on her Ford Interceptor. Nevertheless, five hours of sleep a night would have to suffice until she felt more in control of this case. She quickly began to focus on today's list. Actions taken today must be as safe and meticulous as possible, she mused.

Jen parked in the lot behind Ann's Coffee Shop and entered. Jerry was already seated with a large cup of coffee and *The Summit News* in his hand. He stood up and motioned her over.

"Well so far the paper is fairly positive in the covering of our team. We are the front page news which is not unusual for a small county paper, you know. Nice picture by the way, he pointed at her front page mug shot staring back at them.

"Well, that's scary to look at first thing in the morning," she said sliding into the booth. She scanned the article quickly and decided that it was written pretty much with her own descriptors. Definitely good to know that the local media might just do accurate reporting.

"So Jerry, my instincts tell me that our suspect is still in the county. His job isn't done. I'm thinking he's hiding in Summit County.

"Yeah, I've been sort of thinking the same thing. Unless of course, they fired him because of his failed attempt." Detective Jerry Neal tossed another creamer into his coffee and stirred. "Actually, I don't think bringing in more guns would be wise for anyone at this point," Jerry added then stared deeply into his coffee cup for more answers. "The sniper is playing like a local for now. When is Bill's shift over at the hospital?" he asked.

"Noon," Captain Jen said, "so we can begin our search for the suspect now. Agreed about the guy living here. Someone else must be the eyes and he waits for orders is my guess. The crime lab sketch artist from Summit has arranged to meet with Libby this morning. We'll have a composite by this afternoon. You want to check with Silverthorne and Dillon Lake Park areas? Maybe chat with the Forest Service and alert them? I'll start in the Breckenridge area. Guess we need to call him a short term transient for now. How long do you think he's been here?"

"My guess would be since the newspaper got hold of the cold case story," Jerry answered, "so at least a week, right?

"Absolutely. Okay then, we are looking for Libby's description of a man who has been in the area for a short time. Doesn't do bars and keeps a low profile. Lets meet at the hospital at noon. We'll have our team meeting in Frank's room. I have a suspicion that he would like that. Before I leave here, I'm calling Bix and ask her to alert her friends about this guy. Who knows, he might possibly be hanging out in a gulch somewhere. Housing is at a premium in the county so camping would work."

"Good point. I wouldn't know how to go that deep into the social structure here to get that job done. Bix is a good source," Jerry said then took his coffee cup back over to the counter for a refill. He turned around and verified, "Noon then?"

"Yep," Jen waved at Jerry as he disappeared out the door. She connected with Bix by phone. "Hey lady, you busy today?" she asked.

"Dithering around here then going to see Frank later. What's up?" Bix asked.

"How about calling a few locals and letting them know that we all need to keep our eyes out for Frank's shooter. I can send you a crime scene photo by computer before noon. I'm just thinking that if he was hold up in a gulch somewhere or simply walking the streets, it is possible that we might get lucky and spot him."

"I'll get on it. Maybe the folks at City Market could be helpful, Jen. If you like to eat, you end up there at some point," Bix added.

"Think I'll start there then," Jen said.

As the morning progressed, neither Jerry nor Jen had found any signs of the guy. The snow was melting off the ground faster than their progress; mud season was upon them literally. At 11:45

Captain Jen started for the hospital. Maybe a fifteen minute meeting in Frank's room would be enough for everyone, she thought. Libby was coming over from the office and eating her lunch with them so the wheels were turning. Jen had canvassed at least half of the reservation businesses for their suspect's rental with no luck. As she entered the hospital parking lot, her officers including Frank on crutches, were parading out the front door. They seemed in pretty good spirits. She pulled up to the group and asked, "What's up?"

Libby leaned in Captain Jen's car window and whispered, "Frank is escaping and heading down to the office. He plans to become our office duty coordinator for the next month. Doctors ain't totally happy with the arrangement but finally grumbled approval." Libby let a smile escape her lips as she said, "Mr. Congeniality will play nice on the phones is the promise. I'd say it just might work. At least then I could get some work done."

Jen saw the logic behind this new event. She couldn't quite see Frank totally playing nice but it could work. What with the ski areas closed now for the season, tourist traffic was sparse. Unless snow melting became a sport, the office would be quiet.

Their meeting back at the office was short. Everyone wanted to get a start on their own projects. Libby promised to show Frank how to handle the radio communications and computer duties before she began her investigation. Captain Jen found herself back in Breckenridge finishing the reservation businesses at 1:30.

By late afternoon Jen decided to slip home and

check in with the cats. Low and behold, some private time had opened up for her. Since her condo was on the second floor she and the cats went out on the balcony to eat a meal in the sunshine. Across the valley was the Ten Mile Range of Mountains embellished by ski runs. The only activity on them was white patches of snow retreating in the warm sun. How nice was that, she speculated. Summer would have its way. Spring wasn't going to happen again. Mud season to summer was the mountain norm, she mused while petting her furry friends.

Jen's phone rang breaking her reverie. She checked out the caller ID and discovered it was Bix. "Good afternoon," she answered.

"There has been some developments. The senior citizens who birdwatch and hike weekly are meeting in McCoy Gulch. With the help of the composite picture, they believe the man has a campsite there. Right now the seniors are holding a bird lecture meeting right down the road from him. Sally said that a couple of folks were keeping an eye on him from the bush. They plan to stay until we get there. "I'll drive! My truck will not be recognized. I can get you there in 15 minutes."

"I'm on my way!" Jen sprang out of her lawn chair buckled her belt holster on then grabbed her hydration pack. She figured that Code 2 to Bix's house would work. As she began down the road with lights and no siren, Jen radioed the office.

She was met with a gruff voice announcing calmly, "Summit County HAPT Headquarters. We're happy to help you or find you, whatever works." It was like talking with a smiling bear, Jen thought. Couldn't have been a better salutation from any other officer, she reconnoitered.

"Frank, Captain Jen. We have a possible sighting of the suspect in McCoy Gulch. Code 30. All officers respond immediately Code 3. Will stop at Bix's house then proceed in her truck. Please advise HAPT. Use my phone GPS to find me. 10-4"

"Done! 10-4" was all that came back to her. She had left the airways on and could hear Frank getting the troops organized." He must have had a list of the codes. It was all happening according to protocol. Frank knew where the gulch was and how long each officer would take to get there. "Officer James, you are 20 minutes ETA," he directed Libby. "Code 30."

Captain Jen suddenly knew that it was all going to work out. Frank had even sent an alert to the Breckenridge Police telling them that HAPT cars were moving through town. Frank could have been a talented drum majorette in another life! Unbelievable! How super was that Jen thought as she pulled into Bix's driveway.

Bix had her Ranger Truck backed out with motor running. Jen pulled in, parked and hopped in the passenger's seat. "Ready," she pronounced. The truck tires squealed as they flew up the road and out on Highway 9 south. The traffic wasn't bad so Bix was pushing 65 in a 55 mph up the switchbacks that began the gradual climb over Hoosier Pass. Bix swung a right and hit the gravel road head on. The truck climbed up McCoy Road quickly. "Almost there," Bix shouted over the gravel noise.

"I have backup on the way," Jen shouted.

"Frank is manning the phones at the office. He'll be on desk duty for the next month at least. How many birdwatchers are there? Just trying to get a feel for the situation," she added.

"Somewhere around a dozen I think," Bix answered. "They weekly hike or ski through a gulch identifying the birds and generally having a great old time. These fun people are serious birders. The minute the snow starts melting, they're hiking. The Forest Service relies on migration information from them in the spring and fall. They should be at the bottom of this hill," Bix yelled as she descended down a muddy road with huge ruts. She was able to pick a path and keep the axle intact. Bix stopped the truck and parked behind a couple of Subaru Foresters.

Jen slipped on a jacket over her uniform and followed Bix over to the group of seniors who were intent on listening to the speaker.

"The Stellar Jay lives at high altitude summer and winter. In the spring the jays do migrate down to Dinosaur Ridge outside of the Denver Urban Area to join their cousins, the Blue Jays, for their yearly gathering...." The speaker droned on while glancing toward a campsite some 50 feet away. Three of the ladies in the group circled Jen and whispered, "We've been driving him crazy for the last half hour. He went inside the tent some 10 minutes ago. We're afraid that Sally really has exhausted her speech. Stellar Jays are really very common. Boring.... Can we pack up and go?"

"That would be an excellent idea and thank you so much for your help today. The group picked up their paraphernalia and proceeded to depart. Captain Jen waved at the senior guards to relieve them of duty. She touched Bix's arm then whispered, "Bix, keep an eye on the road and let me know when you see a patrol car coming?"

"Will do," Bix said then casually wandered back up the road. She stopped every few feet and used a pair of binoculars like she was birding. The group spilled out on the road and chatted as the tables, pamphlets and refreshments were cleared away and stashed in their cars. Sally, the speaker, then whispered, "You want us to move up the road out of sight and direct your officers?"

"That would be absolutely great and thank you so much," Jen said then smiled. "You all have handled this situation perfectly. We'll let you know how it all this plays out. Right now it would make me very happy to get your group away from any possible danger. I do hope that this is our guy."

"So do we," said a gentleman from the back. Lets go eat, everyone. I'm starving." With that, the group jumped in their cars and were gone!

Jen walked slowly over to Bix's truck and hopped in the driver's seat. She started the motor then casually pulled it onto the road near the bridge to block the suspect's vehicle. His Land Rover was parked next to the tent. Fortunately, he had camped far enough up on the north side of the gulch that the descending east road exit was on Jen's side. The occasional shaded snow piles and the small river bridge helped limit the suspect's options. He was vehicle trapped. From the cab of the truck she listen to the radio communications on her phone. It sounded like everyone was now less than five minutes ETA. Jen flipped the release on her hand gun and waited. It was going to be a long five minutes.

CHAPTER 11

SUDDENLY SUSPECT!

Captain Jen Holly checked her watch; three minutes left before the team's arrival, she figured. Suddenly the suspect sensed his plight; he shot out of his tent like a missile! His small black pack a blur as he escaped. The shooter launched rifle fire in Jen's direction then quickly ran up the old mining road that ascended southwest toward the rear of McCoy Gulch. His cover was rifle and distance at this point! The sniper was no stranger to strenuous altitude running as he covered the distance.

Jen Holly leaped out of Bix's truck and shouted, "Stop Police!" to no avail. He was on the move. It took Jen less than a second to make her decision. She waved to Bix, grabbed her hydration pack then hit the radio airways. "In pursuit of suspect fleeing on foot. Phone on for tracking, climbing southwest. Jerry, Tyler, Libby; helicopter assistance. 10-4."

She moved parallel to his departure in full run through the bushes and out of rifle sight.

"Done," came Frank's response. "Your signal is strong, 10-2. Go. 10-4."

Jen nodded to herself listening to orders flying over the airways. She was still in a full run; her focus was on the suspect. The rest of the pieces had to fall into place on their own. It was time to see how the team, as a whole, would function.

She turned her shoulder radio volume down to a whisper after hearing Frank's voice saying, "10-99 in pursuit."

What direction this chase would take was totally up to the suspect at this moment. Half a mile of bush then his ascent became an old rockslide with packed snow; the difficulty slowed progress for both suspect and officer. The word 'militant' popped into Captain Jen's mind. This guy was planning his escape by challenging her ability. He had discarded his rifle as he climbed up the rockslide. Jen marked the rifle location with a signal beacon then carefully mapped her ascent as she met his challenge. She also left some of her heavy belt equipment next to his rifle. Gun, radio phone and water were the components that she needed. The quiet drip of melting snow was now her only companion.

The rockslide footing was tricky at best, Jen determined. She would set her step on a boulder then apply pressure to see if it would hold her weight. This technique was truly Colorado's two step for climbers. The rockslide was fairly sturdy; the stability was a relief. After the rockslide came the ledges and tailings.

Jen's conditioning and practice now took hold

of her being. The ascent became steeper and more tedious at this juncture. How Jen placed her fingers on the rock ledges became her focus; secure your hands and then pull up seemed the mode. The smell of dirt and moist small crevasses filled her lungs. Sweat began to trickle down her back from the sheer exertion. Her lungs heaved air in and out as the climb became incredibly steep. When Jen looked up, she could only see blue sky; the towering granite ledges totally limited her vision. This extreme vertical mass winked at her.

There was a mysterious undeniable bond forming between suspect and officer. Jen could hear his breathing and effort as he heaved his body up the ledge. High mountain silence dominated their atmosphere; they were somehow in sync sharing this ascent. Their climbing position on the rocks was now some 50 feet apart. The proximity became intimate in nature; it had become their reality. No emotion, Jen thought, but calculated progress in continuous motion. The challenge cast its web around them shutting out the world. It was a bizarre tango to experience, Jen mused. Up they went together.

***

Libby slammed on her brakes then pulled onto the shoulder of Highway 9 leaving a dusk cloud in her car wake. Frank had cancelled her orders and now directed her to the Dredge Parking Lot in Breckenridge. What was going on, she wondered? Officer James did a U turn then hit her siren and lights in a Code 3. Frank was now directing Jerry and his dog to the parking lot also. What the hell, she thought?

As Libby approached the lot in Breckenridge, she was surprised to see a police helicopter idling. Jerry Neal motioned her over and yelled, "Get your emergency equipment and let's go! Captain Jen is climbing toward the southwest Impasse rim in pursuit. We need to get in position on the rim!" He pulled out his pack and rifle from his SUV then strapped a pack on Tyler his dog. Libby followed suit and grabbed her pack out of her patrol car trunk. Within five minutes the officers were safely in the air. Libby placed the headset on and waited for Jerry to explain.

"We're going to descend down by rope and get ourselves in position," Jerry said eyeing Libby's expression of shock then acceptance. "Frank is sending a text to Captain Jen mapping the area that shows where we'll be located. Hopefully, we can maneuver the suspect into an ambush. Toss your extra ammunition into Tyler's pack. He can move between us if needed."

Five minutes later they were positioned over Impasse rim in the idling helicopter. Libby was first to descend. She had just buckled her harness and tightened her helmet. Officer James now understood exactly why the team had elected to wear hiking boots with their uniforms. Action meant exactly that, action within a moment's notice. With a nod Libby jumped and felt the harness tighten around her body. Her focus was on the terrain below. Libby didn't see any humans on the ground below nor any

foot prints in the remaining snow. She calculated
that Jen's pursuit was still in the climbing stage
over near another back bowl.

If this maneuver had been for training, Libby
would have had time to be amazed by the view. The
rim was simply the top plateau of this 12,000 to
14,000 feet mountain range. One side descended to
I-70 Interstate and the other Highway 9. There was
an incredible amount of rugged terrain in between
those two highways. Enough space to let a savvy
suspect escape if the team wasn't careful.

Libby inspected the terrain below her and
prepared to land safely. She got ready for impact
and said a small prayer!

***

Detective Bill Smith had finally arrived on
scene. He had been a little envious of Jerry and
Libby when he heard their orders. His envy lasted
only for a few moments. He and Jen had talked
about his leg and his continuous reconditioning.
They had decided that he still needed to heal after
the last shooting incident. Bill had been caught in
crossfire pursuing a suspect. He had spent a month
in the hospital and a year in rehabilitation. Now,
how well he functioned was totally up to him and
his training. Yeah, it was best that he handled the
crime scene logistics. Being a good detective was
priority, he concluded.

The seniors had met him above the crime scene.
He stopped, collected their names and information.
Naturally, they were excited and relieved that the

police had responded. "Pretty tidy campsite," said Sally. "We're thinking he knows something about hiding out. Not at all friendly by the way. Actually, bordering on rude," she concluded.

One of the gentlemen added, "His equipment by the way, seemed state of the art. Haven't seen that many lens attachments for a camera in a long time. Takes me back to my photo days. The guy was no amateur for sure," he nodded and got support from the group with his assumptions. "Lets go eat?" he suggested hopefully.

Sally then turned back and held Bill's arm for a moment and said, "Well good luck, young man, and say thanks to that nice officer who came with Bix. Very sweet." Sally and the troops then headed up the road and out of the gulch. What a resource, Bill mused. Locals. You can't beat their help, he thought.

Detective Smith then drove down to the crime scene. He found Bix sitting in her truck waiting. She got out and pointed to the chase happening on the south rim of the gulch. Her binoculars were aimed toward the action. The two small figures were heading up Impasse Mountain, Bill noticed. "How long have they been up there?" he asked.

"I'd say 30 minutes and counting," Bix said handing the binoculars to Bill. She leaned on the truck hood and watched intently. "Captain Jen sure is giving him a race for his money."

"Good," Bill said. "So what happened, Bix?"

"The guy flew out of his tent when Jen moved my truck across his escape route. He didn't hesitate at all. Shot off a couple rifle rounds in Jen's direction to get her attention. Since then I've been watching from here. There hasn't been anymore shots fired just a lot of challenging climbing. What happens now?" she asked looking at Bill.

"We've got a helicopter dropping two officers down on the rim. The intent is to set an ambush."

"Good. Well, get the bastard. I'm heading for home I think. Not sure if I even locked the door on my way out. Plus, Simon was having a fit. Schnoodles want to be in the action. You guys will let me know how all this ends up, right?"

"I'll call you. Right now I'm going to have a look in the tent there and wait for the crime lab. By the way, did you get a look at him? Was he the guy in the picture?" he asked.

"I think so. He had blond hair for sure and was tall. Well, good luck." Bix left her binoculars with Bill and drove out of the scene. She knew that it would take all the fleeting daylight before this encounter would be over. She aimed positive thoughts toward Jen especially. That young lady had become very important to her. "Stay safe, Jen," she mumbled as her truck climbed up the road.

Bill opened the tent flap and was truly astonished by the amount of equipment inside, foreign and American in nature. His gaze spotted several Canon 300mm and 70-200mm lenses. Some of the equipment was German and Swedish. Bill documented with pictures after putting on his rubber gloves. He eyed a police scanner, Uniden BCD436HP Home Series, perched on a small table. The dial was set for their frequency. Hell, the scanner certainly explained why the guy had rushed from the scene. He knew they were coming! The sniper had also left his Streamlight Laser Sights. Bill had to assume that the suspect wasn't carrying that rifle now unless he had three arms. The man had calculated how he would escape and when to discard the rifle. No one could climb that cliff carrying a heavy rifle, specifically, a Whitworth .45 caliber rifle. The remaining ammunition told that story.

Yep, the guy was a professional sharpshooter and assassin to be more exact. Jen could be in for the climb of her life, Detective Bill Smith concluded. Hell, to do it without ropes was bad enough, he assessed, but this assassin was the real thing. The snow spotted terrain was the other crucial culprit. Shit, this pursuit was ugly. Bill tabled his anxiety and continued his job; there was nothing that he could do except work.

Smith came back out of the tent and thought about the camp location. The shooter had established his campsite high enough that he could see what was coming up the road. Also, it was obvious that an attack on him would not come from the north since he backed the tent near a steep incline. Fortified and professional was the Detective's conclusion.

Bill returned to the interior of the tent and meticulously took pictures then searched for any documents. It wasn't surprising to him that there was no identification left behind. He looked under the mattress and through all the equipment. Nope, this guy was good, he mused. Dead end. The suspect didn't even smoke. "Shit," he grumbled.

While he waited for the crime lab to appear, Bill began following what he thought was their trail. He checked his tracking device. There was a signal coming some 50 feet up from the campsite.

Bill's knee began to ache about the time that he came upon the suspect's discarded rifle and Jen's belongings. He marked the scene with evidence tags and continued taking pictures. Some 15 minutes later, Bill came back down and waited. His job here was pretty much done for now. The outcome was now in Captain Holly's hands. The Detective sat down on a boulder and watched the climb develop with the aide of Bix's binoculars. "Be safe, Jen," he mumbled to himself. "Hold tight."

***

Captain Jen Holly suddenly heard the familiar 'bing' sound of her phone. It seemed like such a shocking interruption , however, she did wonder who would text. Habits did die hard she told herself. Still…maybe…Frank? Captain Holly stopped, debated then pulled out her smart phone.

Sure enough there was an text alert from Frank. Specifically, a topographic map of their location. Frank had marked three positions on the image: her position, the suspect's position, then the team's positon, a half mile deep into the curved alpine bowl of Impasse Mountain. The indented contour of the bowl would allow for some safety in footing, she calculated. It looked like an amphitheater filled with winter's old collection of snow remnants. Those white shrines could give the team some cover and room to maneuver, she assessed.

What was the plan, she wondered? As Jen pocketed her phone, an idea began to take root in her mind. It had all the markings of an ambush. If she could get him to move across the face of the ledge, the suspect would be led into the back bowl. Now all she needed to do was get him started in that direction.

Almost on cue the suspect pulled out some smaller rocks from a ledge where he was perched. Obviously, he had taken a break and decided to hurl rocks at her position. His new action meant that he was getting tired of the climb and needed a break. This race was now in a dead heat, she judged. Jen hugged the ledge face as debris from his rocks threatened.

She pulled out her holster gun and upped the ante on this action. If the guy started a rockslide, she would be toast. A bullet zinged off the rocks near his position. Would he stay put or take off again, Jen wondered? Bullets beat rocks at this point; he continued to climb.

Maybe the suspect did not have a hand gun with him, she speculated. That, or he didn't have extra ammunition. Or, maybe he didn't have a holster for the hand gun which was in the backpack. Yep, the latter assumption seemed more provable to her at this point. It did seem that this suspect was not going to reveal any of his intentions until the climb became safer. Smart, she concluded.

Jen had intentionally missed him. She had aimed her warning shot north of his location. He now angled his climb higher but south toward Impasse's back bowl. The ambush just might work, she reconnoitered if they could stay alive.

The scary realization that climbing without ropes put your heart in your throat exploded into her thoughts! They now had just entered a difficult area of rock tailings. Just when she thought it couldn't get worse, it did. It was like being in a flour sifter that constantly shook. You climbed two steps up and froze while clinging and praying then feeling your body sliding slowly down inch by inch. Chaos was not far from reality; it was frightening.

A trickle of rocks showered down in her direction. Jen concluded that he hadn't intentionally sent them her way; the precarious climb was the culprit. The mountain in some weird fate was indeed sending them across the face and into the bowl. This difficulty had brought the challenge to a new level. Would both climbers reach the back bowl or would someone fall?

After the field of tailings, the mountain presented more ledges. Climbing perpendicular was becoming impossible. Jen sensed that each body lift produced another chill of anxiety. That thought became her consciousness; it perched in the dark shadows ominously. "Concentrate," she whispered to herself. Jen's mind gathered in all of her strength as she understood how precarious this ascent had become. She was now beyond tired.

Abruptly, her left leg started shaking from the exertion then her right foot slipped! Jen's fingers clawed and tried to hold her body weight in timeless suspension! Her right foot finally found a smaller ledge below. It had been a very long 10 inches of freefall for Jen.

A gasp of air had escaped from her mouth during the short fall. Her fearful reaction couldn't be muffled. He had heard it. Both climbers froze for a second. Jen exhaled air slowly while waiting for his reaction. There had been no advantage for him; she was still here and he was still there. He began climbing again. Rocks pummeled down in a silent trail after each climber's lift. The option to climb higher was bordering on the impossible; it was a fact.

The mountain demanded them to move sideways or fall. Both climbers began to focus on the bowl some 25 feet south of their location. It meant that they could stop climbing higher and go lateral. The alpine green foliage of the bowl beckoned to them. There were no other safe alternatives. Jen began to sense that he had made his decision.

The sniper began to move sideways sliding from one ledge to the next. His movements became faster as he realized the rewards of this tactic. His technique became speed. The pursuit took a new twist. The shooter was some twenty feet from the tranquil bowl and moving confidently. The race was on! Jen kicked her chase into the next gear. Her legs began to utilize new muscles in this routine. The mountain had changed the game again and they would adjust.

She glanced around at the expansive area coming up. There was one more field of rockslide to cross before they were in the bowl. Jen slid across like a monkey clinging to vines. This terrain was old; the rocks had settled into the dirt to stay. Her progress easier; there was a downward trend in their destination. They approached the entrance to the bowl energized.

Downward she went in a gallop. She felt her knees now taking the brunt of the pursuit. Keeping her body from going too fast became another challenge. Jen consciously applied her body brakes. They were moving in the right direction and that had to be her only thought at this point. "Come on in said the spider to the fly," Jen whispered as she concentrated on her footing.

CHAPTER 12

AMBUSH!

As Captain Jen Holly entered the bowl, she paused to text Frank about the new developments. She placed an marker on the map text and hit send. Hopefully, Frank would figure out just exactly where this ambush needed to take place then send it to Jerry and Libby.

She cautiously moved into the bowl. Jen was letting the suspect get farther into the distance at this point. She hoped that he would assume she had become tired and wasn't able to keep pace. "You go, boy," Jen mumbled. This freedom just might put him at his ease making their surprise even more effective. The 'bing' of her phone brought Jen's attention to the screen. Frank had written 'k.' Who would have thought that she and Frank Mason would become texting buddies? Another crazy life twist, she mused.

Jen had now reached the alpine meadow.

Miniature plants growing in dirt welcomed her. The terrain had now become so much more accessible. Wow! What a concept! The trap was being set. Hallelujah!

Jen was very content to monitor the sniper from a distance. She didn't want to start a bullet cascade now. No, let him run just like a fish, she thought. Reel out some line before you tugged hard!
Jen concentrated on her descent.

***

Libby James and Jerry Neal were huddled over Libby's phone trying to identify the terrain in the bowl where they were to be located. Their eyes glanced up and scouted the contour until they saw what Frank had marked. There was a steep cliff south of the field position. Anyone moving into the bowl would avoid the cliff by hiking north and directly into their trap. It would, essentially, filter him into the ambush. They identified a cluster of rocks perched in the ravine where they could hide.

"It has to be there," Jerry said as he pointed down the decline from their position.

Libby glanced two more times at the location then nodded her head. "I believe so. The rock cluster must be the same. Plus, we can find cover over there for the arrest. You okay with that, Tyler?" she asked the German Shepherd who simply panted and stared at her for instructions. Libby liked working with a dog on the team. It added another dimension to your senses, she decided.

"Let's get setup. I'm going to take Tyler over to the top of the hill and show him where the suspect will enter the area. That way he can alert us before the guy appears." Jerry and Tyler immediately left Libby to establish her own cover.

She found a large boulder that allowed her to remain hidden yet watch the path into the ravine. It would give her the freedom she needed. When the shooter was close enough, Libby could then have a clear view of his actions. She would be on the west, Captain Holly would be on the east and a steep 500 feet precipice would be on the south leaving him only traveling north into the trap. It could work, she calculated, especially, with Tyler alerting them of his approach.

Jerry and Tyler located Libby's position then moved to the north closer down toward where the shooter would enter. The suspect would be trapped by terrain and police. Their tactic was that their little surprise party would convince him to give up. That was the hope. 'Surrounded,' was the message.

Tyler had crawled some 20 feet lower than Jerry's position. He was intently listening and watching. The K9 was now totally in the hunt. His head turned back and forth as if following the signals from a satellite. Libby wondered if he would bark to alert them. She didn't know the dog protocol for such a situation.

The silence of high alpine was almost unbearable at this point. A breeze moved the thin air slightly. Mother Nature was perfectly content to sit back and watch. The reality would be of their making not hers.

Libby could feel her hands sweating on the assault rifle. Her eyes glanced around the environment wildly making sure that the shooter didn't drop from the sky. This ambush was her first. Yes, she had done all the training and passed all the tests with video reenactments. However, they were just games when it compared to this moment. She wiped her sweaty hands on her pants and stared in Tyler's direction.

All that training brought her down to this one test. No, it was more than a test, it was her living history; a vortex where a significant event transformed one's future. Would she live to talk about this landmark or was this 'the end?' A life transition stared her coldly in the face. Libby pulled herself back into the reality of this moment. Jumping ahead would only leap to negative conclusions, she assessed. To stay in the moment and be aware was her best hope.

Tyler then quietly turned and moved toward Jerry. He began his journey crouched low to the ground then pulled up into a full fledged run to Jerry's side. Jerry's ears strained to listen. There became a steady thud of running footfalls breaking the silence; the unfaltering noise of a human's breathing in thin air replaced the serene tranquility. All these components perceived before the man finally appeared. The sniper's profile slowly rose on the horizon. His eyes were locked on the path; a vacant stare of fatigue dominated his countenance, Jerry realized.

The man had been climbing for at least three grueling hours. Fatigue could be a game changer,

Jerry considered. How rational was this suspect? Had his stress level influenced his risk factor? This confrontation was far from certain, Jerry assessed. They really had to be careful; assumptions could be their enemy! "Stop, police!" Jerry shouted while raising his rifle.

The assassin jerked in shock, raised his handgun then fell flat on the ground firing a continuous array of bullets toward Jerry's position. Giving up wasn't an option for this guy. The suspect then scurried behind some bushes for more cover. He then, constantly firing, moved west toward Libby's position.

She kept cover until he got dangerously close. "Halt, Police," she yelled! She assumed the stance. The man answered Libby's command with a barrage of bullets. Libby ducked then returned fire from another position. He assessed the situation and retreated to the east running from bush to rock then firing.

The shooter's hopes were dashed when Jen appeared some minutes later. He was trapped. The man could either charge the officers and kill as many as he could or….

Jen suddenly sensed his resolve. Their ill-fated bond was undeniable. She knew what he was thinking; she was aware of his choices. "It doesn't need to end like this," she shouted. "We can negotiate. Your testimony could get you a lesser charge. Stop and think what's at stake here," she begged.

Strangers in so many ways, yet, two humans joined by their horrendous climb. Jen would never really be able to explain it or truly understand it but she now knew exactly what he was going to do. Nothing really could frighten this man; death was simply another option. The man smiled at Jen, shrugged good-bye then raced for the precipice; the assassin let out a war whoop and jumped into the wind. No hesitation whatsoever; he was gone.

The team rushed toward the edge. They stood watching the body silently drifting down the 500 feet. His arms were out to the side as if he were a bird flying. There was no sound as the body collided with the jagged rocks below. It bounced onto a plateau near the bottom of the ledge, face down. Silence.

"I was hoping for another ending to this whole situation. I should have known from the beginning," Jen murmured. "He just wasn't ever going to give up; it wasn't in his blood to stand down." Jen turned from the ledge and radioed Frank to give the formal report.

Captain Jen Holly then petted Tyler and went over procedure for the records with Jerry and Libby. She then collected their guns and proceeded to record the action. She retraced the confrontation by taking pictures of the shell casings and officer positions. Everything was bagged for evidence then marked and tagged.

Jerry clicked pictures of Jen's approach into the confrontation and followed the procedures for her. Their work was finished as the light began to fade. It was close to 7:30.

Long day, Jen mused. She was exhausted but oh so thankful that all her officers were safe. She glanced at the ledge then silently said good-bye to what might have been. Human choice so real and final. Actually, this strange comrade flew into his own freedom at the end. She shook her head and wondered. Some ten minutes later the hospital team in the helicopter hovered and collected the suspect's body. They pulled him up on a stretcher then headed back to the morgue.

The HAPT officers then decided to hike down Impasse Trail. Jen instructed Frank to send Bill to the trailhead. They packed up their equipment and evidence bags then left. The shooter had taken his guns with him of course; it was like he had never existed, Jen thought. She figured that the man was probably satisfied with how it had ended. He had successfully erased his evidence from the scene. Would they find his gun? Probably long after the case would be closed. That figures, she mused.

When Detective Bill Smith pulled up to the trailhead, he was met by three exhausted officers. Bill knew better than to ask a whole bunch of questions. These people had done their job and deserved a little space. He simply offered water and waited.

Jen's phone did another 'bing.' It was from Frank. 'Made chili. Come to 301 Lode Ridge Road in Frisco. Bring pickles.' Jen could only muster a smile and passed her phone around in the team circle. Silent smiles acknowledged the text.

"All righty then," Bill said. "We best stop at City Market and get those pickles. I'd hate to be a rude guest." He handed the phone back to Jen.

"Also my guess would be that we need to find

some dessert to go with that chili. Something tells me that Frank has one mean sweet tooth," Libby said.

"Amen," the team added then climbed into Bill's Ford Interceptor. Dusk had settled; they drove with lights on to Breckenridge for pickles.

CHAPTER 13

DIG DEEPER

The home was amazing. Décor colors of soft green and warm orange were highlighted by indirect lighting. The interior design was professional; the host must have preferred this subtle ambience. Frank Mason was such an oxymoron. His multi million dollar home had vaulted wooden ceilings, expansive floor to ceiling windows plus a hearth fireplace adorned with a wood fire, of course. The atmosphere was incredibly warm and inviting plus the furniture was characteristic of a skier's paradise. There weren't any hunter dead heads adorning the walls thank heavens, Jen observed. The crown jewel of the downstairs, however, was the kitchen. Julia Childs would have been proud, Jen mused with a chuckle. And then there was Frank wearing a chef's apron announcing in huge font, 'Don't fuck with the Cook!' Nice.

Frank moved causally around the abundant

room even though he was on crutches. The gas stove was located in the center of the kitchen for convenience. Utility cookware adorned the walls like decorations. Adding another subtle ambience to the kitchen was the amazing chili aroma now dominating Jen's senses. The spice fusion was so incredible and inviting. It was like being swept into another world.

Suddenly, Jen realized how hungry she really was. The entire team now felt hunger taking control. How cool was that, she had to ask herself? The conversation completely jumped from the case to anticipation. If she looked closely, Jen could detect how tired and relieved they all were. Time to reflect would come later; now was the time to relax and enjoy.

"So here's your pickles, sir. Hope Kosher Dills fit the ticket?" Bill said placing the jar carefully on the granite counter top.

"Perfect. Ooooh, do I spy carrot cake?" Frank's eyes lit on Libby's offering.

"Well, a little dessert did seem appropriate," Libby placed the box next to the pickles.

Frank nodded and said, "Perfect. Dinner is served. Somebody grab the bowls out of that cabinet over there." Frank gestured toward the designated cabinet with a large ladle that he then popped into the steaming chili stockpot. The bowls and plates were piled with chili, cornbread and pickles.

The living room became quiet as everyone concentrated on their dinner. Contentment ruled. The coffee, perched on a convenient warming plate, was an excellent touch. The group relaxed.

Jen began to sense that this wonderful team needed to share what had occurred today. After accepting her promotion, she had chosen to value team interaction. Simply said, they needed to understand each others' perspective; to comprehend individual reactions was vital. The team had to be confident that their back would be covered in all circumstances.

Silence, she had learned through mistakes, would only create distance. Plus, total comprehension wasn't always obvious, she knew. People had to work at it; they had to appreciate individual nuances. A person could miss so much by assuming how another individual felt. How stupid was that? It wasn't clairvoyant or clever but stupid. Open it up, she commanded herself. Frank had started the process by welcoming them into his home. Now, as the Captain, she had to move them forward. How this opportunity did occur, however, surprised Jen.

Chili devoured, the team sighed and settled. Bill took the reins and opened that door unexpectedly. "Holy shit what a fucking day! Do you have any idea how high you climbed, Captain Jen? My neck ached watching your progress. That guy was like Spiderman and you were right on his ass! It must have pissed him off. Did you ever look down?" Bill asked.

Frank then opened a bottle of B&B and poured a shot into every coffee cup. No one refused his offering. The tantalizing liquor took hold of the moment. The team's conversation morphed into an easy comradery letting egos be set aside. It was the right catalyst for opening the confessional.

"Shit, yes, I looked down. The lump in my throat was like a rock," Jen admitted! "The man was like a Timex watch; he just kept climbing higher! Suction cups was all I could figure."

The teams' laughter erupted like therapy. Everyone took a drink in unison then settled deeper into their chairs staring at the fire.

"Well, since we are coming clean on our little adventure today, I have to admit that my legs were shaking so bad before the ambush that I thought there was an earthquake," Libby confessed. "If Tyler hadn't come over and licked my face like a service dog, I would have shook right off the earth! Thank you, Tyler," she said petting his head as he moved over to sit by her.

Jerry then smiled as he thought of what to say. "Quite honestly, I have never worked with text being such a huge help. Dogs I understand but I jumped right out of my shoes when Libby's phone 'binged.' The maps were amazing, Frank. How did you come up with the idea to text us?"

"Well, I have to admit that the office looks like a tornado hit," Frank said in apology. He smiled sheepishly just thinking about the chaos. "We're at my house because it's a fucking disaster down there. I flew around that room searching drawers and generally creating havoc. If it hadn't been for the young lady downstairs in the GIS Office, the maps wouldn't have happened. After I borrowed those, it became easy," he added.

The group then got up in unison while making

plans to organize the office tomorrow morning. Together, they stuffed the dishwasher with the chili paraphilia. Cleaning done, they finally sat back down with heavy doses of carrot cake and more coffee.

Captain Jen Holly, wearing a proud smile, began to set the tone. It was time to form their new direction and be thanked properly. "I can't completely express how proud I am of you all. Today was incredibly hard on all of us. You couldn't have completed the tasks any better. Stepping up to the plate is so meager of a comment. Thank you for having my back and keeping this investigation moving forward.

I know that at sometime in the future you will think something like, could we have stopped him from jumping? I don't think so. This suspect was extremely professional and remained an enigma to me. Bet he was invisible in many ways. I climbed with him but will never know him. He smiled at me before he jumped and then released an amazing war whoop. That was the extent of his emotions. Nothing more; nothing less." Jen watched as the team absorb her comments. She moved the conversation on, we did a hell of a job today."

She paused and stared at the fireplace flames before continuing, "Somehow, we must dig deeper and work harder from this point on. Unfortunately, we are no closer to solving this case than we were yesterday. All we know or sense, is that our suspect was professional. Was he hired by individuals or by a corporation? Either way, what did that entity know or want from Johnny McPherson? For that matter, we are still waiting to find his body." Jen took a sip of coffee and sighed. "Each day the snow melts and each day we need to dig deeper. So with that said, what are your individual directions going be?"

Bill spoke first again, "I want to interview the CEOs of the corporations and family members thoroughly. Maybe even Sadie Russel's CEO because computers are the name of the game. I can't help but feel that the motive is corporate motivated."

Captain Jen Holly nodded.

Libby James then offered her thoughts, "I want to know why there was an attempt on Frank's life. I can't seem to get it out of my head that the key and the mine, itself, is really important to the case. Maybe Frank's history with McPherson will uncover a motive. It can't just be that Frank looks like Johnny McPherson; there has to be more," Libby took a breath before she continued. "Plus, I am truly enjoying bringing our office up to date with my computer skills. Guess I want to do a little of everything. That's my learning curve," Libby finished then sipped her coffee.

Jen nodded again.

"Well, I need to get back to Buena Vista and touch base with my Chief," Jerry said. "I am sure that the work was just piled on my desk. Possibly later, if the body hasn't been found, Tyler and I can take another crack at it?"

Jerry glanced at Jen and got 'the nod.' "How about you, Frank?" Jen asked.

"Well hell, I got to tell you that I am actually

enjoying the office communication. It's like a chess game. I know Summit like the back of my hand. I can't run up the damn mountains as fast as the rest of the team but there's nothing wrong with my brain. I'm hoping you won't send me out to pasture but let me do the communications' job permanently," Frank added staring directly at Jen.

She smiled in approval at Frank. "You did a great job today. You sound like an old teddy bear on the phone. I like that." Jen smiled and nodded in acceptance.

Her eyes then sought out Jerry. "When there is a search and rescue the chances of you being activated are certain. Naturally, we all know Tyler's value. More treats should be bestowed on our hero and official officer," she said and tossed Tyler a cracker. "As your Captain, I will pick up the pieces, budget, communicate with the media and lead to the best of my abilities. I will never hesitate or avoid situations like today. My philosophy has always been 120 percent. Right now my instincts about Johnny McPherson are, however, strangely skeptical. Where is his body?"

"What are you saying Captain Jen? Surely, you think the body is there, right?" Frank asked sitting up in his seat.

"I am merely saying that his body definitely needs to be found if we are dealing with a homicide. This case can't go to court until there is a body. I'll also work to uncover any information that I can about my climbing partner. Maybe his choice of provisions just might tell a story. Now everyone, go home and get some well deserved rest. I will see you tomorrow one hour later than usual for check-in. Frank, please be on time and cover," she added.

"Will do, Captain Jen," Frank said.

He walked them to the door and then sat back down wondering exactly what the hell the Captain meant. It was beyond his comprehension that Johnny might just be alive? Surely, she didn't mean that? Impossible, Frank thought.

***

An hour later from her new condo, Jen called Bix to tell her what had happened. "The suspect simply flew off the ledge after smiling good-bye. Deep down I knew that option was a possibility but when it happened, it was a shock," Captain Jen added.

"I can imagine," Bix said softly. She could feel the emotional baggage that Jen would carry. "You always would wonder if you could have somehow changed the ending. Totally impossible, but you would wonder. So what's next?" Bix asked.

"Well, the team has sorted out what they want to do and it all makes incredible sense. Frank will handle the office. Bill is now Lead Investigator and Libby wants to learn it all. Jerry is on call as usual. I will pick up the slack," Jen added.

"What does that mean?" Bix questioned.

"Media, lead organizer, and then my own kind of investigation."

"And you will be working on what part of the investigation?" Bix asked. She felt her curiosity growing.

"Simply said, I need a body, Bix. By now Johnny McPherson should have turned up somewhere in that gulch. I have had the medics up there at least two times in the last week. No body. I just don't understand it. Or…?"

"He's alive or kidnapped? Really? Seriously?" Bix questioned. "No one has seen him for months. His girlfriend, Sadie, hasn't heard from him. Or…so she says…. Wow, now you have me thinking about the possibilities. Very intriguing. You know, I might just drop by and see Sadie Russel in Denver tomorrow. Sadie and I have known each other for years," Bix added. "With your permission of course," she added.

"You definitely have my permission. Call Frank at the office tomorrow and tell him where you're heading so he can relate it to Bill and Libby. Denver, huh?" Jen said wondering aloud.

"I am going down to pick up Bernie Holden at DIA later in the afternoon. What if I should simply talk to Sadie around lunch time? I could call her tonight? Maybe say that Johnny's friend, Frank, feels that there are clues he should have noticed and would she have any idea what they might be?"

"Bernie Holden is coming tomorrow? Wow that date slipped up on me. Wonderful. It will be great to see her. Seems like years ago that her father's murder was solved." Jen chucked and then connected the dots, "Guess it was only two summers' ago. How is she doing?"

"As well as expected. The wounds are healing now that the trial is family history. This will be her first trip back to Colorado since his death. I visited her, as you know, but this is Bernie's first venture. Hopefully the time has been long enough for healing."

"Speaking of time, you sure that you have time enough to see Sadie Russel?" Jen questioned.

"No problem. Maybe Bernie and I can help in some way when we get back in Summit. That is, if she can handle getting into another case. Might be good for her. Who knows?" Only Bernie would know the answer to that question, Bix mused. She couldn't wait to see Bernie Holden!

CHAPTER 14

TEAM WORK

Detective Bill Smith found himself standing in front of a small obscure office space on west Colfax. The title on the window declared International Mineral Recovery Foundation. This was the second company on his list right after Slope Incorporated. He had made it down to Denver by early afternoon. The general questions going through his mind right now centered around what all these people wanted from McPherson and how did they interact with Johnny.

He stared for a moment at the dirty store window analyzing this location. It was totally unexpected. Not a high-rise like the other corporations. It was like they didn't want to be discovered. He checked the address one more time just for giggles. Yep, this was it. Needless to say, the word 'recovery' in their title was an interesting detail for Detective Smith. They 'recovered' what and why, he wondered?

As Bill went in, the darkness and stale smoke
smell, hit him. It was downright annoying; Bill
paused to wait until his watering eyes could adjust.
If a foundation wanted to hide, this part of Colfax
would provide that cover. You also had to figure
that maybe it wasn't a wealthy organization. That
was a possibility.

The older gentleman seated at a dusty desk at the
back might be able to shed some light on Bill's
theories. "Hello, sir? I called this morning about
your foundation? Detective Bill Smith from
Summit County? Did I talk with you on the phone,"
he asked?

Now that Bill's eyes had adjusted, he was able
to look around. There were shelves on all the walls
filled with maps and geological books. The dim old
fashioned lights did little to help his inspection. He
moved slowly toward the back until he was standing
above Mr. Thomas Gipple. The gentleman, adorned
in a tweed suit and bow tie, smashed out another
cigarette in his nasty ashtray. Gipple, annoyed that
someone was bothering him, sighed loudly. The
image of a busy man just really didn't translate for
Bill. The man, obviously, didn't want him here.
That, was an interesting fact.

Bill pulled up the vacant dusty chair from the
corner and sat. He pulled out his pad and pencil and
stared at Gipple waiting to be recognized. When the
old gentleman's eyes finally landed on him, Bill
asked, "You don't like talking with people, sir?"

"No. No. That isn't it. It's just that there should
be very little public traffic in my door. We're not
selling anything or looking for new business, young

man."

"And I am not here to inquire about purchases." Bill held up his badge for clarification. "I am only seeking information about International Mineral Recovery Foundation's interest in Johnny McPherson and his property in Summit."

Bill waited patiently while Gipple sorted out his options. The pause was long and drawn out. He began to wonder if the old guy had thought that Bill had been dismissed or he had gone to sleep.

Suddenly, Gipple awoke from his reverie and replied, "What do you need to know? Our interest in Mr. McPherson's mineral rights occurred over a year ago. It hardly is new news or earth shattering. Mr. McPherson denied our foundation's request to prospect the mine on his property. End of story."

"What did you expect to recover?" Bill asked carefully. He waited with pencil poised.

A long bored sigh then erupted from Gipple's mouth. It filled into a reluctant void of voluntary information. Bill was becoming irritated with this pompous smoking puff bag. "Sorry that you feel the need to withhold information. We either talk nicely or I will feel the need to pick up your sorry bones and deliver you to the nearest police station. We're talking, Mr. Gipple, whether you like it or not so cut the crap."

Gipple's eyes popped out and dilated somewhat. He took a breath and began, "The Foundation recovers remaining fossil fuels from the older and neglected mines in many countries. It is an international attempt to consolidate the remaining ore deposits left in the earth. The McPherson Mine was just one of many. Mr. McPherson declined our offer which by the way, came with a considerable stipend of money offered. His refusal closed the inquiry. We do not hassle our clients. Going that route is cost prohibitive." Gipple's mouth then snapped shut like a crocodile.

Bill found himself leaning up in his chair. Gipple had opened a door about motiving clients that wasn't totally clear. Smith sensed the possibility of force as a potential. Why would Gipple even mention it? "How did you know that there were remaining fossil fuels on his property?"

"Well Detective Smith, all the old patented mines have that potential. A prospector would comb the mountains for minerals and usually one mineral would lead to another. The potential is always high."

"Can I see the survey information that your foundation had about Johnny McPherson's mine? It would help our investigation."

"Simply said, there wasn't any. We only asked to take rock samples from the area in and around the mine. Mr. McPherson denied our offer and efforts. McPherson was adamant that he wasn't interested so our hands were tied. We moved onto other mines."

"Can you give me the name of a mine that you did inspect in Colorado?"

"Well, the Bobby Mine in Idaho Springs allowed us access some years back." Gipple volunteered.

"Do you remember whom you talked to at that mine?"

"Sorry. It has been years ago. I don't have that

information at this office."

"Could you check with your main office and get me the information."

Gipple's face glazed over as he smugly said, "You will need a warrant for that information."

"And what is the contact address for our warrant?" Bill asked.

"That would be Berlin Germany," he handed Bill the business card written, of course, in German.

"Thank you, Mr. Gipple. Oh, I do have another question. Did you ever meet Johnny McPherson?"

"Once," he offered.

"Did you have any problems communicating with him?"

"No. He was very clear that his mine was off limits and we needed to not contact him again," Gipple said. "Keep in mind that this meeting was years ago. I can't even remember what the gentleman looked like. We simply dismissed him; he was not a potential client."

Bill thought that the word, 'dismissed' was fairly strong for a foundation that didn't hassle . "Does your foundation have any other offices in the United States?"

"San Francisco actually. It is a small office much like this one," Gipple offered. "Our main business office is in Germany as I have already told you."

"Do you have a brochure that explains your interests and process?"

Gipple let out another huge sigh and opened a small drawer at the bottom of his desk. He fished around in the contents for a few seconds and then pulled out a worn brochure and tossed it to Bill.

Sure enough there were all the addresses on it in English of course. Bill felt that he had been given the crown jewels. "Thank you," Bill said and got up out of the chair. "By the way, how many Colorado mines has your foundation inspected?"

"Nearly two hundred," Gipple supplied the answer rather quickly, Bill thought.

"How long has your foundation been prospecting in Colorado?" Bill inquired now that he was getting answers.

"For the last decade."

"Have you purchased the mineral rights on any of these properties and or the entire properties?" Bill kept pushing.

There was a slight hesitation in Gipple's countenance as he weighed his response. Bill could tell Thomas Gipple felt that this topic might be a slippery slope. "I would say approximately 50 out of 200."

"That many, huh? Properties or just mineral rights?" Bill kept going.

"We purchased both on twenty of the properties."

"Don't suppose that you could give me the names of those properties?" Bill ventured.

"Warrant," Gipple responded in a cloud of smoke as he lit up another cigarette hoping to ward the detective off.

His ploy worked. Bill turned to leave then as an after thought asked, "Oh, has your foundation done any business with Walter Connally of Slope Incorporated?"

"Never heard of them," Gipple said as he

exhaled then aimed a toxic cloud of fumes at Detective Smith. Bill departed; Colfax air smelled incredibly good to him as he deeply inhaled on the sidewalk. Very interesting Bill mused as he unlocked his car and got in.

It was now time to let Libby's computer skills uncover all the information that they needed on this foundation. He had no doubt that Gipple had withheld. Bill took pictures of all sides of the brochure and did a text to Libby. He could feel so much just below the surface. Trolling for answers was definitely appropriate, he thought.

Bill now headed toward Slope Incorporated again. Howard Carlson's secretary had been instructed to fork over all the land survey work done on the McPherson Gulch to Bill today. Warrants were wonderful things he mused as he pulled onto I-25 going south.

***

Libby had just verified that the key was a security box copy and the patent was owned by a bank. She was about ready to hit all banks in Frisco. They could at least tell her if it was one of their keys. If she could narrow it down then only one warrant would be needed.

The text 'bing' set her back down in her chair. Bingo. Bill had just sent her the informational brochure for the foundation. She enlarged the content images and set up a new file for them. She plugged in all three addresses and hit the search button. The computer purred as it began searching

the world for information. By noon Libby would
know what questions to ask in her research. Data
always led to more questions. Libby figured she
could probably check the banks in Frisco then come
back and begin to research the foundation during
lunch. Monitor then munch sounded marvelous!

***

Captain Jen Holly had followed the trail up into
McPherson Gulch. A person could now walk
without snowshoes. The ground was soggy but
accessible. The sound of dripping water was
everywhere. From the bridge's crime scene tape to
the alpine meadow was in an extreme melt. There
were large piles of snow stubbornly clinging to the
shade but it would all disappear soon. The warm
sun now ignited color throughout the soft radiant
meadow. It was almost surreal in nature, Jen
realized. She had to smile at the small delicate
crocus blooming; life would muscle its way to the
surface without hesitation. She approached the
cabin area and paused to analyze the avalanche
impact. The snow had melted down a couple of feet
exposing the ground in places. It was an entirely a
new scene.

The debris from the impact dotted the area
telling a specific story. Jen eyed the foundation of
the cabin. There was the indentation of the crawl
space now visible. Many of the cement blocks and
wooden walls, broken and crumbled, were thrown
around the area by the sheer force of the avalanche.
The trail of debris illustrated the avalanche

direction. From the angle Jen could determine where to look for any of the cabin remains. She gazed up at the area where the shooter had placed the howitzer; it all made sense now. Jen would remind herself later to have an avalanche expert come up and analyze the movement just in case the court needed that information.

She walked through the parade of debris. Her eyes scanned the discarded objects slowly. The Captain adjusted her mind as she searched. A casual afternoon hiker would literally be shopping the area thinking about objects and collection. The police officer would search for evidence. Both perspectives were valid at this juncture. There were some footprints wandering in the same direction that she was walking. Captain Holly took pictures and wondered if the medics had hiked the same route. It was a question that needed to be answered. She would borrow their boots for identification fairly soon.

This area was truly an archaeological dig for now. Someone could research a man's life from what remained here. His personal thoughts, needs and ambitions left to the wind, rain and snow. Kitchen items, books and bedroom items, abandoned to decay in time comprised the Johnny McPherson collection. At this altitude the debris would take a couple hundred years to perish. No. All this stuff would need to be picked up, examined and thrown away. Alpine was definitely a harsh but gentle environment. Decay was not a option in this gulch.

As Jen walked through the remains, she couldn't

help but feel an existing aura around her. The silence of high altitude felt almost uncomfortable. Her mind was replaying the devastating screams of rage that all avalanches cause; it was eerily silent now. Was this aura negative or positive, she couldn't decide? Silence usually nurtured the positive. How odd, she mused; time moves on.

Room remnants mixing together created a new history. Camera ready Jen clicked some general pictures. She took some quick panorama pictures of the foundation remains before she walked. Who knew what would be important or simply filed away? One thing was for sure. There was obviously no body to see.

Maybe she needed to look inside the larger mounds of debris just in case. Jen pulled on rubber gloves and gingerly lifted the top layer of one collection with a stick. Her eyes began to check the second layer carefully. Her stick froze as it uncovered a rock sample bag from under a kitchen pot. The sample bag was made of sturdy duck canvas. Jen had seen one of these bags in the GIS Office some months ago. Halo Lab. was printed near the bottom of the bag. The laboratory address was below the survey information that a prospector would fill out. The information, however, wasn't filled in on this specific bag but there were small rocks samples in the bag. Jen thought about it for a second then placed the bag in her pack. Who knew? It was worth a try.

Captain Holly adjusted her inspection technique once again. There had to be some general conclusions for her to take away. She began to sort in her mind the topics of various books scattered about. It seemed that two topics were of major interests, minerals and computer program technology books. The majority of the mineral books were from Arnold McPherson's prospecting days. Except for a couple that had been published in the 1990's. Johnny, obviously, had an interest in the mine also.

The computer books and laptops plus other computer paraphilia needed also to be inspected. Maybe it was time to send Libby up here to see if any of this equipment might just come to life? It was worth a try, Jen thought. Who knew? It definitely was Johnny's most recent living history for sure.

***

Bix Bixler opened the large doors of the Benter Technological Communications' high-rise. Obviously, corporate consulting had to be big business, she surmised. Her stare was focused on the amount of CEOs listed on the directory when Sadie Russel found her.

"Bix, so happy to see you. How long has it been? I have to say that I do miss my friends in Summit County. That gulch not so much," Sadie grimaced. She gave Bix a welcoming hug then stared at her for a moment before she asked, "Are you really working for the police now?"

"I'm helping a good friend who asked me to contact you, Captain Jen Holly. She just took over the leadership of HAPT."

Sadie's expression registered clarification so Bix continued with more information, "She was one of the officers that I met during that murder case over in Buena Vista? Ever since then, we have been close friends. So I guess the answer is 'yes' with extenuating circumstances. How have you been, lady? Last time I saw you was at the memorial service for Johnny."

Sadie looked down for a moment as she processed the question. "I miss him so much, Bix. It was like nature ripped my heart out. Avalanches are so horrible. He disappeared within seconds. My world simply stopped."

The sigh that heaved from Sadie's heart was strong and deep; Bix felt it and knew it. She gave Sadie a second hug with more feeling. "I am so sorry, Sadie. I can't image. He was such a good man trying to live his life the best way that he could." Bix paused to let her words sink in before she continued, "I feel driven to help Jen uncover what actually happened. Mother Nature wasn't at fault, Sadie. The gulch was invaded by an assassin who was hired to kill Johnny. I believe we owe Johnny McPherson's memory real answers."

Sadie was startled by Bix's comments. She put her arm around Bix's shoulder and guided her toward one of the empty conference rooms. They entered in silence and turned on the light. Sadie began to process what Bix had said. To just leave grief alone had been the easier path back then; she had done that willingly. It had been safe and oh so mentally plausible. Sadie, timidly, ventured forward now, "I am not sure that I am ready for this kind of conversation, Bix. Who would want to take Johnny's life? Even thinking about that possibility destroys any peace that I have found since the accident."

"I understand that completely. We try to heal as best we can, Sadie. The truth, however, needs to come to the surface; this case has been ruled a homicide because of new evidence. There is no statute of limitations on murder. Bix gazed deeply into Sadie's eyes trying to confirm the inevitable certainty of a new investigation. It would continue whether she was in agreement or not. The case would demand closure. "It is now classified as a cold case," Bix continued. "The police are obligated to keep investigating." Bix took a breath before supplying more details. "I am truly thankful that Jen has been assigned to the case. I also think that I can help in some way. Will you give me permission?" Bix reached out and took Sadie's hand. She knew how important it was for Sadie to condone the investigation. Her insights could make a huge difference.

Sadie stared at Bix for a few seconds. Her eyes searched her friend's face before she answered. "You do have my permission as long as I deal only with you. I trust you, Bix."

"Thank you, Sadie. There will become a time when the police will have to interview you simply to make things official. Please keep that in mind. I will help you all that I can," Bix stated.

"So what do you need to know?" Sadie asked settling back in her chair. She braced herself for the conversation as best she could.

"Was this company, Benter Technological Communications, after Johnny's talents in some way? Or, were they hoping that he would throw some business their way?"

"I would have to say the later. My CEO, Jim Neitz, approached me a couple of times to see if Johnny would consider recommending BTC work. I had a feeling that they wanted his approval not his expertise. No. There was no competition. At least Johnny didn't mention it."

"Did you feel that BTC really needed Johnny's help?" Bix asked carefully.

"Oh no. Absolutely not. Look around, Bix. These people are filthy rich and doing quite well. It was more a courtesy of one company to another, big fish to little fish. Johnny actually thought BTC was a good company."

"You know, Detective Smith will have to talk with BTC about the connection. It is purely good police work to consider all involved business corporations. What other companies did BTC have business contacts with that might be important?"

"Come to think of it, the company did a financial speculation project for Slope Incorporated. Howard Carlson had to be involved so that situation might be important."

"Were you working on that project?"

"Actually no. I saw a folder on one of my associate's desk purely in passing. I didn't inquire about it or care at the time."

"Was that before or after the avalanche?"

Sadie's face registered her grief again. The word 'avalanche' was definitely a trigger for her. She paused, swallowed and then continued, "Before the avalanche. Probably in October if my memory serves me right. So long ago." Her eyes fluttered as her mind created the timeline. Sadie then waited to hear the next question. She silently braced herself now realizing how disagreeable facts can be; their details biting and gnawing at her heart.

"I want you to know that my next questions will simply be asked because they have to be. I think it will be better coming from me than a police officer." Bix, once again, placed her hand over Sadie's before she started. "Were you and Johnny having any personal problems?"

"No."

"Had Johnny talked with you about any other business contacts that were threatening him?"

"Not really but he had decided to donate the entire gulch to the Summit Open Land Foundation. We talked about what a good idea that was. The future of the gulch was a huge responsibility for him. He figured that upon his death, Open Land could preserve it. I sure didn't want it and Martha and Howard would have considered it a financial investment. Johnny wasn't buying into that at all.

He honored Arnold McPherson's legacy too much to consider letting the property become white gold. Johnny saw it as something to appreciate for its beauty and history. I promised him that I wouldn't tell anyone about his decision. He was quite adamant about that so I haven't said anything…" Sadie's eyes then stared at Bix as she admitted, "until now of course. Bix, I am hoping that I have done the right thing here. With Johnny gone, my obligations have changed. Right?"

"I think so, Sadie. The question now becomes, who knew and how? And, I truly do believe that Johnny would want you to share this information. He would want any motives revealed so that justice could be done."

Bix hesitated before she could get the nerve to ask Captain Jen Holly's incredibly uncomfortable question. It truly was an awkward question in this white gold tragedy. "Sadie, what would you say if I told you that there is speculation about Johnny McPherson being alive?"

CHAPTER 15

REAL AND RAW

"Speculation! What in the world does that mean? Bix, surely Johnny would let me know if he was alive? To even suggest a secret hiding place is a cruel joke! Who is voicing such a mean hearted accusation?" Sadie's eyes burned holes through Bix Bixler.

Bix's face absorbed the pervasive sting of Sadie's reaction; she was demanding the truth and Bix needed to provide it. Bix leaned forward in her chair and clarified, "Captain Jen Holly has to investigate that premise. You see, Sadie, his body hasn't been found. We're in total snow meltdown up there. The avalanche has revealed a major amount of debris but 'no body.' It just doesn't make sense. Jen has done thorough searches; one with a K-9 and the medics, twice. Nothing."

"Nothing?"

"Captain Holly would be remiss in her duty if she didn't look at all the options. I decided that as a friend, I needed to be the one to tell you. I hope that you can understand."

Sadie leaned back in her chair and exhaled softly. She desperately tried to wrap her mind around this new development. Suddenly, it dawned on her that there might be a glimmer of hope arising. Could Johnny have walked out of the gulch and gone into hiding? And if so, why? So completely into hiding that he wouldn't even contact her? Was he truly in love with her or really didn't trust her? She had to wonder…. Sadie shared her doubt, "Why would he do such a thing, Bix?"

"Could he have feared for your life in some way?" Bix ventured.

"I…I don't know," Sadie stammered. It all seemed so unreal and so incredible to her. The shock shot through her heart letting an array of feelings surface. She whispered, "We have so little time with the ones we love no matter if it is a lifetime or a few moments…we have so little time. Should I dare think that I have a second chance?" she gasped! "God help me, I'd forgive any reason that he would offer. I loved him…I love him!" Sadie's response gained force. Her expression transformed quickly into the present tense of hope. A little light forming.

***

Bix Bixler thought about Sadie's revelations as she entered DIA two hours later. She checked the arrival board and found the gate number for Bernie Holden's arrival. As she proceeded to the gate, Bix couldn't help but visualize Sadie's pale face as the realization had taken hold. Life, once again, handing out another curve ball, Bix thought. Just when you got comfortable with the status quo, here came another pitch. The intensity of Sadie's emotions had rocked Bix to her roots. She could still feel her hands shaking.

Bix had tried to make sure before she left that Sadie wouldn't totally accept the option that Johnny was alive; hope was one thing but total acceptance was another. Nothing had been resolved either way. She wanted to protect Sadie just in case the body was found in some obscure location. Bix had said that much to Sadie three times as they had finished their conversation. Was three times enough? No. One heard what one wanted to hear. Bix had done what Captain Jen needed but it sure felt inadequate at best. The verdict was still out there with no one solution insight. Bix was sure of one thing only at this point; Sadie hadn't been in on any murder plot. Her emotions were too real and raw.

Suddenly, Bix realized that she was standing at Gate A waiting for Bernie Holden to arrive. Speaking of real and raw. Love was again demanding adjustments. Bernie wasn't a second choice in lovers; Bernie was a first choice. Bix had spent the major part of her life accepting second choices. How stupidly poetic was that? Her eyes began to search the crowd pouring from the gate.

There she was! Bix couldn't miss her because she was so damn tall. Bernie's green eyes and red hair was radiating above the mob. "Bernie!" she yelled trying to make her short stature taller.

Without any hesitation Bernie found her, leaned down and kissed her; no words but a kiss. Bix could feel the force of emotion engulfing her body. From mouth to toes her energy exploded. For this specific moment the deep sensuous kiss was all that mattered. Two women lost from the public world and traveling into their own profound moment. Both women accepting the gift that life had given them. Lesser infatuations all forgotten and put on the shelf. The kiss was real. It was an enduring connection that she couldn't stop and wouldn't stop. Wonderfully raw and magnificently real.

***

"Yeah!" Libby James screeched. Her enthusiasm totally out of control. She jumped out of her chair and pumped her arm in triumphant. Frank peered over the communication's board at her to make sure everything was all right. "Sorry, Frank, but sometimes the information is just too good to be true. Would you believe that The International Mineral Recovery Foundation is clandestine in nature? Quite frankly, it looks huge and all powerful. Maybe indeed the world's Wizard of Oz. Gipple lied to Bill. The San Francisco Office occupies a whole high-rise in its glory! Man, this data is incredible. Wow, check this out," Libby's eyes landed on a small footnote at the bottom of the fourth page. 'For more information, contact Agent Marshall Tate of the FBI.' Libby picked up the print-out, ran over to the communication's board and silently pointed at the small footnote for Frank.

"You're right. 'Wow' is damn near right on," he mumbled while staring. "Bill isn't going to believe this when he gets back here. Do you think we struck gold?"

"I think so…." Libby's mind was now spinning. So many questions and so many answers were out there. She quickly texted both Bill and Jen adding the four page summary as an attachment. The International Mineral Recovery Foundation information was now ready for others to decide the next step. Her job was done on that investigation for now.

Libby then decided to concentrate on her own next step. She had gotten a hit at one of the banks. Mountain Bank had identified the key as theirs but the branch office in Breckenridge had the security box number for the key. Libby saw an opportunity to leave and head to Breckenridge. Her energy needed a release at this point. Why not?

"Frank, I'm out of here. I am going to the Courts and get a warrant if there's a judge present then onto Mountain Bank. The safety deposit box key is from the Breckenridge branch. Finding out what McPherson has stored away seems pretty damn important right now."

"You go, girl," Frank said with a smile. "Libby was out the door before Frank could blink. "Kids," he chuckled. He couldn't help admire Libby's enthusiasm at this point plus she was the queen of computer research. No question about it.

Frank's eyes then scanned the HAPT email website. He figured that was part of his job now. One of the emails that he saw was from the FBI

Headquarters in Washington. This curious email had just come in. He checked the address carefully and found a phone number to call. Frank then called the telephone number listed on the email just for kicks.

"FBI," said a pleasant female voice on the phone.

"This is Officer Frank Mason of the HAPT Police Department in Summit County, Colorado. We just received an email supposedly from your office. Can you verify that indeed it was sent from the FBI and that Marshall Tate is the agent who sent the email? I guess I also need your code number so I can verify that this is truly the FBI."

The lady laughed and answered, "Oh yes sir this is the FBI Headquarters in Washington D.C. I will now send your office our code if you like. Of course, I will need your email address."

Frank spent the next half hour verifying the legitimacy of the email. He finally felt comfortable that it was all on the up-and-up. All the codes had been exchanged and he had gotten a specific number to call so that he could talk with the agent directly. This case was sure as hell getting interesting he thought. What was his obligation here about this inquiry? Frank decided that it was appropriate for him to give this agent a call. Getting some general information for Captain Jen certainly wouldn't hurt and could save time.

Frank cautiously dialed the number and waited through two rings.

"Agent Tate. Can I help you?"

"Yes, sir I believe you can. I am Officer Frank

Mason from the Summit County HAPT Police Department in Colorado. I believe that you sent an email today inquiring about our investigation concerning the International Mineral Recovery Foundation?"

"Yes. Yes, I did." Frank could hear Tate shuffling papers before he responded, "Officer Mason, may I ask why your department is investigation this foundation?"

"It is concerning a homicide case here in the county. The victim had been contacted by the foundation prior to his death. We're trying to sort out what that was all about."

"I see..." said Agent Tate. "The FBI will need your office to stop all communication with this foundation. It is of national importance."

A huge silence then ensued. Frank was speechless. What in the hell could he or should he say now? He felt like they were getting their hand slapped. The silence played on.

"I'm sorry. Are you still there, Mason?" Agent Tate inquired.

"Yes sir, I am still here. I believe that Captain Holly will need to verify the FBI request with you. She will be back in the office this afternoon."

"Can't you patch me through by radio now?" Tate asked rather impatiently.

"Sorry sir, she is out climbing to the murder crime scene on the side of a mountain. Communication would be difficult at best."

"I see. Well that definitely makes it a different environment than what I am used to."

Frank could hear the condescension building in

Tate's voice.

Agent Tate continued, "I suppose later today will be fine then. Please give her my information and I will be looking forward to the call."

"Will do, sir." Frank was now teetering on the edge of anger. If he had been in Leadville, the phone would have been thrown across the room. How different this HAPT situation and position was for him. You can teach an old dogs new tricks, Frank decided. Raw anger wasn't going to cut it here he understood that now. Frank took a breath and continued carefully, "I do need to tell you that our investigation could be truly hindered by halting our inquiries. It certainly would be a rare case when one criminal branch can not investigate all potential suspects. I would hope that the Captain can convince you or, at least, find a way to compromise with the FBI." Frank waited to see what the arrogant bastard's reaction would be.

"The lines are drawn on the FBI stance. Like I said, it is of-"

"National Security. Yes, I heard you and will relate the message to my Captain." Frank simply hung up and sat back in his chair. He had kept his temper under control which was a real miracle. Son of a bitch; such a typical stance for the FBI, he thought. These guys always felt their business was the only significant business. "We'll see about that , Mr. FBI." Frank grumbled to himself with a devious smile.

***

Detective Bill Smith had gotten a rather large folder from Howard Carlson's secretary. It definitely looked like Slope Corporation had more than a little business with McPherson. Obviously, they had invested quite a bit of time and money into the McPherson proposal. Bill couldn't wait to open that file and check out the venture.

In fact, all three companies were now candidates on the suspect list. Captain Jen had texted him to contact Jim Neitz at BTC before he left Denver. Sadie Russel's employer had also sought McPherson out for reasons unknown. Bill was able to set up a meeting with him for later in the week. It had been a very successful morning to say the least. From what Neitz said, Bill sensed that BTC was more witness material than suspect. That would be a nice, he reconnoitered.

On a whim, Bill decided to celebrate. There was a restaurant in Idaho Springs that his wife, Bonnie, had suggested he try during his many trips down to Denver. He took exit 241 off I-70 and followed her instructions to Miner's Street. She had then refused to give him anymore directions. She simply smiled and said that he would know it when he saw it. Sure enough there it was. Norm's Diner was on his right. It was a silver 35 foot Winnebago Trailer resting on cement blocks. The Winnie was like the food trailers near the capitol in Denver only there was a kitchen attached to the back. The trailer came with a TV antenna and awning of course. Curiously, there were also Tibetan Prayer Flags waving from the front door. Bill couldn't wait to see the inside.

He pulled into the parking lot, grabbed the McPherson folder for a look-see and locked his car. What could it hurt to read during lunch? Why not get a general feeling about all this stuff right away.

Bill opened the diner door and entered the 1960 décor. He speculated that Norm had emptied his garage to create this insanity. It was over the top. Round economical tables with posters substituting for wallpaper. Joni Mitchell, *The Wall* by Pink Floyd, Beautiful Day, Joan Bias and Crosby Stills and Nash were a few that he recognized. Incredible. Memorabilia including glittering guitars and vinyl records dangled like wind chimes from the ceiling. The atmosphere was total rock and roll. He and Bonnie should donate their *Hair* poster from San Francisco to Norm. The restaurant would be a great resting place for it, he speculated.

Bill took a small table by the window. A young lady wearing an Ellen name tag brought over the menu. The menu cover was entitled, *Stalking the Wild Asparagus.* How cool was that? Even the old literature was introduced. As he opened it there was another shock. Organic! Norm had to have a green house behind the kitchen. Bill ordered a bison burger and spinach salad with the greens of the day. Nice.

Settling back feeling super comfortable and lucky as hell, Bill opened the folder. His eyes scanned the potential survey maps first. Yep, McPherson Gulch would have made a great ski area. He could just feel Slope Incorporation savoring over their offer. The young waitress placed his coffee on the table with a smile. Bill then sipped and read the financial numbers next. It was a surprise how huge the McPherson proposal had been. No company would want to lose it, he knew. It did seem like a fair offer, however. He hunkered down to inspect the numbers closely.

Bill was almost too engrossed in the Slope information to see the two men who had placed a lock pick metal strip in his car window and quickly unlocked the Interceptor's door. Ellen, his alert waitress, was far more aware than he was. "Hey mister, check out your car!" she shouted.

Bill's eyes shot up as he ran from the diner as quickly as he could. Unfortunately, the bald 300 pound 'big guy' was guarding the diner door and tripped Bill on his way out. The gun butt came smashing down on his head. Blood spattered on his suit as 'big guy' rolled him and landed a right hook on his nose then pummeled his face with enthusiasm. Bill, fortunately, found the strength to roll and regain his footing. He charged directly into 'big guy's' pot belly hitting him with all his force. There was an audible groan as the giant toppled.

'The little guy' was now hot wiring the Ford Interceptor. Bill leaped over the mound of flesh on the ground screaming at 'the little guy' in the driver's seat. "Stop, Police! Get out of there, you fuck!" Bill pulled his gun. The little guy understood and moved out of the car with his hands up.

Bill suddenly felt 'big guy' behind him. The giant tackled him once again and pounded his face into the dirt. Before he passed out, Bill felt the giant's gun barrel poised above his temple. It didn't take a genius to know what was inevitable. Lights out!

Detective Smith missed Norm coming from the back of the diner with a baseball bat in hand. The cook stopped 'big guy' with one forceful whack on his back! It had turned into an even fight; definitely not what the thugs wanted. The two bastards then changed their tactics and retreated. Both men began running toward their escape car. The use of guns forgotten.

Bill staggered to his feet about the time that the two jumped into their car and sped out of the parking lot in a nasty smoke cloud. The lunch crowd gave a boisterous cheer from the diner windows. Their relief was obvious. Norm must have wisely corralled them inside before entering into the fray. Ellen, the waitress, was now clicking pictures of the retreating car. "We got them," she declared. Ellen then inspected Bill's sorry looking face and asked, "Mister, can I get you a towel? Your face looks awful sore," Ellen said eyeing him with concern.

"Please," he answered. Norm patted him on the back and proceeded toward the kitchen while calling the local police. Ellen disappeared to get a towel.

The aborted assault was over as quickly as it had begun. A crumpled blood stained cop stood trying to absorb this sudden unpredictable event. Bill shivered as he touched his bruised face; the pain reminded him how incredibly fragile life can be. He should have been dead seconds ago. The significance of that phenomenon shocked him like a bolt of lightning.

Suddenly, he remembered the folder that he had left on the table inside. His heart leaped into his throat and then on cue, Ellen returned carrying the towel and his folder. "Thank God," Bill whispered casting a smile of appreciation toward Ellen. He let a huge sigh escape from his mouth. This inconceivable moment had been extremely raw and definitely real, he admitted.

CHAPTER 16

CLUES AND CLUELESS

Libby and Captain Jen waited for Frank to finish telling them about Agent Tate of the FBI. They had settled on the couch and chairs in the office after discussing Bill's encounter. Captain Jen had placed a 'Closed for Meeting' sign on the door. Bill was on his way back, thank heavens.

"So what did you say to Tate?" Jen asked Frank just a little apprehensive. Frank's temper was a well known fact.

"Used my best decorum and said that you would call him hoping to find some sort of compromise. Of course, he then mumbled that the FBI was all powerful because of 'National Security.' He did say that he would take your call. Good luck with that one," Frank added.

"Well, we do have to inform the FBI of our intentions. I will confer with the Chiefs before I call Tate. Now, we need to research these companies quickly; McPherson Gulch and HAPT are definitely under siege.

We need to consider all the companies and suspects. Bix, who met with Sadie today, felt that Johnny's murder and the possibility of him now hiding out, was a total shock to Miss Russel. It would seem that BTC contacted Johnny without involving Sadie. However, BTC had a contract with Slope Incorporation. Therefore, Howard and Martha Carlson could be up to their eyeballs in that negotiation. Jen moved the conversation on, "What did you find in the safety deposit box, Libby?"

"We now have a copy of the latest survey on the gulch and Johnny's old will. He left Martha and Howard Carlson the gulch in the old will. The Carlson kids would have inherited only money. In the old will Johnny had indicated that his wish was to sell the property to a responsible party whatever that meant. Sadie Russel, however, was indicated as the executor and would inherit a million dollar life insurance policy not the property. It was legal will. Even his grandfather's diary was to be given to the Historical Society.

Oh and Frank, there was a clause where Johnny directed his executor, Sadie, to give you the survey information to deliver to someone named Gray and to request that you, personally, would oversee the selling of the gulch with Sadie if the Carlsons decided to sell that is. Libby searched Frank's expression to see if all this rang a bell.

There was a pause while Frank searched his memory. Suddenly, his eyes lit up in recognition. "Holy shit!" Frank yelped slapping his hands on his knees. "Now I do remember that conversation . It was at least three years ago and during a night of drinks. Around midnight Johnny finally got to the point. It was about that survey report. My instructions were not to open it unless the future of the gulch came into question. That whole conversation was pretty fuzzy. Well hell, Johnny must have decided later that I should deliver the survey to Milton. Hope Milt is still alive."

"Who's that?" asked Libby and Jen in unison.

"An old crusty prospector who knows more about mines in this area than anyone else. Old guy lives in Stringtown over in Leadville," Frank added. "Guy's got no phone and lives without electricity as far as I know. He drives an old wreck of a truck and mines gold in the summer. His gold mining is his income as far as I know. Of course he drinks a lot, naturally. You want me to try and find him?"

"Definitely," Jen said. "Let's keep his name and what he is suppose to do confidential. After Bill's unfortunate encounter, I don't want to involve anyone else. Whoever instigated the assault on Bill is sending us a clear message. Working for HAPT right now seems dangerous, don't you think?" They all paused to think about that implication.

"You know I could put on my old mining clothes then slip out in my wreck of a truck some evening soon and head over to Stringtown," Frank suggested.

"That would be a dangerous undercover assignment, sir," Captain Jen commented. "We'd need to get Chief Hagen in on this. He could have one of his officer do surveillance; you know, just driving by Gray's house once and awhile. I'd want you monitored as best we can," Captain Holly added.

"Then let's get Harry to watch Milt's house for me around 10 tomorrow night. He's the only cop over there who can pull off casual surveillance as far as I am concerned."

"I'll talk with Chief Hagen this afternoon. Are we good on all this? Any questions?" Jen asked.

"One," said Libby. "What is Stringtown?"

Frank took the question. "It used to be the area where the gold industry smelters were located in Leadville during the 1800s. Anyway, the residents of the area were usually poor people who lived on a string; you know, not a lot of income. Goes way back in Leadville history."

"We have one more topic to discuss here. My findings from McPherson Gulch," Jen said then dug in her backpack. The Sample bag of rocks came out first. "Frank, run these down to GIS and get them surveyed. Libby, take a sled up into the gulch and retrieve all the computer parts that might give us some more information. Document with pictures where they are located of course. Actually Libby, take Bill with you. I will ask that you all travel with partners from now on. We don't want anyone else left out there by themselves.

I will be conferring with the Chiefs about Agent Tate this afternoon. Maybe I could take a look at that diary also; I am curious why it seemed important to Johnny. And speaking of Johnny, no, I did not find a body. Nothing." Captain Jen then looked directly at Frank. "Maybe ask Milton Gray if he knows anything about Johnny. We seem to have a Leadville tie here."

***

"Frank, have you learned how to arrange a conference call yet? Maybe you could arrange a meeting with the Chiefs?"

"Figured you asked so I checked the instructions on this monster machine and we're a-go, Captain Jen. You want me to call the stations and get a time scheduled?"

"Please." Jen said then turned another page in the old diary. The first twenty pages were pretty boring to read. Arnold was definitely a geologist at heart. The pages were full of his survey findings. He created a detailed list of the minerals found in the mine. She had to wonder why all the detail? She supposed that all miners needed to understand the composition. It apparently had been fairly decent because Arnold McPherson really got involved in the mining after his wife died. He surveyed all the potential tunnel openings in the mine and then made his decision which tunnel to dig.

Using a pick and wheelbarrow, Arnold related his exhaustive search. Day-after-day he slaved away. It looked like he was determined to strike it rich if the gold vein was there. He began using small amounts of dynamite to speed the progress. For fifty pages Arnold had dug deeper but couldn't locate the vein. He hesitated about bringing anyone else into the mine to work. Jen flipped to the last ten pages and found Arnold complaining about his health. Could be that he was getting older? Could be stress? Of course miners would each day hope that the gold vein would appear before their money would run out. She also calculated that Arnold was nearing his late 70s; he was no spring chicken. Still, Arnold wrote that he had shut down a couple of the tunnels for health reasons. Curious, she thought.

"Got your call organized for 1:30, Captain," Frank interrupted.

"Great." Jen checked her watch. She had fifteen minutes to organize her thoughts.

Frank sat back and marveled on how well Captain Jen handled her bosses. She got permission to basically tell Tate to fuck off. In essence it was decided that their murder case trumped the FBI Investigation until the FBI could prove how this case would become a danger to National Security. Sort of a 'put up or shut up' scenario, Frank assessed.

He decided to head down to the GIS Office with the rock samples. Why not? Captain Jen had the call under control. Actually, he was pretty sure that Halo Laboratory was still in existence. Maybe there was some history data available. Sure wouldn't hurt to contact them and find out. Frank slipped down the stairs with ease. He had gotten a handle on using these damn crutches. Frank opened the door of the office using a crutch as a door stop. "Hey Katie, got another project for you guys."

"Super, Frank. You always brighten my day. Come on in," said Katie Faith from behind her computer. Her blond ponytail swished expectedly as she got up to take the rock sample from Frank and give him a hug. Having the HAPT Office upstairs sure was a new exciting event, she thought happily.

After Jen finished the phone conference she quickly talked with Carl Hagen, Leadville's Chief. "I've got a favor to ask of you."

"Oh yeah. What is it?" Carl asked in a gruff but friendly voice.

"Could I possibly come over and talk with you this afternoon. Not sure I want to mention my business on the phone. FBI involvement does seemed to add paranoia to phone conversations, doesn't it?"

"Yep, young lady it does but you won't need to come over. I'm in Frisco sitting in the Moose Bar finishing lunch. Come on over and pull up a barstool."

"Be there in five. Are you buying?"

"I could be persuaded."

Captain Jen shot out of the office before Frank had come back. She would text him now so that he'd know the door hadn't been locked. As she pulled up to the Moose Bar, she eyed the Leadville Patrol Cruiser near the entrance.

Her eyes began to adjust to the dark bar ambience as she saw Carl sitting at the bar. He motioned her toward a table at the back and nodded to the bartender.

"What can I get you?" asked the barkeep.

"Coffee, thanks," Jen said and headed to the table.

Carl had a beer. "Coffee?" he inquired.

"Well I have to admit that Frank's coffee is pretty damn strong," Captain Jen said.

"No kidding. The man drinks slush," Carl

chuckled. "Why do you think I sent him your way? He smiled then continued. "Actually believe it or not, Frank tells me that he's pretty damn happy," Carl added as he stood up and pulled a chair out for Jen. "Young lady, you have won him over."

"Well, that's good to hear," Jen said. "He really is turning into a great communication's specialist. He knows his way around Summit and the local population talks to him. He also seems to fit with our team. His knowledge really helped in our first pursuit; I feel good about the situation."

"Dandy. I will consider Frank's move one of my miracles then. And by the way Captain, good job with your first manhunt." Chief Carl Hagen then swirled the last of his beer and swallowed before he continued, " I would have to admit that when the Chiefs sat down and bullied me into hiring you, I was skeptical. That is until I monitored your pursuit up the side of Impasse Mountain. You got mountain goat training in ya?"

"I have to admit that I do like climbing. The team will be starting a class on doing high climbs after the McPherson case. It certainly will be needed if we have a tourist hanging out on the side of any mountain," Jen added. "I hope our team does become indispensable to this area and I figure our training just might be the key."

"Better you than me…. So, young lady, what do you need from this old crusty Chief?'

***

Bix and Bernie were starring at the Henry

Holden memorial bench in front of them. The family had donated the bench to the town of Buena Vista . The Holden murder case had so disrupted the town that the family felt it was the least that they could do.

"It's nice, Bernie," Bix said taking hold of her hand. "I'd bet the town does appreciate it. Besides, the park needed another bench," she added assessing the space. Simon stretched out his 12 feet dog leash and was sniffing furiously. There was a frenzy of smells present in the park, dog heaven. "Glad we came over today. It couldn't be nicer weather," Bix added.

"Yep, you're right on both counts. By the way, I think the Holden clan is planning to return again next summer. Two summers off from our RV vacation is probably enough," Bernie added. "What do you think? Want to make a reservation with us?" She glanced at Bix, "I'm hoping that you will."

"I'd have no problem with that," Bix said. If we hadn't agreed to meet Arlene Holly today, I'd say let's stop at High Mountain Vista RV Park to visit." Bix checked her watch and then suggested an alternative plan. "Maybe we should call Bob and Chelsea later this week. Get them out of the reservation business for a lunch this week. They can always use a break. Actually, we ought to do the hot springs in the morning then lunch. You want to be my date?"

"Sounds like a deal," Bernie said with a smile. She had been planning this vacation for months and it really felt wonderful to be able to take time off worry free. The Holden family had hired on a rancher to manage Billy's property while he was off in Washington being a senator. Her father's house was vacant so the manager and his family lived there. John's son, Matt, had inherited Henry's ranch. Matt was still in college deciding what he wanted to be for now so the plan was working quite nicely. Her brother, John, was overseeing the properties while she was gone. Usually, she and John directed the ranch activities centering around all four ranches. What with the extra help, the Holden properties were now thriving. There even had been talk about hiring on more hands.

Bernie let herself sink into her reflections silently for another moment. Wasn't that part of taking a vacation? You got away and could then look back objectively. Who would have thought that the Holden family could make it without selling mineral rights, but it had happened as if there had been some heavenly interaction. Maybe that was what destiny was all about, Bernie mused as they walked back to the car. She clasped Bix's hand more tightly as her thoughts continued. The positive energies walking forward; the negative energies frozen in one place. Keep walking, Bernie, she told herself and it will all work out.

The ladies arrived at Bix's Wrangler and unlocked the doors. Simon had gotten a nice airing at the park so the schnoodle was ready to continue the adventure. He didn't really mind Bix tossing him in the back instead of the co-pilot seat. Bernie could have the seat for now. He liked Bernie. Having her stay with them was a great snuggle in the morning after Bix got up to make coffee. He and

Bernie then caught a few more winks of sleep together. Plus there was always the bonus of more hiking and traveling when she was here. It was all good, Simon yawned.

***

Detective Bill Smith found himself back in the office the next morning. He and Libby had brought down a few of the master drives from Johnny McPherson's computers yesterday. Libby didn't have much hope for their condition because of the extreme weather in the mountains. She was now over at the computer store with some of her geek friends. If there was anyway to get the drives going, Libby would find it. One could always hope that something would come from the computers or the McPherson will. The puzzle pieces were now laying on the table; it was up to the team to fit them together.

Bill had noticed that Frank felt some apprehension about going over to Leadville tonight. Actually all one had to do, was look at Bill's face to understand the potential danger involved. Went with the job, he assessed.

So Detective Bill Smith now sat in his comfy office chair in the afternoon sun. The warmth would help soak out some of his aches and pains. To say that he was over the assault couldn't be farther from the truth. You just didn't flip your recovery like some light switch. It didn't matter whether the event was inevitable death or an event like he had experienced. The assault was ever present. This morning when he walked out of his house, he found himself keeping a watchful eye; his mountain security had been shaken down to its' roots. The mental scar would be ever present along with a new physical scar on his chin as a reminder. Cops needed to be careful, period.

Bill started reading the Slope folder. Any clues that he could uncover about these companies had become incredibly important. He felt that two questions had to be answered; how motivated were these companies and had any of these companies been involved in instigating illegal force in their past? Bill decided to contact Denver Police to see if Slope Incorporated had been implicated in anything. He had just gotten off the phone with Denver when Captain Jen walked in.

Jen walked straight across the room and laid her hand on Bill's shoulder as she closely inspected his facial damage then spoke, "So sorry, Bill. I wish that I could have stopped the assault. Who would have thought that stopping for lunch would end in an altercation? Whoever went after you must have had their muscle ready to use; it was so quickly organized."

"Yep. That seems to indicate Slope Incorporated. However, they knew what was in that folder. Why would they want it back in such a hurry? Which brings me to the thought of intimidation as the motivation or to implicate another company."

"Throw us off the track?" Jen questioned then processed Bill's premise. "Yeah, the assault could be connected to any or all of the above. I agree with you. This case needs full out investigation on all of these companies. We need clues that lead somewhere. Right now I feel clueless; we don't even have the body. We don't even know what kind of case we have. Shit!" Captain Jen's impatience had surfaced. Both Bill and Frank could feel it and agreed with a nod.

"When Libby gets here," Jen ordered, "divide up the research and dig like hell. Sounds like the computers are toast but it was worth a try. You guys did dust them for finger prints?" she verified. "Who knows what might show up? Old methods ain't all bad."

"For sure," Bill said then concentrated on the folder again.

Frank checked the office emails. There was silence as everyone went to work and got into their own space. Frank did make a note to follow up on the gulch evidence as best he could, rocks and all.

With a sigh Captain Jen moved forward. "Frank, let's do the Agent Tate call. Make sure that we record the conversation, and, that you inform him of the recording before I pick up," Jen directed.

"Can do." Frank went to work and had the phone ringing in five minutes. After the fourth ring a recorded message said, "Sorry that I am away from my desk. I have been ordered into the field and will not be back until Friday. Please record the necessary information and I'll get back to you Monday."

Frank and Jen stared at each other in surprise. "Well that just figures don't you think?" Frank mumbled.

"Yep, it does. Well Frank, let's use this time then to go over tonight's events. By the way, I am going to visit my mother tonight, Arlene Holly. She lives above her art gallery in Leadville. That is simply my normal routine," Jen added. "I'll be minutes away. Chief Hagen has set up surveillance and he knows where I'll be. It was Harry that you wanted to drive by, right?" Captain Jen verified.

"Damn straight," Frank said.

***

Bix and Bernie sat with Arlene Holly in one of the restaurants in Leadville. Italian food was the choice by Arlene who had closed The Single Frame Art Gallery for an hour's lunch. She couldn't resist an invitation from Bix who had become her daughter's closest friend. During the last year she and Bix had begun meeting for lunch now and then. For Arlene it was a good way to check up on her daughter without prying. Plus, Bix was great company.

She eyed Bernie Holden with interest. Both Jen and Bix had talked about this lady. Arlene had realized early on that Bix was romantically involved with Bernie. She couldn't wait to hear more on that subject, however, her need to get some answers about her daughter was priority right now. First things first, she decided. "So tell me how is HAPT doing? It sounds like they are extremely busy with the new case," Arlene pried.

"I'd say that they are doing one hell of a job. Jen is so busy that she has asked me to help a little,"

Bix said. "I wish that I could do more but I don't want to push. And from your look, I'd says that I need to explain about her latest mountain pursuit. Right?" Arlene enthusiastically nodded her head. Bix paused before continuing, "It was an incredibly difficult climb. I figure the Chiefs were impressed and so was Jen's team." Bix hid behind her menu hoping that Arlene was satisfied.

Bernie listened with interest but stayed quiet and examined the restaurant menu also.

"She was in extreme danger wasn't she?" Arlene's eyes stared through Bix's menu. There was no room to hedge, Bix decided. "Yes, I had my heart in my throat as I watched. The climb was extraordinary. Jen had trained well for that pursuit. She is highly skilled and talented, but you know that, Arlene," Bix added to soften her words.

"Lord help me I do. I don't like to admit it but I do," Arlene sighed. "How proud I really am doesn't cover it," she revealed modestly.

There was a pause while the ladies stared at their menus and processed the conversation. During this silence, an old scurfy Leadville local wandered into the restaurant and approached the 'take out' counter. "Ya got my orders?" he demanded.

"Here you go like always. Two coffees, right?" the waitress confirmed.

"Like always," he grumbled and left without tipping as usual. The waitress shaking her head then came over to the ladies to get their order. The lunch crowd was small today so there was very little wait time. In a flurry the ladies ordered. Arlene then eyed Bernie intently.

187

"So you are from North Dakota? I am sorry that the murder circumstances in Buena Vista were so awful for your family. It would have been nice to meet you then but I understand totally."

Bernie smiled sadly, Bix observed. Coming to grips with the mountains again had to be difficult for her. Grief was such a living form. It surfaced so often in unexpected places. The stark surprise happening without permission. Healing always so tentative and nebulous. How did one begin to live with loss; sadness embracing time maybe? Living history should never apologize to grief, Bix decided, just let it be.

Bernie looked intensely at Arlene then replied, "You're right. Circumstances do complicate our lives. However, there wouldn't have been a reason to even meet Jen if the circumstances had been different. Your daughter was there to help my family deal with the murder. Jen's police work made closure possible for us," Bernie admitted. "I couldn't have asked for a better response from anyone. Jen came into our lives for that purpose. Amen," she beamed.

Arlene was about to comment when her phone rang. She was surprised to see Jen's name in the display window. "Well speak of Miss Holly. Excuse me for a moment," she said, "Hi honey, what's up?" She listened for a second then nodded. "Of course. See you tonight then. Bye. Well, that's a surprise. Jen is coming over for dinner tonight. I sense an alternative motive here but it's fine by me. You take what you can get with a busy daughter. Now where were we? Oh yes." Arlene reached over and placed her hand on Bernie's then admitted, "Sometimes, I am so proud of Jen that it takes my breath away. Thank you, Bernie. I needed that."

"You're welcome," Bernie said as their lunch arrived.

Bix was truly touched by the conversation. She quickly stared at her lunch not wanting either lady to see her emotional catharsis. "Looks wonderful, Arlene. Nice choice of restaurants," Bix commented changing the subject.

CHAPTER 17

IT STARTS!

Officer Frank Mason had just entered the Leadville City limits when he saw Harry's patrol car sitting at the corner of Mountain View Drive. Frank watched the police car follow him and then casually turn off on 8th Street. Frank smiled at the subtlety that Harry was exhibiting. "Nice," he mumbled. Frank wandered onto Harrison Street and down to Elm so he could make a pass by Milton Gray's cabin. His eyes scanned the property. No cars present so he proceeded to Milt's favorite drinking hole, The Old Bear Inn.

The bar was located on down Highway 24 on the right hand side. Frank parked half a block away, placed the survey in a satchel that he could carry and crutched back to the entrance. For 60 years old he was moving right along on those damn crutches, he calculated. "Not bad, "Frank murmured to himself for confidence.

The darkness inside was exactly like entering a

bear's den. The stale beer aroma assaulted his
senses; Frank decided that it was not quite as
offensive as bear's stench but pretty damn close. He
stood in the doorway for a moment trying to adjust
to the gloom. If possible, the interior of the bar was
darker than outside on the street, he assessed. There
were large cumulus smoke clouds coiling around
the rafters and enclosing the dusty old chandeliers.
The light was so feeble that Frank had to cautiously
move into the middle of the room before he could
locate Milt. Far down at the end of the well-worn
bar sat the old prospector on the same stool that he
had occupied for years. Habits die hard, Frank
thought, as he moved in Milt's direction. When he
was almost ten feet from Milt, there was finally
recognition.

"Well shit is that you, Frank? Thought you'd left
our town for greener pastures? You know, gone
where the money is. What brings you here?
Slumming?"

"You bet, you old fart. Is that stool taken?"
Frank asked leaning his crutches on the bar then
sitting before Milt answered. Milt tossed his
cigarette ash in the general direction of the
overflowing ashtray. "I heard you'd been hurt
climbing a mountain like a damn fool. Guess I
heard right."

"Well not exactly. Someone decided to use me
for target practice. Unfortunately, they didn't miss
their target. The good news is that I should be off
these damn crutches by next week. So how the hell
have you been?"

"Other than I can hardly get up out of bed in the

mornings from my damn arthritis, not bad. Hell, the winters are getting harder to deal with each year. So what's the occasion for your visit?"

"Well, I've got something to show you from Johnny McPherson's stuff. Our team is investigating the McPherson case; it used to be a cold case but now has turned into an active homicide," Frank said then watched Milt's face for any reaction. There wasn't any. Interesting, Frank thought. The old guy was not the least bit surprised.

"Figures," Milt mumbled. "Johnny was too smart to be surprised by an avalanche. He had so much equipment up there that if you hiccupped it would register on that man's machines. I ain't seen nothing like that in my life. Want a beer?" Milt asked throwing down the last of his beer then motioning to the bartender. "Two more and this guy's buying," Milt said pointing at Frank.

"I could do that. After our beer can I drive you over to your cabin so we can sit in the light and check out this survey?" Frank asked.

"Maybe we could move on over to the restaurant here and you could buy me a meal before I look at that survey?" Milt ventured.

"That'll work too," Frank said wondering if there was something at the cabin that Milt might not want him to see. Well, he could deal with that later. Right now Milt's advice about the survey was priority. Johnny must have felt that Milt's knowledge of that mine was significant. He hadn't recommended taking the survey to a company but only to Milt. That fact hadn't been wasted on Frank. There were very few old prospectors left in the area who understood the mining discoveries and how it all connected together. "Can we catch those beers in the restaurant?" Frank asked.

The bartender nodded and motioned to the waitress to fetch and carry.

Frank and Milt then moved themselves toward the kitchen door at the back of the restaurant. Granted, the light was low in there but not to the point of needing a flashlight. They found a table where the kitchen fixtures illuminated their space. They ordered two burgers and fries. Milt also added a piece of apple pie to his order not missing a beat. Frank noticed that there were only two other diners in the restaurant. Probably tourists who had found the town locked down at 10.

"So are you glad that you left old Carl Hagen's command?" Milt asked between bites. "You're working for a woman, right?" he threw in as the ketchup drowned his fries.

"Yep on both counts. I don't miss much, you know, especially, the commute over here. Carl was okay but it gets old after awhile. Same police problems over and over. My new job ain't boring that's for sure. I'm working the radio for a change," Frank added.

"You're what? Holy shit, you talking with tourists and officers? How the hell is that going?"

The burger was surprisingly good, Frank thought. He swallowed before answering. "You may not believe this but I like it. Captain Jen thinks I sound like a friendly old bear on the phone. For me, it's a whole new role.; you know, playing nice. And, working for a lady ain't hard at all when the individual climbs like a mountain goat and plays fair. I am even getting the hang of all the computer gadgets that the office uses. So far, Captain Jen, is treating me just fine," Frank said then popped in the last bite of burger.

As Milt's pie arrived with two enormous scoops of vanilla ice cream on top he said, "So let me see those papers that Johnny wants me to look at." He shoved in a huge bite of pie and waited while Frank got the papers out of his satchel. Milt inspected the survey moving back and forth between pages. Frank watch closely for reactions. As Milt read the fourth page his body twitched ever so slightly. Milt then went back to page two and reviewed the contents. Finally, after at least ten minutes, Milt leaned back into his chair and said, "Nope. Nothing out of the ordinary. Don't see no signs of a gold vein worth mining." Milt then inhaled a scoop of ice cream in one gulp and added, "He probably just wanted me to verify what he already knew."

Abruptly, the bar side of the establishment exploded into a chaotic barroom brawl! Bodies ricocheted off the walls rattling the entire structure. Dishes cascaded and bottles flew! Tempers exploded into a testosterone soup of heated high pitched voices. Punches were aimed at anyone in view! Two drunks mounted the bar and threw bottles at the fight instigators. It was pure bedlam straight from a cowboy movie!

Milt and Frank moved toward the restaurant's swinging doors to get a better view of the insanity. A stranger was fending off a couple of the rowdy locals. The drunks whooped and punched at him!

Organized, it was not. With that, the kitchen crew flew out the back kitchen door along with the two frightened tourists!

The brawl ensued even though the participants were obviously getting tired. There were now more cuss words flying than punches, Frank noticed. His eyes searched the brawl pile looking for the stranger again. The guy had disappeared from view. Frank figured that he was either at the bottom of the pile unconscious or had escaped out the front door. Frank was trapped at the back. Nevertheless, he decided to help the bartender try to control the mob.

Frank moved into the room cautiously pining one of the drunks out of the fray with his crutch. His attention was focused on the remaining pile of combatants hoping that the stranger would emerge. The bartender was yelling while tossing some of the old guys off the pile. Unfortunately, the bartender hadn't seen the drunk with the bottle behind him. Before the bottle came crashing down on his head, Frank stabbed his crutch into the drunk's stomach! Frank was now in it, crutches or not!

Fortunately, Harry made a timely entrance and proceeded to yell at the top of his lungs, "Police! Stop!" Frank moved to his side giving Harry some help; or, as much help as a cop on crutches could do. They began to divide the mix and regain some order when suddenly a smoke bomb was heaved through the front door! The cloud of smoke smothered everyone.

The coughing frenzy of intoxicated men fused into a stampede charging out the front door! Milt ran back and grabbed his pie then followed Frank and Harry out the door! Some men who couldn't afford another arrest disappeared immediately into the night. Harry barked orders at the remaining bedraggled gasping crowd! He corralled as many participants as possible and called for assistance.

Frank went back in to gather up his satchel and papers before the local cops arrived. The survey papers were gone! Someone had come in through the back door and taken them. The kitchen door was wide open! He crutched over and peeked out. Nothing. There was a telltale scent of car exhaust present. He quickly realized that the fight was a diversion. "Holy Shit," he shouted. Frank phoned Capt. Jen immediately. "They got the original drafts of the survey! Thank heavens we copied them."

She had picked up on his first ring; she was on her way. "Hell, don't stop here," he yelled. The survey papers were the target! Check Milt's cabin and Highway 24. There should be a car escaping in either direction by now! Milt's with me. Get the son of a bitch in the car who stole my satchel with the survey papers! I have a description of the one fight suspect that got away. He is definitely beat up."

Jen radioed Carl immediately. "Frank says the target was the survey papers. Car moving fast out of Leadville. Pursue and approach with caution, 10-4!"

"On it. We'll put up blockades on 24 right now! 10-4. Did you hear that, officers; now get the hell to work!" Chief Carl Hagen ordered.

Jen turned on Elm Street and headed for Milt's cabin. The cabin door was thrown open and off its' hinges. She pulled up and approached the scene with her gun drawn. As Jen entered the front door, she yelled, "Police!" The back door slammed shut as she moved through the house. She raced toward the back and saw a blond headed man running down the alley. He turned onto 3rd Street as far as Jen could calculate. She called it in while in full run. "In pursuit of burglary suspect on foot, 10-99. Suspect heading west on 3rd Street on foot. 10-34. Assistance needed, 459 in progress."

"10-97 on scene 4th Street," Carl Hagen yelled. "Nothing here. Heading onto 3rd!"

Captain Jen had lost him. Somehow between 3rd and County 31, the man had disappeared. Vanished into thin air. Somewhere in that vicinity the suspect must have entered one of these homes. Suspect either lived in a house or it was a forced entry. Jen also had to take into consideration that the suspect had been picked up by a vehicle. She hadn't heard any approaching vehicles but it was a possibility.

Chief Hagen came down the street in front of Jen. She stopped and placed her hands on her knees catching a well deserved breath. Running full out at 10,000 feet wasn't easy, she determined.

"Which way did the fucker go?" Carl bellowed as he slammed on his brakes.

"Good question," Jen said between her gulps of breath. Either picked up by a vehicle or is hiding in this vicinity. Captain Jen regained her posture and looked around. The neighborhood looked quiet and asleep.

"Well, we got the town locked down," Carl said inspecting the surroundings. What's your guess?" he asked.

"Could be in a garage or in a house? Have no idea. Last time I saw him was at the corner back there." Jen pointed never taking her eyes off the area. "Wonder if both incidences are related?"

"Good question," Carl said looking at Jen. "Gonna call both Chief Anderson and Marten so that we got all areas locked down. Any vehicle description that you got?"

"Need to check with Frank but I think all he sensed was the exhaust fumes. What a mess," Captain Jen grumbled.

"Now don't get your tail feathers ruffled. We'll go door to door starting at daylight which ain't too long at this point. I'll get a couple guys up here to watch this area real closely. Anything moves, they'll know. The net's set Captain Jen, that's all we can do. Have faith." Carl couldn't help himself, he gave her a big old hug.

"These guys just seemed to get ahead of us somehow. Maybe there was more than one group involved?" Captain Jen said out loud. "Getting tired of playing catchup, Carl."

"I hear ya. We can only do the best that we can so let's get busy."

***

Jen decided to stay at her mother's apartment on the couch tonight so she could join the canvasing at sunlight. Somehow, she just knew that one of these guys hadn't left town.

Frank came over, before he left Leadville, with Milton Gray in tow. He had placed Milt in protective custody and was transporting him to Summit County. At the moment Milt was in Frank's passenger's seat yelling like crazy. Frank and Jen were talking over the top of the ruckus as Arlene Holly watched from the upstairs window.

"Damn straight he's involved somehow," Frank verified. "Two clues to that situation: when I handed him the survey, he talked about Johnny in the present tense and wasn't surprised to hear we thought it was an attempted homicide." Nope, he knew that the papers would be coming. Plus, there's something on page four that shocked him and that is what I need to find out. Planning on interviewing him all night or until I get the answers," Frank said then added. "If that's okay with you?"

"Absolutely. I think I'll call Bill and send him to Breckenridge. He can set up the room and give you support. Libby can handle the road surveillances with Chief Anderson. You guys get us some information from good old Milt. We need some answers."

"I'm on it," said Frank as he crutched down the sidewalk; he then stopped, turned and tried to apologize, "I'm sorry, Captain."

"For what? Doing your job? Now get going and bring me some answers!" Jen said.

Without another word, Frank got into his truck and was off to Summit County.

***

Chief Carl Hagen had lied about going home for some rest. He went back to his office and began calling various Leadville realty companies trying to get a handle on the rentals near 3rd and 4th streets. The motels and hotels were also on his list. He even began to create a list of residents who occasionally rented to folks. It should all be checked out before the morning search even began.

Carl was determined to find out if there was an intruder staying right under his nose. He didn't much like the idea of a stranger disappearing in his town. Leadville was his responsibility and Carl was taking the night's events personally. Some son of a bitch just might think that he could hide his sorry ass in Carl's town. "Good luck with that," Chief Carl Hagen grumbled.

Three hours later as dawn began to wake Leadville, Carl got a reliable tip from the Do Drop Inn Motel's night manager. He had registered an out of towner yesterday who had insisted on total privacy and a accurate map of Leadville streets. There was to be no cleaning staff in his room until he left Sunday. He had made sure that the internet worked before he would check in. "Well, well…" Carl whispered and smiled as he hung up the phone. They just might have to pay this stranger a visit in the next 30 minutes. Carl dialed Jen then proceeded to get ready to apprehend the suspect. Carl radioed Harry who was so wired after the brawl that Carl knew he was out and about.

"Harry, get your ass over to the Do Drop Inn and stakeout room 23. If the guy in there moves at all, I want to know. I'm calling Judge Hedge right now and get a warrant. If the guy farts, I want to know; you hear me?"

"Yes, sir. Loud and clear," said Harry as he did a u turn then proceeded toward the Inn. Harry used a Code 2 to cover the mile back to the motel which was located right on Highway 24. Yeah, the guy could have run down there from 4th Street or even from the bar. It was perfectly centered for a quick escape. Harry could feel his adrenaline rising as he approach the motel. He turned off all his lights and parked so that he could see both the front and back of unit 23. This guy wasn't going anywhere on Harry's watch.

He quietly transmitted, "In position now. 10-4."

CHAPTER 18

PROGRESS...BARELY

Detective Bill Smith had taken custody of Milt Gray at the entrance of the Summit Jail so Frank could have a break. Bill then left the old prospector alone to stew for about 30 minutes in an interrogation room. Frank briefed Bill while pouring coffee. Together, they concluded that Milt wasn't going to sleep until he gave them answers.

"...so Milt knows more than he is letting on about this whole case, Bill. I can feel it," Frank Mason emphasized as he replaced the coffee pot and blew on his cup. "Johnny always had a soft spot for this old geezer who actually knew his grandfather. Now that I think about it, Milt wasn't at Johnny's memorial even. I figured he simply got drunk instead of going. Maybe I had the wrong motive there," Frank added sitting down.

"You never know how folks grieve like you said," Bill assessed. "So you think that he just might know who was after Johnny? You really do think that there was something in that survey he noticed?"

"Hell yes, I'd bet on that," Frank affirmed.

"Well then let's go get him." Bill placed both hands on the table and pulled himself up, then stopped for a moment. "I'm usually the quiet one in interrogations that goes for the kill later on, by the way," Bill informed Frank. They moved toward the room.

"Sounds like a plan to me," Frank said as he opened the interrogation room door. The older officer hit the floor running as he asked, "So where the fuck is Johnny McPherson, Milt? You haven't been truthful and you know a hell of a lot more than you've admitted. Now get it together and tell us what's going on," Frank yelled as he tossed down his crutches and sat across the table from Milt. Frank had brought coffee for the old guy; he placed it on the table in front of Milt Gray. The room was far more spacious and almost clean he noticed. Breckenridge had some good digs of course.

Milt's mouth snapped open then shut in surprise. Frank's question had startled him. "I know nothing about anything. You're the one who came over to see me. I was just minding my own business when all hell broke loose. I resent the-"

"Don't bullshit me, Milt. You saw something in that survey. I could tell. Page four meant something. I know it did. What was it, Milt? What did you see?" Frank asked.

"I don't know what you're talking about. There ain't no gold there," he grouched pounding the table with his hand. The sound popped with emphasis.

"What do you know about International Mineral Recovery Foundation?" Bill asked quietly.

Milt's head whipped around as he stared at Bill, shocked. The Foundation name obviously meant something to him. "I…I don't know what you're talking about. Never heard of them," he said stubbornly.

Both Bill and Frank could tell that Milt had just told a lie. The old prospector was nervously moving in his chair and looked like a scared rabbit. Push more, Bill thought. "I'm going to give you about five seconds to change your story then we will book you for accessory to murder. You, obviously, know exactly what I'm talking about."

Milt swallowed and thought quickly.

"Five…four…"

"Okay. Okay. Yeah, I've heard of them. They go around the world forcing people to forfeit their claims. Any miner who is still breathing knows about those guys. They then go in and harvest any type of ore that is worth anything. They're the scavengers destroying property and paying the owners less than it's worth. Yeah, I know of them like every other miner who owns an old deposit. What of it?"

"What did they offer to pay Johnny?" Frank asked trying to gather information.

"Not what it was worth, I'm sure. He never told me how much. He did say that he was beginning to feel forced to consider their offer. They was putting the screws to him. Yup, that what he told me before the avalanche got him," Milt stated.

"Speaking of the avalanche, how did Johnny

survive that disaster?" Frank asked.

"Who said he did?"

"I don't think you're convinced about that," Frank added.

"Says who?" Milt Gray shot back.

"Says me, you old fool. How come you didn't go to the memorial, Milt? I sure as hell didn't see you there when I paid my respects," Frank added watching Milt's face closely.

Milt leaned up in his chair and looked Frank right in the eyes. His breath could have knocked over a bull mouse, Frank thought trying not to flinch. "I don't do memorials; never have and never will. Ask anybody who knows me. They ain't for the dead; they're for the living. I drank until I was shit faced instead." Milt leaned back fairly satisfied with his answer.

"Martha and Howard were there," Frank kept pushing.

"Sure as hell they were. Those two were counting on their retirement off of Johnny's white gold. Fake sorrow brought on by real greed. Those two old farts know how to spend money but they sure as hell don't save any. At least Johnny told me that before the avalanche happened of course," Milt said repeating his new theme of denial.

"Like hell he did!" Frank barked back. "Those are things that a person tells after the fact. Johnny told you after the avalanche when you asked who did it? You wanted to know who he was looking for. That's what I think!"

"Who cares what you think," Milt retaliated. "Johnny was feeling the screws tightening before they did him in. He came over and talked to me sitting on the same stool that you sat on tonight. That's where people sit when they want answers from me. When they need to tell me important things. Yes sir, right on that stool...."

Frank decided to take another direction just to see what might happen. "So where was Sadie Russel in all of this? You know, Johnny's girlfriend?" Frank asked.

"Solid. Solid as a rock. Johnny really thought the world of her. I think that they would have gotten hitched eventually for legal reasons. Probably wouldn't have lived together all the time, but would pay taxes and watched out for each other. Both of them had careers. Sadie couldn't take long stretches in the mountains but she sure as hell loved Johnny." Milt continued on with this safe subject, "You know, couples are different these days. A strong woman doesn't take kindly to being controlled by a man. Sadie was her own woman and Johnny liked that. They had a partnership," Milt added shaking his head. Frank felt that Milt's response here was probably true from what they had uncovered so far. The rest of his crap barely measured up, he assessed.

"How about BTC, Sadie's employer?" Bill began probing.

"What about them? Oh yeah...." Milt realized where this topic was heading. He supplied what he knew hoping to go home tonight and feed his dog. "Johnny did say that they were average but okay. He said Slope Incorporated wanted a piece of them. He didn't much want that to happen because of

Sadie though. She sure as hell loved her job. Johnny was trying to help BTC stay safe."

"What did Johnny think about Slope Incorporation's ski resort proposal?" Frank asked trying to keep the truthful flow going.

"What in the hell do you think he thought? It was an abomination to his land and open space in Summit. Hell, how many ski areas does Summit County have to support before it would become too much? The land was worth far more is what Johnny said. The land has to breathe-"

"Where's the body?" Bill Smith said softly as he interrupted the old guy's beginning tirade.

"What?" Milt said putting his hand up to his ear.

"Where is the body?" Bill said again turning up the volume.

The comment registered with Milt. His gaze took on that scared rabbit look again.

***

Libby was on the south end of Breckenridge. She had parked her patrol car in the gas station lot across from Highway 9. The station served people before they left the ski areas going on 9 to 285 then Denver. It was the long way around but a person could choose to avoid I-70 and the majority of traffic. Libby realized that her location was definitely a long shot. Who knew?

Of course then there was the old historic route climbing Boreas Pass into Como then 285 to Denver. In the early spring this road wasn't used often. The road conditions were difficult to say the least. Fresh snow mandated local traffic flow only at this time of the year.

In earlier times Boreas Pass had been the only reliable route to Denver. The old steam engines had traveled year round. These narrow-gauged trains tunneled through the snow on Boreas Pass to Breckenridge. They were muscle trains, with huge snow blower mouths that gnawed and tunneled their way over the pass. You didn't have to worry about spring snow conditions then. Buy your ticket and ride along with prospectors and town folk.

Trains then rotated around in Breckenridge and got ready to haul freight back down to Denver. Libby always remembered one weird story that she had heard about caskets being deliver to Denver. Deceased residents couldn't be buried during the hard freeze at high altitude in the early years. Mourners and occupied caskets traveled down the narrow-gauged track together. Some of the oldest cemeteries like Fairmount and Riverside in Denver became the final resting places for these souls. Fairmount had nicknamed one of their older areas, Miner's Alley. Interesting times, Libby mused as she stared across the highway at the old train exhibit. Quite a tourist attraction now.

Libby's car motor was running for heat what with the temperature near 32. Summer was coming but not quite here yet. Chief Anderson had most of his officers hanging out along I-70, 20 miles north of her position. Chief Hagen from Leadville was searching Highway 24. Officer Libby James felt like an after thought sitting here. Would the suspects really head up Hoosier Pass and into

Fairplay? She weighed that option in her mind as she kept herself awake.

Libby also wondered how the interrogation was going at the Breckenridge Jail. Milt Gray had to be quite a character, she calculated. Libby felt a little jealous right now. Somehow, she was missing the action tonight in both areas but someone had to sit twiddling their thumbs. Bummer.

Then to her surprise, a car hurriedly entered the tranquil scene. It was rushing out of Breckenridge. The car came up on the Boreas Pass intersection and totally ignored the red stop light and left turn arrow . It sped up the road leading to Boreas Pass. Not only had the car made an illegal left turn but there was something about it that just didn't sit well with Libby. She radioed Chief Anderson and asked permission, "Sir, I just had a car run the light at Boreas Pass and proceed up that road. I would like permission to pursue it. I am assuming that they will turn in somewhere but if they don't…well…it's worth a try. 10-4."

"Permission granted. Let me know," came back Chief Anderson's response.

Libby moved out of the parking lot and followed, cautiously, in pursuit. She knew that the entire loop was 22 miles. A car could pass through Como and end up east of Fairplay then escape to Denver on 285. Staying back was definitely her goal. She figured that they would probably turn off somewhere, go inside a nice comfy condo and pass out.

Libby moved quickly down the straight stretch from town scanning the first switch back that wound up the pass. She could see the car now going slower halfway up the ascent. As soon as they disappeared around the bend, Libby shot up the mountain side. At the summit she watched as the car deliberately followed the main road. Libby pulled over and texted Bill and Jen quickly so that they were aware of her actions.

She then passed Captain Jen's condo complex and sped up the second ascent. She was less than a quarter mile behind them. The next mile was continual switchbacks sprinkled with driveways into large condo complexes. The left hand side of the road was dotted with spectacular views. The ski area runs were in full moonlight across the valley; the floor of Summit sparkled with the town's lights. Actually, it was a breath taking drive, Libby assessed. Better, if you weren't in pursuit, she smiled.

Libby hovered at the top of the third summit and watched the car weave down again ignoring all the condo options. It was now a straight run into the back of Boreas Pass. She passed Tyrolean Terrace Condos on the left and could then bet that their destination would be Como. So far the bulldozers had plowed the road for easy access. Now the fun began with the less traveled road. Would the snow be plowed and ruts manageable? Good question, she mused.

The mounds of snow were at least six feet tall on both sides of the narrow road. So far so good, she sighed then called Chief Anderson. "On the Boreas Pass Road toward Como. Road is passable at this time. Blockade requested at 285. 10-4."

"Done," came the answer through the static. Libby now concentrated on the ruts and road. At least if she got stuck, Chief Anderson would know where she was located. "I want to take a train," she mumbled to the empty car.

Her Ford Interceptor slowly crawled over the terrain. Unfortunately the weather had piled eight inches of fresh unplowed snow on this section of the road. The county probably was just beginning to get this scenic road ready for summer. As she climbed in elevation, it was steadily getting worse. Fortunately, being the second car, had allowed her to follow their tire tracks. There was no way to loose the suspects from now on. That was the good news.

Libby passed the old Baker Water Tank on her left where the narrow-gauged trains had stopped to add water before continuing into Breckenridge. It looked like a ghost beacon towering above the snow, Libby concluded. The moonlight now sparkled on the snow illuminating the desolate track. It was becoming harder for Libby to call it a road at this point. She realized that now the conditions had deteriorated to the point of no return. Libby couldn't turn around; 22 miles had become an incredible amount of distance at this point.

Her car moved onward covering another couple of miles at a slow cautious pace. Time was at a surreal standstill; it was now a treacherous solitary pursuit. Libby began to assess her winter preparation kit in the trunk. She just might need it tonight. Barely had she begun to think about survival when her eyes focused on the stuck car some 300 feet ahead of her.

***

Captain Jen Holly ran in the front entrance of the Leadville Police Station ten minutes after she had been called. Chief Carl Hagen was just hitching up his belt with a gun and holster.

"Howdy, Captain Holly, I figured you'd get down here about now. We're ready. Got four officers ready to ram that door flat. Harry's on stakeout at the location as we speak. Got my warrant in hand if the situation needs one. Judge Hedge wasn't happy to be awakened but that's the way it goes. It's not like it happens every damn night in this town. You're keeping us on our toes, Captain Jen. Well, lets go get the son of a bitch."

The anxiety was flowing as the officers pilled into one car and Jen and Carl in the other. They moved out quietly; no sirens and no police lights. The procession paraded down Harrison Street in single file stopping for the lights and attracting very little attention. Leadville had rolled up the sidewalks so to speak, Jen mused. Nothing was happening but that assessment was soon to change.

They pulled up beside Harry's patrol car. He rolled down his window to talk with Carl. "All quiet, sir. His lights went off at 12:30 and haven't seen hide nor hair of the suspect since then. The manager of the inn came out a couple times and brought me coffee. I'd say he'd love to get this guy off his property pretty quick.

"Well hell then, let's make that happen,"

whispered Chief Hagen. Captain Jen nodded her okay as they got out of their cars. The other bevy of officers unloaded the battering ram and checked their rifles quietly. Finally, the troops circled Carl and stared with anxious eyes. "Let's go get that son of a bitch. Remember, you do not fire unless I fire. Is that understood?" Carl waited until each of the five officers nodded and made eye contact. "Roberts and Jones go to the back just in case." Jen watched Carl intrigued with his technique. He had control and demanded it, she assessed.

They moved as a silent unit. Carl raised his hand up for all to view after two guys were ready with the ram. Three fingers became two then one and then the wham of the ram! It was like an explosion as they rushed into the dark room with guns drawn. "Stop. Police. Hands up!" Carl bellowed. The suspect groaned then appeared from under the covers with arms up, wearing only boxer shorts. Jen immediately did the search then went to the bedside table and found his gun on top. She turned on the bedside lamp and was shocked to see the suspect in hot chili pepper boxer shorts that literally glowed. She couldn't hide her amusement.

"Down on the floor, mister!" Carl loudly demanded. The Chief then waited until the guy was spread eagle on the floor. "Okay, now tell us who you are and what you're doing in my town?"

"Check the pocket of my suit coat," was the suspect's quiet answer.

Jen moved toward the closet, found his pocket and brought out the suspect's identification. To her absolute surprise, Agent Marshal Tate was on the floor of the Do Drop Inn in hot chili pepper regalia!

"Chief, we have Agent Marshal Tate of the FBI in our custody," she said starting to feel just a little irritated; amused yes, but also irritated. So now she knew exactly why he didn't return her call. Very interesting development, she calculated.

Her reaction wasn't nearly as explosive as Chief Carl Hagen's who had awakened a judge, paid overtime for officers and generally wasted his time. "What the hell?" Carl roared. "Sir, I believe that there are procedural codes that cover entry into any police jurisdiction. I didn't get shit from you, Agent. I want to know why the hell not?" Carl demanded.

His face was beet red and Jen thought she could actual see the smoke coming out of his ears. His officers stood back watching their Chief blow a gasket. "Then I want your address so I can bill your sorry ass for my expenses. What the hell were you thinking? You can get up, you son of a bitch, and put your pants on for God's sakes. Those boxers are fucking blinding," Carl added in disgust.

CHAPTER 19

ALL RIGHT…THEN

Officer Libby James' situation became obvious at this juncture. No one was going anywhere. One suspect was out in back of their stuck car trying to push them forward. Sure didn't look like it was going to work. Libby decided to reverse her car back 20 feet more so that her position wasn't spotted so easily. The steep rock formations towering above the old train route did add some cover. Libby pulled out her binoculars from her pack on the back seat. From her location, she could clearly watch the suspects. Now, it was a waiting game. She tried the radio which was total static at this location. Libby finally texted a message to Jen and Bill hoping that it would get through. She related her information and radio status.

As Libby decided to retrieve her winter survival kit from her car trunk, she noticed that snow had begun to fall again. She began to estimate that her altitude was almost 10,500 and that her mileage indicated a distance of ten miles from 285. The suspects had almost made it. The falling snow wasn't threatening but served as a subtle reminder that winter wasn't over up here. This silent dusting would provide a couple more inches, she estimated.

The plunk of an incoming text was a relief. Jen had gotten her message. "Stand down," was the reply. Yep, she had already figured out that one. She snuggled in the car then took inventory of her kit; snacks and lots of warm clothing. She plugged in her phone to the car outlet knowing that as soon as the suspect got back into their car, she could start her motor for heat. Her car battery was fairly new which was a bonus and her gas tank was full. Libby slipped off her shoes then put on clean dry wool socks. A sweater, stocking hat and ski pants became her fashion attire as she settled in for the night. A sleeping bag and her parka, folded as a pillow, would become her lounge chair.

Libby had to figure that these guys were smart enough to realize that staying put was the best plan until sunrise. At sunrise all bets were off. She wondered if they had figured out that it was about ten miles to 285. Who knew?

Libby munched on a protein bar and found the most comfortable position that she could achieve while watching the car in front disappear under the falling snow. The hours would slowly tick by. Her watch glowed two thirty a.m.

***

It had been decided by all officers concerned

that Agent Tate of the FBI would remain in handcuffs after he got dressed and extracted from the motel. That way, his cover would not be blown and Chief Carl Hagen would keep his image intact. Everyone piled into the three cars and headed back to the station. Harry had the honor of transporting Agent Tate in his car cage. Jen and Carl discussed jurisdiction with the other Chiefs, Anderson and Marten, on radio as they headed toward the Leadville station. It was decided that the local police still controlled the situation. Marten had decided to contact one of the county prosecutors for a second opinion.

Agent Tate began talking immediately in Hagen's office. "A day ago I received an anonymous email from the Leadville area. It basically said that there was information to be had about the International Mineral Recovery Foundation's involvement in the attempted murder. Something about how it was written made me think that, indeed, Johnny McPherson was alive and hiding out in Leadville," he said.

Marshall Tate leaned his wide shoulders back in the chair and eyed both officers. The shock on Hagen's face was easy to read. However, Captain Holly's look was more a stare of agreement. So she had suspected, he thought. Maybe she was closer to that conclusion than he had thought.

"My task force, HAPT, has been wondering now for a couple of days. The main clue is that there has been no body recovered. We have searched the area at least three times and nothing."

"Why did you think it was so important that

you flew in immediately?" Jen asked.

"The Foundation has illegal international activities going on and we are about ready to send out the subpoena. McPherson could be a key witness in those proceedings if he is alive."

"And then have him go into witness protection? That doesn't sound like Johnny McPherson to me," Jen added. "That gulch is his life," she declared.

"And it might very well be his death if he doesn't come into custody," Tate responded. "The Foundation is playing for keeps, trust me." Agent Tate's piercing blue eyes became intense. "The man is definitely in danger."

"I believe he knows that or he wouldn't have gone into hiding," Carl said. He also asked, "Then this Foundation that you're talking about is the group that set off the avalanche?"

"Well I can't go that far without talking with McPherson and Captain Holly here. Tate ran his hand through his abundant supply of blond hair as he waited for Jen's input.

Both men stared at Jen waiting for her response. "HAPT believes that it could be one of three companies," she said. "We began our investigation a week ago. So far HAPT has taken a cold case and just reclassified it as a homicide. The results are preliminary."

"Three?" Carl's surprise grew deeper.

"Slope Incorporated and BTC are also candidates for the honor. We are currently investigating all three. Johnny McPherson could really help move the case along."

Jen heard a plunk on her phone and looked

down to see that Libby was texting her. "Excuse me, gentlemen, I have some business to take of here. Carl, will you come with me please. We need to chat with the Chiefs for a few seconds. Sorry, Agent Tate, we'll be right back." They scurried into a conference room and shut the door.

"What's up?" he asked. Carl didn't use text and was rather surprised when Captain Jen had jumped up quickly.

"Officer James has followed two suspects up the Boreas Pass Road. They were on the way to Como when their vehicle got stuck. Libby is about 30 feet behind them on stakeout and it is snowing of course. It is Chief Anderson and Libby's premise that these two are our fleeing suspects from tonight's bar brawl," Jen clarified. "The blockade on 285 is set of course," she added.

"Holy shit!" Carl whispered. "All right then what do we do now?" he asked being more mystified by the turn in all the events.

"I think we need to decide if we trust this agent enough to work with him. We need to make a deal so that he doesn't find McPherson and whisk him out of the county. We might never see McPherson again," Jen stated with her hands on her hips. Then a thought rushed into her mind. "Whoa. We need to let Bill and Frank know about all the events so they can push Milton Gray and get some information about Johnny's whereabouts."

"Okay, so this is what I am thinking. I'll contact the boys by phone from this room here. Tell them to break Milt tonight. You go back in there and see what you think about trusting anything the

FBI man says. See if we can bargain with him."

"I think it's a plan," Captain Jen said then with her hand on the door knob, she hesitated and looked back at Carl. "You realize my part of this scheme hinges on instinct? He could say one thing and screw us after he gets the facts," Jen honestly speculated.

"I know that, little lady. Let's go with your instincts and I promise not to hold it against you if the agent is one lying fucker. We'll just figure out how to even the score if we have to," Carl stated and grabbed his phone.

Jen shut the door of Carl's conference room and walked back to Agent Tate. She had less than five seconds to decide how to handle him.

***

Frank's phone suddenly rang in his pocket; he jumped and grabbed it. He was surprised to see Chief Hagen's name. "I'll be right back," Frank said and grabbed one of his crutches to get himself out of the room quickly. "Yes sir?"

"We have the FBI agent in my station. The Feds believe that Johnny is alive and sent them an email about meeting. Agent Tate flew in yesterday and was searching Milt's cabin when we arrived to give chase. Use it on Milt and break that son of a bitch. Johnny's life may depend on what Milt says."

"All right then…we're on it. Any word on Libby's stakeout?"

"Far as we know, she's sitting tight." Carl said then hung up.

Frank texted Bill and let him know the information then headed back into the room. He figured Milt could hold the key to finding Johnny; it was now or never. When he opened the door, he could see that Bill had moved on the text without any hesitation.

"All right, Milt, the joke's over. The FBI was just found going through your cabin. They have admitted that Johnny McPherson emailed them. He is alive so cut the crap. And, I'm going to tell you why you want to confess to what you know. Johnny's life is on the line. The International Mineral Recovery Foundation is in federal trouble and searching for Johnny. They don't want to have tea with him but kill him for what he knows!"

"You're shitting me! This is some kind of a trick I know it!" Milt retaliated. Gray jumped out of his chair and began to pace. This game had changed and he was now sober enough to realize that.

"It's your move, Milt. Johnny is going to need help from the local police on two counts," Frank added. "Think about it. The feds could easily place him in witness protection after they use him in court or the Foundation could simply kill him! Either way, you'd never see him again."

Bill quietly added, "And Milt, you are obstructing justice and will be charged unless you come clean now. Hope you like jail?"

The silence in the room settled in on Milt like a snow storm. Hell, Johnny was in an awful place. And, as a matter of fact, he wasn't in a good place either. Even if he lied his way out of here tonight, the Foundation might find him and twist him like a pretzel to get information about Johnny. Milt's life wasn't worth shit either way. His eyes darted back and forth weighing the options. He and Johnny were in quite a pickle barrel of trouble.

Gray took a deep breath and tried the waters. "If McPherson were alive, and I'm not saying that he is, what are you offering him or me?" Milt asked. "Hell, you lost the assholes who trashed the bar tonight. Why would anyone think that you can help?" Gray shot back. "Hell, maybe you guys are working for the feds or at least with them. Why should you care about Johnny or for that matter, me? So far, you ain't done shit," he retorted. His eyes glowed with anger as he stated his case. Gray looked from Bill to Frank and back again. Something had to be offered to him or else he would stay quiet and that was a fact.

Bill took the lead at this point. "What if I told you that we have the two suspects who messed up the bar in surveillance and they will be captured by tomorrow morning. And what if I told you that the FBI agent is in custody over in the Leadville Police Station? I actually think that we are right on the top of this case and in control."

Milt thought about that for a moment. At least these guys had a few of the situations under control. The only problem was the Foundation or whoever tried to kill Johnny, was still out there. However, then he realized so was Johnny; Milt was the one in jail.

"All right. Johnny McPherson survived the avalanche. He hitched a ride over to Leadville right after. I came home from the bar and found him sitting on my front porch. Johnny has stayed with me off and on since December. He knew that someone had tried to kill him and he has been watching all the players. Johnny figured he was a dead man if he turned himself into the police. Who would believe him and who would then investigate the case? He figured that if everyone thought he was dead he could investigate without having to run and keep his friends safe. We went down to Denver and bought a computer for him plus an old clunker of a truck so he could get around. Naturally, we paid cash for both."

Frank Mason suddenly felt relief.; Johnny McPherson was alive. Why hadn't Johnny come to him, Frank asked himself? Then, Frank began to wonder who else knew. "Did Sadie know that he was alive?" Frank asked.

"No. Just me and it has been harder than hell to keep my mouth shut. After he explained about the situation, I knew that I had to help him. He feels really bad about not telling Sadie but it is for her own protection."

Frank observed a sudden relief in Milt's countenance. It probably had been a hell of a load on the old guy.

"All right…then, where is Johnny?" Frank asked holding his breath as he waited for the answer.

"I don't know," Milt said. "Can someone feed my dog tonight?"

***

Libby's eyes abruptly popped open for some reason that she would never understand. It had been an eerie hollow premonition that interrupted her slumber; she now felt chills crawling up her back. Libby hadn't remembered falling asleep; it had just happened.

There they were! Two figures cloaked in darkness were about 30 feet from her car and approaching. The sunrise had just begun. She grabbed her rifle and sprung out the door rolling in the new 8" of snow.

As she cleared the side of the car and got to the back for cover, bullets ricocheted off the Ford Interceptor. These guys weren't playing around. Libby aimed and fired her rifle just to introduce herself. The two figures scattered for cover. Luckily, Libby had fallen asleep with her phone in a pocket. Now she tried to text Captain Jen with the news.

The suspects were circling her position in hopes of getting a clear shot. Libby crawled around to the passenger side and opened the door slowly. A barrage of bullets hit the ground just missing her. She leaned in and grabbed the keys with satisfaction. It was possible that they wanted her car to try an escape. "Ain't going to happen," she whispered.

Libby crawled back behind the car for more protection. She searched the terrain around her position wondering if she could find a vantage point. Getting away from the gas tank was a priority in her mind. Libby would blow up her car if she had to. The wait for help was going to be forever, she knew. Plus, these guys knew that there had to be other police coming. Their only chance was to try and eliminate her then either take the car or continue on foot.

Obviously, they had no shovel in their car. Libby took stock of what was in her trunk now She did have snowshoes. They seemed more valuable than her shovel. The snow at 10,500 was still pretty damn deep. These two cars weren't going anywhere she now calculated. No, last night's snow had taken that option off the table. Maybe she needed to convince them to chase her?

Libby clicked the snowshoes on and ran directly back from the car. 50 feet back then she slipped behind a large boulder. She fired several rounds and waited for the response. A few shots then silence as they inspected her car. "Good luck," she mumbled without meaning it. Libby watched as they discovered the shovel in the trunk. A few more shots aimed in her general direction as they moved back to their car. One guy started to shovel while the other suspect fired a couple more aimless rounds in her direction.

Libby began to formulate a plan. She would be the mosquito bothering them while slowing down their progress. Just buzzing them from a distance and far enough out that they couldn't reach her unless crawling through waist deep snow. She figured that they wouldn't want to do that. So her plan was hatched, so to speak. Libby moved toward their position traveling along the ridge above the cars. She jumped when a text came in on her phone.

'On the way. Watch the skies. Keep safe!'

Captain Jen had written.

Libby quickly texted back, '10-4.'

Now it was simply a game to delay the suspects as much as she could. Libby moved up close enough to get a good shot. She aimed and hoped. The shovel flew out of the suspect's hand as she heard his yowl! A few cuss words flew as they took cover. If they had thought that she had run away, their hope was dashed. Plus, they had to consider that she was a potential threat. The wounded shovel would testify to that! Libby waited to see what would be their next move.

One of the men turned on their car and tried again to get it moving forward. "Ain't going to happen," Libby repeated. Sure enough, he then beat the steering wheel in frustration and slammed the door. The two began a rather lengthy discussion planning their strategy. Libby waited patiently. Time was now on her side. She moved about 20 feet from her last location just to keep them busy.

The suspects then tried to initiate a gun fight by shooting toward her last position. Libby smiled and fired a couple rounds just to let them know that she was mobile. They fired again at her new position. Libby had taken off immediately after firing. A large cluster of pines were now being used for cover. Each time she moved closer to their position, her routine of finding new cover, firing and moving was working. So far so good, she mused.

The suspects now realized that they had two choices. Run separately toward 285 or hold up in the cars for certain capture or death. They chose the first option and began to gather up ammo and supplies to carry.

Libby then texted Captain Jen, 'We're on the move toward 285. Suspects will possibly separate. Am slowing progress.' She zipped her phone in her parka pocket.

The suspects began to move out with small packs on their backs. They would stay on the road until the descending altitude melted the depth of snow. Eventually, they would be able to split up and try to vanish into the forest.

"All right then…we're on the move," Libby whispered and left the pines to follow her escaping suspects.

CHAPTER 20

UNEXPECTED GUESTS

Bix Bixler and Bernie Holden had just finished dinner when Simon began to growl. They both stood still with dishes in their arms; the progress toward the dishwasher had been temporally halted. Simon's head twisted to one side as he listened and watched through the glass on the front door. His low growl sounded serious to Bix. She put the dirty dishes on the counter and went to the door. It was locked; she checked. As she looked out the glass door, Bix could see nothing threatening. Of course, dogs heard and smelled so much better than humans, she assessed. He could be sensing something coming down the road.

"You suppose we have a four legged intruder?" Bernie asked then finished depositing their dishes in the dishwasher.

"Could be," Bix answered. "What's happening , Simon? We got a bear in the neighborhood?" Bix asked. Simon decided then to explode into a frenzy of barks. Bix turned on the front deck light and peeked out. She still couldn't see anything. She turned back and directly looked down at the little dog. "Well Simon, I don't get it. Nothing there, buddy."

At that precise moment human footsteps could be heard approaching. Bix swirled back around and saw a dark figure walking up the driveway. The man came up the front steps and knocked. Bix couldn't believe her eyes! Standing before her was Johnny McPherson! It was him or his ghost! "Oh my God," Bix gasped throwing open the door.

Bernie moved next to Bix sensing her shock. To her surprise, Bix gave the man a huge hug! "You are truly a sight for sore eyes," Bix held him tightly. Simon realizing that he should know this guy started wagging his stubby tail furiously.

"So sorry to scare you and arrive unannounced," Johnny said. "Quite frankly, with all the events going on, I couldn't think of a better place to come for advice. Am I forgiven?"

"Of course you are," Bix said then turned toward Bernie. "Johnny McPherson, this is my very best friend, Bernie Holden from North Dakota. She's visiting me for a couple of weeks. Well, come in," Bix invited. "Coffee? A drink?" she offered.

"Bourbon strait up. Thanks, Bix," he sighed then gave Simon a head scratch and smile.

"Have you eaten?" Bernie asked.

"Well…not for awhile. Really you don't need to go to any trouble."

"Of course we do. Sit down. I just put leftovers in the refrigerator," Bernie added then sprung into action.

Bix sat down next to Johnny and took his hand. Bernie placed the bourbon and a glass on the table. The man looked exhausted, they both observed. Bernie then watched him pour a generous shot into the glass and down the liquor. Finally, he was able to relax enough to talk, she observed.

"I take it that you have been following the case?" He waited for Bix's nod then continued, "God help me, I am a wanted man. I could escape an avalanche but not all these crazy people. My life isn't worth two cents at this point," he admitted.

Bernie placed a plate of chicken, homemade bread and salad down in front of Johnny. "Shit, that looks great. Thank you, ladies." He ate like a starving man. Between bites, Johnny began to relate his story. "The avalanche didn't totally take me by surprise because of all my technological alerts; I had five minutes warning. I ran to the mining shaft and shut the door hoping that I would be able to get out after it settled. The noise and vibration was incredible. Cats with nine lives have nothing on me. When I emerged from the entrance, the snow hadn't totally covered the door. It opens to the inside which was another wise move by my grandfather."

"Did you see anyone when you came out?" Bix asked. "You know that the avalanche was started by someone, right?"

"I figured that. Before I left the gulch, I wrote down information about the slide. It was pretty obvious when you see how the needle leaped from the explosion at the onset of the slide. Figured, I might need to prove it later. And no, I didn't see anyone out there when I opened the door. I did wait awhile in case someone would be there to shoot at me. It was easy to shovel the three feet of snow in front of the entry."

"Probably a wise move to wait," added Bernie thinking about what she would do in that predicament. She picked up Johnny's empty dishes and deposited them quietly in the sink not wanting to miss any details. If she hadn't been in this case before, she was now. Bernie motioned Simon up into her lap; he promptly fell asleep.

Johnny thoughtfully continued , "Then this month the newspaper ran my cold case investigation article. I was relieved and alarmed by that event. Unfortunately, I can't prove shit yet. I can prove the avalanche was man-made but not what company started it. In fact, I wonder if the avalanche is even related to the more resent events," Johnny added with a worried look on his face. "My life is a mess and I have no control. My friends are in danger and…Sadie. God, how is Sadie doing? I just couldn't contact her because of the danger. She will be so angry. What in the hell could I have done?" Johnny let his question stand unanswered. Bix certainly had no response. People's first reaction is to always keep love ones safe when, in fact, true friends are there to help. It wasn't her place to say anything here.

"Is Milt okay?" he asked finally.

Bix began to fill in the pieces as she answered Johnny's questions. "I went down and talked with Sadie this week. She really misses you. I told her about the case and that the police hadn't found your body. You need to call her as soon as possible, danger or not. She will be so relieved. Then there's Milt being held at the Breckenridge Police Station under Captain Jen's care. Frank is in the process of grilling him about you and the events. You do know that Frank got shot by your assassin, right?"

"I heard. I am truly sorry about that. In fact, I am so sorry about this whole mess," Johnny said feeling the weight and stress caused by his case. "Frank's a good guy and a stand-up fellow and friend." Johnny's eyes then landed on Bix. Why Frank, Bix?"

"You and Frank do look somewhat alike from a distance would be my guess," Bix admitted. "At least that's my conclusion. The assassin must have found your foot prints out of the gulch is what I'm thinking."

"I was wondering about that resemblance but afraid to admit it. Poor Frank. " Johnny paused to process. He looked up at the ladies and finally continued, "I'm coming forward now because hiding is creating danger for too many people. Better they target me than my friends," he concluded. "So I guess the next step is to figure out just exactly how to come forward," he admitted.

Obviously, Johnny's decision had somehow brought him to Bix's front door. Her life could be threated by his unexpected arrival, nevertheless, she was the one person who could help him now. He was glad that Bernie was there; that Bix had someone to watch her back. Johnny's life was at a point where he desperately needed solid advice.

He began hesitantly, "So tell me about Captain Jen Holly and HAPT? Please don't pull any punches. Straight out answers; what do I need to know."

Bix inhaled while Bernie and Johnny intensely stared at her. She realized how crucial her answers could become.

***

"What in the hell do you mean, you don't know where he is?" Frank Mason roared. How frustrating was that, he thought. They had come so far and yet were so far away from the answers.

"Honest to God, I don't know. Johnny has been in and out since HAPT started to investigate. He figured that you guys would come calling at my door. I figure he's camping somewhere over in the Leadville or Independence Pass area. He told me that the less I knew the better."

"So what did you find out about his dilemma from him? Was he close to answering who was after him?" Bill asked trying to squeeze out more information.

"I think he had it down to two possibilities and Howard Carlson was in the middle of one. Of course the International Mineral Recovery Foundation was at the top of his list. When he discovered that the feds were looking at them, he began to lean in that direction. Hell, they're pretty corrupt and probably wouldn't stop at anything to get their way," Milt said with a nod.

"What did you see on the survey, Milt?" Frank

asked.

"Uranium for one thing, a big vein of it. Companies like the Foundation are slowly stockpiling Uranium deposits from all over the world. Uranium makes wars and energy, ya know. You can watch the trend happening over near the Grand Canyon right now. I know it sounds like a long shot but, hell, that company is trying to get a large stockpile. Sabotage green energy and get us back on the nuclear road is their game plan. Johnny told me that if I saw the survey and it was a promising deposit of Uranium, he would dynamite the mine and close it off for good," Milt stated. The two officers leaned back in their chairs and thought about that implication. Frank now totally understood their motive.

Bill finally found his voice and asked, "Are you sure about that deposit?"

"Destroy that survey," was Milt's answer. "The mine belongs to Johnny not the public."

***

"Agent Tate, I'm going to be straight with you right now," Captain Jen Holly confessed. "Your response will determine what actions we take. Summit County will only allow the FBI to assist," Jen stated as she sat back down and stared directly at Marshall Tate. "We owe the FBI nothing in this case. Our local case trumps your investigation. The DA is filing protective custody papers for Johnny McPherson as we speak; the sooner that he is found, the safer he will be. If you even try to transport Johnny McPherson without our permission, we will open up this information to the governor and then the public. Do I make myself clear?"

"Crystal clear," he answered. "While you all just talked, I called the FBI. We are prepared to work with your team in solving this case. I then advised the front office to not request anymore agents at this time. I'm willing to take a chance that HAPT does know what they're doing. The second I feel that my assumption is incorrect, the FBI will bring in more power. Do we understand each other?"

"Perfectly."

"Now where is McPherson?" Tate asked.

"According to Milt Gray, who is in custody, Johnny is camping and staying low. He probably now knows about Milt and is concerned. I think he is close to giving himself up for the sake of his protection and friends. We'll get the word out to the locals and see if we can get some help in our search."

"Will they help?"

"Yes. I am sure that they will see the merit in helping. They are Johnny's friends and he does trust them. When they understand that Johnny is alive, they will help him come in safely."

"I do also need to tell you what other information our team has uncovered in the last 24 hours. The assassin who started the avalanche is one Eric Calvin, a known assassin for hire with ties here in Colorado. His footprints matched the ones at the avalanche scene; the autopsy from Impasse

Mountain was a match. This suspect also has 50,000 recently deposited in his bank account. We know only that he was paid here in Colorado. I will assume that the FBI can run a further investigation into where this cash came from faster than we can?" Captain Jen added just to see if the cooperation would go both ways. She waited for Tate's response.

"Do you have any account numbers on the cash?" he asked.

"Yes." Jen took a slip a paper from her pocket and handed it to him.

Tate got on his phone and put the information into a text. "Done. The office should have our answers by morning or at least after businesses open." Tate eyed her closely and added, "So you figured I'd take the offer?"

"What choice do you have?" she asked.

"There are a few large options out there; please keep that in mind. I am going out on a limb here and taking a chance on you, Captain Holly," Tate said placing his cell phone back in his pocket.

Jen was satisfied right now that Agent Tate would at least look like he was cooperating. They would have to watch him closely from now on, she reconnoitered.

Jen then ventured into the most pressing business at hand. Her attention was definitely needed elsewhere. Carl was a step ahead scheduling the helicopter for the Como mission. She continued, "I do need to tell you that I'm not totally convinced that the suspects of the Leadville assault and theft work for the same company as Eric Calvin did. My instincts say that we have more than one group after Johnny's white gold. His property is extremely valuable. He may be a witness for the FBI but in the State of Colorado, he possesses a fortune in property. To put it succinctly, he is valuable dead or alive," Jen verified. "So Agent Tate, did you pack any warm clothes for the trip and have you ever rappelled?" Jen inquired.

***

Libby figured that their location was at least two miles away from Como now. It was her hope that instead of disturbing the meager population of the little town, they could deal with the arrest in the forest. She had glanced at her phone map and noticed that Como wasn't far from 285. Within the next two miles would be the best option for their capture. Landing a helicopter, however, would be a tall order. It would be another drop from the sky on ropes, she assumed. Libby texted the message, 'one mile south of Como.'

Immediately the plunk sound announced, '10-4.' Now, Libby concentrated on herding the suspects slowly down the road . She, occasionally, let off a round of shots in their general direction breaking the serene silence. It was almost an insult to nature, she admitted but necessary. Invariably, the morning sun began warming the vivid triad of seasonal colors. The deep snow began to melt off the idyllic terrain creating slush.

Right now Libby calculated that the slush was her friend. Any plan to escape into the forest was not an option for these guys; the snow would be deeper in the shadows. These guys were finding that the road was enough of a challenge; the slush produced a forceful suction that pulled viciously at their boots.

Libby then heard a welcoming sound in the far distance; the copter was coming! She sprang into action and fired a good 12 shots at the suspects. They, immediately, moved toward some large boulders on the right. Libby figured that if she could keep them focusing on her and firing, they might not realize what was going to happen. They began to return her fire. The rifle noise echoed in the distance. Good, she thought. Officer Libby James had initiated her own little war!

From her location, Libby could see small specks rappelling safely. She kept up the volley of fire then moving her position closer to them. Now it would be a wait and see game for her. She had upped the tempo of her fire and movement. The suspects had decided to stay behind the boulders and take a rest from tramping through the melting snow. Libby needed to keep them focused on her assault for as long as possible. She, once again, moved to higher ground then reloaded her rifle. At this point she could use up as much ammo as she wanted. The team would have more.

Ten minutes later, Libby suddenly heard footsteps to her left. Her first reaction was to take inventory and make sure that both suspects were still glued behind the boulder. They were. She let out a yell, "Over here!" Libby expected a familiar voice to answer. However to her surprise, the voice

was deep and unfamiliar! "Officer James?" the
voice inquired.

Weaving his way out of the forest was a tall,
blond stranger! He looked like a Greek God in
police gear. Libby's jaw dropped as their eyes met!
She couldn't help herself as the question popped out
of her mouth, "Who are you?"

***

Bernie and Bix found themselves sitting on the
couch after Johnny McPherson had departed. Simon
snuggled in next to them soundly asleep after an
eventful evening. A good dinner and good
company, he thought happily.

Johnny had asked Bix if he could camp on her
old mining claim in Dante's Gulch. She had owned
the property since the 1970s. Her first Colorado
acquisition. Bix, of course, was happy to consent. It
was agreed that they would bring Captain Jen out to
talk with him tomorrow. The stage was set. Now, all
Bix could do is hope that it had been the right
decision.

"So what do you think, Bernie? Did I convince
him? And, I guess, more importantly, was is it the
right thing to do?" Bix said then sighed. She had
reached out for Bernie's hand automatically for
support.

Bernie contemplated her answer. "You know,
when I first arrived and saw that you were involved
in another criminal case, my reaction was to have
nothing to do with it. However, now that I have met
Johnny, I think you did exactly what you had to do.

He is good man and friend. Hell, Jen is our friend also and she needs help. It is the perfect vortex."

Bernie was suddenly surprised by the warmth that gushed into her heart. She had fallen in love with this woman for all the right reasons. "I am so proud of you, Bix." Bernie began to explore Bix's face with her free hand as she continued, "If, indeed, things in life do happen for a reason then bringing these two people together was your job. Johnny needs protection; Jen needs answers. What happens in the end is not your responsibility. You have done all that you can and should do." Bernie kissed Bix's forehead to emphasize her words. She smiled and nodded then promptly fell into Bix's eyes.

Another long sigh escaped from Bix's countenance. How incredibly wonderful was it to feel Bernie's support; her physical warmth so near. Hence, the power of two! Bix reached up and pulled Bernie down into a long deep kiss. Bix's emotions swirled through her body then traveled into another universe; the soft universe of trust. These two old lesbians had discovered the miracle of a new safe haven. How incredible was that, Bix Bixler thought.

***

"I am Agent Tate of the FBI and you are Officer James, my avenging angel of HAPT." He suddenly took her hand and kissed it; the action sent shock waves through them. Their eyes met with a piercing electricity.

Libby could feel a blush exploding onto her face and smoke coming out of her ears. God, how embarrassing she thought. "Nice to meet you, Agent Tate." She said stepping back from the encounter.

"Oh I think it will have to be Marshall," he said towering over her. His height was at least 6'4" Libby estimated . They had both made the physical comparison at exactly the same; Libby stood tall all of her 5'4".

"Well, Agent Tate, welcome to Colorado she said trying to get a grip. Shall we go help the others?" she asked.

"An excellent idea. What a beautiful place," he added letting himself have the luxury of an observation before the mission became the focus.

They both hit the ground running when the shots began. Jerry, Tyler dog, and Bill had taken off in the direction of one escaping suspect while Jen remained, keeping the second guy trapped behind the boulder.

Libby and Marshall then went in opposite directions surrounding Jen's suspect. The tactic was working. The three of them had him pinned down. It was going to be the perp's decision to surrender or get killed. They moved in and returned each volley waiting. The prep tried to move from his position but was met with fire from them. "Nice try, guy," Libby whispered.

The sky had provided unexpected guests not to mention Agent Marshall Tate. The tables had turned in so many ways, Libby concluded. "Surprise," she murmured. Just when you think that life has no more surprises, something amazing drops from the sky and shocks you to your core. Amazing, she assessed.

CHAPTER 21

PUZZLES

Detective Bill Smith stopped next to Jerry Neal and petted Tyler while they searched the terrain up ahead. It was a rather steep ascent with various bushes clinging to the grade. They had on their snowshoes and were following the perp's tracks carefully. His progress had slowed considerably as he climbed higher in altitude.

"I think he's maybe 200 feet above us," whispered Jerry. "I think he'll try to double back eventually. The climb's too steep and the snow is getting deeper. When is the question?"

"Think you're right," Bill said with his binoculars aimed in the suspect's general direction. "There he is," he said and pointed to the left where a cliff reached out. "He'll probably hide in a crevasse up there and try to pick us off as we ascend. Then after he shoots one of us, head back down and try to out run the other. At least that's what I'd try to do," Bill stated with a nod.

Jerry looked at Bill then the cliff and nodded in agreement. "Yup. If he's smart, that's exactly what he'll do; if he knows that there are two of us that is. How about if Tyler and I approach making some noise and keeping his attention while you move in from the opposite side? We could put on a drama to make him think one cop is in pursuit. Might be amusing."

Bill thought about that for a few seconds and realized that the plan just might do the trick. "Let's go. I could be up there in about 20 minutes if I climb without him seeing me."

"I'll wait to hear from you before I move in then." Jerry said. "See you at the top."

The two men moved forward and separated. Bill made sure that he ascended as Jerry made noise or fired at the guy. Tyler barked a couple times keeping the drama moving. It was possible that the suspect might think that he was only being followed by one man and his dog, Bill assessed. Damn, the guy was a good shot; he was always close to hitting where Bill judged Jerry to be located. Of course, Jerry was pretty good at this kind of technique. Thinking and knowing were two different things when you worked with Detective Jerry Neal.

Bill pulled himself directly up the ascent using the bushes for cover. His knee was holding the weight nicely. All his therapy this year had helped. Now all he had to do was be careful and not get shot again. Might be a tall order today, he considered. If he could get through this mission safely, his position on the team would be secure.

Bill glanced some 25 feet up and mapped out

how he wanted to bushwhack the area. The next 30 feet had boulders that would allow him to run and hide behind them one at a time. He could sprint between the rocks when Jerry made noise. So far the distractions were working. There were enough crevasses to help Bill gain another ten feet using this technique. Jerry fired and the perp shot back. Bill made it up another five feet and finally dived into the last crevasse.

The terrain now had become smaller rocks with very little cover. He would have to crawl like a lizard staying close to the ground. Bill felt the anxiety mounting as his lungs heaved from the exertion. Fortunately, the shooter seemed content to focus on Jerry. Maybe the guy was buying it that Jerry and his K-9 was the pursuit team. Bill crawled until, once again, the ascent brought him to another challenge.

The next section of his climb became a narrow passageway where mine tailings culminated into a gushing water spout. The spring waterfall aimed the flow toward a small creek some 75 feet below. The water force thundered throughout the terrain. Bill could hardly hear Jerry or the shots as he got closer to the raging water. He assessed the climb and discovered that if he could cross just in front of the falls, there was a wildlife trail on the far side. Just what he needed! The ascent on his side of the falls was becoming impossible because of the tailings and the treacherous height.

Bill leaned out and checked for a way to stabilize his crossing. There was a stump on the far side some ten feet from him and one precarious stump on his side. He tested the strength of this lone stump near him. Not the best, he calculated. Did he have a choice? Not that he could see. It was either cross or go back down and around. Time dictated that he take this chance.

Bill took out his rope from his pack; it was cowboy lasso time. He measured his loop then let the rope go. Missed. Damn. He sighed and relaxed hoping that his second attempt would be better. Bill let the lasso slowly circle over his head two times then he released the rope. It caught the stump. Bill tightened the rope then secured his side as best he could.

With the rope in place, he eased out onto the ledge letting the cold water spray him. It was a tedious cautious crossing. He didn't look down knowing that his fall would be at least 75 feet. He concentrated on his footing hoping for the best.

Abruptly three quarters of the way across, Bill felt the precarious old stump begin to break away from the moist ground. Its' complete surrender was seconds away; roots emerging! Now! Bill yanked hard sending his body toward the opposite bank. He literally flew over the waterfall! His feet were flying; his arms screaming with pain as he pulled himself the last five feet onto the moist ledge. The landing was incredibly painful but secure. He moved his limbs carefully and was relieved to find that nothing was broken. Bill finally felt the air coming back into his lungs as he rolled over onto his back.

With no time to spare, Bill sat up as he untied the lasso. The poor old stump had landed in the pool of water below he noticed. It seemed to be waving at him in an eerie fashion now. This old stump had been sacrificed and was destined to become driftwood pieces. Better the stump than me, Bill reconnoitered. He then thanked God and the stump before he left the area.

***

"Do you really want to die today?" Captain Jen Holly shouted toward the cornered suspect. His destiny wasn't going to develop into an escape today. It was over, Jen knew. He was surrounded. The question was did this shooter realize it? There was a pause as the guy must have considered her comments. Jen decided to add more information into the one-sided conversation. "We would be able to offer some sort of deal if you surrendered at this time. No one has been hurt up to this point. We are talking about a fight in a bar and resisting arrest only. If you return the survey papers, we can show that you did comply and then reduce the charges."

Jen waited patiently again while the suspect considered his options. The quiet settled. Jen's patience was just about over when he finally did answer, "Then my surrender would mean reduction of charges? Is that what you're saying?" he asked to get it clear in his head.

"Yes," Jen affirmed.

There was another pause as the perp played the scenario. "I'm coming out. Don't shoot!"

"Hands up and leave your weapons on the ground where I can see them," Jen shouted. She watched him lean down and deposit his rifle plus a hand gun on the ground then raise his hands. "Officer James, will you please go gather the weapons and cuff the suspect. Agent Tate, please assist," she added.

Jen then contacted the helicopter and called them to transport. Officer Libby James did the formal reading of rights to the suspect then she and Marshall Tate secured the criminal into Libby's car for now.

Captain Jen's cell rang as she watched Libby. Her display announced an urgent message from Bix. Jen called her quickly and moved away from the scene for a few seconds. Captain Jen made another quick call and then joined the other officers. She had organized her next move. "I will need you officers to hike our suspect to the helicopter landing site then transport him. Make sure that when you arrive in Breckenridge that you contact Chief Anderson, Libby."

"Yes, Captain Jen. Are we to go ahead and start the interrogation at that point?" Libby asked.

"Definitely. Make sure that Chief Anderson is witness to the interrogation. Is that all right with you, Agent Tate?" Jen added.

"I have no problem with that," he said. "Shall we search their car for the survey papers before we depart?" he asked.

"If you don't mind, I would like to inspect the survey while I wait for the snowplow. We can decide the survey's jurisdiction when I get to Breckenridge. Officer James, I will need to borrow your keys and trade you vehicles for the rest of the day. My vehicle is at the helicopter pad in Breckenridge. Go ahead and begin the paperwork on this guy," she said.

"Can I ask what other development has taken place?" Agent Tate inquired. His instincts had clicked in as he watched Captain Holly closely. He knew that she had another lead of some sort.

"At this time I need to take care of some business that has surfaced. I will inform you later when I get to Breckenridge. Fair enough?" Jen asked.

Agent Tate eyed her closely weighing the situation. Did he take her at her word or did he push for more answers. Was she trying to pull a fast one? He did feel that he could at least trust her not to create a breech in their agreement so soon. His decision was to let it go until later in the day. If she had tricked him, the FBI could land big time in Summit County. He settled back on his heels and said, "Very well then until later this afternoon. Shall we get started, Officer James?"

"I assume the helicopter landed not far down the road?" Libby asked.

"First forest clearing about ten minutes ahead. You can't miss it." Captain Jen said. As she watched the two officers depart with the suspect, Jen began going through their car. She took pictures of the car's position then began to search it thoroughly. More firearms were in the open trunk. On the backseat was the original survey.

She sat down in Libby's car and began reading. It was obviously a thorough report and done officially. Of course she had no idea if the various quantities of minerals were high or not. The authorities would have to check those readings. She did understand the presence of uranium. Most basements in Summit gave off radon readings so the findings didn't seem shocking to her. Guess she'd learn a lot more about that situation later.

Johnny McPherson would also be able to shed some light on the subject, she assessed. So he had finally surfaced and, low and behold, gone to Bix's house. Jen had to hand it to him; he did know who to trust. She checked the time and figured that Bix's house would be ten minutes away after she got out of here.

In the distance she could hear the deep motor of the bulldozer that she had requested. Get the suspects car over to the side and then turn Libby's car around. Jen had also requested two officers to run a stakeout for Jerry and Bill. The shots were still active and moving up the ridge. The copter would return to the landing sight and wait for Bill and Jerry.

Jen texted Frank, Bill and Jerry the situation and gave them the contact information for the approaching officers and copter pilot. Frank would need to let the Chiefs know what was happening. Bill and Jerry could then plan how the arrest would go down. Captain Jen had intentionally not mentioned Johnny McPherson. She wanted to meet with him and get his consent to come in first. It wasn't quite policy but close. Her captain stripes would account for her actions, Jen figured.

A plunk noise announced that all officers were communicating. It sounded like Bill and Jerry were maybe twenty minutes out on an arrest. Their plan was solid and Jen would be right here until she knew that the guy was in custody and her officers were safe. The puzzle was on the table now with the pieces turned up. It was time for HAPT to create the picture and solve this case.

***

Libby and Marshall walked the suspect on down the road. The slush pulled at their boots with an uncomfortable regularity. All three of them concentrated on the effort to simply walk. Conversation was not a premium at this time to say the least. Marshall concentrated on placing his boots in previous hiked steps. It was some help but not a lot.

What an interesting place this was, he thought. His eyes scanned the pine trees and rock formations. The snow magnified the blue sky; the air forcefully enhanced the clean pine scent. He felt himself breathing deeply trying to find oxygen while his lungs were overwhelmed by the forest aroma. The city contrast was so apparent.

Even Leadville had been snowless and hinting at spring but here it was behind that seasonal reality. He had never been to Colorado on assignment except for Denver. Actually, his life had been one city to the next. It made sense that Colorado backcountry would be on the list eventually. Funny how a destination could change one's life, Marshall considered carefully.

The mountains had been a nice surprise but

Libby James shocked him big time; finding her had completely thrown him off his game. He had instantly melted into those blue eyes; the depth was amazing. He didn't know her yet he did know her. Maybe he had known her all of his life but hadn't come to Colorado yet? Nevertheless, the event had taken his breath away. Fate had thrown a curve ball right into his life.

His gaze then landed on Libby. She definitely was a small package of complete cop but oh so attractive. Her red curly hair literally bounced as she moved along. Marshall realized that he had to be very careful here. Had his attraction to her influenced his handling of Captain Holly? He thought about that for a few seconds and decided that what Holly had done was probably exactly what he would have done. Maybe not totally by the book but close. What she would divulge to him when she arrived back in Breckenridge would be very telling. Marshall's FBI investigation had to become his focus once again.

Freckles! My God, Libby had freckles. Marshall hadn't noticed them until now. Easy boy, he admonished himself. Slow down and keep calm, he preached.

Libby had some very conflicted emotions swirling through her body also. She was leaping into the universe of 'what ifs.' This guy was way too attractive to be single. Actually, that topic of single hadn't even come up yet. Hell, no topics had been explored. They were total strangers, she realized. He could be a spy working internationally with a FBI cover. Well, maybe not that extreme.

Still, he was a stranger but an extremely interesting stranger and probably married. That would just be her luck, she reconnoitered. Married with five kids was not out of the realm of reality here. The man was just too gorgeous to be single.

Libby sighed assessing her failed dating record. Dating in Summit had been difficult to say the least. Guys were interested until they found out that she was a cop. Her age group didn't own homes in the mountains. They came to ski and take extended vacations from their structured lives. They were briefly here to experiment and were not looking to settle down. No, she hadn't found the right guy up here that was for sure. Shit! Here comes mister married with five kids; she just knew it! Libby pulled herself back from the brink of negativity before she became convinced. There was always hope, she assessed.

Marshall suddenly realized that he hadn't even considered that Libby could be married. She probably was married or dating the Chief of Police for all he knew. Speaking of jumping ahead of the cart, he admonished himself again. Well hell, he could hope that maybe this lady was here for him to meet. Just maybe the puzzle of life had placed them together for whatever reason. The point was that they had met and they were attracted to each other. That, was a fact.

"How much farther is this damn copter pad? This little hike is criminal abuse," the perp grumbled.

Libby replied remembering the name from his driver's license. "Well Mr. Cook, maybe you should have chosen another escape route. Seems like you and your partner should have been a little wiser."

"How the hell did we know that this road led back to fucking winter? The map didn't give no elevation hints."

"There's the helicopter landing site," Marshall said pointing some 50 feet ahead. "Won't be long now, Mr. Cook. What made you head toward Breckenridge instead of I-70 by the way?"

"We aren't stupid. There had to be at least 100 fucking cops lining I-70 last evening. Don't know why cause we sure as hell didn't do anything life threatening." Luke Cook eyed the tall blond guy closely to see how he took that comment. Didn't seem to be any reaction there he observed. The little lady cop didn't say nothing either. Let the games begin, Luke thought. Keep my mouth shut until I find out what happens to Bret. If he's escapes, I need to keep the fuck quiet; killed in jail ain't smart.

The helicopter landed five minutes later, bundled them in quickly then on toward Breckenridge. The pilot could tell that his day was going to be busy. Good money and good hours not bad. His day would be far more enjoyable than the poor sap in back, he assessed.

CHAPTER 22

REVELATIONS

Bill's progress had become less complicated now that he was following the wildlife trail. He was parallel with the suspect at this point. Bill texted Jerry and let him know that he would be above the guy in five minutes at the most. Then it was a process of determining how to ease down on his position for the capture. He figured that surprise was definitely in his favor.

Some 20 feet above him there was a small clump of bushes that would provide cover. As Bill eased himself up and over into the bushes, he realized the shooter was using an old mine tunnel opening for his cover. Luckily, Bill discovered that the mine shaft traveled into the bushes; in fact, it had eroded into a hollow opening near Bill's position. Could he crawl through this tunnel and reach the suspect? It was worth a try. He texted Jerry what he was planning.

A text came back quickly, 'Be careful. Text

when you are ready.'

Bill tied the rope around a sturdy boulder for his rappel. He then tested his knot to make absolutely sure that everything was secure. Next, he found a large limb that had recently fallen on the forest floor. He coiled the rope around it and positioned the limb over the center of the chasm into the mine. Quietly, he lowered the rope into the opening He peeked into the black abyss again; his eyes adjusted enough to see the rope dangling in the center of the hole. His rappel would be some 12 feet down. It looked reasonably dry down there, thank heavens. Bill judged the distance to where the shooter was positioned at the tunnel opening; maybe 20 feet he calculated.

If he was incredibly quiet, his drop might not be noticed. Bill waited until the usual rifle volley happened then flashed his light for a quick second to see the floor of the tunnel. Looked solid, he calculated. It also looked like there might just be a turn in the cavity that would keep his approach out-of-sight. Maybe he wouldn't be such a sitting-duck. Bill stuck his head down in the hole one more time just for good measure. Yep, there was a curve there, good.

The smells of moss and rock penetrated his nostrils. He also detected a slight whiff of sulfur from the shooter's rifle. That meant that the airflow was from outside into the shaft's entrance. Bill determined that his descent would not introduce any new smells. Noise became his worst fear at this time. The rappel had to be slow and deliberate. Bill texted then waited for the barrage of rifle fire from

Jerry.

The atmosphere exploded into rapid fire. The shooter replied with equal enthusiasm assuming that Jerry was going to make an attack. Tyler barked and ran around in a frenzy. It was now or never, Bill thought as he began to lower himself. There was just enough room for his shoulders he noticed. Bill kept his boots from hitting the sides of the dark dank hole so that there would be no debris falling. His shoulder muscles strained, his body was rigid and then his muscular stress began to dissipate as he crouched on the floor. He had hit the bottom. The few seconds that it had taken were so intense that he was sweating; his heart was racing. Bill then allowed his body permission to relax for a few moments as he gathered control. He didn't advance but let his vision adjust to the immense darkness that now engulfed him.

Then in this cold blackness, Bill suddenly realized that he could actually hear the man breathing. Holy shit, he was so close and yet so far away from this imminent danger. There was something surreal about this constant human breath. The revelation created shivers that convulsed throughout his body. Control, he told himself. Nevertheless, Bill conceded that his mind could not resist listening; the sensation was just too real. He accepted this stark cold reality; accepted the fact that this moment would haunt his life forever in unavoidable flashbacks. Nevertheless, the actual moment was still in Bill's control.

He advanced toward the turn. His head darted out and then quickly back after examining the entrance. Bill had seen the silhouette of a black shadow peering out into the sunlight. He figured that the shooter's eyes would have to adjust to the darkness when he turned around in defense. It would give Bill a few seconds of advantage for the arrest.

Still, the 20 feet of distance between them loomed larger-than-life right now. Bill peered out again. There was a rock formation some five feet ahead of his position. Move a few feet at a time; don't get greedy, Bill told himself. He crept low to the ground inching his way forward. The formation did become his safe haven; he could breathe now.

As he glanced out, Bill saw a small concave crevice some 10 feet back from the suspect's position. It was closer than he wanted to be but there were no other options that he could see. He would have to chance it. Bill took a deep breath and proceeded toward the indentation. He focused on his destination.

Suddenly, his phone plunked in a text! The sound was incredibly loud and seemed to echo off the tunnel walls as the shooter reacted with blazing rapid fire! The bullets ricocheted around Bill as he dropped onto the chasm's floor. He had forgotten to put his phone on airplane mode! Damn!

***

"It's time you come clean and shed some light on who sent you to Leadville. Your partner is so close to being arrested as we speak," Agent Marshall Tate said staring into Luke Cook's face. He hadn't left any room for personal space. His hands were flat on the table as he leaned forward.

"You do understand that the suspect who gives us information will be able to cut a deal? One of you will cut a break; the other?" Libby had commented from her chair placing her hands up in a questioning fashion.

"Bret's the one who got us the job. I ain't no leader in this mess. We was suppose to rip off the papers that the old guy had. We did exactly what we were told. How did we know that the damn GPS wouldn't say anything about the snow on Boreas Pass. Hell, I didn't even start the fight. That was Bret's idea. I just snuck in through the kitchen and grabbed the papers off the table. The old geezers were none the worse for wear," Luke grumbled and nodded his head to emphasize his position. "That's all we did."

"Oh I think there's plenty more blame to go around here, Mr. Cook," Libby continued. "I think there's a little avalanche business to discuss. How does attempted murder figure into your arrest?"

"Now wait a minute, we had nothing to do with no avalanche. That's just fucked up. We just arrived on this scene and did what we were told. We was to get the papers, lady. You hear me," Cook emphasized. "Hell, we certainly don't know the area well enough to start no fucking avalanche."

"You could have come back later. You could have left the area after you thought you had killed Johnny McPherson. You know, finished the job," Libby continued.

"Who's Johnny McPherson? I don't know what

the hell you're talking about?" Cook said with shock registering on his pale face.

"How did you know that the papers were in Leadville and in Frank Mason's possession? How did you know about Milton Gray?" Marshall asked.

"Bret was told not me. I just follow orders," Cook said.

"What's Bret's last name by the way?" Marshall inquired.

"Jones, Bret Jones."

Libby texted the Police Data Bank to run their records and see what was there. She had a feeling that the information would be interesting. How involved would this Bret Jones be was a factor. Obviously, Luke was simply a bottom feeder. Yep, both men were bottom feeders with theft and assault on their records. She passed her smart phone to Marshall who examined the contents.

He processed and went on, "I want to know who hired you? I want to know who paid you for the job, now. The FBI has no intentions of making any deal with a felon who is holding back vital information. You hear me, Cook. I am representing the Federal Government and that means Federal Prison time. You need to convince me that you know nothing. I don't think you just follow orders. It's just too neat of an excuse," Marshall stated in a cold threatening voice.

Libby glanced over and looked at Marshall. She felt the malice in his threat and wondered how Luke was feeling. They could tell that he was considering his options. The lawyer word hadn't come up yet. Luke was thinking how much he could divulge before calling for a lawyer. He finally figured that no lawyer was coming for him.

"International Mineral and Recovery Foundation has hired us before. Ain't saying that I'm working for them now but in the past…" Cook let his words trail off. "That's all I got to say now; let me have my phone call," he demanded.

Libby's phone plunked in another text. She immediately got up out of her chair and motioned for Marshall to join her in the hallway.

Something was obviously up, Marshall realized and got up to join her.

***

Bill grabbed his pistol and fired from his prone position on the floor of the cavern. The bullets were flying hot and fast. Both men were locked into the combat. Bill was rolling from side to side keeping ahead of the barrage. He moved back behind the rock formation and sighed in relief. His hand flew onto his phone and wrote the word, 'help.'

Jerry was advancing at this point. His rifle fire was in the mix now setting a new pace to the confrontation. The suspect was literally surrounded. The situation must have dawned on him. Yet, he wasn't talking and he wasn't stopping. He suddenly concentrated his fire on Jerry and moved out of the open.

Bill rushed forward as quickly as he could. The man's AKA was pushing Jerry back in rapid fire. Damn, the man had plenty of ammo, Bill calculated. This might not bode well!

Jerry retreated with caution knowing that they outnumbered the guy. The problem was the power of his weapon. It had become pretty obvious that he wasn't going to give up. Both Bill and Jerry sensed that the perpetrator was heading toward 'death by cop.'

The helicopter came back into view now but kept out of rifle range. It hovered for a few minutes then let the reinforcements rappel down into the area. The troops were assembling. The odds of an arrest were certainly being stacked in their favor. Within five minutes there would be no way to escape for this suspect. It was going to be all over shortly.

Jen had talked with Chief Anderson and they immediately were on the same page. To remain with only two cops on scene was out of the question. The order had been given to send in more men. It took every inch of Jen's reserve not to get on the helicopter. For the first time she began to feel the restraint of her office. Being a cowboy and jumping into every confrontation was over when you gave the orders. She had stopped her search of the crime scene now and couldn't help but listen intently to Bill and Jerry. They had begun to use their radios now that the suspect was out and running.

"He's coming down your way, Jerry. He should be visible south of the brush near the water sprout," Bill shouted.

"10-4," Jerry yelled. I'm going to come up near the pine trees to the right of the water and try to ambush him there. Tyler has his scent at this time and can lead me."

"10-4." Bill yelled. "Will come up behind him and hope one of us will see him before he sees us. Do you think he'll stop shooting?"

"Nope. Maybe Tyler can tackle him before he escapes around me. Gonna try. Do you hear us, officers?" Jerry added. "Don't shoot my dog!"

"10-4," said a third voice in the mix.

Bill came back on one more time and added, "Be careful. The man is moving pretty fast now that he's descending. I'd say he may want to get back out on the road."

"My thought also. Be advised everyone," Jerry said and the communication then went quiet.

The shots in the distance had gotten so much more frequent that Jen knew something was happening. Her mind tried not to think about the words, ' man down.' Keep them safe she prayed and listened. Suddenly there were at least three more policemen shooting in rapid fire. The forest exploded in total war. Jen could hear when the suspect fired. His AKA threw out shells with deadly rapidity; he was moving again. Her eyes followed his progress as he raced in the direction of the road. "Stop, Police!" was shouted by one of the new officers on the scene. There was a long pause while life or death was held in the balance. The perpetrator was making his decision.

His AKA then came alive firing a foray of bullets. It was answered by at least five policemen firing in unison. The bullets penetrated his body with force as he took the direct hits. Round-and round he spun long gone and definitely dead. There would be at least 15 bullets to collect out of his body.

"We got him," came Jerry's voice. "He is down. I am heading over to his body to check his vitals."

"Be careful," said Bill. The woods became incredibly quiet while many people waited for the prognosis of the shooter. "Send the ME to the scene. He's dead," Jerry ended his communication.

Jen could feel her whole body start to relax. No, it wasn't pretty but at least it was over. The suspect had chosen his own destiny in the situation. He probably had a long record of crimes and just couldn't deal with prison again, she thought. Jen then called Chief Anderson and informed him that she would be leaving shortly in Libby's SUV to work another situation in the case.

"10-4," Anderson replied. "Proceed."

Jen did find the silver lining now in her promotion. It was definitely nice to not have to ask permission to leave this scene. She sped out of Boreas Pass as quickly as she could knowing that the little sleepy town of Como had not been terrorized today or last night. She was sure that sooner or later, someone from Como would ask about all the copter noise and rifle fire but not right now. Before she left, Jen texted Jerry and Bill, 'Good job, gentlemen.'

***

"So it's time to make him feel really uncomfortable even if he is telling the truth,"

Officer Libby James said. They had just heard the
news about the assault and shooting. Luke was the
only chance for a complete confession. A
confession that would nail International's
involvement. Names and orders had to lead to
motive at this point and Luke had to know more
than what he was saying.

"I agree so let's do the old slam the door trick
and see what shit hits the fan," Marshall said with a
snide look on his face. He flicked his eyebrows up
and down a couple of times for Libby.

Libby thought it was a great cop look.
"Ready?" she asked with her hand on the door
knob.

"Ready," Marshall whispered.

The door flew open with a bang. Marshall let a
growl out from somewhere deep in his throat. "Well
buddy, you're in for it now. Too many cops and too
much time. Your partner is dead and he deserved it.
We're ready to throw the fucking book at you. Now
get your shit together and tell us why International
hired you cretins to kill and destroy!"

"I told you all that I know," Cook jerked back
in his chair and stared at Marshall.

"No you didn't, Cook," shouted Libby pulling
out her chair. "We're going to have a long night in
here. Who was your connection with International?
Surely, since you worked for them more than once,
the boss had to have talked with you. Who was it?
You need to tell us now!" Libby hit the table with
her fist and glared at Cook.

The tension in the room had really amped up,
he noticed. Damn, Bret was dead. He didn't have a

fall guy anymore. The whole shitting thing was left on his shoulders. Luke began to calculate that if he turned over one of the boss men to these cops, the pressure would become less for him. Maybe he could use that old fart, Gipple, for bait. If he played his cards right, Gipple could take the blame. Hell Bret wasn't around to point the finger at him. No Gipple didn't just sit in his office like a big fat toad. The guy had some power, Luke knew. If he went ahead and got Gipple implicated then the pressure was off of him. If he waited until after the International lawyer showed up, he would be advised to keep his mouth shut about Gipple.

Cook took a long breath then began his new tact with gusto, "It was Gipple, Thomas Gipple who planned this heist. He was the one who paid us to get the survey." Cook then added for good measure, "I swear to God I don't know nothing about no avalanche. That takes a whole different kind of hired help. You got to believe that!" Luke Cook's face erupted into a beet red color as he played out his drama scene. "Now, I want my lawyer."

***

The lone figure sat comfortably in an old lawn chair staring into his campfire. He was watching the coffee pot that had just begun to perk when Bix and Captain Jen Holly pulled up. They got out slowly and waved at Johnny McPherson. He got up and walked toward them. His expression was one of trepidation mixed with relief. Johnny was, obviously, having doubts. Jen understood that feeling. To finally come out of hiding could spell danger. It was a huge step for him, she knew.

"Bix, good to see you and thanks," Johnny said then gave Bix a large hug. "Captain Holly?" he eyed Jen carefully and offered his hand in recognition.

"Thank you for deciding to talk with me. I really need your help," Jen said warmly. She wanted Johnny to feel comfortable with his decision and their first meeting. To bully him was completely out of the question, she assessed. There had to be no egos involved today just the truth.

"Coffee?" he gestured. They sat down on a bench opposite Johnny's chair. He pulled out a couple of mugs from his kitchen pack and poured the hot liquid carefully.

Jen had decided to wear her gun and stay in uniform just in case there was an ambush. She laid her team survival pack on the ground next to the bench. Right now security was priority. Better to stay prepared than be sorry later, she thought.

They had taken Bix's truck to maintain some cover. From a distant, they were just campers having morning coffee at high altitude. Her eyes scanned the area closely as she sipped her coffee. If anyone came down the road, they would see the intruder plus the gulch walls would intensify all motor noise. She listened. Bix and Johnny were aware of Jen's careful surveillance and remained quiet as she assessed the terrain.

Finally Johnny said, "If anyone should approach, they will most likely head on up the gulch over there staying on that gravel road." He pointed with his coffee cup hand. "Kind of hard to see that left turn you took. You got to know the gulch to see how to get here," he added. "Don't you think, Bix?"

"I'd say that was a pretty good assumption, Johnny. Let's turn Jen around so she can get the full view of the gulch just in case we do have company." With that statement, all three began to maneuver the bench position and then sit back down again like musical chairs. Bix ended up in the chair; Jen and Johnny sat next to each other on the bench. Both of them were able to scan the terrain now. The expanse of quiet spread throughout the gulch like a warm giant blanket. They were secure for now.

Johnny stared at the campfire for a moment before he began, "I take it that you have investigated my business contacts enough to know the two potential companies suspects in this scenario?" He poked the fire with a stick and waited to hear Jen's response patiently.

"I believe we have; International Mineral Recovery Foundation and Slope Incorporated. Correct?" Jen said. "What about BTC?"

"Not guilty," Johnny said, "and I have proof that eliminates them. Their only involvement was to turn down Slope Incorporated's offer to pressure me," he said. "I was informed by them that Slope was going after me and offered BTC a percentage of Slope's profit for help. I would testify to that and BTC would also become a witness." He poked the fire again and took a drink of coffee.

"Now we come to my sister and stupid brother-in-law. I have hacked into most of Howard's emails simply because I can without a warrant. The emails clear him of everything except having a big mouth. He and Martha want out of Slope and will retire soon. The company has been doing business using rather shady methods. You need to look real closely at Walter Connally. He's the snake as far as I can tell and I think Howard and Martha will come clean for the right deal. There's no loyalty there anymore. Connally has pushed Howard over the edge."

Jen leaned up in her chair staring at Johnny for a second. "Why do you say that?" she asked carefully.

"Connally only cares about money. I have proof that he is trying to force Howard into helping him. Let's face it, McPherson's Gulch is white gold. Hell any property at high elevation is white gold and especially my gulch. Your property here Bix is white gold," Johnny said as his arms motioned indicating their surroundings. "It's either water or minerals like uranium that motivates these Piranhas. Tourist homes are simply an intermediate step toward environmental ownership. Companies like Slope will eventually be eaten up by monsters like International Mineral Recovery Foundation. It is simply a case of big fish eats little fish. We need to be aware and ready to stop them," Johnny declared. "Our future depends on it." He tossed his cold remains of coffee onto the fire in a final gesture.

Johnny McPherson's insight was a nightmarish perspective of the future, Jen assessed. A concept that could happen. 'Could' being the operative word here. It was a giant leap, she acknowledged. Maybe it all started when water became a lawyer's dream commodity which brought her back to Dillon

Reservoir. History does repeat itself and that was a fact.

Bix now brought the conversation back to their reality. "Johnny, we can only do our small part. We need to stop these companies right here right now. Stop the land grab."

"Agreed," Johnny murmured. "My research can be brought up on your office computer if we can get me into town safely. I am willing to give the information to you if you keep me out of the witness protection program. I will testify only if I live here and nowhere else." Johnny's eyes bore holds into Jen's face; he was dead serious and waiting for her commitment.

"I think we need to make that happen," Jen said. "This case needs to be solved now before anyone else gets hurt. I will do my very best, Johnny. "

Jen's words began to take on a whole new meaning as a Range Rover began climbing up the opposite side of the gulch. Johnny pointed at the flash of light coming from the back seat. Someone was using binoculars to scan the area.

CHAPTER 23

THE PLOT THICKENS

Libby and Marshall Tate glanced at each other. Cook was probably coming clean. The jury was out, however, on his total involvement in the McPherson Case. Libby was beginning to feel like maybe Cook was more a player than they had first thought. From Marshall's expression, she could tell that he was wondering the same thing. Was this guy just following orders or was he giving them? Time would tell. "So tell us about this Thomas Gipple?" Libby proceeded cautiously.

"Like I fucking said, Gipple was the one who hired us for some legit jobs. This specific job was a little shady but what was the harm? He wanted us to get the papers from the old guy so he could examine them. We didn't exactly know what type of papers and it didn't fucking matter. No one was going to get hurt so what was the harm?" Cook emphasized.

"How did you meet Thomas Gipple?" Agent Marshall Tate asked.

"He came to us a couple years ago and asked if we wanted to work for International. Legally, of course," Luke Cook threw in quickly. "The guy needed us to do the footwork on jobs that he didn't want to do or couldn't. He's an old guy, you know." Cook leaned back in his chair feeling a little more confident. These cops seemed to be eating up his comments. Good. Just as long as he could get the focus off of his involvement, things would be okay. The less he was charged with, the better. He had to buy some time before his lawyer showed up and Gipple was the perfect chump to sacrifice. "I want my lawyer now. I ain't going to say nothing else until my lawyer arrives," Cook said and crossed his arms in defiance.

Marshall and Libby then left the room to organize the next move in their investigation. Libby felt that it was time to make sure that Captain Jen knew what was going on and, basically, check in with Frank. "We both need to regroup, right?" she said.

"I think so. I'll go call the FBI Office and let you inform whoever you need to. Let's meet back here in maybe 15 minutes," Marshall said after looking at his watch.

"I will be putting out a APB on Gipple for HAPT, Marshall. I assume you knew that?" Libby said looking at him closely. She needed to make sure that Agent Tate from the FBI would leave that action to the local police. These two officers had to be so very careful about their conduct at this time. The mutual attraction had to be set aside. Two jobs were on the line and they both knew it.

"That's fine, Officer James. My office will monitor the progress only and not need to intervene at this present time," Marshall stated. His voice was cold and all business but his eyes were warm and communicated so much more. He couldn't help it.

And Libby couldn't help but know exactly what was happening. They were on the course to some type of personal relationship. The chemistry was almost explosive. Could they control it and keep within the perimeters was the question. Her eyes watched Marshall walk away and into another office for privacy. She could feel her heart do a flip-flop as she pulled her focus back into the case. Libby let out an audible sigh as she went to find Chief Anderson. The next step meant total communication. Get everyone on the same page would be a challenge. She knocked at his door and Josh Anderson motioned her to come in.

"So the plot thickens," he said. Have a seat. I take it you're here to discuss the next move, right?"

"I assume that an APB needs to immediately go out on Thomas Gipple. I'd like to contact Frank and have him do the communication with Bill Smith and Denver Police. The reason for Bill's involvement would be that he did the preliminary interview with Gipple," Libby added. "He just may want to be in on the arrest."

"I think you're correct. Let's get him on the radio," Chief Anderson said. He pulled over to his radio and did the honors. "Officer Smith, we need to have a quick conference with you. This is Chief Anderson calling from Breckenridge Police. Are you there?"

"Yes sir, I am available. The ME has arrived here in Boreas Pass and the crime scene investigators are busy. I have given my statement and Officer Neal is now doing the same. We should be done here in the next 10 minutes."

"Affirmative. Officer Smith, we have just gotten information from Cook, the other suspect in custody. He has just confessed that Thomas Gipple was the one who ordered them to steal the survey from Milton Gray in Leadville. We need to issue an arrest warrant to have him picked up immediately. Officer James suggested that you might want to be in on that arrest since you interrogated Gipple earlier. Is that correct?" Anderson said.

"Definitely, sir. Could we be ordered to Denver to pick Gipple up and bring him to Summit County immediately?" Bill asked.

"Be so advised. You two can start down the hill and I'll make the necessary arrangements right after we notify Captain Holly. Start immediately," Chief Anderson said then looked at Libby closely as he disconnected.

The two of them hadn't really talked since Libby had left his department. Actually, this was the first opportunity that had occurred. He stared at her closely and ventured into the subject. "I take it that the transfer to HAPT is working out for you?" he inquired.

"Yes sir. I do like my position. Thank you for allowing me to transfer," she said with a smile.

"You're welcome. Now go call your boss and I'll call Frank. He can then learn how to communicate with Denver and relay our directives." His eyes then did a double take. "You know, I think I'll call the Denver Chief, personally, and give him the first heads up as a courtesy. Their meeting was adjourned at that point. Both officers began to feel the expediency of the situation.

Libby disappeared into one of the vacant conference rooms and radioed Captain Jen. Unfortunately, the radio wasn't able to locate the Captain. She immediately went to text and mapped out what had happened so far.

Captain Jen texted back, 'In pursuit not available.'

Libby was startled by the text. She rushed out the door to find Chief Anderson. His office was now on high energy. He was dispatching some police into Dante's Gulch. It was a Code 3 with sirens blazing! Agent Marshall Tate was standing in the doorway watching the Chief closely. Libby stood beside Marshall and stared.

Chief Anderson finished giving his orders then glanced up at the two. "You had better get out to the gulch, Officer James, and take the FBI with you. Your Captain is in pursuit of more suspects. Apparently, McPherson is alive and has been residing in Dante's Gulch. Bix and Jen are there now and their position was spotted by some more perps who are probably wanting to kill McPherson. Kindly bring them all back safely. That's an order," he said to an empty room. Both officers were flying out the front door at lightning speed.

They both got into Captain Jen's Interceptor and hit the siren. Libby maneuvered her way from Frisco and then through all the Breckenridge tourists and stop signs. They finally were speeding south on Highway 9 toward Hoosier Pass. Libby now found her voice, "Did you get all that information, Marshall? I can't believe that Johnny McPherson is alive. This whole case just broke wide open. Wow!" she said breathlessly.

"Guess I can tell you now," Marshall said hesitantly. "I was ordered to Leadville to find McPherson. He started sending emails to the FBI about International Mineral Recovery Foundation a couple of weeks ago. We have been tracking his emails and finally discovered Leadville. The guy's signal bounced around the world and then landed in Leadville. Unbelievable. McPherson's good on that computer, I must say. My directive was to bring him in as a material witness against International. The FBI has just filed a case against International Mineral Recovery Foundation."

"Go on," Libby urged as her blood pressure began to elevate.

'Public lands with abundant mines on them are being grabbed by International and not always legally. Old prospectors and their families have simply disappeared or been forced to sell to the Foundation. Plus, numerous local political leaders all over the U.S. have been offered undercover brides. The money flow is incredible. International has billions and their power has grown. The situation is out of control."

"Why? What are they after?" Libby asked keeping her eyes on the road and glancing into the rear view mirror. They had passed at least five slower cars. It was quiet enough on the road that people seemed aware of their siren. Libby handled the curves like a race car driver, Marshall noticed. She knew how to speed up during the last of the curve. The question now was, how was she handling his information at this point.

"You just got around to telling me the motive?" she asked. "You have been here 24 hours and you're just getting around to telling me about International? We're on our way to a situation that might end up with someone getting shot and you couldn't reveal the details until now? How extreme is this situation?" Libby wasn't exactly angry but she was frustrated. Well, maybe she was angry; pretty damn angry. "Down girl," she mumbled. Whether you agreed with a departmental decision or not, they sure as hell could get in the way. She didn't agree and now resented the hell out of the FBI.

"I'm sorry but you know my position. Information as needed was the directive," Marshall said firmly. "I can tell you that Johnny McPherson is a huge part of our case. What he knows can bring the whole scam down. I'm sorry, Libby."

Libby released a loud sigh then nodded. "I understand, she mumbled. "Bureaucracy! Did Captain Jen know?"

"She knows and we are on a need to know basis. I have been totally honest with her." Marshall glanced at Libby hoping that they were okay now also. He hesitantly changed the subject and asked, "You like her a lot, don't you?"

"Best boss that I've ever had," Libby said without hesitation. The Captain would put herself out there for us at anytime." Libby, abruptly, began to feel just a little nervous about the Captain out there in the gulch. She hit the gas pedal and moved a little quicker. No way in hell was anyone going to injure her Captain!

***

"Bix, can you take Johnny out of here along the south side of the gulch. You know, follow the rim out. Are there any roads near Hoosier where Bernie could pick you up?"

"Actually, there is, 235, would do the trick. I could call her as we descend. Is that what you're thinking?"

"Exactly. I have a suspicion that these perps have gotten into our radio and maybe phones. They seem to be able to track us real closely. That is possible isn't it, Johnny?"

"Yep. It does seem a little fishy that they're here right after you two arrived." I assume you took all precautions?" McPherson asked.

"Of course and we weren't followed until now," Jen added. She glanced up again at the Range Rover and watched as they came slowly back down the road. It was obvious that they were checking for a roads to turn on. "Now get going, you two. Hustle out of here as quickly as you can. Go!"

Bix threw her arms around Jen Holly. "You'll be really careful," she searched Jen's eye for confirmation and a nod. "Shall we call Breckenridge Police when we get back down?" Bix asked.

"No. I've got it handled. Now go!"

With that order, the two left. They ascended into the woods quickly. Bix began to bushwhack toward the tree line of the gulch on the south side. Johnny didn't even have to ask Bix Bixler where they were going. He knew better. This lady had climbed the familiar area so often. It was a given that she knew what to do.

The willow bushes had become much more dense as they ascended. Each climber forged their own path upward knowing that the branches would whip back on the second climber. As the willows thinned out, Bix maneuvered around the ledges and boulders carefully. Their pace was quick but not stupid. They had remained silent simply because climbing was enough use of their air.

The alpine meadow now allowed them to move forward crossing small streams of water from the steep ledges of Evening Sky Mountain. Small waterfalls brought down the last of the snow melt with efficiency. As they traversed the mountain side, old burro trails from mining days crossed their path. The green grass had become spongy and soft under their boots.

Bix glanced back toward Jen's position as she stopped for breath. She calculated that they were probably a mile away from the campfire. "I hated to leave Jen down there," Bix mumbled to Johnny.

"I hear you," he said. "And, I hate the fact that all these lives are now at stake because of my dilemma. It just isn't fair," Johnny whispered. He took Bix's hand for a few moments just for the connection.

"You couldn't have helped it? How could you have known what would happen? You can't blame yourself, Johnny. Life isn't that simple. It finds ways to test us and make us better. You wanted a life in the mountains and that's that. Don't apologize for not wanting to sell out. The land is so much bigger than what we are. Let's go." And with that said, Bix began to move quickly never looking back. They had at least two more miles to cover. Bix calculated that at the next break, she'd call Bernie.

In the distance they suddenly heard rifle fire. The assault had begun and the events began to play out in haste. Johnny and Bix glanced at each other and then hiked just a little faster. They needed to accomplish their part of this showdown.

***

Jen's eyes began to flash around the area. She needed to keep the appearance of three campers. If these perps thought that there were still three guns shooting at them, the farther away Bix and Johnny McPherson would get undetected. Jen judged that her backup was probably 20 minutes out. She arranged three firing positions in the camp. Jen pulled the bench over and then piled Johnny's pack on top. Her second position was from behind a stump in the site. It was possible to roll from one to the other without being seen. Her eyes frantically checked Johnny's camp for more items to pile on the barricade. Finally, she pulled his sleeping bag from the tent then tossed it over the chair. She had now assembled a firing line where three people could be defending the area. It would have to do, she surmised.

In the near distance, Jen could hear a motor as their car moved up the rutted road. They were here. Jen double checked her three weapons, two pistols and a rifle. Her mind spun through the options that she could have taken. She could have disappeared with Bix and Johnny putting everyone in danger or the group could have stayed and not only endangered their lives but Johnny's testimony. No, this was the best idea that she could come up with at the time. The case came first, she calculated. Jen checked her watch. Less than five minutes had gone by. Time was not flying. Jen understood that she was about to cross the line and not be able to retreat. She had intentionally not communicated her plan to anyone. These perps were monitoring the police communications she suspected.

Jen suddenly got an idea that could help her three-gun plot. She pulled out her smart phone to text Libby then activated Frank's phone also. The hope that Frank might pick up the message was entirely possible. "Here goes," she whispered. 'Captain to HAPT ,' she wrote. 'we r trapped Dante's Gulch All three. barricade . Come soon. Tell husband, Simon, we'll be ok,' Jen smiled ever so slightly; clear enough she hoped.

Their vehicle stopped somewhere up the road out of sight. Jen loaded all the weapons and placed as much ammo as she could next to each position. Her guess was that there were at least three of them, maybe more. It was obvious that this was their last chance to get Johnny McPherson before the police had him in custody. Captain Holly knew it was all out war.

The doors quietly shut on the vehicle, all four doors. Okay, there were four of them at least. Jen inhaled as she prepared for the fight. She had to wonder if an AKA would be among their fire power. God help me if they do, she thought. Jen had a few minutes left before her life would change.

***

Libby tossed her phone across the seat to Marshall as it activated. He stared at it then read the text aloud. When he got to the part about Jen's husband, his reaction changed. "She must be really worried about the outcome of this assault. Pretty personal for a formal police communique."

"It would be if Captain Jen had a husband," she murmured. "Simon is Bix's dog," she clarified. Libby then activated her radio to get Frank. He answered quickly with only a, "10-4." Frank had caught it also.

"I do believe that I know what's going on," she assessed. "Captain Jen thinks that they are monitoring our communications! No wonder they are showing up everywhere! These guys have tapped in to our system! Shit!" Libby passed another slow moving tourist then began climbing the first switchback approaching Hoosier Pass.

Frank quickly left the office. He slipped into the public bathroom down the hall with the land phone from an unoccupied office space . Their office could be bugged. Hopefully the bathroom was safe. Frank then called Chief Carl Hagen on the newly acquired land phone. Hagen answered on the third ring. They devised a plan and decided to phone Chief Anderson the current information. Frank also asked Hagen to make all appropriate calls. He ended with the news about Gipple.

Suddenly Katie from the GIS Office came walking into the bathroom. "Frank? What are you doing? This is the Ladies!"

"Oh shit! I am sorry but the office just might be bugged, Katie. Can you used the library bathroom?" he asked.

"Actually, let me go get some paper and hang a sign on the door so that you do have privacy in your new office," Katie said shaking her head. "Your team is always so interesting. What did we all do for fun before you guys got here? I don't know," she said leaving Frank talking with Carl Hagen. The bathroom had definitely become his office. HAPT would function no matter what, Frank assessed. He knew that Libby had gotten the message loud and clear when she texted him with, 'Dispatch a car to Simon's house immediately.' Okay then the plot had thickened, he surmised.

Libby hit the brakes to make the turn into the gulch. Marshall held on for dear life as they began to hit gravel. Rocks flying and tension mounting didn't help the situation.

"I think that Captain Jen is holding these guys off by herself. I think she sent Bix and Johnny back out of the gulch on foot. Captain Jen is there by herself," she assessed while flying over the top of the first hill. "We've got to get there, Marshall. Hold on!"

"Already am!" he yelled as they peaked the second hill. Gravel was flying as the ruts tossed them without mercy. The car's shocks screamed for help! Wherever this road led was totally new ground for Marshall. It wasn't a road but an animal trail! "Good God do they ever plow this mess?" he yelled.

"Once a summer I think," Libby returned. "I'm sorry," Libby yelled back.

"I know. Go!" Marshall said.

***

Quickly Johnny McPherson and Bix began to descend while traveling east. Johnny could tell that Bix was calculating where she wanted to be. Lord knew there wasn't a trail anywhere in sight. Bix was obviously free-wheeling their direction. They now began to maneuver through a thick field of bushes.

Bix could feel the small branches scratching at her legs. She would be bleeding by the time they got out of this mess. Johnny, fortunately, had on long pants so he wasn't feeling like he was being whipped. Bix pulled a huge bunch of branches apart and peered out. They were back in the pines again. Her eyes scanned higher up the ledges behind them while she sought to find the old mill mining remains. Bix calculated that the travel needed to be diagonal to the mill site. She aimed their progress accordingly.

They ran through the pine area. Johnny could
hear the Blue River flowing from somewhere close.
The rapids indicated that they were near. The terrain
had become marshy and definitely more like
wetlands than just woods. They hiked around a few
holding ponds until they came upon a concrete dam.
A Colorado Springs Watershed sign indicated that
they had reached civilization. Both hikers stopped
to look around and assess the terrain. They were
standing on the top of the small dam looking down
on a gravel road. It started right in front them.

"We're out," Bix stated. She got her phone out
of her pack.

Johnny glanced around to inspect their
surroundings. The mountain water was flowing into
a holding pond on their left. The collected flow then
traveled through a small concrete lock. Obviously,
the construction was done to help measure the water
flow for Colorado Springs. It looked like it had been
built at least 50 years ago, he surmised. At least
now there was a road to follow. Their progress
would be much quicker, he knew.

Bix took advantage of their stop to call Bernie
in hopes that a signal could be had. The phone rang.
Bix glanced at Johnny and smiled in her relief.
Their part of this day had now become less
complicated. She really wanted to get some help up
to Jen Holly before something terrible could
happen.

"Hello, Bixler residence," Bernie Holden said.
From her tone Bix could tell that she was feeling the
stress of today also. Waiting was really one of the
harder things that humans are asked to do, Bix

knew.

"Hi. It's me," Bix said feeling incredible relief.

"What's going on?" Bernie asked.

"I am with Johnny now and Jen's up in the gulch fighting off an ambush. She ordered us out. We will be ready to pick up by the time you get here. I'm going to give you some instructions about how to find us. Get some paper and pencil off of the counter," Bix said. She could hear Simon whimpering in the background. He had picked up on her voice; the little guy was so intuitive.

"I tried to call the HAPT office a few minutes ago and no one answered," Bernie clarified as she searched. "What's that all about?" Bernie asked as she rustled around on the counter searching.

"I have no idea. Maybe Frank is on the way to the gulch or my house. Pretty interesting. Okay, you ready for instructions?"

"Yep."

***

Captain Jen Holly felt the sweat trickle down her back as she strained her vision to watch the road. She heard their footsteps first before she saw them. All four of them! Each man carried enough fire power to knock her off the face of the earth. Before they got any closer, Jen began firing. Each perp dived into the bushes and returned the volley. Jen rolled to the center position and fired back then moved on to the left for another round. So far the suspects were busy just keeping up with the chaos and surprise. Soon they would begin to form a plan on how to control the situation. She could see one of them starting to look around the terrain. He was probably the leader, she calculated. Jen had to wonder if their orders were to kill or capture them. Either way, the odds were not in her favor.

She kept rolling from position to position. Jen knew that they had started to communicate and form an assault plan. The man hiding behind a large boulder suddenly rushed out and moved ten feet forward. Two more of them charged toward the gulley while the last one then moved up from the center. Their positions were now at least ten feet closer to her. 25 feet was now separating Jen from the shooters. As one of them would spray her barricade, the others began to creep closer and closer.

Jen checked her watch. It had been ten minutes only. Their rapid fire was mutilating her walls. The bullets were zinging so close! She wouldn't be able to hold from here much longer. Her retreat became inevitable. Where could she go?

Jen inspected the terrain behind her for this retreat. There was quite a cluster of bushes halfway up the incline; she would still have to run 15 feet without cover to get there. Her mind calculated that it would take at least five seconds to reach the bushes.

It had become obvious that these shooters were here to kill Johnny and anyone with him. The information that he possessed had to be buried was her guess. So the quicker she moved out, the better. What would they do after they realized that Jen was alone? Three options flashed into her mind: the perps would be so angry that they would kill her, they could capture her and torture her for information, or they would decide to spread out and see if they could find Johnny's tracks. It really didn't matter at this point what their intentions were. None of the options worked out well for her.

***

Above the third hill Libby and Marshall ran into a barricade positioned on the road. An officer ran back to talk with them. Libby recognized the guy from Chief Anderson's Department. Dan Trout shouted, "Officer James, we got orders to wait for you here so that we can advance together." He removed the barricade and let them enter. "The tourists have been ushered out of the area so we're ready."

"Let's do it," Libby said never completely stopping her car. The second patrol car, parked off to the side of the road, motioned her to take the lead. Excellent, she thought. At this time Code 3 seemed important. The sirens and lights came on as the three cars sped up into Dante's Gulch.

"What do you think we'll find?" asked Marshall while checking his gun and Libby's rifle. Their adrenalin was overwhelming now.

"Bix and Johnny gone and Captain Jen left to play three parts in this drama. God help her!" Libby said earnestly. Her heart was pounding as she drove.

Marshall, without even thinking, placed his hand on her leg for support. It felt like it was so very natural that neither one of them realized what had happened.

The ascent now had turned into a vehicle's worst nightmare. The road damage was not to be avoided. Libby proceeded with caution while the rear tires fishtailed; she could not accelerate beyond the road's tolerance. Gravel flew freely and dust dominated the air. Speed was a ridiculous joke at this juncture. Libby's thoughts raced while her SUV crawled up the ascent adorned with washboards plus cavernous ruts. Vibrations rattling every nut and bolt increased the challenge! The balance of motion took all of Libby's concentration; the dance of compromise was her focus, speed versus safety.

CHAPTER 24

ALL THAT IS HUMAN

Bix and Johnny McPherson had reached the green Colorado Springs gate that blocked car traffic. On the other side of the gate were a few homes along the road . These high elevation residences had incredible views of Summit County. A rough winter for a stellar summer was the choice for these occupants. For the time being, these lots were mostly vacant; the people would build eventually, Bix reflected. Maybe not in her lifetime but they would come.

Johnny placed a hand on Bix's shoulder. Her thoughts, once again, landed in the moment. He pointed toward the dust rising from the road. A car was approaching them. "Our ride has arrived," he commented with relief.

Bernie Holden was speeding down the gravel road toward them in Bix's Jeep Wrangler. Bix focused on the red haired lady in the front seat. Her heart beat faster as she realized her love for this special woman. What a miracle that was.

Bernie pulled up beside them and jumped out. She grabbed Bix and buried her in a huge hug. Simon followed Bernie's lead and danced in joy. He jumped and happily barked running in a circle around the two ladies. Johnny was glad for Bix at this moment; it was good to see that she had found someone. He finally snatched up Simon and tried to slow the little guy's frenzy.

"My God I thought you'd never call," Bernie said. She released Bix from her grip to look at her and make sure that she was okay. "Your legs! What happened?" she asked looking at the scratches and blood.

"Brush that couldn't be avoided on the way down. We were limited with where we could walk. We needed to keep as much distance as we could from the shooters. Fortunately, we got some warning before they arrived at the campsite. Jen got us out of there quickly."

"What exactly is her plan?" Bernie asked. Bix took this opportunity to reach for Simon who was ecstatic to be in her arms.

Johnny answered, "I figure she was going to ambush them so that we could disappear. Got to say, I'm pretty impressed not only with Bix's escape route but Captain Holly's determination. We had no idea how many men were coming up the gulch at that point. It was a pretty big undertaking for any cop. My hat's off to her."

The atmosphere suddenly exploded with a chaotic amount of ammo fire echoing from the back of the gulch. The ambush had escalated. Abruptly,

the lights and sirens of the three police cars entered
the scene. Their eyes watched the cars racing up the
dam road on the north side of Dante's Gulch. Bix
and Johnny felt detached from the conflict. They
were now distant spectators yet emotionally bound
to the action.

"Where are they going?" Bix asked looking at
Johnny with alarm. At that moment Libby halted
the SUV, saw her mistake, turned around then
headed back down toward the campsite road.
"Thank heavens that the police realized where Jen is
located," Bix added with a sigh. "They'll get them
and come to Jen's rescue." Her words became a
silent prayer that they all shared.

It was now time to move, Bernie realized.
"You want me to drive us down?" Bernie asked
sensing the urgency. No matter what happened,
Johnny needed to be delivered to the police. His
safety and their safety depended on it, Bernie knew.

"That would be great. Our instructions are to go
directly to our house and wait there for an officer to
arrive. That's all we know," Bix added as she went
to the passenger's side and slid the seat back so
Johnny could get in. Bix grabbed Simon and
climbed in; the car turned around then raced toward
the highway.

***

The moment of retreat beckoned Captain Jen
Holly. Her future came down to this moment; Jen's
living history was about to be written. The shooters
would take aim and either hit or miss, life or death.

292

To stay behind the barricade would be suicide, Jen sensed. Did they think that she was Johnny at this point? No, it was obvious that they had figured out the ploy. Her uniform probably had been recognized.

15 feet was all that she had to cover, 15 feet. She needed a distraction of some sort. Next to the campfire there was a big metal pot. Jen reached out and retrieved it quickly. Her plan was to throw it as far as she could into the brush by the lake. Maybe she could add a few more seconds to her escape. Any distraction would help, Holly calculated.

"Okay then," she whispered. It had to happen now! Captain Jen took a huge breath from deep inside and heaved the pot as far as she could; she rushed like a crazy lady toward the trees! The seconds passing were gigantic in proportion. Captain Jen Holly retreated knowing that her back was open for target practice! Ten more feet was all that she needed! Her eyes riveted on the trees above; her body strained with the ascent. Destiny was approaching!

The hired assassins aimed then released a fury of rifle fire. One shot exploded as it hit Jen's left shoulder. The bullet's speed was much faster than her legs could run. The tremendous impact forced her body into a spin. Twisted. Hurled as the bullet penetratcd into her flesh selfishly making room for itself.

The pain was beyond her comprehension as the blood began to flow. Jen's world was sliding into darkness. Her body went numb while falling deeper into places beyond reality. Body and soul began to cope with the trauma. She fell deeper. Her mind fought to stay alert but to no avail. Jen's body knew best; she slipped into darkness. The pain reeled through her body as her mind went unconscious.

***

The four men stood over the cop's body inspecting the damage. To the naked eye, the body looked lifeless and definitely not a threat to them. There were no signs of consciousness that they could see. Who cared? She was at least out for the count. One perp removed her weapons and threw them into the brush.

"Well hell," the 300 pound bearded criminal said. "Looks like we aren't going to get any information out of this bitch," he mumbled while probing her body with his boot. "She's bleeding like crazy; can't be long now." He wiped his bloody boot clean on Jen's pant leg. "Let's spread out and see if we can find any tracks for the others. I figure McPherson was camping here and had visitors. Now, we have to figure out where the hell he went."

They moved down the incline beginning the search for tracks. A plan had just been formulated when, suddenly, they heard sirens and lights echoing throughout Dante's Gulch. The four men observed the parade with interest. Just like they had done, the police missed the left turn into the camping site and charged up the road toward the dam.

"Well, I'd call that a bit of luck. Let's get the fuck out of here!" said the bearded thug. The group ran full speed back to their car then turned around in the cul-de-sac. They bounced over the ruts swearing the whole way. Three minutes later they were back on the main gravel road and headed out of the gulch.

***

One breath at a time, Jen ordered. Count your breaths. It was a simple reflex action but oh so powerful. She could feel the cold of the ground; her blood seeping out letting shock in. The point was that she could feel. In the distance she could hear the police car siren. Jen concentrated on that sound. Concentrated…in and out… back and forth. The pain had now become a welcome companion striking her in spasms. Stinging, twitching, keeping her conscious. Keeping her listening. Hoping….

***

Libby had passed the campground turn then instantly realized her mistake. "Damn!" she yelled.

Marshall quickly reacted, "What?"

"I missed the damn turn. We want to be on the other side of the gulch. Shit! We need a place to turn around." Her eyes intensely surveyed the road; it looked bleak in her estimation.

"Up there," Marshall said and pointed.

She blinked her lights to warn the cars behind her then slammed on her brakes. The Interceptor fishtailed as she slowed. The car barely fit into the open shoulder space. There was just enough room to swing around after two tries. As she raced down the slope, she motioned to the other cars but kept going forward. They, in turn, used the turnaround and quickly followed her lead.

Marshall was the first to see the car come rushing out of the campsite turn. It sped down the road throwing gravel in all directions. "There they go!" he yelled.

"Wonder if they have Captain Jen in the car?" Libby questioned. She had a split second to make her decision. Did she turn in or follow the perps? A multitude of choices flashed through her mind. She could imagine the alternatives. Jen could have been shot and abandoned or bound and thrown in the back seat of the escape car. The cop within her told her to follow the perps. "Marshall, call the office and tell Frank to dispatch an ambulance up into the campsites in Dante's Gulch immediately."

She listened as Marshall made the call. Her anxiety heightened with each of his words. It was like she was making the call herself. If there were forceful wishes, Libby then thought them. Jen's life could be in jeopardy at this very moment. Libby could feel the power of her decision. It was one of those moments that would influence her life forever. Libby released a deep breath letting her emotions surface; she was so close to tears. "God, I hope I made the right decision," she yelled.

"You did the right thing, honey," Marshall said. "Law enforcement must follow their orders. It's priority." Whoops, he thought. It had just slipped out of Marshall's mouth. 'Honey?' Oh my God maybe she didn't hear it, he hoped. Marshall calmed down and focused on the chase. "We need to get these fucks before they're out on the highway again! Go like hell; I'll hold on!"

Libby pushed down on the accelerator slightly. Her instincts told her that control would be a big issue as they neared the three treacherous downhills coming up. Could be that the perps would make a mistake as they topped a hill. On the second hill Libby remembered that there were some huge ruts deep enough to blow a tire. Wicked enough to at least give her a chance to diminish their lead. The cars neared the terrain and Libby braced herself. "Get ready, Marshall, rough road coming up! Here goes!" Libby pressed down on the brakes gently keeping some control.

The car in front of her naively raced ahead with perilous speed. As the perps' car mounted the hill, it flew into the air surrendering all control. The motor roared sending chills through Libby's body. It was a slow motion disaster. The car turned to the right and hurled toward the embankment. It came to roost in a cluster of Aspen. The tree branches subdued the force of the landing then deposited the car on the ground. The thud of ruined metal and twisted plastic screamed in devastation. The police cars froze as they watched this chaos. It was right out of the movies. Filmed once after many hours of discussion and speculation. Who would have thought that these perps would destroy their own escape? Libby and Marshall, simultaneously, let out a breath while watching the impact.

"Shit, that was scary," Marshall said as he opened the door and pulled out his gun. Libby followed his lead. They moved, cautiously, toward the belly-up remains. The motor was still running. It was an eerie feeling heading toward the scene.

Libby's eyes scanned the backseat for Captain Jen. At first she was relieved that Jen wasn't there then her mind sought the alternative. 'Officer down', she feared; her heart jumped a beat at the mere thought. "Let her be alive," she whispered softy. Marshall heard her whisper. His glance at her said it all. If there was power in positive thoughts, they now sent them up Dante's Gulch together.

As if on cue, the ambulance raced passed them seeking the campsite destination. Marshall crawled to the driver's side window and tested for a pulse on the first bloody suspect. He shook his head 'no' then moved toward the backseat. "Alive, but barely," was his comment. He carefully pulled the heavy bearded man from the upside down car wreck so they could administer aide.

Libby found the front seat passenger to be alive. The backseat perp was a goner. She turned on her radio to transmit. The Breckenridge police controller acknowledged her call. "11-79 request for second ambulance. Four suspects in car accident on Dante Gulch road. Two alive and two dead. 10-4," Libby finished.

Marshall turned off the engine then pulled the live man clear of the wreckage. He began to apply pressure on the perp's leg; the right leg was almost ripped from his body. "First aide kit!" Marshall yelled.

One of the other officers assisted quickly. It was probably a futile effort rapping the leg but they had to try. The two men got a tourniquet in position and kept applying pressure to control the bleeding. Marshall figured that the leg could be re-attached if they didn't mess up the tendons. It was worth a try.

Libby inspected the trapped front seat perp. The dashboard had smashed into his chest. The damage was anyone's guess at this point. She connected with the radio again and requested jaws-of-life be brought up.

One of the police cars turned around and went back up the gulch to assist. Libby watched them go and would have given anything right now to be with them. Her hope that the ambulance would arrive soon and take over this situation was paramount in her mind. All she could think of as she pressed on the open wound was Captain Jen laying on the ground needing help. Her duty with these perps seemed less important yet it was duty. The police oath was hard to follow sometimes. A friend's life was at stake.

Her thoughts were brought back to the moment. It became obvious to her now that her perp's life was slipping away. There was a final hiss as his breath ceased. The man became limp as his life force left the body. Libby felt a hollowness as she tried breathing air into his lungs; unfortunately, his lungs could no longer hold air. There was no resistance. She kept up her efforts until the ambulance came sailing over the first hill. The medics raced to the scene carrying every device they could.

Regrettably, the count of survival had now diminished to one. That call was not Libby's to make on her guy. She continued pushing air until the medic relieved her. He placed a stethoscope on the man's chest and listened checking again and again. The medic then shook his head and checked his watch for time of death.

***

The moving ambulance paused, pulled over, when they saw in their rearview mirror the police car signal to lead the procession. The patrol car eked passed them then turned onto the campsite road. Sirens off, lights on, the SUV began its' approach. Branches scrapped the sides of both vehicles. The bottom of the heavy ambulance occasionally hit the dirt road with a thump; the ambulance risked vehicle damage in order to get to the cul-de-sac. One passenger medic kept his head outside of the vehicle trying to spot rut depths and signal warnings to the driver. They had gone into creep mode but still moved forward.

The police car in front of them was able to move faster even though progress seemed so slow when a cop's life was on the line. The car finally reached the cul-de-sac. The two officers raced out and began searching for the Captain. One of the men ran toward the lake. The other man circled the campsite then began to widen the perimeter of his search. He slowly began climbing the hill.

"Nothing!" yelled the officer down at the lake. He ran back to the campsite and moved outward from there. The other man silently kept up his search technique. Halfway up the hill, he found her!

"Up here and hurry!" he yelled.

The ambulance had just come to a stop and the two medics pulled out their kits then rushed up the hill. All four men gasped trying to catch their breath after climbing at 11, 500 elevation. Rushing, was no easy task.

The medics turned her body over carefully; all four men inhaled and waited. Would Captain Holly be dead or alive? It was the moment of truth that had captured their full attention. Breath held in unison; time stopped. The two medics froze for one moment and concentrated.

Captain Jen Holly's eyes popped open and stared up at them! They all jumped then smiled openly. "She's alive and kicking," Officer Dan Trout yelled from the second row of observers. "Thank God!" He immediately moved away from the four and began to broadcast the news. Few details needed to be conveyed at this point. She was alive was all that people needed to hear!

Captain Jen Holy was then wrapped warmly and placed on a stretcher. The IV's were in place and onboard. Her arm was wrapped tightly to slow the bleeding. All four men wanted to help carry her down the decline. The processional moved cautiously forward trying not to bounce the stretcher. They, carefully, lifted and loaded Jen into the back of the ambulance. One medic and Dan Trout jumped into the back. Officer Trout held her hand tightly keeping her with them. He wasn't going to let anything happen to her on his watch. The other officer jumped into the police car, turned on the sirens and lights and escorted the ambulance back to Frisco.

The hospital knew they were coming and prepared the emergency unit. Calls immediately went out from all the departments all over the state. 'Officer down,' was never taken lightly throughout the ranks of the police force. There would be representatives from other districts offering their assistance as Jen would fight for her life.

***

Chief Carl Hagen took a deep breath before he made the phone call to Arlene Holly. Calls to mothers were never easy. He had met Jen's mother a few times over the years. Carl knew what a wonderful lady she was. Naturally, that made this phone call so much harder for him. "Hello? Arlene, this is Chief Hagen. I am afraid that I have some bad news for you."

"No, she's alive right? Please dear Lord tell me that she is alive!" Arlene Holly moaned.

"Yes. She is alive and on the way to the hospital in Frisco. That's all I know. I'll be over in five minutes to get you."

"Thank you, Carl. I'll be ready," Arlene said. It felt like a nightmare; it was such an incredible surprise and so unexpected! Her day had become a disaster; her precious daughter was going to the hospital. The words slapped Arlene in the face. She felt like the world was now upside down. She hung up the phone and spun into action!

It was the phone call that every family member of a police officer hoped would never come. Arlene felt that since Jen had become a Captain, her chances of an injury would be reduced. That duty would put her more in the office than on the road. Didn't seemed like that was going happen. This case was way too close to home. Johnny McPherson was a good man and didn't deserve any of this; neither did her wonderful daughter.

Arlene flew around the gallery shutting down the appliances and locking the front door. Should she write a sign for the door? No, Arlene decided. Her thought was to wait until after Jen's condition was stable. Mothers had to have some privacy when their children needed help. Arlene knew that she could only focus on Jen's health at this moment. Phone calls would be too distracting. Lights out in the gallery and Arlene was on the curb waiting for Carl as he pulled up.

He didn't hesitate for a second. Sirens blaring and lights on, he pulled a U turn and flew out of Leadville. Neither adult said anything right away. Carl radioed in that he was on the way to the Frisco Hospital. ETA was 30 minutes.

As they neared Copper Mountain and I-70 Highway, Police cars located on the road shoulders joined in behind them. The procession now had 10 cars. Carl's police cruiser was the only one with a siren; the rest followed with lights on in solemn silence. One Summit Cruiser passed them and sped up the highway with lights in motion to lead the escort. They were now snuggled in safely within the solemn parade.

As Carl pulled up to the hospital emergency entrance, he noticed the ambulance was still sitting in place at the emergency door. He rushed around to the passenger side and opened the door for Arlene. He took her arm warmly as they approached the entrance. A nurse was stationed at the door. She recognized Chief Hagen and assumed that this was Captain Holly's mother, Arlene.

Nurse Betty Sanders came forward to greet them. "Chief Hagen, thank you. And, you must be Arlene Holly." Betty's smile and countenance reassured Arlene slightly; her blood pressure began to settle. "Bix called me a few minutes ago. She wants me to take very good care of you and your daughter." Betty nodded at Carl relieving him of this duty. He was very appreciative as he went to find the other officers out front.

As Betty ushered Arlene through the entrance, she began to talk, "I'm Nurse Sanders; please call me Betty. Actually, I have met your daughter on several occasions so the Holly family is in good hands. So glad to meet you. Please come in and let's talk privately," Betty said taking Arlene's hand.

Carl Hagen was relieved. He knew that, indeed, Arlene was in good hands. He walked toward the main entrance where several officers were stationed. They would probably know more about the confrontation than he did at this point. He had listened to some of the events about Dante's Gulch but hadn't caught the report on the perps' car accident yet. He had considered listening on the way from Leadville but decided that Arlene really didn't need that. He wandered over to the front door as Chief Anderson came out to greet him. Their faces were solemn as the information was shared. Both men had been shaken by the events; it was a lot to process. The HAPT Unit had so much to handle right now. The case had become so incredibly dangerous. Crooks were coming out of the woodwork; the Chiefs wanted it to stop now.

CHAPTER 25

TURN THE PAGE

Nurse Sanders escorted Arlene Holly into a small conference room. They sat down in two lounge chairs for their conversation. Arlene stared into Betty's eyes. The pause was momentous.

"Tell me the whole truth. Don't sugar coat anything," Arlene demanded. Arlene noticed that she was holding her breath while waiting for the answer; answers had played through her mind on the way over from Leadville, obviously. The scenarios constantly surfacing then changing from dread to positive. It all whirled and landed in this very moment.

"I can honestly tell you that Jen was very lucky. Having said that, please keep in mind that bullets are never kind. This particular bullet sailed right through her shoulder muscles missing most of her veins except for one, the Cephalic Vein. It nicked that vein so she lost a lot of blood. The surgical team was able to repair the vein damage. Nevertheless, the nerve damage from the bullet's entry won't be apparent until later. As she heals, we'll be able to answer more questions. When we get down that road, make sure that she does lots of therapy. Right now healing must take place. Loss of blood definitely takes a toll on the body."

Arlene let out her breath and tried to process all that Betty was saying. "How many transfusions and how long was the operation?"

"Actually one transfusion on the way down from the gulch and then two more here. The medic team was able to reach her location fairly soon. I can say that if they had not gotten there for another 30 minutes, Jen's outcome might be totally different. She would be on the way to Denver in critical condition. As is, she is critical but close to stable. The hour and half operation does place her in ICU to wake up; not totally out of the woods but almost. We'll bring her out of ICU later tonight if her vital signs remain the same. Bullets are horrible things," Betty finished and sighed. Hang in there," she whispered and grasp Arlene's hand.

***

Officers Jerry Neal and Bill Smith had been listening to all the events on the scanner. Frank had gone over to Bix's house to pick up Johnny McPherson and deliver him to the HAPT Office. A few seconds ago, Chief Hagen had come on the scanner to report on Captain Jen's condition. He apparently was at the Frisco Hospital. The two

HAPT Officers did a high five when they heard that Jen was almost stable. Their whole mood changed as they approached Gipple's location on Colfax Street in Denver. International Mineral Recovery Foundation was going to get a shock today. They needed to pay for what they had done to Captain Jen. Bill slid into a parking spot and then prepared for the arrest. Jerry had called ahead and let the Denver Police know their location. They were now waiting for backup. The word had spread about the Captain's conditions and Denver was happy to assist. A police cruiser pulled up beside them less than five minutes later.

Jerry got out and stood between the two cars while Bill rolled down his window. "We need to take Thomas Gipple alive from that building," Bill said while pointing at the designated location.

"You want us to head around back and come in simultaneously?" the Denver Officer asked.

"Sounds like a plan," Jerry said. "Let us know when you are in position and then we'll start in the front door."

"Will there be any other perps in the building?" Denver asked.

Jerry looked at Bill for that answer. Bill thought for a moment then replied, "Last time that I walked in unannounced, it didn't seem so but International does own the entire building. I have no idea what is upstairs."

"Shall we smash the back door then head upstairs while you two handle the perp?"

"I think so. Better safe than sorry," said Jerry. "We have apprehended four perps in Summit. Only

one perp is alive after a disastrous road accident. He
is in the hospital. I'd say they are playing for keeps
here and professionals. Take no chances,
gentlemen. Our assumption is that all of the active
players are apprehended or dead but who knows...."
his voice trailed off.

"We'll cover the back then head upstairs in
pursuit."

"Good," Bill added as he double checked his
gun. The Denver cruiser pulled into a vacant
parking spot some 20 feet ahead. The two officers
came back in vests, helmets and battering ram for
the backdoor. They quickly headed up the alley then
disappeared into the shadows.

Bill and Jerry moved toward the front door
watching the sidewalks for pedestrian traffic or
anything unexpected. They moved quickly into
position and waited. Less than two minutes later,
the Denver Officers radioed, "In position. 10-4."
Jerry nodded at Bill to begin the assault. Bill took a
breath and whispered, "Go!"

Both teams rushed the building. Bill and Jerry
heard the bolt lock shatter on the back door. Both
units then announced, "Police!"

Thomas Gipple was sitting in his office chair at
the back as usual. The smoke rising from his never
ending cigarette filled the air. Bill could see the
shock registering on his face as he clutched his
heart in case of a heart attack. "What? Oh my God!"

"Both hands up, Gipple." Bill rushed over and
applied handcuffs while Jerry inspected the entire
room for anymore perps. "Clear," he yelled. "You
have the right to remain-" Bill began.

Suddenly, there was gunfire from upstairs. Shuffling feet indicated that there were at least two men plus police up there. The police were yelling, "Stop, this is an arrest. Hands up!" to no avail. Shots continued.

Jerry motioned Bill to get Gipple in the SUV while he would join the situation upstairs. Bill nodded then whipped Gipple out of the building while finishing his 'rights.'

As they approached the SUV, a body flew out of the upstairs' window. Bill secured Gipple in the cage and ran over to inspect the body. Fortunately, the body wasn't a cop; unfortunately, he was dead. Bill called for an ambulance then proceeded back into the building. He ascended the stairs in time to hear an officer call for backup, "Code 30!" Bill flew into the action hoping that all officers were okay.

***

Libby and Marshall charged into the hospital. They headed to the main desk for directions. In the distant hallway, they suddenly saw Chief Carl Hagen and Chief Josh Anderson talking. Libby couldn't conceal her panic as she approached the two officers. Her eyes probing quickly for answers.

"She's going to make it. She was lucky, if you can be lucky, when a bullet's got your name on it. Captain Jen is in ICU and hasn't awakened yet," Chief Anderson said with a half smile. His relief was apparent.

"Thank God," Libby said.

"Now the Captain would like you two to get down to the HAPT Office and keep Johnny McPherson safe. Frank is there all by his lonesome," Chief Hagen said. "Now git! We'll keep you informed of the events here. Oh, and by the way, good work in the gulch," he added.

"Thank you, sir," Libby replied. She and Marshall left the hospital quickly and headed toward the office. Fortunately, the office was less than five minutes ETA.

Marshall was finally going to meet Johnny McPherson. In fact, he would be responsible for McPherson's safety while the man was in custody. The FBI needed to be informed soon, he calculated. Right now, he would honor his agreement with Captain Holly. There was no need to bring in more agents if the situation looked secure.

Libby was so relieved that she had made the right decision in the gulch. Her hands had been shaking at the hospital. She hoped that neither Chief had noticed. It was like a cloud had been removed from over her head. Captain Jen would survive this horrible ordeal. Looked like the good guys might just win this one! Whew.

Their SUV pulled into the parking lot. Libby radioed Frank to tell him where they were.

"Come on up. We're snug-as-a-bug. We'll remove the barrier from in front of the door so it will take us a couple of minutes." Libby could hear Frank talking with Johnny as she and Marshall approached the building.

Marshall stopped Libby with a warning hand then pulled his gun. "We need to do surveillance of the building on our way up. I'll take the top floor; you the bottom?" he said checking with her. She nodded and went to work opening office doors to make sure everything was normal. A few seconds later she joined Marshall who had just finished the second floor.

Libby knocked twice then opened the door. "Frank, we're here." She inspected the chaos in the room. Frank had used the filing cabinets for the barricade. It all looked secure at this time. The two men were anxious but okay.

Agent Marshall Tate approached Johnny McPherson quickly. He glanced back at Libby then said, "Mr. McPherson, I represent the FBI and we need to take you into custody. You will need to sign papers that indicate your intentions to testify at the International Mineral Recovery Foundation trial. These papers will transfer your custody from the HAPT Team to us eventually. It is a formality that must be taken care of before we go any further. Captain Jen has been duly informed of this arrangement. I am Agent Marshall Tate, by the way."

***

As Arlene Holly got ready to enter the ICU, Nurse Betty placed a hand on her shoulder. "Don't be surprised by the amount of equipment and 'do-dads' attached to Jen. It is mainly monitoring equipment. She's still asleep and should be waking up soon. The procedure is usually 15 minute visitations in ICU. I'll come back when you need to take a break." Betty Sanders smiled and left Arlene alone to enter the room.

Even so, the warning hadn't prepared Arlene for what she saw. The reality rocked Arlene down to her toes. Her darling daughter was attached to every tube possible! The room was cold with only the continual machine beeps monitoring her condition. Arlene rushed over to the bed and grasped Jen's hand. Jen was cold to the touch, her long black hair was tucked under a surgical cap. She looked so small and helpless.

Her strong independent child could have died, Arlene realized. She hated the bullet; she hated the man who shot her! She hated the job. God, she hated the job. Why couldn't it be someone else's daughter and not hers? Jen could be home with three or four babies but not here. Arlene's temper spiked. It just wasn't fair. The tears sprang from her eyes. Were they motivated by sadness or anger? Arlene wasn't sure and she really didn't care right now. It just wasn't fair.

As she turned to leave the room and give Carl Hagen and every other police officer a piece of her mind, a small little voice whispered the eternal word, "Mom?"

***

Bill hit the floor immediate upon entering the room upstairs! The perp was behind a large desk at the far end of the room. His fire power was, of course, fully equipped and lethal. The room itself was lined with numerous computers monitoring world information; stocks, mineral commodities, banks and the International's conquests. The company was running quite a business here on Colfax Street, Bill assessed. The blue monitors cast an eerie glow on the confrontation area. Each time a stray bullet would hit a monitor, a small explosion would erupt then smoke and then, lights out . The Denver Officers and Jerry were located not far from the stairway entrance. They had not made much progress.

The perp let out a volley of shots at the officers keeping them at bay. Jerry then began to crawl slowly around the perimeter of the room. He wedged himself between the interior wall and the desks. His approach was fairly quiet because of all the constant hum from the computers; Jerry moved slowly. The Denver group began to send off fire as he moved closer to the perp's position then a volley would come from the perp.

Bill decided to send a little more diversion into this drama. If he could add more distraction then this assault might just be over before anyone else got hurt. He leaped six feet over behind another desk close to the center of the room bringing the perp's focus away from Jerry's approach. Three shots from Bill ricocheted off the top of the perp's desk sending large splinters of wood flying through the air. The perp fired back in Bill's direction with equal intensity. The wood chips floated; decisions were in the air.

More cops moving around spelled more trouble for Nick Russel. He hadn't signed on for this shit. He was a computer nerd for God's sake. An illegal nerd, but a computer tech. This mess was way over the top of his job description!

The assault from two different directions meant his surrender was getting near. Surrounded and out numbered had certainly shifted the outcome. It became obvious to Russel that he had two choices. Either commit suicide like his partner or fucking surrender. Nick wondered how many years in prison would he have to serve when he surrendered. Yup, he had decided surrender was the decision. When? Now, that was the question. Could he indeed handle more prison time? It was such a dilemma. He then heard in the distance more sirens approaching. When they arrived, he would be set up for a firing squad by zillions of excited cops! Shit.

One of the Denver Officers voiced this conclusion out loud. There was a long pause as Russel considered.

Jerry was now close enough that he could take this guy if he had to; he waited to see what the perp's decision would be. Seconds ticked away. The silence in the room would not last long, Nick realized. His time was limited.

"I'm coming out," Russel said.

"Throw your guns out on the floor now," Denver demanded. Another pause took place then 'thumps' as the guns began to pile up.

"Coming out with hands up. Don't shot!" Nick Russel slowly rose from behind the desk. His eyes were large and his forehead was sweaty as he allowed himself to become a target.

As Jerry stood up so close to him, Nick was in total shock. Russel had jumped with surprise; he would have been dead shortly he realized. There was no doubt. Jerry's position would have made his escape out the window impossible. His choice was of little satisfaction, however; Nick Russel was screwed anyway he looked at it. Could he make a deal? Maybe there were more options here but if he ratted out on International, they'd kill him in prison. Best to keep his mouth shut for now and see if he could determine what his information would buy him. Witness protection was a slim possibility but his only way out. Get with the feds immediately then go from there. He could help hang International in a court room. Would they see his value as a witness? God, he hoped so. The choices then were isolation in a fucking cell for the rest of his life or witness protection. Fuck!

CHAPTER 26

ACTION!

"Oh Jen honey, you're awake! I am so glad. I was so afraid of what might happen. How do you feel?" Arlene Holly finally took a breath and asked.

"Mom, slow down. My mouth is dry can hardly talk. Can I have water?" Captain Jen Holly asked sending her tongue out of her mouth to explore her crusty lips. Jen then tried to swallow. Her throat was now cleared of tubes but her sore throat was a whopper. The oxygen tube was still stuck up her nose she noticed with displeasure. Waking was not a pleasant experience at this point.

Arlene Holly hit the nurse's button to see what was possible here. She immediately slipped into a mother's nurturing mode, thankful and attentive. Jen could have asked for the world and Arlene would have conquered it!

Betty came into the room wearing a smile when she saw that her patient was awake and cranky. "So how are we doing?" she asked beginning the ritual of checking vital signs.

"Water?" Arlene asked.

"I can do that. Little bit at a time though. Let's make sure that you can keep it down." Betty reached for the pitcher and poured a small amount into the plastic cup with a straw. " Do you know who I am?" she asked hoping that Jen was back both physically and mentally.

Jen drake greedily. The relief of water soothing her throat was good. Not great but good; her throat still was incredibly sore. "Betty Sanders. You're on the wrong floor. This is ICU," Jen processed.

"You're right on all counts. Bix ordered me down here to make sure we treated you correctly. How's it feel to have two mother hens?"

"Overwhelming but wonderful. When did I get here?"

Betty looked at her watch to add up the hours. "You arrived around 2 P.M. and it's now 8 P.M. so six hours give or take. Not long for someone who just had major surgery."

"How am I doing?" Jen asked.

"Not bad at all. Your arm experienced quite a trauma not to mention what any operation does to the whole human body. Plenty of time to rest and get your strength back, young lady," Betty said giving Jen's hand a cordial pat." I'll be back in a little while to check on you. Looks to me like getting you out of ICU could happen this evening." Betty filled Jen's cup up with more water. She handed the water to Arlene, smiled and commented, "Keep her calm and maybe it is about time for a nap. She has to be pretty darn tired at this point."

Arlene took the hint and moved in close to Jen for a little mother-daughter conversation as Betty disappeared out the door. Jen drank more water greedily then let her body relax.

"When did you get here?" she asked Arlene.

"Four hours ago. Chief Hagen brought me over as soon as he heard on the scanner about you. We had an escort from Leadville all the way down I-70. He must have been driving 90 all the way. I've never covered that much ground that quickly before. For a gruff old guy, he sure took care of me. I owe him."

"For the last couple of days, Carl's been a huge help. Carl Hagen was against HAPT. Did you know that?" Arlene shook her head 'no.' Jen continued, "I always figured that the other Chiefs decided to form the unit when the county was missing a Chief in Frisco. That way, they could vote it in without Carl's approval. Funny, Hagen has become my guardian angel. Don't tell him that I said that…he…." Captain Jen Holly fell into a deep calm sleep holding her mother's hand.

It was just like Jen to be thinking about being a cop at this moment. Laying in a hospital bed but still all cop, Arlene thought. She stared down at her daughter's beautiful face; Jen was snoring softly in a deep sleep. A mother really couldn't be more thankful, she admitted.

Arlene's thoughts about yelling at every policeman in the hospital had evaporated. Jen's conversational topic had made her wonder if Jen had, somehow, known how angry Arlene had been earlier. "Impossible," she murmured as she softly moved Jen's hair back under the cap. Yet, what did a critical patient really sense, she wondered? There had to be a place between coma and consciousness where awareness sat listening. The experience had to be incredibly nebulous. Arlene slowly released Jen's hand, tucked the sheet up to her chin then kissed her forehead as mothers do.

It had been a long day. Arlene hoped that the cafeteria was still open. Her body was way overdue for some type of nourishment. Lunch had been eons ago. Arlene had decided to stay at the hospital and keep her daughter company. Tomorrow she could make phone calls and greet reality. Right now the gift of life simply glowed for her. This miracle was all that a mother could ask for in a lifetime. "Thank you, God," she whispered then left the ICU room.

***

"So tell me what you do know," Agent Marshall Tate asked Johnny McPherson as they all sat down on the couches. Libby had slipped out a recorder for the event and done the preliminary police policy information. Now, the time had come for some type of answers. Just how important was this person to the case? Marshall needed to find out so he could report to the FBI front office.

He carefully began the interrogation, "I know that International has been responsible for many of the attacks against you. Will you explain your connection with International Mineral and Recovery Foundation for the record?"

"You will need to know for the record that

Captain Holly promised me that I could remain in my gulch after I testify against International. I will need your verbal confirmation of her promise before we begin. I do not want witness protection after my testimony. The decision must always be mine." Johnny McPherson waited until the FBI Agent contacted his office. The conversation was short; they needed his testimony. What choice did they have?

"Witness Protection will be your choice or not after the trial," Marshall Tate affirmed.

Johnny then began his testimony, "They contacted me in October of last year. It started with them inquiring about purchasing the old McPherson Mine. I was surprised because I didn't know that anyone was interested in my grandfather's mine. I use it for food storage only and have never considered the mineral potential."

Marshall took a few notes then continued, "What did you do next?"

"Naturally, I checked on International to see what the internet could tell me," Johnny offered.

"And what did you find out?" Frank asked then glanced at Marshall for permission to speak. Marshall nodded. It was good question at this point.

"I found out that they were as corrupt as you can get. Their policy was to bully a land owner into selling to them. Hell, it didn't matter how; they just would get the job done. Their tactics were scum."

"What did you do after you got this information," Libby ventured into the interrogation process.

"I politely declined to negotiate with them,"

Johnny answered.

"What was their reaction to your response?" Marshall asked.

"Hell they sniffed around down at the Breckenridge Court House. They learned that I had done a survey years ago. The Registrar's Office did not have a copy which aggravated them to no end."

"How did you come across this information?" Frank asked.

"Why the courthouse called me to chat and wondered who these rude people were. It was a courtesy call only by the way," Johnny added. "Locals get some advantages."

"What happened next?" Libby asked. She couldn't help but lean up at this time. It was getting interesting. Johnny was beginning to fill in the missing pieces.

"They offered me a hell of a lot of money for just the mine. You see, they have a technique that mines out mineral deposits without messing up the biome so they say. Research says that's a joke after you sign on the dotted line. Milt Gray told me that information, by the way. He knew some prospectors over near Durango that had signed and watched these fuckers ruin their property especially the water supply."

"And, what was their response when you rejected their offer?" Marshall asked.

"Well they got nasty and threatened me by saying a refusal could have dire consequences for my family and or Sadie. So at Thanksgiving I warned Martha and Howard about my intentions to donate the gulch to Summit upon my death. Sadie was fine with my decision."

"How about Martha and Howard Carlson's reaction? Let the record show that the Carlsons are Johnny's sister and brother-in-law," Libby stated quickly.

Johnny continued, "They weren't happy but finally understood. I mean Howard figured he was retiring. He did mention that one reason to retire was because he wasn't feeling the love at Slope anymore. He said that they had changed. Did he mention my intentions to Connally? I have no idea."

"Did you agree with him that Slope wasn't all that clean?" Marshall inquired.

"Pretty much so. Connally was really annoyed when I refused to consider his offer for his ski area last summer. I figured it was a bunch of worthless threats until the avalanche. Now, I'm not so sure on that one. The avalanche happened less than a three months later. Who knows?"

"Am I hearing you saying that you think Slope Incorporated was responsible for the avalanche. And that International Mineral Recovery Foundation could be responsible for all, or some, of the other threats on your life?" Agent Tate wanted a clarification of Johnny's testimony at this time.

"I think so. It looks like a double squeeze to me. My Summit property was the single motivation for both companies. My computer analysis just might prove it with a little help from the FBI and HAPT. I'm worth more dead than alive at this point; the gulch is valuable," Johnny finished, "white gold."

***

Jerry and Bill had Thomas Gipple and Nick Russel, two employees of International Mineral and Recovery Foundation, in the back seat of their patrol SUV. They had just hit the Eisenhower Tunnel entrance. The detectives had turned down the scanner information except when something about Captain Jen's condition would come on. They had been monitoring her condition since their departure from Denver.

As they left the tunnel, Bill got a text message from Libby informing them about how the interrogation was going. He quickly texted Libby back about the appearance of Nick Russel. Bill had been checking out who the guy was from the Police Data Bank. This Nick Russel had a half sister named Sadie; they were estranged from each other according to the information. So the plot had thickened. Bill finished his text with advice, 'Call Chief Anderson concerning Sadie immediately. Need to transport.'

"Excuse me for a second," Libby said then moved out of the office into the hallway to call Chief Anderson. "Chief, this is Libby. Detective Smith said that I need to connect you?"

"Yes. I have just sent Officer Trout to Sadie Russel's job location. He is ten minutes out and will bring her back. We have checked and she is at work today. I assume that you have heard who her brother just happens to be?"

"Shall I mention Nick Russel to Johnny and see if he knows anything at this point?"

"Handle it carefully and the answer is yes." Chief Josh Anderson ordered. "Be subtle for now do you read?"

"Absolutely, sir," Libby answered. The police simply wanted the connection piece verified. No more at this time. Libby understood completely. She disconnected then moved back into the room. She was careful not to alarm Marshall and Frank now. Her face became a total blank.

Thomas Gipple had babbled all the way to Summit County. He was full of threats about any kind of arrest. Bill and Jerry were getting pretty sick of listening to the guy.

"You people will hear from International! They do not take lightly to the arrest of their employees let me tell you. I want a lawyer immediately! Your actions border on kidnapping. I am being detained against my will. There will be a lawsuit," Gipple sputtered. He nervously twisted his hands. Gipple's cigarette addiction had begun to make him jiggery. The man just couldn't stop talking.

Bill texted Libby that they were 15 minutes from the office. He couldn't get out of the car any sooner. Gipple was absolute spooky.

Jerry just drove concentrating on the road. Somehow, he was able to tune the idiot out for now. Gipple's comments were being recorded. That was enough, Jerry assessed. Let it be.

***

Captain Jen Holly awoke to find herself in an empty hospital room. At least she was out of ICU.

The beeping had stopped. The lights were low and the door was open slightly. She peered into the hallway and was able to hear hushed voices.

What had happened in the case so far? Had they picked up the suspects who had shot her? The questions began reeling through her head. She looked around on the cart near her to see if her phone was there. Nope. Jen figured that the nurses had been instructed to keep her quiet. Shit.

Jen hit the nurse call button. Maybe she could figure out how to get hold of her phone. Betty's head peeked in the door. Ah, you're awake. Want some more water? No food until tomorrow morning are the instructions." Betty began taking the vitals and then glanced at Jen. She knew. "Would you like to see your mother? She is out in the waiting area. I could go get her?"

"That would be great or maybe I could call her on my phone to save you a trip?" Jen ventured.

"Good luck with that one, young lady. You know the worst patients are doctors and cops. Ain't gonna work. Been there and done that before. No phone at least not tonight. Sleep is your call, young lady. I'll go and locate your mom." Betty left the room having won the first battle.

***

"Should we keep a police officer outside of Milt Gray's home in Leadville tonight?" Agent Marshall Tate asked. "Do you believe him to be in any danger?"

Johnny thought for a moment weighing the

question carefully. "If possible, I'd say that isn't a bad idea. Whoever is after me does realize that I have left Leadville but who knows. Please do keep Milt safe," Johnny requested.

Libby was also beginning to understand the potential threat surrounding their witnesses and suspects. "How about Sadie? Is Sadie safe, do you think?" Libby asked.

Marshall and Frank watched closely for Johnny McPherson's reaction and answer.

"I don't see any reason that she wouldn't be," Johnny answered. "I have intentionally kept her out of the situation as best that I could. She works for a company that isn't involved as far as I know. I checked them out at the beginning of this mess. I couldn't find any connection."

"Could it be possible that there is someone in Sadie's life that could be involved other than her company? Say… a relative or anyone she is close to in some way," Libby carefully asked. "Any family members involved in computers?"

Marshall and Frank watched Libby maneuver into the new information.

"No, why? What are you getting at?" Johnny asked. Sadie's parents are in Florida and totally retired. She has no sisters or brothers as far as I know. So what are you thinking?"

"Just the general questions that police need to ask," Libby hedged. "We certainly wouldn't want to leave anyone out who needs protection. Surely you can see our concern." Johnny nodded. He seemed satisfied for now, Libby assessed.

At this time Frank Mason began to sense it was

time for a break. Maybe a good night's sleep for all. "Would it be possible for Johnny to stay at my house this evening since it is getting late? We can finish this interrogation tomorrow? Maybe a couple of police cars stationed near my house would do?" So that's the way they left it.

Bill and Jerry were to head to Breckenridge and do their interrogations there tonight. It was advised that Johnny's interview continue tomorrow after any new information could be obtained from Thomas Gipple and Nick Russel. Johnny McPherson would be safe for the rest of the evening. The police escort to Frank's house arrived shortly after and gathered them up.

As Libby stared at the two men leaving she had to admit that they did look like brothers. Seemed like the only coincidence in the entire case, she mused. Well, it was over for tonight, she thought.

Both, Libby and Marshall suddenly realized that they had been left alone. Tonight, was all secure; tomorrow, would be another day. The evening dusk was beginning to settled in over Frisco. It had become oddly quiet; the town would sleep soundly.

CHAPTER 27

KABOOM!

As Libby unlocked her patrol SUV the silence loomed between them. Marshall's eyes darted from the door handle to Libby. He got in slowly and began to feel his pulse rising.

"Where are you staying?" Libby asked as her hand froze on the ignition switch. Her nerves were frayed from the day's events yet she felt a new surge of anxiety hit her at this moment. It was all about Marshall she had no doubt.

"The motel near I-70, Antler something," he said. Marshall pointed straight ahead. Funny, but I can't even remember the name of it. Been a long day."

"Yes it has," Libby offered. Her tongue was tied. The attraction between the two had been overwhelming today. Libby realized that she had used him for strength when the action went south. Reality had become linked with their intimacy if that is what you could call, holding hands. It felt mental too; he was in her head. She drove the car slowly out of the parking lot and headed for his motel.

Parting really felt terrible to her right now. "You want me to pick you up tomorrow morning for the interrogation?" she asked. Right now it was a pretty lame question in her mind but she couldn't think of anything else to say. Maybe he needed time to call a girlfriend and assure her that he was all right. Maybe he needed to conduct business with the FBI. Hell, maybe he just needed some space since he had dropped in. He had fallen out of the sky and found her immediately. People did need time to adjust, good or bad.

Marshall couldn't stop glancing at Libby. He was trying to memorize everything about her. The way her hands touched the steering wheel, the quirky smile on her incredible lips, her red curly hair that never seemed out of place and her warm deep voice that surprised him each time he heard it.

He had never been this attracted to someone before. His life had been filled with women who were compromises. Marshall had to literally convince himself that he had been in love with them. But Libby, God it was overpowering! He knew nothing about her except that he wanted to know everything. There were so many questions that they needed to ask each other yet right this moment, it didn't matter. He wanted Libby more than anything he had ever wanted; he wanted her now. His body was on overdrive.

"Here?" she asked in a whisper as she drove into the motel parking lot. Her voice felt weak; her heart was pounding so loud that she could hardly hear anything else. Libby turned off the motor, tried to breathe and turned toward him, waiting.

There was an incredible long pause that deepened as these two human beings sorted out the next move. Libby began to fall into his incredibly deep blue eyes. The intensity was like an electric shock, warm and almost spiritual for her. What was he feeling she wondered? Did they both feel the same way? Would they find out?

Marshall suddenly pulled Libby into his arms. He felt the warmth of her body as her arms tightened around his neck. He pulled back slightly so that he could search her countenance. It felt right. His fingers traced Libby's beautiful lips then he kissed her, exploring the depths. The explosion rocked both of them; darkness and warmth all at the same time. Tongues diving deeper. Marshall had never been so attracted with such force as he felt now. Her smell was incredible. He was home opening the door of a warm familiar place; his body became totally alive.

Neither one of these people could talk. They stared into each other's eyes trying to cope with what had just happened. Marshall pulled himself out of the car and came over to the driver's door. He opened the door and offered her his hand . Libby took his hand as she had done all day without any hesitation. It was such a simple gesture yet said so much. Marshall pulled her out and walked toward his room; the distance felt like miles as they approached a new beginning without a word of explanation. The key gave way to intensity.

***

"Okay catheter out, young lady. You will now need to start moving around," Betty stated. The door had been closed but now she opened it. "Kindly, take it easy today," Nurse Betty Sanders said as she organized her paraphernalia. "You will become tired easily and that is to be expected. That left arm will be painful even though you have a cast; pain takes a lot of energy to combat. Do not overdue, young lady," Betty pointed a warning index finger in Jen's direction.

How many times had Jen's mother, Arlene, done that same gesture? Too funny, she thought. Visons surfaced from her memory. Nurturing was such a part of life, she reasoned.

"Now, I was wondering if you'd like to take a couple steps over to that chair before I leave?" Betty inquired pointing in the direction of the chair.

It looked like four steps, Jen figured. "Okay..." she said then rotated her legs to the side of the bed too quickly. Unfortunately, she had bumped her cast slightly on the bed frame. The pain exploded; stars burst into Jen's vision! Her body yelled as she winced in shock while her head went dizzy. Jen tried to collect herself. It was going to be a long recovery she knew in that moment.

"You okay?" Betty asked offering support on the right side of her body.

"I think so," Jen whispered. She lifted her weight from the bed and stood carefully. Her feet began to move in little tiny steps. Betty was good support. Well, maybe it was going to more than four steps. Ten steps later, Jen was seated in the chair She closed her eyes and then realized that Betty was still there watching her closely. "Think I'll sit here awhile before heading back to bed," Jen said exhausted.

"Good plan," Betty nodded. "I'll be back in ten minutes and we can journey back to bed then. Okay?"

"Sounds like a deal," Jen mumbled allowing her eyes to close." When she opened them again, Betty was gone. Jen relaxed in the chair, eyes closed. Well, it was obviously going to be a long physical comeback but there was nothing wrong with her mind.

Jen began to wade through all the information that she knew about the case. Her eyes popped open when she realized that she needed the recent reports about police actions. Where was her phone? Her bet was that she would find it in the pocket of her pants which were in the closet.

Jen, carefully, pulled herself out of the chair and shuffled her way to the closet. Her body had learned how to avoid moving her left shoulder so no stars. Dizziness, yes; she waited until it all cleared. With her right hand she opened the closet door and felt in the pocket of her pants. Yes, there it was! All right then she rejoiced. It was a small victory but it really felt great. Jen then slowly shut the closet and shuffled off to bed.

The call to Frank ordering her laptop and other reports was such a relief. She could function now and that was incredibly important to her recovery.

Jen hid her phone under a pillow just like she had done during her teenage years. She couldn't help but punch the pain button to get some relief now. Captain Jen Holly made a mental note to avoid pain medication as much as she could. However in defense now, Jen's journey across the room felt like she had climbed a mountain. Jen allowed herself a nap as her reward. A smile remained on her face as she slept soundly.

Two hours later Arlene, looking refreshed, entered her daughter's room. She had talked with Betty before entering and had gotten encouraging news. Now, her job was to put the brakes on Jen's activities. Both older women had sensed that Jen could be a very difficult patient. Arlene smiled remembering how Jen had handled an occasional sick day when she was in high school. Her idea of getting well was reading an entire book then going out to play baseball! Lordy!

"Hi Mom," Jen mumbled coming out of her sound sleep. Her eyes felt heavy as focus returned.

"Well hello. I hear you had quite a morning and I think maybe more activity than Nurse Sanders thought." Arlene lifted a laptop and folders into view. "Frank came by about 30 minutes ago. He said that you had ordered this information over the phone?"

"Well there's nothing wrong with my head," Jen said trying to justify the behavior. "Besides, you know how I am."

"Yes I do and this injury is far more serious than sniffles in high school! Honey, you could have fallen and ended up flying to Denver for surgery if the wound had reopened. Think about it as you're taking solo flights around this room. It's damn dangerous and you know it," Arlene said not being able to keep all the anxiety out of her voice. Her concern was real and justified.

Kaboom. Jen suddenly did realize how stupid her choice had been. She used more responsible choices when she had climbed than what she had done this morning. She needed that arm for the rest of her life! What in the hell had she been thinking or maybe not thinking. "I'm sorry, Mom. It was stupid as can be. It's just so frustrating to find myself in here when I should be out with the team."

Arlene moved closer and took Jen's hand. "I understand but your health is on the line; your life is on the line for heaven's sake," Arlene said softly. "I am aware that all your life you have ignored illness. Denial helps you handle recovery but this isn't a mere cold; this is a hospital where people go when their life is threatened. Now, shall we compromise? Go ahead and use this computer but if you need to move out of that bed, you call a nurse or me?"

"I can do that. I promise." Jen held out her good hand to get possession. There was a lot of evidence to catch up on and she knew that her research could make a difference. Someone had to get back to basics and make sure that their actions weren't being manipulated by other entities. Focus was the key in her mind and she was determined to help solve this case.

Arlene hesitated then sat the laptop and folders on the bed. "Do not overdue even your head. Your team seems to be working just fine." Arlene pointed at Jen in motherly fashion and said, "Now mind!"

"Yes, ma'am." Jen smiled as her mother walked out of the room. Her mother had been right and Jen would honor her promise. Reading had, however, always been part of her healing process. That, would never change. Jen had the strength to read and, eventually, she would heal. It was her routine.

***

"All right, Russel, you know that you're facing jail time so stop the fucking whining. You were caught red handed working for International Mineral and Recovery Foundation illegally hacking your sister's emails then you began shooting at the police. Do you really think that we're going to buy any bullshit about this company made you do it? People do it. Those are the choices," Bill yelled pushing Nick Russel with his aggressive index finger.

"All right! Yes, I was working in a sort of sketchy area but it doesn't make me guilty. Yes, I did resist arrest but that's all!" Russel said withering lower into his chair.

"Not that easy," Jerry commented. "Resisting arrest is probably the least of your worries right now. Are you aware that International is about to be taken down by the feds? Yeah that's right. We have one of their agents right here in town. He is ready to take you back to DC. All hell is going to break out at your company. You can either confess to us or end up dead."

"What do you mean by that?" Nick jerked alert in his chair. His situation was beginning to dawn on him.

"You think the Foundation will keep you alive when they figure out that you are such a weak son of a bitch? A top notch lawyer will come in and cover up the Foundation's involvement then use you as a scapegoat. I have no doubt that down the line before you testify, an accident will happen in prison. Nick Russel will no longer be alive to testify. You're bound for a casket."

"That's crazy. I'm just a small player in all of this mess. Surely they can realize that? I don't have any information about their dealings. I have no value!" he yelled.

"Our thoughts exactly, Nick," Bill said. "You are a small link that is disposable. You are a throw away item."

The silence in the room fell onto Nick's shoulders like a heavy load of bricks. The Foundation really didn't need him. They did need that old fart, Gipple, but Nick's situation was different. Gipple could afford to wait for a lawyer; he could wait and not talk with the police. Russel, however, realized at this juncture how precarious his situation was. Turn state's evidence and plead out was definitely an option. "Let me think," he mumbled.

"Seems like it's a no brainer to me," Bill stated. Bill could feel Russel beginning to understand his role in this whole case. Nick was definitely a weak link. His situation could be pleaded out and then he could end up in witness protection. It wasn't right but the little worm did have incriminating evidence to share. Hell of a world when you could shoot at cops then end up with a whole new life instead of jail."

Jerry got it. He knew exactly what was expected of them. Get the little shit to comply and turn state's evidence. It was time to serve him a spoon full of sugar here. "Think about it, Nick. You do have value. It just happens to be with the feds and local police. Our department needs to implicate the Foundation's attempts on Johnny McPherson's life. We have a case to solve. If you help us, we can help you get protection. Is it a deal?"

Both officers sat back in their chairs hardly breathing. They could open this fucking case up right now!

***

Libby tore off Marshall's shirt and felt her hands exploring his chest then sliding down caressing his slender waist. Her hands, like magnets, found his penis, warm and erect. She let out a yelp.

Marshall had moved them toward the bed while scarching out every inch of her breasts. Her shirt and bra were tossed on the floor. Their guns were piled in a heap on the only chair in the room. His hands had frisk the guns off both of them with methodical speed. Now his reward was Libby's firm breasts. Marshall's body had exploded into fireworks. He let out a huge moan that filled the room with his need. Her touch so warm.

Marshall then tore off Libby's pants as quickly as he could. They now stood naked clamping their bodies together as if there was nowhere else to be. They both became aware of the moment; the intimacies of each other's flesh. They fit; it was incredible.

Libby melted down onto the bed as Marshall lowered his body. He was on top of her; his eyes penetrated into her heart. Libby had never felt this much energy; their closeness had thrown away all hesitation. He was her life right now in this moment.

Marshall memorized her body as he searched each inch. His lips kissed away doubt and celebrated with approval . God, he approved and loved. This woman was more than he had even expected. It was passed making love on the surface; he was ready to go deeper. Deeper into her moist warm being. He wanted to fall into this person and never come out again. To stay held by her arousal; to be captured in this miracle. Marshall's penis slowly began to penetrate Libby. They moved gently at first. Positioned their bodies together; it was so important and so amazing.

Suddenly, Marshall needed to go deeper and faster. They moaned together in pure ecstasy. Libby was welcoming him deeper and faster. Deeper....Kaboom!

***

"All right then what do you want to know?"

Nick Russel said with resignation. "Let me say that I want to be protected from the Foundation. I know how powerful they can be. I want to live, damn it."

"That can be arranged," said Bill ready to break the case open like a ripe melon. "Keep in mind that your interrogation will be recorded for the use of both HAPT and the FBI. How much you reveal, can and will, determine how the government decides to protect you on down the line. You have HAPT's full cooperation here in Summit County."

"First of all, HAPT would be very interested in your sister's involvement in the case," said Jerry.

"My sister? What in the hell are you talking about?" Nick Russel said in defense.

"We have uncovered the fact that Sadie Russel is, indeed, your sister. It is obvious that she is in a relationship with Johnny McPherson. Surely you two have talked about him in detail," Jerry pushed.

"All right," Nick said throwing his hands up in the air. "I hacked her fucking computer. Okay!" An expression of resignation fell across his face.

Bill began to feel how important this testimony could be. What an incredible high Bill allowed himself to admit; opening up any case was definitely a rush. Jerry was positively beaming. The atmosphere in the room had become electric. Almost as good as sex Bill reconnoitered but not quite. Kaboom!

CHAPTER 28

BACK TO BASICS

As Arlene opened Jen's door early next morning, she found herself walking into a HAPT meeting, snacks and all. Her daughter was in bed sitting upright; the officers had circled the bed for the meeting. Chairs had been brought in from the waiting room, Arlene surmised. "Oh excuse me. See you later Jen," she said then shut the door quietly.

Betty found her a few minutes later. The two ladies really couldn't say anything. Both shook their heads and smiled. Betty, feeling like it was her fault, finally said, "I couldn't stop it. Suddenly, here were all these officers on the floor knocking at her door. She was sitting in bed, like a good girl, ready to lead the meeting. Who would have thought it?'

"I should have known," Arlene admitted. "Oh well. I'm off to shop. I don't get over to Summit that often and I'd like to stick my nose in a couple art galleries over here. I'll be back later."

"I don't blame you. Have fun." The ladies

adjourned.

Captain Holly waited until the door had closed then continued, "Finish Johnny McPherson's testimony today, Frank. Have we put an APB out on Sadie Russel yet?" she asked looking around the room.

"Did that first thing this morning. Denver Police will deliver her as far as Idaho Springs around 11 today. Who do you want me to send down to get her?" Frank asked.

"Libby, why don't you head down and bring her up for a visit? I think that approach might be less intimidating."

"Yes, Captain. Who should I contact in Denver to make the connections?" Libby asked.

"Get the information from Frank. Frank, make sure that I know exactly how the connection is going," Jen added. "Are we all right with having our meetings here until I am dismissed?"

The team nodded. Agent Marshall Tate then said, "I will be contacting my boss within the next hour for my FBI report. "The FBI will, of course, need to gather up all these people for testimonies and protection fairly soon. I will advise my office that all suspects at this time are safe and needed here, just so you know. I would like to be in on the McPherson interview again today. I assume that is all right?"

"Excellent," Jen said encouraging Marshall. "Team, I have one request to ask today. I would like you to arrange for Russel and McPherson to pass each other in some hallway. I want to know if there is any recognition whatsoever. Secondly, what is the Dante Gulch's suspect's name?"

Frank supplied the answer to that question from his notes. "He is one Jim Hailey. Bill says he's the same guy who hit him at the diner in Idaho Springs. So that ties those two events together. Unfortunately, he is not ready to interrogate yet. The doctors say it will be at least 36 hours. Specialist did extensive work on that leg yesterday. We have Frisco Officers outside of his hospital door since he arrived."

"Okay, so let's divide up the suspects like this," Jen continued. "Libby, bring Sadie to the Breckenridge Police Station for her testimony. Jerry, will you be the second officer on that interrogation? Marshall, after the McPherson interview, will you and Bill try your hand with Thomas Gipple? I figure you two would know his profile better than anyone else. Bill, spend some time reviewing your last discussion with Gipple then review Slope's involvement for later."

Jen then concentrated on Jerry. "Maybe you could help Bill before the Gipple testimony this morning, Jerry?"

"Done," Jerry said feeling glad to be included. He did like the efficiency of HAPT. Things got done on schedule over here.

"Anyone have any problems with the day's assignments so far?" Jen asked. The room was silent.

"And Frank, I want you to arrange the little drama with Russel and McPherson somehow after Marshall is done with Johnny. Also, get complete details from McPherson about his meeting last Fall with Slope's boss, Walter Connally. Please record that session and bring it to me. Oh, and everyone today, make sure that you mention Jim Hailey during your interrogations and watch for a reaction of some sort there."

Frank was the first to ask the question that everyone was beginning to wonder. "Captain Jen, can I ask what you're thinking here?"

"After reading all the files, my gut feeling is that Johnny is correct. International Mineral and Recovery Foundation is not behind the avalanche but is involved in the survey crimes. Slope Incorporated arranged for the avalanche by hiring Eric Calvin. We have an avalanche arranged to kill Johnny in December; months later, the mineral survey became the target. The only common denominator is the value of McPherson Gulch known by these money grabbing companies.

I want to know if Sadie helped her half-brother or not and, was she involved with either company? Sadie's interrogation now becomes incredibly important. And Frank, get that reading on Nick Russel and Johnny. Has Johnny McPherson ever seen Sadie's half-brother, Nick Russel, before is very important? That's a huge question in my mind. Back to basics, ladies and gentlemen. Convince me one way or the other here."

Nurse Betty Sanders could have heard a pin drop as she entered Jen Holly's room. The officers were obviously processing something; it was your typical pregnant pause, Betty thought. Yup, it looked like a bomb had been dropped. Well…well….

Betty then went ahead with her routine and said,

"Time for meds, Captain Holly. Please remember that you are a patient in a hospital after major surgery. I hate to adjourn the meeting but this patient is my responsibility and the hospital is my boss. Can you meet later, Frank?" Betty said taking control.

"Hell of an idea. We got our orders. Meeting adjourned," he said. The officers, carrying their chairs, trooped out of the room.

Jen began to beam with satisfaction as she stared at the closing door; the meeting had gone well. Her leadership had been tested; the compromise successful. Jen concluded that maybe life didn't always give you what you wanted but life could supply what was needed. Betty watched Jen come back to the present as she held the dreaded cup of pills. With a smug satisfied expression, Jen tossed the pills down with water. It was nap time. Good.

***

"Well, that was a surprise," said Marshall as he and Bill headed off to interrogate Thomas Gipple. I wasn't here for the avalanche but it did start there, didn't it?"

"Sure did and none of us were there. At that time there wasn't any HAPT and there wasn't a Captain Jen. The incident was handled by the Leadville Police Department. So yeah, there is a huge gap," Bill said unlocking his car. "We came into the avalanche picture when Frank got shot. The cold case then became an active murder case with a sharpshooter named Eric Calvin. He then would be later found in McCoy Gulch camping."

"That's the suspect that flew off the cliff? The guy Captain Holly pursued? Right?" Marshall asked.

"One in the same. We thought at the time that he was internationally hired. However, evidence shows that he worked out of the United States. He was expensive to hire so companies used him, we had decided. I'd say very professional and oh so invisible."

"I'll send his name through the FBI Databank," Marshall added.

Bill was damn happy that the feds were cooperating and helping. "Eric Calvin is all that we have so far. It may not even be his real name. Haven't gone deeper yet due to all the activity," Bill added. They had just entered the Summit County Jail parking lot. Bill turned off the motor and stared for a second. "Wonder if Thomas Gipple of International would know Calvin? We haven't established who he worked for if we follow the Captain's thinking. Calvin is an unknown commodity. Captain Jen would like to find that he was hired by Slope Incorporated."

"Does open up a whole new concept, doesn't it?" Marshall said looking at Bill. They then proceeded to map out their strategy.

Bill texted the team and reminded them to try Eric Calvin's name during interrogations today. Somewhere along the way, someone should show recognition. Calvin was a loose end right now and needed to fit in one of the schemes, mineral or ski area. Which would it be?

***

Officer Libby James checked the text as she pulled into Idaho Springs and waited for the Denver Police. Eric Calvin, Bill Hailey and Nick Russel were now the surviving hired criminals. The question was who hired each one, relatives or companies? It was getting interesting, Libby thought. Actually at this point, Sadie Russel needed to be placed on their suspect list. Libby texted everyone that thought.

The Captain had sure opened up the whole can of worms in their meeting. At least no one could say that HAPT had become focused on too few alternatives. It was a wide open case at this time. Actually, it wasn't even a murder case anymore but attempted murder. "Wow," Officer James mumbled. The surprises just kept piling up, Libby realized.

Her personal life was also wide open. Libby couldn't believe how Agent Marshall Tate had changed everything. He had become such a force in her heart in such a short amount a time. She had to keep her perspective somehow. Marshall would be heading back to Washington soon; that, unfortunately, was a fact. Their professional and personal lives were so different. Libby had always been an outdoor girl. City living had never appealed to her; the mountains had always brought her strength. Now, her needs were changing.

Would Marshall ever consider relocating? People either fell in love with the mountains or moved away. Libby had watched friends try to settle into the mountains. Friends either adjusted and discovered that their health improved or they ended up on oxygen with trouble eating and sleeping.

Exercise had always been Libby's solution. She couldn't go to gyms with their low ceilings; viewing the sky was her forte. When Libby got home from work each night, she always went for a hike then settled into her evening. Computers were part of her life but she made sure that it was a balanced life. Nowadays, one could be a computer tech and live up here most of the time. No, moving to the city had never been an option that worked for her. She had intentionally chosen her lifestyle and job. "Wow," she murmured for the second time.

Nevertheless, her pulse now elevated every time she looked at Marshall. Was that enough emotion to even think about change? They both had futures in their own environments and professions. Did Marshall love the city and was he totally drawn to that life style like Libby was drawn to in the mountains? Their professional goals were such a giant hurdle. Could she adjust to the city life and work there? It was quite a dilemma, Libby reconnoitered. "Slow down, girl," she told herself. Their relationship was so new and wonderful. Why spoil it with a dose of reality, Libby told herself. Enjoy the moment she half heartedly decided.

The Denver Patrol Car pulled into the parking lot. She could see Sadie in the back seat. Miss Russel looked worried and conflicted. By this time, Sadie had found out that Johnny McPherson was alive. Speaking of conflicting lifestyles. You had a flatlander and a mountain man trying to make a-go of it. Libby began to wonder if she could gleam some perspective from these two. How many years had they dated? Seemed like she had read five years. Libby could visualize the huge amount of computer communications that had transpired between the two. Difficult? Yes.

"Officer James?" said the Policeman tapping on her window.

Libby came back to the present and hit the window button. "Hello. I am here to transfer one Sadie Russel to Summit County," she said.

"Do you mind if I take down your badge number and verify who you are? Captain Holly called us to make sure that this move was correct."

Libby showed him her badge and sat tight while he put it into the computer for verification. Captain Jen sure wasn't going to take any chances. They needed this lady to make it to Summit. Libby began to realize that the trip back home could be dangerous in more ways than one. Her awareness level peaked as Sadie Russel was delivered into the backseat of her SUV.

"You're cleared, thanks for waiting. Looks like this case has really got you guys going," the officer said.

"You got that right," Libby replied.

"Want us to follow you as far as the Eisenhower Tunnel? It's a beautiful day and a scenic ride wouldn't hurt," he offered.

"That would be great," Libby answered with zero hesitation. The two cars started west with no lights or sirens. They looked like a speed patrol monitoring I-70.

Libby settled back into her seat and then checked out Sadie in her mirror. She wanted to put the lady in a more relaxed mood. Right now Sadie looked nervous as hell. Captain Jen had given her the order to not intimidate Sadie. So far her ride had been definitely intimidating.

"So were you shocked to hear that Johnny was alive?" Libby asked.

"Relieved is the word that I would use. I can't imagine having to hide out for six months in fear," Sadie added. "Poor Johnny."

"By the way, I'm Libby James. Sure glad that this situation could work out for you two. I can't imagine the circumstances. I'm just starting a relationship where distance could make a huge difference. I can't imagine…."

"Neither could I at first. Johnny and I finally adjusted to our distant lives. We figured it would work out as I got ready to retire. We'd see each other every other weekend. The computer email took the edge off of our frustrations. Then the avalanche destroyed us. Now all of this…." Sadie's voice trailed off softly. "Am I under arrest?" she asked. "The Denver Policemen wouldn't say. I would like to know."

Libby smiled and then offered, "Not as far as I know. There has been some extenuating circumstances however."

"Well, that's good news." Sadie processed the information closely. "What circumstances?" Her eyes explored Libby's expression in the rearview mirror.

"We wondered if you knew Bill Hailey or Eric Calvin?" Libby casually asked.

"They don't sound familiar. The names really don't ring a bell," Sadie said.

Libby pulled the pictures up on the computer screen in the front seat. "Do they look familiar?"

Sadie leaned up and concentrated. Nope. Never seen either one of those guys. Sorry." She leaned back then added. "Should I?"

"No. We could always hope though. It was a long shot," Libby said with a sigh.

"Is that all that's new? I mean you could have asked me in Denver about those two."

"Well, there is another suspect who has been arrested in this case. Nick Russel." Libby's eyes focused on Sadie.

The shock registered. Sadie's face paled as her body went rigid. "You mean my half-brother?"

Libby nodded and kept quiet.

"I was adopted by his father. At the time it was a nice gesture but not so nice now. Nick has been in and out of jail. I truly haven't seen him for at least eight years. After my parents retired, I completely lost track of him. That decision was my choice."

Sadie's eyes stared out the window lost in old thoughts, Libby surmised. "Did you know where he worked?" she asked carefully.

"I had heard that he had become a hired hack some years ago. My parents said that he'd work for any company who had a shady reputation," she added.

"How so?" asked Libby.

"Greed is the best way to say it. Strong

companies who would muscle their way into illegal activities for profit. Reputable companies knew Nick's reputation and wouldn't hire him." Sadie nodded then directly looked at Libby again. "Please don't tell me that Nick's involved in all of this? Surely he wouldn't. Nick has never ever met Johnny. How would he know anything about my situation? I haven't seen him for years. This can't be happening." Sadie's face went red in frustration and anger as a thought occurred to her. "Don't tell me that I have been hacked!"

Libby could actually feel both emotions filling the car. Sadie was in a tailspin trying to process the possibilities. The topic had shaken her completely. Nick's involvement was obviously something Sadie had not considered. Libby was of the persuasion to believe her. That being said, Sadie's half-brother was actually sitting in a jail cell now. "Are you sure that Johnny has never met Nick?" Libby inquired.

"God no. I don't think that I have ever mentioned Nick to Johnny. I figured that Nick was out of my life for good. It just didn't seem important at this point," Sadie finished. "It's been almost a decade since I've seen him. He never really was part of my life before. I was ten years older than him."

"Could Nick Russel have gotten enough data about you to hack your personal computer?" Libby asked.

All the history came rushing back into Sadie's memory. Her parents anguish and embarrassment as they fought their prodigal son. Sadie gave up more of the story to Libby without hesitating. "Nick was

a very talented computer genius. I can remember
him trying his hand at hacking into companies many
years ago. My parents got to the point that they took
away his computer. Lot of good that did. I had left
for college and came home one Christmas to hear
about my half-brother's antics. He was on
probation and into drugs. Never saw him that year
or ever again. We all washed our hands of Nick.

Distance helped me keep away from Nick's
problems. My parents moved away to Florida and I
was off working in Colorado. The stress that he had
brought into the house was horrendous. We all
escaped except Nick."

"Would he know where you're working now?"
Libby asked.

"He could, I suppose. Especially if he wanted
to find out or was ordered by someone. "Shit,"
Sadie moaned. The whole concept became clear to
her. "Then he could have learned from our
communication all the information that any
company would need to know. Everybody would
know that Johnny McPherson was donating his
property. My entire relationship with Johnny could
have been violated." Sadie digested all the
implications. Her very private world was suddenly
becoming public. The courts would dig and reveal.

There was a long pause as both ladies realized
the implications. In one way it was all good. HAPT
could clear Sadie but her relationship with Johnny
might just be in shambles. Libby pulled over to the
side of the road at the tunnel then waved as the
Denver Police turned around and headed back to
Denver. She then opened the door of the SUV and

got in the backseat with Sadie.

"Sadie, I want to clear you if I can. I am going to have to ask you for your computer right now before we go any further." Libby took Sadie's hands to soften the request. Sadie would have to trust Libby or find a lawyer quickly. Libby continued her explanation, "You need to decide if you want me to get a warrant before I open it or simply allow me to investigate so I can prove that Nick hacked it. That's a lot of trust to offer a stranger I know. I just don't see any other alternative. If not me then the courts."

Sadie stared at Libby intensely. "Can you keep Johnny and my relationship somewhat private?" she asked. "I realize that I must shoulder this blame in what has happened. Nick Russel is involved because of me. I need to take that responsibility," Sadie added. Tears fell from her eyes.

Libby could see the sadness and anguish surface. Sadie was feeling the weight of circumstances that were beyond her control. Libby could only hope that it would work out for them. White gold was the motive not their relationship. It simply had just happened.

Officer Libby James began cautiously, "All I can say is that I can try to preserve some privacy for you. Once this case goes to court, I then will have no control. The DA might be satisfied with using only what I offer them. However, legally, your emails are all evidence. Having said that, your compliance might create some restraint on their part.

Now with a warrant all bets are off. The

prosecution would classify you as a hostile witness. The court could decide to try you as an accessory to the crime. Of course they would have to prove that but they could try. Sadie, we're at the crossroads here where you must be read your rights before you say another word. You can ask for a lawyer right now and we can then talk about the weather for the rest of the trip. That's fine by me; it is the law. Libby then did read Sadie her rights and finished with the age old question, "Do you understand these rights?"

"Yes." Sadie said never taking her eyes from Libby's face; she then handed over her computer. "The password is McPherson's Tunnel 2010."

***

"So when did you hire Eric Calvin?" Agent Marshall Tate asked Thomas Gipple. Tate then ventured into a clarification, "Since we're still waiting for your lawyer, we could get some preliminary information out of the way, Mr. Gipple."

"Who's Eric Calvin? Never heard of him. God I need a cigarette. You have any?" Thomas Gipple asked almost shivering from addiction.

"Nope," Detective Bill Smith answered. "But maybe if you were a little cooperative, I could see if one of the guys out there has one?" It was blackmail by smoke but fair, Bill surmised.

"Then go fetch me a cigarette," Gipple snarled.

While Bill went to find a smoke, Marshall began to press for answers. "Then you knew Eric

Calvin?"

Gipple's hand made a 'v' for cigarette as he sat silently.

Bill returned with the contraband and a lighter. Gipple lit the cigarette and inhaled deeply until he began to cough. After the nicotine reached his lungs, Thomas Gipple's whole body seemed to relax. "I've never heard of Calvin. International had no one on the payroll named Eric Calvin. Sorry," he finished with a smirk of satisfaction.

"How then did your company orchestrate the avalanche?" Bill inquired.

"Very simple, we didn't. That little splash of news worthy information was way before our time. The newspaper article was interesting though. It got us thinking."

The door suddenly opened and a dark suited lawyer entered without any introduction. He tossed a pack of cigarettes on the table for Gipple and sat down. Gipple grabbed the smokes lightning fast and secured them in his pocket. "We'll need some privacy to organize our thoughts," the lawyer announced.

Bill and Marshall then left the room. They both headed toward the coffee. How did the lawyer time his entry so perfectly, they wondered?

"Okay so if that's true then we do have two separate crimes like the Captain thinks," Bill reasoned as he sat down and added cream to his coffee.

"Sounds like it. If one can believe that nicotine can make someone confess. I am likely to believe that," Marshall added. "Sounds like it was easy for him, especially, if there wasn't any connection."

"Yep," Bill said. "So what happened with Johnny McPherson this morning?"

"He also believes that the two crimes weren't done by the same company. He went into detail about someone setting off avalanches; it sounded pretty damn technical to me. You don't just hire someone but you get a specialist and no, he did not recognize Eric Calvin's picture."

"What did he think would motivate someone to want him dead?" Bill asked.

"The announcement that Summit Open Areas was getting his property was his bet. The first announcement happened during the Thanksgiving family event. However, it was hard for him to think that his sister just might be involved. He just couldn't see it. And no, he didn't have any information about Nick Russel either."

"Interesting. Did he think Sadie Russel was involved?"

"No. She really didn't want to be involved in that family business, Johnny said. She really hated talking about wills. They had decided to take out a life insurance policy for each other and that was it."

"Did he know about her having a half-brother?"

"That piece of information really seemed to be a surprise for him. He voiced the opinion that Sadie had never mentioned the guy. We'll see what happens when he and Nick Russel pass each other in the hallway."

Bill then started counting on his fingers just to get it straight in his mind. "So International Mineral Recovery Foundation hired Luke Cook's gang for the Leadville survey heist and the attack on Libby. Then International hired Nick Russel for hacking and Jim Hailey's gang for attacking me plus the Dante's Gulch assault on Captain Jen. Have I got it right?"

"Yep," Marshall said as he licked his coffee spoon and placed it on the table thoughtfully. At least the case was coming together for him, he thought Their group of prisoners was enough to hang International. The FBI would be so happy. The case was almost ready for trial.

Nevertheless, Marshall's personal life had become so very complicated. Suddenly, Agent Marshall Tate just didn't feel single anymore!

CHAPTER 29

FALLING INTO PLACE

Libby and Jerry met at the office before they opened up the Sadie Russel formal interrogation at the jail. Jerry had gotten wind of all of Johnny's evidence. Tyler was asleep in his new bed next to the couch. "So the Thanksgiving dinner in McPherson Gulch could be important or not so important? Nick Russel could have alerted International through Johnny and Sadie's emails?"

"Yep and Martha and Howard Carlson could be cleared," Libby verified. "Talking about their Thanksgiving should not be considered a crime. Gossip yes, but conspiracy?"

"Would be hard to prove," Jerry said. "It looks like Sadie Russel just might be a witness able to verify how the information got out. Martha and Howard Carlson just might not be involved. One would hope so for Johnny's sake. Having your sister in jail would not bode well for him. Howard could have simply blabbed at the office leaving

Connally no choice but to hire Calvin for the avalanche. Kill Johnny McPherson before the new will was signed; it would be his last ditch effort.

Libby fingers flew over Sadie's computer keys. Fortunately, Sadie's entries were dated, she observed. Libby had gone back to November 2015 entries. Her eyes scanned through the emails. "Okay, so here Johnny says that he intends to tell Howard and Martha on turkey day. Sadie asks what will be their reaction? Johnny says that he knew their intentions would be to sell the gulch. Martha would talk about their kids and their future. None of the kids liked to visit the gulch. Johnny would announce that he would leave the kids money not the land. Johnny finished the topic by then saying the family would be satisfied with money." Libby scanned down more emails. "No communication again until the middle of December?" she questioned. Libby looked at Jerry for an answer.

"Sadie probably stayed up in the gulch for the rest of her vacation," he offered.

"Of course. So what happened is totally in Sadie's memory now," Libby stated. She clicked off the computer and thought for a few moments. "Let's change the interrogation into a testimony, recorded of course, but here in the office. Bring it down a notch and treat Sadie as a witness instead of a suspect?"

"I'll go pick Sadie up and why don't you phone Captain Jen just to make sure that we're all on the same page."

"Done."

***

Frank Mason requested that Nick Russel be brought into another interrogation room. Agent Tate and Frank had finished up the McPherson testimony. Now Johnny wanted to head over to Leadville and make sure that Milt was okay. Frank had requested an officer from Frisco to accompany him.

Johnny McPherson was sitting in the open area of the Breckenridge Police Station waiting for his escort. Nick Russel was coming down the hallway from the opposite direction. He passed right in front of Johnny. They both glanced at each other while Frank observed. Zero reaction.

Just to make absolutely sure, Frank asked Johnny, " Have you seen anyone in the station today who you recognize? There's lots of suspects floating around?"

Johnny said, "Nope, nada."

"So you're okay with waiting until this evening to see Sadie?" Frank questioned.

"Guess I don't have any choice in that matter, do I?"

"Sorry but it is better for both of you and, especially, the case. What is said before you meet could be really important."

Johnny sighed and looked down at his hands. He knew that the minute he had stepped into police custody, he was no longer in control of his life. "It's just hard, Frank."

"Hell I know but we all are trying as hard as we can. You know that," Frank said then placed his hand on Johnny's shoulder. "It all is so important at this point. Who you identify and what you have seen. Hell, even on the off chance that you might see someone here in the police station. Please stay vigilant and aware. You'll let me know if anyone or anything comes to your mind, right?"

"Of course. So far all I see are strangers tangled in their own troubles."

"How about earlier? See anyone anywhere that you recognize but can't remember?" Frank ventured.

"Nope," Johnny stated as his escort appeared at the door. "Now that guy looks like he might want to go to Leadville," Johnny pointed.

"I think you're right. See you this evening, buddy."

"Thanks, Frank. I do appreciate all that you have done," Johnny said. "You're a damn good friend."

"So are you, Johnny. Now go find Milt and make sure they're taking care of him and his dog in Leadville."

Frank watched Johnny leave then called Captain Jen. "No go on Nick Russel. Neither of them batted an eye. I'd say they are definitely strangers." Frank listened to Jen's response. She seemed okay with the situation. "So I ain't to go back to the office you say?" Frank said then listened. "Okay I'll stay here and have a chat with Nick Russel. You want family details from him and any confrontations with the police or his parents that I can get recorded? Will do." Frank clicked off his phone and headed for Nick Russel's interrogation room.

***

Thomas Gipple was a dead end for now. Bill and Marshall Tate got nothing more. The lawyer talked and Gipple smoked. The old fart was a health hazard to say the least. Marshall had hinted that when International Mineral went on trial, maybe Gipple could make a deal to reduce his sentence with the government. Gipple's eyes flashed some interest through the cloud of smoke. The lawyer had missed that communication, Bill noticed. Yep, the government had done its' homework on this case, Bill surmised. Gipple and his International Mineral lawyer shuffled out of the room at this point satisfied with their defense. It was over for Summit with Gipple, Bill knew. The FBI could take the whole lot of them and HAPT would be left to investigate Slope Incorporated.

Marshall then left the room to call the FBI and see what his next orders looked like. Transportation of witnesses and suspects had to be scheduled soon. The International Trial would be transferred to Washington leaving the avalanche investigation here. Probably an okay arrangement, Bill considered. International Mineral and Recovery Foundation would be on trial for years. Good luck with that, he thought.

Bill called Captain Jen who relayed that Sadie Russel had now been classified as a witness and not a suspect for the time being. Slope Incorporated then needed scrutiny. If they could find Eric

Calvin's name on any employment list from Slope the evidence would surface. Even a blank check for 50 thousand drawn during December would go a long ways. Follow the money trail, he calculated.

Bill had issued a warrant for Slope's employee hire list for the last two years. It would be a couple of hours before that information arrived. Captain Jen had instructed him to work out of the Frisco Police Station now and stay away from the office. Sadie Russel's testimony at the office had become crucial.

Libby was digging deep into the emails and would probably be able to prove Sadie and the Carlson's part in the case.

It was a relief that HAPT was now back on the original Avalanche Case. Bill thought it was pretty ironic that both cases centered around property value. The vortex of power and greed had sent havoc through this small but prosperous area. Bill shook his head and kept digging. It would all fall into place, he predicted.

***

Jen texted Libby all the questions that she could think of for Sadie Russel. It was like she had read Bill's mind plus she was curious about who Sadie confided in personally. They would have to show that Sadie had or hadn't told anyone about Johnny's plans. Did both companies know that Johnny's property was headed for the open space destination? In that case both companies would have seen the value in killing off Johnny

McPherson before he changed his will. The motive was in place.

Jen hoped that Eric Calvin who had flown off Impasse Mountain could be tied to Slope. She had spent time with the man on the side of that mountain. His involvement was of special interest to her. He was methodical in his surveillance of their cold case. Calvin must have come back to McPherson Gulch and accidently shot Frank thinking he was Johnny McPherson. He had stayed around since December to monitor. He was a careful man. Jen's body shivered slightly as she thought about their climb up Impasse. Eric Calvin's flight off the cliff was lodged in her memory forever.

As if on cue, Jen's hospital door opened. Bix and Bernie peeked in, two very welcome ladies. She hadn't talked with them since Dante's Gulch. "What a wonderful surprise; I am so glad to see you!" Jen reached out with her good hand and grabbed their hands. The connection felt so good; these two ladies were family.

"So glad to see you too." Bix replied. "You look great considering what has happened. Bernie and I have been so worried. Arlene has kept us in the loop, bless her heart," Bix affirmed.

"Did we hear that you are conducting your team's movements from bedside? Command Center is the way Arlene described it," Bernie joked.

"We won't keep you long, Captain Jen," Bix said.

"You two are always welcome anytime. Sit! There's a slack in the action as we speak. Interviews going on all over the place. I never believed how much work one can do from a hospital bed," Jen said with satisfaction. "So what are your plans, Bernie?" Jen asked. "I hope you have found time to enjoy your vacation?" Her eyes explored Bernie's face intently.

"Totally," answered Bernie. "I feel right at home what with another murder case to solve. There's never a dull moment with Bix as you well know."

Jen smiled and said, "I guess that just might be true." Jen hesitated and then asked, "So how long are you able to stay, Bernie?"

"Got to head back in a couple of days. The ranch can't be left to handle itself much longer even with my brother caretaking. It ain't right. You can ask just so much of a brother, you know."

"Well, be sure and say hello to the Holden clan for me," Jen said.

"Will do. Bix is coming out for a visit this winter to ride the range by the way. We'll need to get Simon a ticket also," Bernie added glancing at Bix.

Jen could tell that the plans had been made. "Good. Well if you need a certain police captain to keep an eye on your house, Bix, I'm here and ready."

"That is a great offer and thank you." Bix's eyes then began to twinkle as she changed the subject. "So we have got something for you speaking of work. Bernie and I went for a hike yesterday and we found ourselves up on the Impasse Mountain ledge," Bix ventured.

"Near where the helicopter had picked up Frank's shooter," Bernie clarified.

"Yeah right. Just out for a casual hike. Really?" Jen chastised.

"Well maybe not but…" Bix then opened a brown paper bag and pulled out a small black pack with two finger. She displayed it like a trophy and shot a glance of amusement at Bernie. "We found this pack on the ledge. We didn't open it but left that for you to do," Bix said. "Found it some fifty feet away from the yellow tape area like someone had thrown it away before landing," Bix commented. The look on her face was classic, Jen noted.

Bernie beamed also as she described the location. "I took a picture of the exact area with my phone before we removed the pack."

"Maybe Eric Calvin left me a clue after all," Jen said excitedly. She peeked in the dark pack then emptied the contents on the bed. Nothing, except ammo and a rain jacket. The pockets were empty also. Then Jen's eyes spied the attached key chain with an empty bullet casing on it. It dangled from one of the pack's zipper pockets. With one eye closed she inspected the interior. "Well, well what do we have here? Toss me those tweezers on Betty's tray over there, please."

Bix held the empty casing with a rubber glove while Jen extracted a piece of finely rolled paper from the interior. Bix then with the tweezers carefully unrolled the paper. Written on it was a row of numbers and the location address of 1112 Federal. They stared at paper in silence.

Jen then put the address in her computer added the descriptor, Denver area. Handy Dandy storage came up. "Must be unit 77 and the combination," she calculated. Thank you, Eric Calvin and thank you, ladies," Captain Jen said happily. She felt like a kid at Christmas!

"You're welcome," Bernie and Bix said. They then realized how busy Captain Jen was going to be.

"Well we better be heading out of here or Nurse Sanders will have my head." Bix said.

"I don't think so. I know, by the way, who put Sanders on my case. It wasn't the hospital but a certain concerned citizen." She eyed Bix sternly then added, "Thanks. Sanders has kept me in tow. I do have a tendency to get crazy when I'm cooped up. Between my mother and Nurse Sanders, there's little room for any stupid mistakes on my part."

"Good." Bix leaned over and kissed Jen's cheek and Bernie patted her hand fondly. The two ladies then left as quietly as they had entered.

Jen stared at the shutting door and marveled at Bix and Bernie. Who else would think about hiking up there and finding that pack? It was one more piece of the puzzle falling into place. Thank heavens, Jen sighed and promptly dialed the police office in Denver. Just might get lucky, she thought. You might be testifying anyway, Eric Calvin, even from the grave, she calculated.

Jen then made a note to call the ME. She had decided that she would pay for Eric Calvin's burial. No one had come forward to claim the body. It really wasn't surprising. However, there had been a bond in that pursuit that Jen couldn't explain; she

owed him a proper burial. The team didn't need to
know. Maybe a small funeral could be arranged.
Bix and Arlene would come. They could say
something. Any life was worth that dignity.

***

Jerry ushered Sadie Russel into the office. They
had stopped by and picked up some breakfast
muffins. Nice touch, Libby thought as she hoped to
find a blueberry muffin in that sack.

"Sadie, good to see you again," Libby said with
a smile.

"Thanks, you two, for springing me from the
jail. I hope you're finding what you need on my
computer," she said pointing in Libby's general
direction.

"Thank you for sharing both the computer and
breakfast," Libby added. "Let's sit on the couch;
I'm starving."

They sat down. Libby pulled the recorder over
and then eyed Sadie. "We need to record your
individual statement now so that after you meet
with Johnny, the defense can't say that the two of us
coerced your statements. Purely procedural," Libby
finished.

"I understand," Sadie said with a nod. "So what
do you need to know?"

Jerry and Libby glanced at each other. Jerry
was very willing to let Libby take the lead. "Let's
go back to Thanksgiving dinner 2015. You and
Johnny were hosting that dinner in McPherson
Gulch. Is that correct?"

"Yes, Sadie supplied then continued, "Johnny had invited his sister and brother-in-law, Martha and Howard Carlson."

"Did Johnny McPherson have any agenda to share during the visit?" Libby asked.

"He wanted to explain his intentions about leaving his property to be open space in Summit County. Their reaction, unfortunately, was just as we expected. Martha whined about her children not receiving their inheritance. It was ugly but at least the emotions were out in the open. Finally when Johnny informed Martha that her kids would get a considerable amount of money from his estate, she quieted down. They also realized that I had no intentions of contesting Johnny's decision. I think Martha Carlson left feeling better about it."

"How about Howard?" Jerry asked.

"Howard has plenty of money," Sadie said. "I do think he would have liked to present the property to Slope Incorporated just to act like a big fish one more time but he is retiring next year. I think he's finally realized that it just doesn't matter. Come to think of it, Howard did mention that there was no love lost between the company and himself. His admission kind of surprised Johnny and I. Maybe the company disclosed that they were happy to get rid of Howard, big salary and all."

"So he agreed?" Libby asked.

"Well, not exactly. Howard definitely thinks money and power are far more important than holding onto land. Johnny, of course, said that Howard's company didn't need to destroy another piece of property in Summit for pure greed. Johnny, like always, talked about the promise he had made to Arnold McPherson. He had promised his grandfather that he would honor the land."

"How did their conversation end?" Jerry asked.

"In a truce as usual. They never understood each other so their conversations always ended in a truce. Family is family."

"Sadie, the next question is very important so please think before you answer," Libby cautioned. "Did you tell anyone, friend or business associate, about that conversation?"

"No. Actually that's an easy question for me. Johnny and I discussed our relationship and business affiliations years ago. Our agreement was that nothing needed to go out of our bedroom so to speak. I would never discuss such private information with friends or company."

"Did you and Johnny discuss it later in any emails?" Jerry asked.

"Yes, of course," Sadie confessed. There was a pause as everyone processed that information.

Libby decided to hit that one dead on, "When is the last time that you saw or talked with your half-brother, Nick Russel, just for the record," she asked.

"At least eight years ago. I truly have not kept track of his activities nor cared to," Sadie answered. Her eyes radiated intensely.

"Have you ever seen or heard of any of these men?" Jerry asked getting the pictures out: Jim Hailey, Thomas Gipple, Eric Calvin, Luke Cook."

"No," Sadie answered as she examine the group of mugshots.

"Have you heard of Milt Gray and Walter Connally?" Libby asked just for balance.

"Yes. Milt is an old prospector from Leadville that Johnny dearly loves. He's also quite an authority on mineral surveys according to Johnny. Walter Connally, now that you have brought up his name, did get mentioned during Thanksgiving dinner. Howard identified him as his CEO who knew everything about property values according to Howard. Johnny called Connally 'the bully of greed.' Johnny had worked for Connally and didn't come away from that job very happy. Howard then shut-up. We moved on into dinner."

"Have you ever had any contact with Slope Incorporated?" Libby asked.

"No. I only know that both Slope Incorporated and International Mineral Recovery Foundation are huge companies that manage their own computer works. My company is small potatoes next to those two." Sadie ate her muffin for a moment then looked directly at Libby and asked, "Was I really hacked?"

"Yes," Libby replied.

Sadie's eyes closed for a moment as she processed that mess. As all this turmoil fell into place, Sadie realized that she and Johnny were now front page sensations. McPherson Gulch, in all its seclusion and majesty, had awakened an avalanche of controversy. Who would have thought it?

***

"Would you want me to send the FBI to

Arizona's Slope Incorporated Office to do a raid?
We could tie up all their business information from
the that office before the Slope would have a chance
to cover their tracks. I could even deliver Connally
to Summit County tomorrow evening" Marshall
told Captain Jen Holly the next morning during the
HAPT meeting.

"Nice power," Jen answered mulling over the
request. "Sure, why not? That certainly would
eliminate all the red tape for us. Wow. Thanks,
Marshall."

Agent Marshall Tate nodded and exited the
hospital room while dialing his home office. His
offer would payback HAPT for their aide in the
International Mineral Recovery Foundation Case.
Simple request when you were the FBI. His boss
would wake up the Arizona FBI Branch. He
chuckled quietly waiting for his connection.

Libby James began relating Sadie Russel's
contribution to the case at this time. She ended her
summary with, "I do believe Howard Carlson is the
informational leak. Do I think that he and Martha
Carlson arranged the avalanche? No. I think Slope
Incorporated saw their opportunity slipping away.
Kill Johnny McPherson before he had an
opportunity to change his will is what I think. I
would like permission to dig deeper into the files
that Bill brought back from Slope, if that's okay?"
She looked at the Captain.

"So granted. Bill, why don't you help Libby
this morning? Seems like we need to understand
Howard's connection and Walter Connally's
involvement before he arrives in our county. Jerry

and Frank take custody of Connally when he gets here. We want it to be official and by the book. Marshall will probably want to join us in the interrogation room in Breckenridge. Please make sure that he is welcome.

And now ladies and gentlemen, I can tell by the nurse standing in my door that it is nap time. This afternoon I am out of here! Not that I'm counting or anything. Right Nurse Sanders? I must say, I will miss you," Jen smiled coyly at her. The group broke up without another word and disappeared.

CHAPTER 30

SAID AND DONE!

"BOOM! I've got it! $50,000 to one firm called, Mountain Comet Liquidation!" Libby yelped. Couldn't be much more clever but oh so clear."

Bill leaped out of his chair and inspected Libby's computer monitor. Sure enough there was the deposit from good old Walter Connally himself. It was made one week after Thanksgiving. "What a fucking turkey," Bill mumbled. "We got him."

"Wonder if we could find any evidence either way in Howard Carlson's emails about his involvement or lack of?" Libby now changed her approach and settled in her chair. Howard Carlson and Walter Connally had communicated quite a lot during each day, she assessed. "Let's start with the emails right after turkey day."

"Sounds like a plan," Bill mumbled as he settled in for the long haul. "Coffee?" he asked Libby.

"Sure. Why not. Looks like we'll be here for a while," she answered.

Officer Frank Mason had volunteered to handle Sadie and Johnny's meeting. He had decided to take them to lunch and instruct them to not talk about the case until after the Connally interrogation was completed and the arrest was made. He felt like their chaperone at this time. Well that was all right, he reconnoitered. Actually, it was pretty damn cute, he admitted.

***

The FBI raid happened around noon after Marshall had ordered it. He stayed put in Summit and waited for Walter Connally plus the business boxes of evidence to arrive on the FBI's private plane. Marshall had also requested six agents from Denver to scan the information incase there was any significant evidence about Slope and International joining together. Probably not but it would at least give HAPT some aide. He figured that the amount of data would be more than anyone wanted to scan. Yep, six guys might be able to pull it off in a couple days. The home office in Washington was fairly happy with his results at this point. They had hinted that maybe he should be back by next week. That prospect loomed in his thoughts.

As he waited anxiously, his mind settled on Libby. Last night they had been together again. What an incredible woman. His pulse just jumped when he thought of her. Each night had become a gift at this point. They both knew that his stay was coming to an end. Neither of them had the heart to bring up the topic. Marshall could already feel the pain that separation would cause. It was like half his heart would remain in Summit. What to do was a dilemma.

Marshall had watched Libby throughout this case. He could tell that her roots were so deeply ingrained into the mountain environment. It was funny that during his life, environment had really meant nothing. The job advancements had satisfied him. Being a Navy brat had established that occupational ties were priority in his family. Now, he realized how incredibly vital a place could be. It was even drawing him with some hidden force that he had never experienced before. The mountains were so fucking strong, the sun so warm and near, and the lady so intense. What to do? How to live?

Evening started when the door of the Breckenridge Police Station burst open and two agents adorned in typical black suits entered. Marshall escorted them into an interview room to get all the information. There was an hour conference while Connally got processed.

Captain Jen Holly pulled herself out of the chair in her condo. She had already gotten her uniform on with the help of her mother who had moved in for the time being. The cats were happy. Chief Hagen was on the way from Leadville to Breckenridge. He would drive her to the police station and then watch the interrogation.

Libby and Bill had been notified that Connally was now in Breckenridge. They began to organize their research and printed quickly. Fortunately, they had time to create a summary. Bill rushed down to the SUV and started the engine. Libby locked the office door and secured the file under her arm. They were ready!

Jerry had convinced Chief James Marten from Buena Vista that he needed to be in on this interrogation. He had to promise the Chief that he would call him immediately when Connally confessed. Jerry smiled to himself; gossip was a powerful tool. Then again, to have the newly created HAPT Officers be so successful was a feather in all the Police Departments' hats. The mountain communities would shine; the image would be great!

Plus, HAPT had successfully worked with the FBI. No one's ego had gotten in the way. Marshall was a good guy and Jerry had noticed that he was smitten with Libby which certainly didn't hurt anything. Cool. Jerry gave Tyler some doggie biscuits and water then hopped in the driver's seat as they headed to Breckenridge.

***

Libby immediately handed the file on Walter Connally to Captain Jen. Agent Marshall Tate and Chief Anderson scanned the information quickly also. Hopefully, Connally was toast.

It was decided that those three would be the basic interrogation unit. Captain Jen, however, did send Bill, Libby and Jerry into the room first to read Walter Connally his rights and get the recorder plus cameras set for the interrogation. Chief Anderson thought that was a pretty nice touch. These officers had worked harder than hell on this case and deserved some recognition. He made a mental note to remember her actions. HAPT had done a hell of a job, Anderson assessed. He had been so damn impressed observing Jen lead from a hospital bed. Another nice touch.

Captain Jen was beginning to feel the pain coming back into her shoulder. She had stopped taking anything for the pain eight hours ago. She knew that some devious lawyer would hope to prove that her medicated condition would taint the interrogation.

Jen had to be in the room for the interrogation; it was her first case as HAPT Captain. From the email information it was beginning to sound more like Connally orchestrated the avalanche without Martha and Howard's knowledge. Thank heavens for Johnny McPherson that it didn't look like his sister and brother-in-law were involved. True, Howard had a big mouth and had told his boss, Walter Connally, about Johnny's decision to rewrite his will and give the gulch to open space. It was a foolish mistake by Howard but that was all; his ego got in the way. Big mouth, Jen concluded.

An hour ago, Jen had gotten a call from Denver about the storage unit that Bix and Bernie had uncovered. It revealed 50,000 cash and a voice recording of Connally and Calvin's meeting. The tape had confirmed that Connally employed Eric Calvin for the avalanche. Obviously, Calvin hadn't trusted Connally either hence the recording was terrific evidence. "Thanks Eric," Jen murmured as she entered the interrogation room.

***

"How the fuck did I pull off an avalanche?" Walter Connally screamed. "You people are ridiculous! That's bullshit!"

"Walter, you need to let me do the talking during this interrogation," Arthur Jones, his lawyer, cautioned. His advice seemed to be ignored as Walter Connally tried to manipulate the situation. His self-importance as CEO of Slope Incorporated outweighed the government's involvement in his mind.

"So you really think that there is no evidence against you?" Jen asked. "Seems like your emails to Howard Carlson were pretty clear. It would seem obvious to you that Howard wasn't going to inherit McPherson Gulch. You damn well were going to miss out on a considerable amount of financial profit. We're suppose to believe that you were simply raving mad and never followed through?" she asked.

"You're damn right! I never decided to kill Johnny McPherson. Hell, we have plenty of projects on the table right now," Walter bragged and leaned back in his chair. "I'm a good business man," he yelled.

"May I ask you, once more, to let me control this interrogation, Walter?" Lawyer Jones asked.

"Oh, shut-up. They have nothing," Walter stated.

"Oh I think you're wrong there," said Agent Marshall Tate in a quiet but stern tone. The pause filled the air with tension as Marshall calculated what to say next. "You now have the FBI on your tail. For all we know, Slope and International Mineral are working together. You not only are going to be tried in Colorado for attempted murder but the Federal Government will investigate every file in your office. My guess would be that you are going to jail, Mr. Connally, and in a federal facility. My guess would be that Slope Incorporated has more than one case pending."

"That's not right," Walter yelled as he leaped to feet. His face radiated bright red. He stared at Lawyer Jones waiting for his denial and protection.

There was another long pause while the lawyer reconnoitered. "I will need to see your warrants for Slope's business records."

Chief Anderson then spoke up, "Done and done. We have both federal and the state of Colorado on the warrants. Chief Anderson put the warrant copies on the table. Your office is being cleared out as we speak," Anderson added while staring at Walter Connally.

"All right this interrogation is over," said Lawyer Jones slamming his hand on the table.

"No it's not," mumbled Walter in a softer tone. I'd like to know what the hell you think you have on me before I leave this room."

"Ever heard of Calvin's Mountain Liquidation Company, Mr. Connally?" Jen asked softly. Her eyes pierced Connally's face.

The room fell silent as Walter processed the information. He had done a double-take glancing around the room. Connally knew his name was on the cash withdrawal and he knew that they were very close to what 'liquidation' really meant in the title. Damn. "I was merely liquidating stock for Eric Calvin. That's all."

Jen leaned up and flipped the switch on another tape recorder. The blood drained from Walter Connally's face as he listened to his own voice arrange the damn avalanche. The recorder left zero doubt of who was responsible. Walter inhaled slowly then said softly, "We didn't mean to kill anyone. It was meant to successfully clear away all the buildings in McPherson Gulch to scare the hell out of Johnny McPherson. That's all."

"Mr. Connally, you need to stop this interview now," Lawyer Jones yelled.

"They know, you stupid fuck. Now sit back and shut-up," Walter demanded.

"Was Howard or Martha Carlson in on the avalanche scam?" Captain Jen held her breathe while waiting for the answer. "Anyone in the immediate family?" she added.

"The Carlsons are idiots. They should have contested the original land title and not let Johnny inherit the whole fucking gulch. Land is gold and that's all there is to it. No. Howard wasn't in on it. He's too weak and stupid." Walter dismissed the topic with a wave of his hand.

Then his countenance became more confident as he leaned back in his chair to negotiate. "Now, I just might know some information about International Mineral Recovery Foundation. Of course, it would be my bargaining chit." Walter Connally then stared directly at Agent Marshall Tate. He was ready to be swept away by the FBI.

"Now, I will keep quiet and stand with this worthless lawyer who will bargain with you later. This interview is now over. I'm done."

And so he was done and toast. Walter would be tried for attempted murder in Colorado and then promptly shipped off to Washington for the International Mineral Recovery Foundation's tedious trial. The Federal Government would take him into custody so that they could bargain for his evidence.

Jen wouldn't be surprised that within five years, Walter Connally would leave prison for time served. Courts had a funny way of processing suspect evidence. How valuable would his contribution be to the FBI's case? Might be just valuable enough to get him out with time served. He'd have a ruined career but he would be out of prison. Case closed.

***

The stars were magnificent now that darkness had enclosed the atmosphere. Occasionally, a falling star detached itself and fell leaving a trail like a pencil on paper; the sky was so close at 10,500 feet. Bix and Bernie were blissfully relaxing in the hot tub. Their focus was on the sky; underwater, their hands were clasped. Jen's phone call had caused some disruption but all was comfy again.

Captain Holly had been directed to enter the premises and go directly to the hot tub for further discussion. It was Bernie's last night in Colorado.

She and Bix were now sharing the feeling of peace and commitment in their relationship. They had become a couple and that was a fact. Miles apart in residences but definitely a couple. It wasn't a question of would they be together; it was more a question of how and when.

Jen pulled into the driveway and let the day's duty melt from her countenance. She sat for a moment and simply breathed. It was so nice to be able to come over to Bix's house and leave the 'captain stuff' behind for a few hours. "Thank you, Lord," she murmured.

Jen shut the car door and proceeded to the refrigerator where a cold beer was waiting. Her arm was still in a sling but she had adjusted fairly well to life. Captain Holly then unbuckled her holster and discarded her weapon on the kitchen counter. She wandered out onto the deck eyeing the stars, the gas fireplace glow and the two heads above the hot tub water surface.

"Good evening ladies. You sure look comfy," she said then sat down in a deck chair. It was a warm inviting atmosphere, Jen realized. Just what a worn-out cop needed. The beer tasted incredible as she sighed in relief. "Life is good," she murmured.

"Definitely," said Bernie. "Warm and toasty. Can't think of a better place to be," she added. Her complexion was rosy red from the 103 degree water.

Bernie's serene tone said it all, Jen concluded. These two had come to an understanding. Their relationship had become more than just visits. Love was in the air and Jen could feel it. She was slightly jealous. Actually, more than slightly jealous. "So I asked the lady in the GIS Department out today," Jen confessed. Her eyes darted from each of their faces to catch the reaction.

"Woot! Great news," Bix said with a large smile. "Finally! Katie, right?" Jen nodded.

"I take it that it has been brewing for awhile?" Bernie interjected.

"Too long," Bix answered giving Bernie's hand an extra squeeze.

"Bix is right. Got to say she's spot-on what with the case and the new job," Captain Jen confessed. "I have put my personal life on the back burner; my bad," she admitted. They all silently processed that information.

Jen then took a sip of beer before revealing another new development. "By the way, Libby and Marshall are going fast and furious. If they truly believe we all don't see it then they're crazy," Jen stated. "Plus, Marshall has thrown his hat in the ring for the Sheriff's job in Frisco. Guess he likes it around here."

"Well…well. I hope it works out for those two young people. I do like beautiful endings," Bix replied.

"Any other applicants for that job?" Bernie asked.

"Well, now that you mention it, Bill seems interested so I don't know what will happen. Now that HAPT's future is solvent, he might just stay put. Don't know."

"Getting interesting as usual," Bix said. "Oh! Did you hear that Sadie and Johnny have gotten engaged? And, the architects are constructing a new home for them in McPherson Gulch. One with all the conveniences located closer to the road."

"Plus, it will be a fortress with a gate at the river and cameras with other surveillance equipment installed," Bernie added. "They will know about any intrusions. Sadie will be able to drive right up to the door. Modern living and loving," Bernie concluded.

"Well, not all modern," Bix clarified. "Johnny is building an authentic replica of his grandfather's cabin on top of the old foundation. McPherson's Funnel will possess an actual museum; the McPherson history will be well-preserved and protected. We come from our roots, you know. Johnny and Sadie will honor Arnold McPherson's life. I like it," Bix added happily.

"That is so cool," Jen said falling deeply into the moment while staring at the gas fireplace's continual flame. All the events of the past month suddenly funneled into her perspective. "Life is never all bad is it," she affirmed looking intensely at the two heads in the hot tub?

"White gold avalanches can only last for so long. People will recover and the snow will melt," Bix commented then gave Bernie's hand an extra squeeze.

THE END

BOOKS CAN BE FOUND ON AMAZON AND CREATE A SPACE.

NOVELS:

THE RED QUEEN CAPER
THE WHITE GOLD CAPER

Simon Snoodle Publishing

ABOUT THE AUTHOR

The first book that I ever read on my own was a mystery. For some reason while other children were picking up the reading skills, I found myself having nothing but difficulty. The pages were simply blurs of words. The next summer, not to be outdone by my brother, I picked up one of my mother's adult paperback mysteries and faked it. I faked it until one day that summer, comprehension began. Heck with the children's books; I was hooked on mysteries forever!

For 34 years teaching became my profession, Drama and English. The interpretation of the written word motivated me into the educational field; I taught student levels 6th grade through College Prep. over the years. Eventually, retirement has blessed me. I now find the time to write mysteries and explore my favorite environment.

I followed my ancestors to Colorado and have spent 25 years in the mountains. The respect that I have for high elevation is incredible. I am addicted to hiking and being outdoors. Writing mysteries and hiking simply blended together into the Colorado Mountain Mystery Caper Series.

Janet McDermott

21584363R00222

Made in the USA
Columbia, SC
20 July 2018